ANNE LEONARD has degrees from St. John's College, Annapolis (BA), the University of Pittsburgh (MFA), Kent State University (PhD), and the University of California, Hastings College of the Law. She lives in Northern California with her husband, son and two black cats.

Praise for *Moth and Spark*:

'Fun and beautifully crafted. The novel is something like a Russian nesting doll: it's a Jane Austen novel inside a *Princess Bride*-type fantasy romp inside a much darker Tolkein-esque story of politics, war, magic, and dragons. An impressive debut'
Charlie Lovett, *New York Times* bestselling author of *The Bookman's Tale*

'*Moth and Spark* is a soaring adventure . . . it's beautifully written, with a beautiful romance and a rich plot with engaging characters'
www.realitysabore.blogspot.co.uk

'A rare gem . . . A fantastic read all around'
www.thebookswarm.blogspot.com

'*Moth and Spark* is an excellent novel and a heck of an addition to the fantasy genre'
www.matthewscottbaker.com

'A nice breath of fresh air being blown into epic fantasy'
www.lytherus.com

'I loved the dragons. I loved the plot . . . Anne Leonard's debut had me falling fast for it'
www.thebookcellarx.com

'Immensely readable, hard to put down'
www.fantasyreviewbarn.com

'Astounding writing . . . a story you can really sink into. One of those powerful debut novels that is unlike anything you've ever read before'
www.bookwormblues.net

ANNE LEONARD

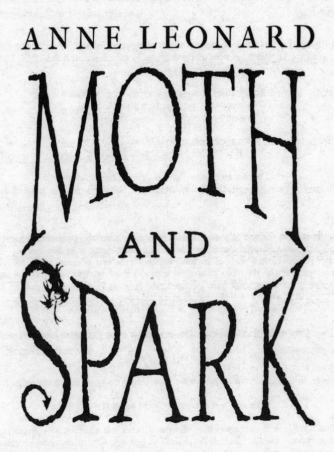

MOTH
AND
SPARK

headline

Published by arrangement with Viking Penguin,
A member of Penguin Group (USA) LLC,
a Penguin Random House Company, New York.

First published in Great Britain in 2014 by
HEADLINE PUBLISHING GROUP

First published in paperback in Great Britain in 2014 by
HEADLINE PUBLISHING GROUP

1

Cataloguing in Publication Data is available from the British Library

ISBN 978 1 4722 1485 0

Typeset in Guardi LT Std by Palimpsest Book Production Ltd, Falkirk, Stirlingshire

Printed and bound by Clays Ltd, St Ives plc

Headline's policy is to use papers that are natural, renewable and recyclable products and
made from wood grown in sustainable forests. The logging and manufacturing processes are
expected to conform to the environmental regulations of the country of origin.

HEADLINE PUBLISHING GROUP
An Hachette UK Company
338 Euston Road
London NW1 3BH

www.headline.co.uk
www.hachette.co.uk

To

ADAM

and

BENJAMIN

At midnight on the Emperor's pavement flit
Flames that no faggot feeds, nor steel has lit,
Nor storm disturbs, flames begotten of flame,
Where blood-begotten spirits come
And all complexities of fury leave,
Dying into a dance,
An agony of trance,
An agony of flame that cannot singe a sleeve.

—W. B. Yeats, "Byzantium"

The fact is, that you were sick of civility, of deference, of officious attention. You were disgusted with the women who were always speaking, and looking, and thinking for *your* approbation alone. I roused, and interested you, because I was so unlike *them*.

—Jane Austen, *Pride and Prejudice*

PROLOGUE

1

Riding, riding, he had been riding when the dragon appeared overhead and came slowly, inevitably, down. It was a cloudy day and he was in the Fells. The air still had plenty of winter in it here, high up. There were two men with him from the garrison. There had been no purpose to the ride besides itself; he had been sick of the dirt and smells and noise and press of soldiers in the hold and needed to clear his head with exercise and open air. Then the dragon's cry, sharp and compelling as a hunting hawk's, but longer, fiercer, more dreadful. He had heard it a hundred times and it still made the hair on the back of his neck rise and his skin prickle. He was prey, and his body knew it.

The horses knew it too and reared and neighed in terror. Corin was nearly thrown, and one of the soldiers was. The dragon descended. It folded its shimmering blue wings with a rush of hot air that smelled like sulfur. Long ivory claws gouged the earth. It was huge, its snout at least the length of a tall man's arm. Silver scales on its sides glistened even under the grey sky. It crouched, tail switching back and forth, nostrils steaming.

By the time Corin had his own horse under control, the second soldier was kneeling beside the first, whose leg was clearly broken. One horse had not gone far, but the other one was out of sight. "Go back for help," Corin said. "There's nothing you can do about a dragon." He did not even touch the hilt of his sword. It was useless.

The dragonrider came off the dragon in a smooth and graceful slide. Corin's horse trembled and sweated but did not move. He would stay mounted as long as he could. When he glanced over his shoulder he saw that the soldier was obeying him and returning.

The dragonrider had dark skin and black hair, and when he spoke it was a different accent from the Mycenean Corin was used to. "Lord Prince." The tone was hard, mocking.

"Rider." He felt the dragon looking at him, and he was careful to keep his eyes on the man and not the beast. One who stared too long into a dragon's eyes would go mad.

"I have for you a message."

"Speak it."

"The Firekeepers have chosen you to free them from their slavery. Already you walk in Hadon's dreams. He fears you, so he will bring down war. He makes alliances with your enemies and turns your friends against you. This is your task, this and no other: to free the Firekeepers from the Empire. They will lend you their power, so that you will be as them though still a man, until you have done this. They will do what magic they can for you.

"Dismount."

Corin's legs moved of their own accord. He walked stiffly toward the rider. The rider held out a small golden flask.

"Drink this."

"No."

Faster than anyone could move, the dragonrider had hold of him and forced the liquid down his throat. It was sweet and thin and it burned. He struggled, but it was no good. One swallow, two swallows, three. His mouth had the taste of iron.

The dragonrider stepped back. Corin staggered. He felt feverish.

The rider said, "You will forget this until the change is complete. When you remember it, then it will be time for you to begin your labor. The Firekeepers will watch, do not shirk it."

Darkness closed in on him, and when it lifted he remembered nothing of the dragon or the rider. He was sitting on the stony track beside the man with a broken leg, waiting, while his horse nuzzled among the rocks to see what thin new grass it could find.

2

The canyon walls were black. Sharp glasslike chips of stone and rough dark cinders lay on the ground. When she looked up the towering walls to the top, all she could see was the deep blue of sky. No trees, no grasses, nothing but stone and sky.

She walked. The ground was ashy. She heard the wind.

Then she walked among men, and they did not see her, and she knew she was a shade, a phantom. There were dozens of them, dark-haired, strong. Soldiers, she thought. They had rigged ropes down the sheer cliffs, with harnesses. More and more came down slowly, like spiders dropping in jerks and starts. They had baskets with them, baskets lined with firecloth and coals. The dragons' bodies were stiff and dark. Men walked heedlessly by them, as though they were nothing more than rock, and gathered the eggs.

Smooth round eggs with a mother-of-pearl sheen. The eggs reflected the black walls. The men carried them gently.

She came to the end of the canyon. A tall crack in the rock breathed icy air at her. She slipped through, untroubled by sharp edges. She could see in the dark. Inside was a large cavern, with a long crevice running across the center. Cold air rose from it, steaming and curling like smoke. Beside the crevice lay the body of a man.

She knelt beside him while the cold air coiled around them. His skin was the waxy white of death. His lips and fingernails were blue. There was no mark on him. With a gentle touch she opened his eyes and saw that they were as black and hard as the canyon walls. She placed her hand upon his cheek and wished him peace.

Featherlike, she drifted down the crevice. It was a long way. Ice crystals clung to the walls. The air grew colder and clearer. The stone was the pocked and circled roughness of lava gone cold. At the bottom another body lay. This one had been burned. It disintegrated into ash at her touch.

There were ashes everywhere. Many dead, she realized. There had been a conflagration. And then it had gone out.

The seeing twisted, and she spun further and further back.

The crevice glowed with heat. Flames shot up as though from a furnace. On the roof of the cavern was the shadow of a dragon. It writhed in pain. It screamed, and fire jetted to the cavern roof in a white-blue glow. A man with eyes that flashed silver stood on the edge of the crevice and drew the fire to him. He breathed it in. His skin shimmered. He became a puff of ashes that fell softly down.

And another man came, and another, eyes flashing silver, then turning to stone. They breathed in the flame and became ash, and the fire faded. The dragon's shadow dimmed. Its writhing slowed.

One more spin, and she stood in the canyon. The sky was a blackness that breathed fire and had wings of smoke. It was made of coal. Red sparks showered from its body. Its claws had the shiny brightness of fresh blood.

It reached down and ripped her open.

She faded into darkness.

Which became the darkness of sleep and waking in her own soft bed, and there was grey at the window. She heard dawn birds and kitchen noises and the rattle of a wagon along the street. By the time she had washed and dressed, the dream had so vanished from her mind that she did not even remember she had dreamed. She had not a single thought of dragons.

CHAPTER ONE

Corin stared unhappily at the dingy little inn that was the only public place with a roof on it for miles. He considered riding on. He had slept in such places before and would again, but he was not sure he had the stomach for it that night. The wood and paint were sun-blistered and faded to dull grey, and the yard was a trampled patch of bare earth with some chickens pecking at it. Next to a corner of the building, a skinny mongrel scratched itself vigorously. The rusting pump by the porch was probably the only source of fresh water. He certainly wouldn't get a room to himself, and what bed he did get would be full of fleas. Houses that looked equally downtrodden were strung out along the road. A shutter somewhere banged in the gusty wind.

Beside him, Bron said doubtfully, "We could just pay him for his trouble and keep going." They had sent a man ahead to find lodging when it became clear they needed it. The sky was a lowering dark yellowish-grey that promised rain at any moment.

Corin looked over his shoulder at the eight other men. They had been riding from dawn to dusk for a week, and another push still wouldn't get them home this evening; they had nearly sixty miles more. All of them, himself included, were saddle-weary to the bone.

He took the map out of his cloak pocket. Wind threatened to tear it away. They were fifteen miles west of Lyde and it was about that far to the next town of any size. It was the main east-west road, but this was farm country, and all they would find along it were scattered villages, none likely to be any better than where they were. Baron Stede's estate was about seven miles northwest, and they could impose on him. But in Corin's experience working soldiers did not mix well with lords or gentlemen, and the additional formality and time such visits required were rarely worth the better beds. Especially with Stede, whose obsequiousness was matched only by his dullness. The fleas at least were honest in getting his blood. And democratic too; they didn't care how royal it was. The thought of hot water for a bath almost changed his mind, but the wind and the darkness of the clouds decided him.

"No," he said, "let's stay, but I don't want to know a damn thing about the kitchen."

Bron gave him a glance to see if he meant it, then dismounted and started giving orders to the men. Corin got down slowly and barely noticed when someone led his horse away. He hoped the stabling was adequate and decided Bron would have told him if it weren't. No point in looking. One of his boots had been chafing at his ankle for the last hour or so, and he dropped to one knee to adjust the laces. He was stalling, and he knew it, so he screwed himself up and went in.

The captain had as usual arranged things so that he barely had to deal with the innkeeper. So far as the man knew, he was just another soldier. The inn itself was better than it looked from the outside. It was crowded and noisy. Oil lamps dispersed darkness and a few windows let in fresh air. The common room was tidy, the glasses clean, the food tolerable, and the wine surprisingly decent. Perhaps, he reflected sardonically, he had been leading a rough life too long and his tastes were changing. The last six weeks had been rough only in comparison with palace softness, and he did not allow himself to take the thought seriously.

The table-maid was very pretty, with golden hair in a thick braid to her waist. She flirted and laughed and teased, all charmingly and without favoring anyone. But she was no harlot; when one of the men put his hand on her hip she slapped it away with the efficiency and ease of a motion she had made a hundred times before. The soldier's discomfited expression brought laughter from the others, and Corin hid his grin behind his wineglass. When she topped off his glass several minutes later he found himself quite aware of the smoothness of her neck and arms and the pleasant roundnesses beneath her practical and modest clothing. In Mycene with a body like that she would be someone's slave. She was lucky to be Caithenian. He watched her a little longer than he should have.

His muscles relaxed slowly with the food and wine. He was not only weary from the travel but still preoccupied by the events of the past weeks. His father had given him a straightforward task: one of the commanders of the northern holds had died of lung-fever in midwinter, and Corin had gone to install the new commander and perform an overdue inspection.

That part had all gone well enough. The north was beautiful in spring, with clear sunny skies and thousands of birds everywhere, the Fell Hills bright and beyond them the mountains rising sharp and distinct, white tips gleaming. Even the high ground above the treeline was colorful with the small creeping flowers that bloomed for a few weeks a year. When he rode on the open plain he saw the distant huts and wool-sheds of the shepherds. The barks of the sheepdogs and the bleats of the sheep were loud over the wide lonely land. There was no danger to look for from the north; the Fells and the mountains were sparsely inhabited by very poor people struggling for an existence as far north as anyone had ever gone. The holds had been used only for military training for decades. He should have enjoyed the solitude that he never got at home.

But things could not be that simple, of course. There were dragons. It was a rare day when he did not see one flying overhead, sometimes circling, looking for all the world as though it were doing its own inspection. On occasion they flew low enough to frighten the horses with their scent. And that was not at all the pattern of things; Emperor Hadon usually kept his dragons within the heart of the Empire, not patrolling the bleak northern edge of this small vassal kingdom. No love was lost on either side between Hadon and the king, but Hadon had always kept with history and tradition, ruling from afar and leaving Caithen mostly to its own affairs. Like kings before him, Aram had never made trouble. If Hadon had sent dragons here now, it meant he was up to something. He was watching where he had no call to watch.

Worse, it was a taunting and unsubtle reminder of Hadon's power over the dragons and over Caithen to bring them this close to the

Dragon Valleys from which they had been seized and where they could no longer go. The dragon had been the symbol of Corin's house once, before the Empire stole the dragons five hundred years ago, claimed the country with them. The dragon crest was Mycene's now. Corin hoped bitterly that the dragons would rebel, throw off their riders and come back to the caves that their blood remembered. Caithen had never mastered the dragons as the Empire did, he could not say they were his dragons, but they belonged in his land. It did not matter that they were deadly.

Nearly as disquieting were the stories the soldiers brought back from the shepherds and farmers and villagers they talked to, oddly compelling stories that lodged themselves in Corin's thoughts and would not leave. There were stories of huge white wolves creeping down from the mountains and slaughtering sheep by the dozens, of goblins, of two-headed calves that could speak, of witches laying curses and shadow-stealing, of necromancy. A woman in one village had the Sight and predicted doom. There were always such stories somewhere; natural philosophy was still the province of the rich and educated. The poor would have their gods of tree and stream and hollow, their hedgerow cures and charms. But those things were not usually tossed about in tavern gossip. For them to come out now meant fear of something else that was too hard to face. He had seen the hex signs, the wardings, on the farmhouse doors and the roofs of barns. On the sides of the roads were little primitive pyramids of stone for guarding and shrines with offerings of food. People expected evil.

It made no sense, not even accounting for the uneasiness the dragons cast. The winter had been milder than usual, and the spring days were clear and pleasant. The woods were thick with deer and the meadows with game. There was no severe sickness, no spate of dried-up wells, no vast quantity of dead or deformed lambs. The Sarian bandits who plagued other parts of Caithen had not made their way into this wild country. The farmers he met were busy and taciturn but not struggling. The alehouses were full of laughter. It was always someone else who had had bad luck.

Yet sooner or later the talk turned to whispers of corruption, of savagery, of a violent unnatural world. Spirits and demons walked the earth, fire springing up in their footsteps, women miscarrying when they passed. Wraith lights led travelers astray and horses refused to ford familiar streams. Dogs howled and snapped at nothing. The garrison soldiers were a superstitious lot, and they became twitchy. After a while the tension was heavy enough that Corin had his own nightmares of singing bones and red-hot cages and miles of gallows. He caught himself making the signs against evil, throwing salt over his shoulder, thinking the nonsense rhymes to ward off faerie. He slept uneasily, and he saw the signs of sleeplessness in the men around him. It was hard to think logically, to keep account of tasks, to be civil. He was clumsy and irritable. Bron's surreptitious worried looks at him became more frequent. And he began to forget things.

Small things at first, what he had had for breakfast or where he had put his cloak. But they grew larger. He spent an evening talking with the new commander and afterward could not repeat a word of the conversation. He sat down to write letters and half an hour would pass between one sentence and the next. He found himself and his men miles south of the garrison one afternoon and did not remember leaving. He remembered preparing the night before, waking that morning, but he could recall nothing since dawn. When he tried to remark on it he spoke words that were entirely different. Something had to be done and he could not think what. An irrational insidious voice told him that he lay under a spell, and for all that he tried to shrug it off and convince himself nothing was wrong, he kept coming back to it.

Now, a week later, it should have seemed absurd. He had not had a nightmare for three days. But he could not shake the feeling of failure and lost chance, the nagging certainty that he had forgotten something important he was supposed to do, that hung over him. He was afraid to ask Bron, because he thought the captain might tell him something he did not want to hear. He glared into his wineglass and drained it quickly.

The table-maid appeared a few minutes later and refilled the glass. His fingers brushed against hers as he took it. She glanced at him. Their eyes met. He thought that she would not slap his hand away. He wondered if she knew who he was.

He was tempted, but she was too young and too ignorant. It would not be fair. As soon as he finished eating he stood up, taking his glass with him, and went outside. Rain was not falling yet, but he smelled the moisture in the air. The wind was stronger. It pressed his clothing against his body and tossed the leaves of a nearby tree upside down. The unpainted wood of the porch was cracked and warped with age, but it seemed solid enough. He put his glass on the railing and leaned outward, looking into the greyness. To his relief, none of the soldiers came out after him. He was well liked by his men, but they knew to leave him alone when he was in such a mood. A foul, ill-tempered mood, he admitted to himself. If they shunned him it was as much for their sake as for his.

A wagon rattled along the road. His legs were tightening up. Walking might be a good thing. When he went around the corner the full force of the wind struck him, bringing tears to his eyes. He ignored it. Behind the inn was a good-sized vegetable garden, yellow and white with blossoms. He saw peppers, beans, melons, beets, chard, onions. There were many plants he was too city-bred, or too wealthy, to identify. The garden was well maintained, and large enough that it was a significant labor. There must be one or two other servants besides the girl; cooking, gardening, cleaning, and laundering on the scale that this required was too much for any one person. Although it was possible that nine nights out of ten they had no guests. He doubted it; the crowd of people inside had suggested it was rather popular among the local farmers and villagers. What would happen to them when . . . when what? Once again it slid away.

He walked around the barn, the wash-house, and the inn itself before returning to the porch. It was far too early to go to bed, and there was nothing to abate his restlessness. The rain started. The dog scampered onto the porch and looked beseechingly at him. He went back in, hoping there were no leaks in the roof. He refilled his glass and went upstairs.

The room was better than he had expected, though tiny. The bed frame was well constructed and had a real mattress rather than a straw pallet. Besides the bed, the only other furniture was a small table, wobbly when jostled but sturdy enough to hold the glass. The floor had been swept and the linens looked clean. The door did not shut perfectly—he had to put his shoulder against it and push—and the windowpane was cracked and dusty. The ballast ropes were fairly new. Corin gingerly raised the frame a few inches, and it held.

He paused. There was a carved and painted hex on the outside sill. The paint was fresh. He ran his fingers lightly over it. A protection against wandering spirits. It should not surprise him, not in a country inn like this where likely no one could read. But it did. It was the newness of it, he decided, made from raw fear and not unthinking custom. For a moment he imagined he could feel his fingers tingling with galvanic power.

He pushed the thought aside and sat down on the bed. The rain hammered on the roof. It fell in heavy grey sheets, making the fields in the distance almost invisible. The only source of light in the room was a pair of thick ugly candles. No inn like this could afford glowlamps. Corin found the firestarter and lit them with a quick click.

The flames bent and fluttered. He watched the red and gold flicker and elide into each other, and he thought once more of dragons. He raised his glass ironically. To the Empire.

At nearly midnight, he was about to go to bed when someone knocked. Rain still slapped loudly against the window. He opened the door. Bron stood in the corridor looking worried. Before Corin could say a word, Bron spoke urgently. "Sarians, sir, a dozen of them, they just fired a barn two miles east. One of the boys got here ahead of them."

It was too troubling to swear about. The bandits harried the eastern fringes of the country. They had never come this far west.

"How much time have we got?" he asked as he buckled his sword belt back on.

Bron shrugged. He was ten years older than Corin, a few inches shorter, and eminently capable. "Ten minutes? Not long. But they're on foot."

"Do the people downstairs know?"

"No, sir. Alric headed the boy off before he went in."

Ten to twelve. They should be able to defeat the Sarians handily, but Corin wasn't going to take anything for granted. He said, "Get all the people here into the common room and put two men at the door. Can we rely on the horses in this rain?"

"I wouldn't," said Bron. "Too much mud."

"All right." Corin put on his cloak and cap. It was going to be a hellish fight. None of them had any armor more substantial than their leather vests. The Sarians weren't likely to either, though.

The rain was torrential, the darkness thick. They waited on the porch. The smell of the smoke and the glow of the burning barn were evident even in the storm. Huge puddles glimmered on the dirt yard. It would be treacherous footing, slick and full of holes and lumps hiding under the water. The wind was not blowing as hard as it had been earlier, at least.

Two of the soldiers had bows. Bron put them at open windows on the second story of the inn. With any luck they would be able to bring down a few of the Sarians before the battle turned to hand-to-hand fighting. Two, maybe three shots each before the darkness and the close quarters made archery untenable.

Corin held his sword ready. It was an excellent blade, and he was a good swordsman. The soldiers were all superb. He was not too worried about the outcome. He was far more worried about the fact of the Sarian presence at all. But allowing himself to think about it was too much of a distraction. He forced himself to pay attention to the rain and the men standing by him on the porch.

The Sarians made no secret of their coming. They were chanting loudly and carrying torches. Corin's heart sank when he saw that; they were the greenfire war-lights that water could not extinguish.

The men's faces were painted white, contrasting sharply with their red hair.

Corin could not hear the bow-twangs over the rain, but he saw the flicker of darkness in the light before two of the Sarians toppled over. A third cried out. That was enough warning for the others, who flung the torches down and drew their swords. The metal shone green with the reflected light. The shadows were huge. One more man went down with an arrow in his throat as the bandits advanced.

It was impossible for Corin to plant his feet in the mud. He would have to step lightly instead. Two of the Sarians were coming at him. They were taller and heavier, all of them. Bron interposed himself but one of the men got around him and swung at Corin. He parried easily but from the shock of the blow he knew the other man was stronger. Water beaded on the white paint on the Sarian's face.

Corin was dimly aware that the two archers had come out from the inn, but he dared not look. His opponent had the advantage of him in reach and was skilled with the blade. The swords clashed against each other over and over. The mud made it nearly impossible to hold his line. A white light flared blindingly from one of the abandoned torches, flickered. Movements became jerky, hard to follow. Shadows moved maddeningly over the ground. The puddles reflecting the light were sleek.

The Sarian advanced on him, pushing him toward the building. He was going to be trapped against the wall if he was not careful. He parried the next blow and darted to the side, turned, so his back was to open air, risky as that was. Again the swords clashed.

He was lighter, he should be able to use that. He quickened his own slashes and forced the man slowly back to one of the puddles. Somewhere else in the yard a man screamed in pain. He could not tell whose voice it was.

The Sarian stepped into thick heavy mud that gave under his weight. He tried to lunge but the mud slowed him enough for Corin to get past his guard and strike him on the forearm. There was a ringing sound as the blade hit against a metal cuff or bracelet of some sort. Corin's arm shook with the force of the clash. He kept hold of his sword.

The man pressed him again. He chilled briefly with fear. That pushed his body into harder, faster action. The sword felt weightless. It moved in the patterns he had practiced almost daily since he was a child. He did not have to think what to do. Even with the staccato light he could see clearly. Another slash to the man's arm, and this time he hit not metal but flesh and bone, and he pulled back and swung again. The Sarian parried but more weakly.

Corin drew back once more. The man still lay open, and he surged forward, left palm on the pommel. The Sarian's sword slid ineffectively against his and dipped down. He was through, pushing the blade into the man's chest with all the strength he had. Dark blood bubbled out of the man's mouth. Corin withdrew the blade. It grated hideously against bone. The Sarian was falling, slowly, backward with buckling legs. Blood poured from the wound. The man's sword fell.

Breathing hard, sweat burning his eyes, Corin took his first look around. He saw immediately that he was not needed. Only two Sarians were still standing, and each had three soldiers ranged against him. They fell almost simultaneously. It was over.

He stepped onto the porch and wiped his face uselessly with his wet sleeve. Rain had already washed most of the blood from his own sword. There was a pain in his side from exertion.

Bron joined him. "All dead," he said. "No one hurt on our side except Alric, it's minor."

"Put the bodies in the barn," Corin said. They couldn't stay there, the blood would disturb the horses too much, but they needed to be searched and looked at. The barn was dry and they could have a light.

Bron gestured backward at the torches. "What about those, sir?"

"I'll take care of them," Corin said grimly.

"By yourself?"

"Yes." Bron knew as well as he did that ordinary Sarian bandits did not carry the war-lights. He twisted his cap to wring out what water he could. Bron stepped aside as he came down the steps.

There were five of the war-lights. One was flickering white, and one had gone out. The others still shone with green flame. Heat radiated from them. They smelled acrid and stung his eyes. He picked one up and found the knob on the side, turned it. The flame flared up. Quickly he turned it the other way. It extinguished with a snap, leaving no fading glow or ember. He touched the metal wick and pulled his finger away at once. It was still quite hot. He jabbed the wick into the damp ground and screwed it ruthlessly until he felt it bend. When he pulled it out it was coated with mud. He worked it back and forth at the bend until it snapped.

After he had done the same with each of them, he gathered them up and walked to the barn. The rain fell faster, whipping into his face. He was so wet already that it did not matter much.

Inside the barn, he dropped the war-lights with a clatter and looked around. The barn was large enough to belong to a much more prosperous inn, but old and in some disrepair. To the left was a walkway with about a dozen stalls on either side and a large covered pen at the end. To the right were bales of hay stacked fifteen high and ten deep, large feed barrels, mostly empty, and a row of hooks. There were some loose hay bales and two battered stools in the open area. The floor was dirt and gravel and was relatively clean, though the smells of horse manure and wet hay and leather lay over everything. The only light came from a lantern hanging from the ceiling on a long chain. It had been disturbed, and the shadows swelled and shrank like waves as the light moved slowly to and fro. The horses were shifting and huffing; if things were not kept calm they could become difficult. Three of the soldiers were attempting to settle them. There were no horses besides their own.

The bodies were laid out neatly on the floor. A dozen Sarians, all tall and red-haired, all strong. There was no look of starvation about them. If they were bandits they had been doing remarkably well. Bron and Alric were already searching. Alric's forearm was bandaged neatly with no blood showing. To Corin's relief none of the deaths had been messy. That made it easier on everyone.

The Sarian bandits had been a problem for most of the last four years, but only on the fringes of the country. They were cruel and vicious. Their targets were lone farms and poor villages well away from main roads and large towns. They were also luckless deserters of Tyrekh's army, pushed westward by the forces they dared not try to go back through. They fought with knives and slings and staffs, not with good swords and war-lights. It was a hard, makeshift, and harried existence. These men were not of that sort.

He squatted beside a body and looked carefully at it. The Sarian had been one of the ones who died from an arrow, and there was little blood. Someone had cut his shirt open. From nipple to nipple, and from each nipple to navel, was a burn-scar in a straight line an inch wide. In the center of the triangle was a smaller triangle, inverted. Corin winced reflexively, seeing them. He was not surprised—he had heard of these brands, honor-marks—but he could not help imagining the pain. The nipples had been pierced and ringed. From each ring hung a sliver of bone. These were elite soldiers, the cruelest Tyrekh had. And that led to only one grim and inescapable conclusion: Tyrekh was on the move.

He gestured at the burns. "They'll all have them," he said, "or at least some of them. It's ritual."

"Bloody stupid ritual, it must kill some perfectly good fighters," replied Bron, who was nothing if not practical.

"I think that's the point," Corin said. He stood and thought.

Six years ago Tyrekh had come out of the east from Sarium, on the other side of the nearly impassable Black Peaks. He had taken four other countries under his control over three years. He was said to be a sorcerer, a half-god, a fey immortal. His soldiers worshipped him, which made them fearless. Corin knew of at least six assassination attempts that had failed, resulting in impalement for the men who had been unlucky enough to survive their tries. Aram had flatly refused to send anyone himself after seeing what happened to those from other countries. Nor had he risked many spies, and those only the best. The Sarian troops were armed with weapons of fire and strength such as no one had ever seen. They were cruel, rapacious, and unstoppable. Tyrekh took the field himself and whatever resisted him was left shattered behind. Kersage, Readh, Torent, Al Marini, Veniti, Arragon, great cities all, and now their palaces were destroyed and their people were slaves, and Tyrekh's governors sucked away anything that people still had. After taking Illyria, he had ceased, apparently content not to reach farther west into Argondy and Caithen, and there had been three years of nervous peace since. No one would be surprised to learn it had ended.

"I'm going back in," he said. "I'll need someone to take a message when you're done. Make sure all the men know to keep quiet about the fight. Put the torches in one of my bags."

Bron nodded. They looked at each other. Speech was pointless.

Corin went back to the inn. He changed into dry clothes, took writing materials from his saddlebag, and went downstairs to wait. The common room was still noisy and raucous; he could not even hear the rain. He suspected that some of the men in the room were too drunk to have been aware of the danger they faced.

He did not want to call attention to himself. He sat at a table and began composing mental messages to his father. They all had a tone of panic in them. He should have stayed in the barn and helped search; it would have kept him occupied and made it go faster. Dignity be damned. He scowled.

After a while he realized the uncomfortable feeling inside him was fear. He did not try to talk himself out of it. Caithen was a small country; its strength lay in spies and not in soldiers. The Caithenian army had increased fivefold in the last six years, but it was still small and inexperienced in comparison with Tyrekh's. As much as Corin hated Mycene's overlordship, he knew that it made the Emperor bound to protect Caithen. But if the Sarians were already moving in, they had plenty of time to slaughter before they were challenged by Imperial troops.

Someone approached him. He looked up. The serving girl with a pitcher of beer. He accepted a drink, more to have something to keep his hands busy than because he was thirsty. She had a charm on a cord around her neck, and her hand was going to it frequently. She knew or felt something. He watched her, because it was easier and more pleasant than thinking about war, but he no longer had even the smallest flicker of desire.

His mug was still nearly full when Bron came and sat down. "Only one thing besides money," the captain said. He put a small leather pouch on the table.

Corin opened it. The leather was rich, soft and finely grained, not something a bandit was likely to possess. Inside were a few coins, an extremely battered map, and a green stone carved in the shape of an animal fang. The Sarian gods were animals, wolves and bears and sharp-beaked birds. He touched the stone. A luck piece or ritual item of some sort, no doubt. It had failed the man this time. "Have you got someone ready?" he asked Bron.

"Yes. Rine."

He laid out his paper and scrawled a brief message. *Twelve Sarians west of Lyde with war-lights. Soldiers not outlaws. I am making all haste.* He blew the ink dry and folded the paper. The only thing to seal it with was cheap wax from a candle in a wall-sconce. He doubted it would hold, but it was better than nothing. Rine could be trusted not to read it.

"I'd prefer he go the whole way," Corin said, sliding it to Bron. "He can answer questions. But it has to get there whatever way is fastest, he can give it to a courier. And interrupt my father no matter what he's doing."

Bron took the letter and left. A group of men burst into a drinking song on the other side of the room. One grabbed the table-maid by the shirt and pulled her to him. She emptied the beer pitcher on him. Despite himself, Corin grinned. That was spunk. He hoped she made him pay for the beer too. He watched a moment longer to be sure no harm came to her.

Then he went silently back to his room and stretched out fully clothed on the bed, sword at hand. The peace was well and truly broken.

CHAPTER TWO

꧁꧂

When they reached the capital the next day, it was drizzling and getting dark, and they were all splattered with mud, wet, cold, and uncomfortable. It had been a slow and miserable ride, forty miles on rutted muddy roads before they reached a paved surface. Rain had fallen sporadically all day.

Six hundred years ago Caithenor had been a walled city. But wars and time and profit and lovemaking had done their work, and now it sprawled for several miles in every direction beyond the newest of the walls, which was four hundred years old. Tyrekh would have no need to use cannons to take the city.

The gates had long since been torn down, but the entrance arches still stood, narrowing points that were always packed and crowded with people moving in each direction. The men on duty at the old guardhouses were there only to watch for disturbances, not to keep people in or out. On a sunny day or a moonlit night, the city was brilliant with reflected light from glass windows and towers and gilt domes, from sparkling mica in the stone of the buildings and streets, from the fountains bubbling and leaping everywhere and the wide band of the slow river that curved through the low hills. At sunset or sunrise on such days the city burned red and gold. Now there was no dazzle or shine, only the looming bulk of greyish buildings. Crystal edifices were sullen and dirty in the wet. The lit streetlamps made glowing circles of silver in the mist but gave very little illumination beyond the circles' edges.

There was little point in shouting *Make Way* at the entrance arch, because there was no room for anyone to go. They had hooded cloaks; in the darkening evening they rode in without anyone taking notice. The streets were full of damp people in festive garb, all of it looking a little wilted and sad, and after a while Corin realized the Summer Fair must have started. It was wretched weather for it. As though to taunt them with the nearness of home, rain began to fall extremely hard almost as soon as they passed through the east arch, and the last few miles were among the worst of their journey. He was gladder than usual that they did not have to go through the poor parts of the city, with unpaved streets and ramshackle buildings. In this kind of weather it would be like riding through a foul swamp. The hills washed their filth down onto the Flats, and the river cast its up.

Slender white-barked trees grew at even intervals on either side of the street. Sprays of yellow blossoms, heavy and sagging with wet, hung profusely from the branches, and petals covered the sidewalks. They rode past shops and inns, theaters, galleries, public houses. Eventually the shops gave way to mansions surrounded by wide lawns and brick walls, the homes of wealthy commoners and lords. To Corin they seemed dead and unreal compared with the clutter and bustle of the villages he had spent the last week riding past. If they were empty who would know? For a disconcerting instant he had an image of himself riding through a silent town with brambles overgrowing the cobbles and birds nesting on the windowsills. He was relieved when the palace gates rose up before him, when through the slash of rain he saw lantern light and the familiar angles of the guardhouse.

Lights streamed out of the windows and glimmered in the puddles on the flagstones, but with his head down and his hood up all Corin could see of the buildings was a shadowy mass of stone. His horse, realizing it was home, put on an unexpected burst of energy, and he had to rein it in.

He stopped at the ordinary entrance to the main building—the formal entrance was hardly ever used—and dismounted. The horse blew but stood still. Three stable-boys hurried down the granite steps to take the horses. Corin took the saddlebags off, then handed the reins to one of the boys. The soldiers dismounted, leaving their horses likewise, and the men went up the steps in a cluster. There was a roofed area at the top where they shook some of the water from their cloaks and boots. The guards held the doors wide-open so they could crowd through quickly.

The vestibule was puddled with water. One of the guards took

Corin's cloak and offered him a towel from a large stack on the chair beside him. He dried his face and hair and neck gratefully, discovered that his shoulders and chest were still dry. His pants clung to him. He looked resentfully at the mud on his boots and made a mostly futile effort to scrape it off. A cat darted out from under a bench and dashed away.

As often was the case, the large entrance hall was clustered with people. He had hoped to sneak in unnoticed, obviously an impossibility. He made himself look cheerful and walked in. The tiled rust-red and black stone floor was muddy. The glowlamps on the walls only made the darkness outside the tall arched windows more noticeable. Light reflected on the polished wooden window frames in soft blurs of gold.

There were an inordinate number of young women in the hall, and he resigned himself to being on display. This was the last year he could reasonably expect to make it through the summer without ending up betrothed to someone; at twenty-five he was getting too old to stay unmarried. He suspected his mother was beginning to despair of ever making a good match. Various shades of rose seemed to be the fashion this season. It was not a color he found particularly attractive on most women. He thought absently of the girl at the inn; she had been prettier in her ordinary clothes than half these women with their silks and flounces and elaborate hair. They were all alike, flittering and fluttering, smiling brightly, pushing and shoving one another with elbows out to throw themselves in his path. He was the grand prize, and everyone knew it.

He caught the eye of one woman, whose bold, provocative smile was at odds with the round youthfulness of her face. It was impossible for his eye not to follow the line of her dark ringlets over her white skin to the tightness of her low-necked gown. That was one who would end up in trouble if she weren't more careful. His glance slid to the face of the woman next to her, and he nearly stopped in his tracks; she was stunning, black-haired and slender with the most astonishingly beautiful face he had ever seen. She had not been at court before; he would have remembered her. Their eyes met. She blushed and looked down. He felt hot. He kept walking and hoped no one had noticed.

When he passed into the corridors, he let himself relax again. He would be expected immediately, but he was entitled to change his clothes and make himself presentable before going to see the king. He left the war-lights in his room. He would have them destroyed later.

The guards outside his father's study looked more tense than usual, high-strung with alertness. He hoped it was not a sign of trouble. Like the city gate guards, they were a formality; no one in the palace was going to try to harm the king. They should not have had to act as though they really were on guard. Perhaps his news had not been the first.

In the antechamber the clerk's desk was empty, though his lamp was still on. Two pages were playing a lopsided game of chess at a small table. They jumped up hastily when they saw him, jostling the table. He noticed with amusement that it was the boy who was losing who steadied the board to keep it from sliding. A few captured pieces rolled on the floor.

The other boy said smoothly, "The clerk just went in, my lord." He was well on his way to being an accomplished courtier and sycophant.

"Thank you," Corin said. He heard voices through the door, which was slightly ajar, but could not make out the words. He hesitated a moment, wondering if he should go in or wait, then heard footsteps. Quickly he stepped back and waited for the clerk to come out.

Bryden, who was normally unflappable, looked far more relieved to see him than he had any right to. That was hardly good. He said, "He'll be glad you're back, sir. Go on in."

Corin looked back at the boys and said to the losing one, "Bring your knight out," then went in. Aram was standing. His desk was much more cluttered than usual.

The king started to say something but was interrupted by the low bark and long growl of his black dog, Sika, beside him. Her hackles were up as she stared at Corin as though he were a stranger, instead of someone she had known all her life. He was so startled that he froze.

"Lie down," Aram said.

The dog did not move. Corin took a step forward and she growled again, teeth bared. "Come here, girl," he said, holding out a hand. He had had long absences before and she had always greeted him eagerly on return. He looked at his father. "Has she been like this?"

"No," Aram said. "Has something—"

Sika charged, knocking Corin to the floor. Her teeth were almost at his throat. He felt the hot breath, the saliva falling on his face. He was jolted by the fall, but not enough for the reflexes and training of years to be dulled. With his arms crossed over his neck and face he kicked at the dog. There was shouting going on, hard to hear over the barks. He rolled over and up, lunged forward and caught the collar. Aram's hand came down next to his. One of the guards was right beside him, sword drawn.

The dog went silent, then relaxed into a lying position, whined softly. The men stared at each other. Corin carefully held one hand up to Sika's face. She licked it. Her tail whisked against the floor.

Corin stood up. His heart was pounding, and his hands trembled from the release of urgency. His voice was steady though when he said, "What the hell was that?"

"I have no idea," Aram said. He released the dog's collar. "Do you want me to put her out?"

He considered it. There was a reason she had done that, but the thought kept sliding away from him.

"No," he said. He looked at the guard. "You can leave, thank you." He wiped his forehead. "Have you got anything to drink?"

"Sit down, I'll get it."

The chair was very soft, the most comfortable one he had sat on in weeks. The room was dim, only a few of the lamps lit. Corin closed his eyes. The fire roared pleasantly, like the sea. He looked up long enough to take a cup of wine from his father, who said, "Take your time about it. Have you eaten?"

"No. The Sarians—" he began.

"I had your message this morning," Aram said sharply. This from the man who was nearly always even-tempered and patient. "There's no rush, and I want you clear-headed."

Corin knew better than to protest. He had learned a long time ago to pick his battles. He sipped. Good wine, how could he have thought the inn's wine decent? Aram spoke to someone at the door in soft words Corin did not try to hear. He stayed quiet, the only sounds the rain and the fire and the occasional rustle of papers on his father's desk.

It was not long before a servant came with a meal for him, steam still rising from the soup. The man put the tray on a square side table and left as quietly as he had come. The king kept working while Corin ate. The meat was tender, the sauce flavorful, the bread light and free of grit from the mill. By the time he finished he felt more alert; he must have needed the rest and food more than he thought.

He pushed the dishes to the side. Usually when he got back from a journey he would ask after his mother if she was not present, find out what work he needed to take up, listen to the king's summary of events. He refilled his cup and said, "What are we going to do?"

Aram looked hard at him, then moved from behind the desk to a chair opposite Corin's. He was dressed formally but had loosened the buttons at his collar. He was not much of one for pomp. His hair was the same dark brown as his son's, well flecked now with grey, but his eyes were almost black. He said, "You don't know everything yet. I got word three days ago that Tyrekh has begun moving his soldiers across the Illyrian border with Argondy. I'd have sent for you if I hadn't known you were nearly back."

That was what Corin had feared. He was already resigned to it. "What about Mari?" he asked urgently. His older sister was married to an Argondian duke. Tyrekh's soldiers had no compunction about killing anyone; if she had been married to a cobbler it would have been as necessary to get her out. Argondy was a soft country of rolling hills and wide plains, crowded with small villages and towns, crisscrossed with roads. It was an easy land to traverse and would be an easy land to conquer. The eastern border with Illyria followed a line of hills but was no obstacle; it had been drawn in a treaty several hundred years ago and reflected no significant natural boundaries. Tyrekh had brought his men out of the harsh steppe lands of

Sarium, across the high and deadly Black Peaks, then through the increasingly gentler countries to the west. Argondy would present no challenge to him.

"She is safe enough, she was on her way here for the summer and across the border when it happened. She has the children with her. I sent troops to meet them as a precaution. I don't know about Ves, though. I doubt he will flee until there is no other choice."

Corin nodded. Mari's husband was no more a coward than she was. "I hope you sent enough. The men I fought were probably not the only forerunners." It was all too easy to imagine other such bands of soldiers making their way at night along untraveled country lanes, drawing closer and closer to the capital.

"What exactly happened? I heard most of it from your man, but I want to hear from you."

"It was typical Sarian outlaw work, but if they were bandits I'm a seamstress. We were staying at a wretched little inn in Stede's barony when we heard they had fired a barn. There were a dozen of them, with five war-lights and good clothing. They were all in excellent condition and fought well, though not well enough. If they had been bandits they would have scattered as soon as they saw they were losing. Some of them had the warrior marks, too."

"Well," Aram said softly. "Well, well, well."

A draft touched Corin's skin, and he shivered. For an instant he felt as though he were being watched. A gust of wind blew rain hard against the windows. They were thick glass in iron frames, unlikely to be broken by even the fiercest storms, but he started at the noise. He was glad he had gotten inside before the weather turned this much worse.

"What's the matter?" Aram asked. "You're on edge."

He shook his head and felt his damp hair. "Just expecting to be rained on again." His father would see through the lie but would not press it.

After a moment, Aram said, "I had the sense from your reports that there was something you didn't want to commit to paper."

It was strange, there in the north, he tried to say. His tongue tangled as though he were speaking another language while drunken. He wondered if he would be able to write it. If only he could remember everything. He hoped he had not left a trail of forgotten ill judgments. He felt sweat on his forehead. His body sang to him that something bad had happened.

"Corin?"

"The dragons." His mouth did not want to shape the word.

"Tell me."

It was hard to say. "They were observing." Faltering sometimes, the words slipping away, he described the constant presence of the dragons. He remembered the way the sun sparked on their wings, the curl of the garrison pennants in their passage. "I don't know if they were watching that hold alone, or others. There's not—since—I haven't seen others. But I can tell you that I was not the only one. To notice. There were plenty of men looking up. No one said anything. I take it there's been nothing from the spies in Mycene to suggest anything amiss."

Aram shook his head. "Nothing."

"I don't like that." The spies were too good for silence to be convincing. Someone should have known why Hadon sent his dragons north.

"It may be the least of our worries," Aram said. "You saw them the entire time you were there?"

For a moment he was mute. Then he found his voice. "Yes," he said. "They'd been seen by others before I got there, too." The words were clear, spoken by someone else. He could not remember if it was true.

Aram broke a wooden stylus in half with a loud snap. That was something he never did either. He said, "Then whatever plans he's making in that tangled mind of his, it's probably not to do with the Sarians. Set it aside if you can for now."

Corin looked sideways at his father. Now it was Aram who wasn't saying all he thought. He decided not to push it. The king would tell him when he was ready. He said, "Does Hadon know about Tyrekh?"

Aram said, "God knows what his spies have told him. But I sent to him as soon as I heard, we should have his response in a day or two. We can only hope there's time."

"What have you planned?"

"Coll's beginning to organize the troops, and we sent out more scouts. I called a formal war council. Most of the dukes were on their way here anyway for the summer court, so it will take place fairly soon, perhaps even tomorrow. I told the ones who have already arrived, but they're to keep it quiet. You can tell Bron, but no one else."

Summer court, he should have stayed away. He hoped his younger sister Tai was coming too, she would keep him sane with her dry wit and mischievous suggestions. She had married last fall and he was still not used to her absence. He was very glad she had not been made to marry one of Hadon's sons.

His gaze went to the dog, who was sleeping on her pillow in the corner. Why had she jumped him? "Tell me what else you know about Tyrekh's movement."

They pulled the chairs closer together and spent some time going over the details of Aram's reports. It felt like something acted, done over and over. Three years ago Corin had spent many hours staring at maps, discussing numbers and formations and movements of soldiers, planning defenses. There was not much in the way of alternatives, and Tyrekh would deduce the plans accurately. They had little choice in what they did. The land forced them into certain stances.

A river ran the length of the Caithenian border with Argondy. The northern half, coming down out of the Fells, was steep and rocky. The river was swift and cut into deep gorges with sheer treeless sides or cascaded down falls several hundred feet high. South the land softened to low hills, but the river widened to a lake, eight miles wide and a hundred miles long, with marshes and bogs on either side. Eventually it narrowed back to a river, but it was still as wide as a mile in some places and even boggier. Several crossing points could be made across the lake, but ferrying an army was impractical. The only viable entry for a large mass of men into Caithen from Argondy was the main road with its many-arched bridge across the river. It was still hill country there, and an army would be vulnerable to ambushes and attacks from above. That was the sole tactical advantage Caithen had. It would take a few days of steady marching through the duchy of Harin for Tyrekh's troops to move far enough west into Caithen to be able to go quickly and in the open.

Eventually Aram pushed the papers aside. He rose and walked to one of the bay windows. Corin had the sense that he was waiting for someone or something else. After a moment of indecision, he joined his father. Their reflections were wavy from the water running down the glass. Sika got up and came toward them, her claws clicking on the floor. Both men tensed, but she only wagged her tail and sat.

Aram turned from the window to stare at Corin. "You can't let yourself get killed, Corin, not even in battle. If the worst happens, you'll have to hide somewhere so you can fight back later. The spies will survive. You know what is in place."

"But—"

"I'm not giving you a choice."

Aram was right, he always was. "Yes, sir."

"Good." He put his hand on Corin's shoulder.

"What about you?"

"You don't really think I'm going to get out of this alive or free, do you? I'll try to, certainly, but if I can protect only one of us it has to be you. You're young, you can keep an insurgency going for another generation if you have to."

It depressed him. He said nothing, and after a moment his father's hand dropped. The king returned to his seat. Corin went to the map table and looked at the map of southern Caithen, the coast along the Narrow Sea. The best port for ships to put in was Dele, and it was an easy march from there over gentle country to Caithenor. The Sarians were not either shipbuilders or sailors, but the Argondians were.

"We have to secure the Port of Dele," he said. "Once Tyrekh gets hold of the Argondian fleet, he doesn't need to come overland."

"Yes," Aram said. He sounded distracted. Corin glanced at him. He was leaning forward with his chin resting on clasped hands, looking into air. The grimness on his face was one that Corin had seen before, but not often. It was hardly surprising. The king said, "Was it peaceful in the north?"

"Yes," Corin answered. It was an odd question. He felt words threatening to slip away again. "But the people are all afraid of something anyhow," he managed to get out. "Spirits. Curses. It's nonsense." There was a white emptiness in his mind that he could not go around. He had forgotten. The thorny briars would grow instead, blocking him, stabbing him when he tried to push through.

What was he thinking? Was he going mad? For a second he felt it, everything around him a waxwork, a reflection, unreal. Then he grounded himself fiercely in the crackle of the fire and the smooth darkness of the wine in his cup.

Aram said, "It's superstition, yes. But it's riding the back of something else. Fear can't be tamped down forever. It's the same here. Everyone knows Tyrekh has yet to be dealt with, even though no one will say it. The waiting is coming to an end. Bad things are going to happen, Corin. Don't let them take you unaware."

The heaviness of it settled in him. He had been told that history had tides, but this felt more like a chain, one cold thick link added at a time. He had the sense that Aram was speaking of something more than Tyrekh.

"I won't," he said. What else could he say?

Neither of them spoke again for a few minutes. Corin randomly turned pages in the map book. He lingered over a map of the northern mountains, with their fierce names—Tower Peak, Mount Fang, the Bloodhorn—and wondered if there was anything there that Hadon could be looking for.

He was about to excuse himself when someone knocked. The king called an entrance as Corin sat back down. It was Joce, which sent a shiver of apprehension through him. The Basilisks were Aram's secret servants, not called upon for ordinary matters.

They were remnants of the race of true wizards, nothing like the conjurers and magicians who claimed to be able to cast spells and tell the future. Every village had its witch who murmured over potions and laid the cards to no effect. In cities men tried secretly to conjure up the dead and find the path to immortality and got nothing for their trouble but a reeking mess of oils and entrails and candlewax. It was not so with Joce and his people. A thousand years ago, longer, they had been able to do all manner of things: change into animals, call the wind, speak mind to mind, see in a puddle of water what happened miles away. They needed no incantations or tinctures of antimony. But power over people was not something most of them sought—there were always a few, the evil sorcerers of tales and legend—and as the ordinary men built armies and made laws, the wizards were hunted and driven into hiding, killed or enslaved. For a while kings tried to keep them as advisers, but all the jealousies and treacheries of courts brought that to an end. If they were not killed, they were discredited, and the kings with them. They diminished, the learning and power diminishing with them, and when the persecutions of the Fires came three centuries ago they were destroyed.

Or so it had always been thought. Aram's grandfather had found them out, hiding and desperately poor, but not yet completely powerless. That king had been overly fond of his wine and his women but not dim-witted, and he bargained to provide protection for them all in exchange for the service of a few. The pledge had been kept unbroken ever since. The wizards who served, the Basilisks, were deadly, superbly trained in armed and unarmed combat, and virtually fearless. Much power had been lost, but they still could hold a man immobile with a single glance, or throw up illusions to protect themselves. They had enough of the shapechanging power left to disguise themselves as other men for a short time. Aram's grandfather had called them *Basilisks* because of their paralyzing stare; Corin thought it might also have been a private lament for the loss of the dragons.

It was a tightly guarded secret; Corin was not sure if even his sisters knew. The spymaster knew only that they were Aram's personally selected men, to be used for the most dangerous or important spying. Joce had been a spy among the Sarian soldiers for nearly three years. There was nothing distinctive about his looks, which had caused more than one person to not pay him enough attention. Sika padded happily over to him; he was good with animals, as most wizards were. He gave her his hand to lick.

Aram said, "What is the latest from Dele?"

"Nothing new, my lord. All's been steady for some time."

"When were you to go again?"

"Next week."

"Leave it for now," Aram said. "I want you to roam about and find the weak places here. That includes people. Lay traps if you need to."

"Weak against what?"

"Tyrekh."

Joce appeared unsurprised. Corin had never seen him startled. He said, "Anyone to exclude?"

"Not this time. Consider everyone from the washmaids to the dukes. If something takes you into the city, go ahead and follow it. Don't speak to anyone about this."

The first time Corin had heard his father give orders of this sort he had thought they were uselessly vague and redundant. He had learned the importance of redundancy soon enough, but it had been longer before he understood what Aram was doing with the broadness of his commands. Some parameters did not need to be stated. Joce knew the few people he never had to watch. He was like a cat. He would prowl and wait and sniff out everything, vanishing into shadow if he was seen, and he would notice what Aram would never have thought to look at.

"How long?"

"Come back in three days, or sooner if you find something. Corin, have you anything to add?"

Memory rose in him, a white face with water beading on it. "Why would Sarian soldiers paint their faces white?"

Joce said, "There's something in the paint that makes them stronger and more fearless. It dulls pain. Tyrekh gives it to his best."

"Eight of us killed twelve of them," Corin said. "Nine hand to hand, three went down from bowshots."

"You have good men. But—" He stopped.

"But what? Say it."

"War against Tyrekh is not an even match like that."

We've the Empire, Corin thought. He did not speak it. Tyrekh might move faster.

Joce said, "Is that all, my lord?"

"Yes," Aram said.

Joce bowed and stepped back. On impulse, Corin stood up and walked beside him to the antechamber. The room was dim and deserted, though the shadows of the guards in the hall could be seen.

"Be careful," he said, clasping Joce's forearm in the soldier's gesture of good luck. The man's body jerked hard at the touch.

It was an insult. But it was clear to Corin that it had been a movement of the body that could not have been prevented, like a dead muscle twitching when a current ran through it. Joce looked almost frightened.

"My lord," he said after a few seconds that seemed to last years, "you're dangerous." He held out his arm, and there on the skin were burns the size and shape of fingertips, red and new.

Corin felt as though he had received a blow to the stomach, but an anticipated one. "Who might know?" he whispered.

"I don't know, sir. I'll think about it." He had regained his composure. "Shall I ask the others?"

"No. Not yet."

"You'll need them later."

"Why?"

"Power."

"Whose?"

Joce looked at the burns on his arm. "Yours," he said softly.

Their eyes met and held for a long moment. Then Joce broke the contact with a bent head. Corin stepped back into his father's room and shut the door again.

Aram did not ask why he had gone. Who else had he touched? His father. No, Aram had touched him. Not the boy taking his horse, or the guards at the entrance. The dog had attacked him, he had burned a wizard's skin. Something was happening to him. The answer lay in the north, among the things he had forgotten.

"Corin?"

He came back. "I'm sorry, I was drifting. What was he watching in Dele?"

"Ordinary corruption. You know the sort."

Corin did. Where there was trade there was evasion of law. It mattered for the revenues but it was unlikely to matter in the face of war. "Will it interfere with securing the port?"

"Anything could, but I don't think so."

Corin nodded, then, to his embarrassment, yawned.

"You must be exhausted," Aram said. "Other things can wait. I'm sure your mother would like to see you."

"She doesn't have any unpleasant surprises for me, does she?"

"Such as a bride? You're still safe there."

"Good."

Aram laughed. "Get on with you," he said.

Talk to Bron, Corin thought. Ask him what I did. He might remember things. He said, "Good night."

It was not as late as it felt, and after he had seen his mother—Talia greeted him with a brief embrace and the unwelcome news that an imminent war was not an excuse for avoiding the courtiers—he bathed, then read quietly in his sitting room. It was cowardly of him, but he did not want to think about the war any longer. Not tonight. A window was open enough to let in the sound and smell of the rain, and the fire was bright and smokeless. The glowlamps were brighter than he wanted, so he kept them off.

Someone knocked. It irritated him. He had not told the guards to keep people away. A mistake, that was, especially when it was their only useful function. He had already locked the door, so he had to go open it himself.

When he saw Seana he felt only weariness. He let her in but did not latch or bolt the door. She put her arms around his neck and kissed him. Her lips were soft and smooth, the tip of her tongue warm. It did not arouse him. She was wearing a dress with off-the-shoulder sleeves and a rounded neckline. He put his hands on her shoulders and stepped gently out of her embrace. Part of him noticed coldly that he did not burn her.

Her earrings were tear-shaped blue opals set in gold, and she wore a matching ring on her right hand. An opal pendant rested at the top of the cleft between her breasts. Her wedding ring, ornate gold edged with diamonds, glittered in the firelight. Her perfume was spicy with a hint of bitterness. Her red-brown hair tumbled down her back.

She took his hands in hers and moved forward, so that they were only a few fingers apart. It was quite clear what she wanted, and usually he would have been undressing her by now. Especially after six weeks surrounded by only men. Corin did not love her and she knew it, but they had a comradely sort of friendship. They had been occasional lovers for several years, when it suited them both and her husband, the Duke of Osstig, was away. The duke, who was more than thirty years older than she was, had to be aware that she was unfaithful to him—and it had not only been with Corin, nor had he been the first. It was widely known to be an unhappy marriage. In the unlikely occurrence of a divorce, the lawyers would be kept busy for years. Corin did not let her share his bed when her husband was at court. Adultery was bad enough, he would not compound it with indiscretion.

As attractive as she was, he did not want her tonight. The face of the woman in the entrance hall, the beautiful woman who had blushed, intruded into his thoughts. That was not what held him back from her, though. Perhaps he was just tired. Tiredness had never stopped him before.

He sat down in one of the formal brocaded chairs and looked at her. She took the hint and sat in another, said, "Was it a hard journey, Cor?"

"No, just dull and wet," he answered. And I've come home to a war. But he wouldn't say that to her, she would think he was brooding. She was intelligent but had little patience for long consideration and by far preferred acting to thinking. "Are you chilled?" he asked, looking at her bare shoulders.

"Not especially," she said. She tugged almost nervously at the pendant. The motion of her hand emphasized her breasts. He wanted to cover them instead of touch them. "How was the north? Cold?"

"At times," he said, remembering the thick frost that had furred the buildings some mornings before the sun was on them. "It made one work, instead of sitting lazily." He could not believe how banal this talk was already, they might as well have been at a state dinner. Did he really have nothing to say to her if they were not in bed?

He tried. "I'm not used to being back yet. My head is still full of military lists and assessments. What have I missed?"

She tossed her hair. "Nothing really," she said. "Oh, there's plenty of gossip now that the summer court has begun, but you aren't ever interested in that. You're about as stiff as a stone wall, Corin, whatever is the matter?"

"Nothing," he said. He stood up. "It's not a good idea tonight, Seana. I think you'd better leave." He took her hand and raised her from the chair.

"Simoun will be here tomorrow," she said, touching his chin. "Are you sure?"

There had been other times when he had declined her, and she was never upset or spiteful. He had no worries that she would make trouble. But there had always been a sense of *not this time, later though*. That was not how he felt now.

"I'm sure," he said. He leaned down and kissed her cheek. "I'll see you later."

She trailed her hand down to his waist, then turned without hesitation and left. For a moment he stared out the open door into the wainscoted hallway, watching the flicker of light on the wood. The guards had moved discreetly away; he told them he was not to be disturbed.

His book no longer interested him. He went to bed, and dreamed of violent things.

CHAPTER THREE

T am roused with a start. The rain was very loud against the window; that must have been what awakened her. The room was stuffy. She lay in bed for a while, but sleep did not return. She found the firestarter and lit a candle. It was a red taper that burned clearly, the holder beautifully glazed. It was the small items like this that made her aware of the wealth of the palace.

She could turn on a lamp if she wished, but that felt too much like getting up. There was a window seat piled with cushions, and she took the candle over, placed it on the floor so it would not reflect in the glass. After a moment's thought she opened the window about an inch, letting in the noise and the cool air. The scent of the wet stone reminded her briefly of forest; it made her feel wilder than the palace was. She got a blanket, light and soft, from the closet and wrapped herself in it while she looked out at the darkness.

Even four stories up she heard the rain drumming on the stone below. Her rooms overlooked a courtyard with a plain grassy area and a few modest flower beds in the center. An arcade surrounded the courtyard, the pillars functional and unadorned. She could not see any of it now, but in half a week it had already become quite familiar to her. When she walked through it she had hardly been able to tell which of the many windows was her own. It was uninteresting but adequate; she had been afraid she might overlook the furnace sheds or the washyard. In the palace, windows went with rank, and she had none.

That had mattered much less than she expected. Her brother's wife, who was a baron's daughter, had received permission from Queen Talia to bring Tam to summer court. Kinship to Cina seemed to be all Tam needed to be accepted among the minor nobility who were the core of the courtiers. The unmarried women whose rooms were in the same wing were the daughters of counts, barons, baronets, and knights, some of them rich in land but poorer in gold than herself. Wealth earned in commerce was no longer vulgar in Caithen—she supposed it might be elsewhere in the Empire—and her brother, who was both clever and lucky, had plenty. Her father was a doctor, respected both for his profession and his skill in it, who also had a widespread reputation as a scholar among physicians and natural philosophers. He was not poor either; he was the man the rich and the nearby country lords called on at every sneeze. Tam could reasonably expect to leave at the end of summer with an engagement to a minor lord.

She had not come husband-hunting, though, which set her apart from the rest of the women; she had come because she was curious. It was not something she dared admit to anyone. The honor was a real one, and she could not diminish it by comparing her position to that of a spectator at the circus, entertaining as it was to watch the games of courtship that the others played. She liked Cina—everybody did, she was very popular—and did not want to embarrass her. So she smiled and flirted and charmed and talked like all the others. To her relief she had not yet caught any man she would have to let down, though she had had to work consciously at not favoring any man twice. Fortunately no one suitable had caught her eye either.

She was a well-bred and well-educated young woman, even an accomplished one. She spoke three languages besides her own and could draw, sing, play the piano, and do embroidery, all of it inoffensively. She could converse on poetry and morals with equal grace. She had improved her mind by extensive reading. But her education did not end there.

For the last five years she had gone with her father when he went, once every week or two, into the dark places of the poor to treat them without fee. She dressed wounds, mixed medicines, sat by the dying. She helped her father with his experiments and his writings. When he saw something interesting under the glass, it was she who drew the picture for him. She had done other work too, assisting her brother with his accounts, shipping lists, and other such things. He had clerks, but there was always more work to do, and he trusted her to ensure he wasn't being cheated. The young men she had met here would have only scorn or, worse, pity, for her for doing such things, and therefore she would not marry any of them. She was not averse to men or marriage, but she was averse to idleness and indulgence.

Her father had not wanted her to come to Caithenor. Partly it was because he thought it was too frivolous, but his greater fear was that this might be the summer the Sarians moved west. He knew what it meant if they did. He had been to Sarium twice, once before Tam was born, and the second time eight years ago, when Tyrekh was building his army and looking hungrily westward. Sarium was a harsh land of arid steppes and icy mountains, which were rich in iron and tin and other metals, silver and traces of gold. There were also fields of coal, in which the Sarians delved pits and widened them until the land for miles was nothing but craters and dust. They were clever with machines, with forges, with mixes of salts and metals, with distillations of drugs from many different plants. The coal and the metals and the other things the Sarians had, fine goat wool and medicinal plants, beautiful rugs, they traded in the powerful kingdoms to the east for goods they needed. In the steep and narrow but very long river valleys—slashes in the land, her father said—they grew grain and raised goats and small cattle and built their cities. Her father had learned a great deal there, which was why he had made the dangerous journey twice.

But Tyrekh thought there was no reason to trade for what he could take, so he came west across the Black Peaks instead, and took. And took and took. Tam's father had told her some of the things the Sarians did to their own people, horrible things that she did not want to think about. He had told her three years ago, when they thought Tyrekh might come to Argondy and Caithen, because she had asked him. She hated what she heard but could not tell him to stop. The Sarians made use of the land to punish, and they made use of their metals and machines and chemistries to frighten and control. To kill.

It had been peaceful in Caithen, but her father was not reassured. He thought Tyrekh had already waited too long. Occasionally men he knew from Illyria or Liddea, ground down with fear and suffering, came to their home. They told grim stories of slavery and death.

Tam's father listened, and waited, and thought she should stay at home in her shabby and insignificant city.

She and her mother persuaded him that all of Argondy and half of Caithen lay between the Sarians and Caithenor. Her brother was in Dele as he was every summer, making bargains with traders from across the Empire, shipmasters, and bankers. If war came he was in much more danger than she was. Hyrne grudgingly gave in, yielding his daughter to the fripperies of court.

The candle flickered and went out in a sudden strong draft. Tam stayed where she was, letting the darkness fold itself around her. It made her aware of the age of the palace, built a thousand years ago and added on to piece by piece, as the world changed and different things were needed. Without light the room was stripped of all its modern touches and had only the walls it had had when it was built centuries ago. Who knew how many other people had sat here and looked out on rainy nights?

Age itself did not impress Tam; her own city of Dalrinia was dotted with buildings that were hundreds of years old, and some of the roads were even older. Caithenor too, she was told, had its share of ruins and overgrown lich-fields. Civilizations had risen and fallen for millennia. Remnants of walls and foundations were scattered across the landscape, buried, built upon. She had been to the City of Silence in the west, where no grass grew and the only things that moved were the tiny dust-devils in the streets, and every stone house was full of stone people. There was no record, no memory, of what had happened there, only stone and dust. Coins, knives, shards of pottery, the rubbish of the past, were constantly being unearthed as fields were tilled or foundations were dug. A gift from the Old Ones, people said, flinging them aside. The past was everywhere in Caithen, and therefore unremarkable. But here there was a continuity to it; the building continued through time, but the roots were ancient and undisturbed. If she could strip off the graceful layers she would find something unmovable and strong. For a thousand years, long before warring lords had been united under a single king, this place had been a center of power. She could not help feeling humbled.

In the next room, the clock struck softly. Three. She should really go back to bed. But there was something very pleasant about sitting here, safe, alone, watching rain. It was quiet and still as the palace never was between dawn and midnight. She pulled the blanket more snugly around herself.

A steady light appeared in the courtyard, coming from the walkway opposite her. It moved but did not flicker—someone was carrying a lantern. He put it down and leaned against the nearest pillar. The yellow light reflected on the wet stone. Not dazzling, but bright compared with the darkness. She frowned in perplexity. Even if it was a guard doing rounds, he could have seen immediately that the courtyard was empty. There were no high bushes or walls anyone might lurk behind. Who would stay and wait on a night like this? On any night, for that matter. But the man continued to wait.

A few minutes later, a second man joined him. All Tam could see of either one was dark hair and men's clothing. The dark hair could have been blond in the wet night. They were talking, she could tell that from the gestures, but the rain drowned out their voices. The lantern was so steady that it had to be of excellent make and use expensive oil; these were not a couple of servants gossiping. The palace was huge; there must be dozens of places where two men could talk in private. It was not just privacy they wanted, then. They could not be seen to have any connection to each other.

The hair on the back of her neck and arms rose. It amazed her; she had not thought that happened anywhere except in three-volume novels with dashing men and swooning ladies. She realized the men were looking up toward her window. Her body had known. They could not see anything, she was sure of that, not with the candle out and the rain rippling on the glass. Maybe they had noticed the window was open a bit. Or they were looking at all the rooms. She stayed entirely still. They turned away.

She remained motionless. It was not the freeze of a frightened rabbit. But if they looked again the patterns of darkness might have changed. She had no idea if they could tell whose room it was, or if they would even care, but she did not want to leave a trace of her accidental spying. The men wanted secrecy and she was breaking that, even if they did not know, even if she did not intend it. Whatever required this sort of meeting was either criminal or illicit.

They talked longer. One was taller and thinner, and his cloak was so well cut he had to be a lord. There was a hint of deference in the second man's posture that made her guess he was a commoner, perhaps even a servant. That was not much to go on. Even if she had been able to see their features through the rain and the shadow, she would not have known who they were. And if she did, what would she do with that knowledge? Nothing. If she told a guard, she would only be laughed at. There were probably dozens of other intrigues. Wherever there was power to be gained, there was plotting. Following them to find out more was out of the question. It would be the end of her reputation to be out of her room at this time of the night. Three years ago she might have anyway, but maturity had calmed some of her impulses.

A light came on in a room on her floor on the western side of the courtyard. The light was shockingly bright by comparison to the lantern. It was a glowlamp, and the curtains must be drawn aside. She counted windows and decided it was Alina's room. A few seconds later Alina herself came to the window, a robe wrapped around her. She opened the window casement.

The men walked around the courtyard until they were under her window. The taller man stepped out into the open where Alina could see him. She leaned out. If either spoke, Tam could not hear.

Alina looked around, then, apparently satisfied, dropped something. The man caught it deftly. He inspected it, then went back to the walkway and handed it to the other man. Alina's light went out, followed by the lantern.

Tam waited for a while, then got slowly up. Her body was stiff, she must have sat longer than she thought. The assignation had all the hallmarks of a romantic tryst between secret lovers, yet Tam thought that unlikely. For one thing, there had been two men, and for another Alina had no reasons for secrecy. She was too interested in getting married to waste her time on someone ineligible.

Infatuation made for odd behavior, though. And love and marriage did not often coincide where wealth and power were.

She sighed. Something about a secret romance made even those who did not want one feel left out. Well, she would be sensible again come daylight.

Daylight came, but not sun. The clouds were thick and low and dark, making the day grey and dreary. Tam breakfasted with Cina in the Sun Room, most inappositely named on such a morning. There were small tables set far enough apart for privacy, large leafy plants in huge pots, and tall windows open to the east. A door led out to a neat grassy square with a tall hedge of brightly flowering bushes on the opposite side. It was favored by the courtiers as a pleasant middle ground between eating alone in one's rooms or dining in the noise and hubbub of the hall, but they were early enough that it was mostly empty. The room felt cold, and Tam was glad of the warmth of her coffee through the thin delicate porcelain. The cup was gold rimmed, with a graceful pattern of a vine. Another of the little touches of beauty that signified wealth.

It was the first time she had been alone with her sister-in-law since they had arrived, and they chatted of what Tam had seen so far before Cina said, "I've shopping to do this morning, will you come?"

Tam gave it thought. Had the weather been good she would have assented; she had seen only a bit of the city on her way in and she wanted to see more. Dalrinia was considerably smaller than Caithenor. But puddle-dodging and wet dashes from store to store did not appeal to her, and she said, "Not today, thank you."

"What will you do instead? It's hardly a day for strolling the gardens."

"Explore the palace, and then I expect I'll read," she said. The library was extraordinary, and even though she could not take books out—that was a privilege of nobility—she could easily spend hours there. It had books in it that were so old they were written by hand. The most valuable were locked up, but there was a displayed manuscript of the Treaty of Pell dating back seven hundred years that she was itching to get a longer look at.

"You're not bored already, are you?"

"No, of course not. But on a dreary day like this people will be squabbling, and that's no fun."

"There's something to that," Cina agreed. "At least everything else is calm."

"Really?" Tam asked, thinking that tension probably swirled around and under many of the conversations between jealous men and women.

"No full-blown scandals yet or serious rifts. Those will come later. Court is still young. Keep your eyes open, Tam, and not just for love affairs. It's about preferment and power too, and you're not experienced."

"I'm not an innocent, Cina," Tam said, grimacing.

"I know that. But it's different here from your home. Just be careful."

"Well, I haven't anything to offer someone, so no doubt they'll all lose interest in me soon."

"You've beauty and money. That's enough." Cina drank some tea. "You can see through most scoundrels, but some of them are very good at it here. Charming, handsome, and without a scrap of conscience. Don't form any attachments without talking to me first."

"If it's such a lair, why do you come?" she asked before she could help herself. "I'm sorry, that was a stupid question." Cina came because she always had, because she was expected to, because there was nothing to do at home. Her friends came here. She had no children to care for yet.

Cina brushed a crumb off her dress. "I love your brother," she said, "but in summer he has no time for me." She said it quite calmly and spread butter on a piece of fresh white bread. She raised the bread to her mouth, then lowered it. "Tam, I would not have brought you if I thought you'd run into trouble. You're clever and you aren't full of romantic sensibilities. But you haven't grown up with these people. All I'm saying is to watch your step. It will suck you in before you know it, and getting out isn't all that easy."

"Anyone in particular to warn me of?"

"No. That is, there are, but names will only make you feel that other men are safe." Cina looked away from Tam. A page was approaching with a note.

"My lady." He ignored Tam.

Cina said, "Excuse me," and took the paper, read. "Please give her my assurances that we will be there," she said. As soon as the boy was gone she said, "Dinner tonight with Lady Elwyn. There will be a mesmerist afterward, if you care for that sort of thing." She passed Tam the note. "She has a son, I expect you're being scouted."

This was what she had contracted to by coming. "Will he be there?"

"Probably. He's quite safe. You won't be the only one, though; she picks six or seven of the likeliest every year." She ate the last bit of fruit on her plate.

"Every year? How old is he?"

"He must be close to thirty now." Cina stood up. "Are you sure you won't go into town with me?"

"Quite."

"Enjoy yourself. Don't go poking into anything you shouldn't."

Tam finished her own meal after Cina left, decided against more coffee, and made her way slowly and somewhat thoughtfully back through the corridors. It was early enough that not very many people were about other than the occasional guard. They did not do anything in these public areas of the palace except stand unobtrusively in corners and watch, pretending not to be bored. She supposed that in other places they had more responsibility, but it could still not be much. There had not been any sort of violence against the government for years. Tam wondered if her father would see the guards as a reassurance or as a reminder.

The palace was actually a collection of buildings spread out over acres of land, and she had not explored it yet at all, though she had pored over a plan of the grounds. Many areas she had no need to go to: the archives and the bureaucrats' offices, the storehouses and barracks and guest residences. There were stables, a coach-house, a smithy, outdoor cook pits, a laundry, boiler-houses, and a large plaza for swordfighting or wrestling or ball. Between the buildings were green well-kept lawns or neat and colorful flower beds, vines covering arched entrances or hanging down from roofs, and slender elegant trees. Some buildings were joined to each other with enclosed pathways or graceful footbridges. Many lawns had a fountain in them. On the main building, there were balconies from which plants hung or water poured, caught in basins to be pumped up again, over and over. Trees in large tubs shaded terraces at many levels.

Much of the first two floors of the palace was open to palace guests. Silver moved and shimmered everywhere: water falling smoothly down a wall of reflective marble, ribbons of metal turning noiselessly in columns from floor to ceiling lining a corridor, light swirling on a ceiling with no apparent source or pattern. Tam could not tell what animated the movements. In the corners of a wide arched chamber, metal birds sang sweetly and clearly from glass trees that changed colors with the notes. It was artistry of a skill she had never seen before.

She passed rooms for small gatherings or large parties, for dining or for making music, for playing games or looking at art. In one room was a table with an inlaid chessboard of silver and reddish-gold, with intricate and polished pieces. Someone had moved a soldier forward two squares. Impulsively, Tam countered by bringing out a knight. She was a good player, but such an anonymous move was all she could expect to do here. Women played cards. The adjacent room was entirely empty except for the large pendulum swinging slowly over the mosaic circle in the floor with the degrees marked in gold. The center of the circle was a dragon, wings lifted, tail curved. The flames curling from its mouth had been worked in gems.

Next she came to a writing room, with several small tables, ink, pens, and paper. She lingered for a moment, thinking she ought to write her parents. Then she went on. She stepped into the formal Great Hall, all pale marble and gold, huge, empty. A large balcony overhung the room at the end opposite the pair of immense and gilded doors that was the ceremonial entrance to the palace. She supposed the balcony was for speeches or pronouncements before a crowd. There was a lonesome feeling to the place. Stern-faced portraits of past kings and queens lined the walls. Near the front was one of the king that must have been painted for his coronation. He looked quite young and serious. She wondered how much it resembled him now.

She decided to leave the remaining official rooms and go back to the more ordinary spaces. The halls instilled quietness in her, solemnity even. Not so with other people, who appeared to care not a whit who else heard their conversations. She was not ignored, but looking at her did not stop people from talking. Everything was suddenly quite crowded. She took turns this way and that until she found herself alone except for guards in a narrow corridor. Feeling as though she could breathe again, she walked more slowly.

She had not walked very far when a guard called out. Startled, she turned. He was not paying any attention to her; his exclamation had been addressed to a man coming in from another door with a drawn knife. Tam froze. Her body went alert with fear. The guard was hurrying toward the man.

Then she saw that the courtier—he was dressed too finely to be a servant—was staggering. His face was so white she wondered how he could be standing. There was a glassiness in his eyes, and his pupils were dilated. He dropped the knife. The guard bent down to pick it up as the man stumbled toward Tam. She realized he was not just sick, he was dying.

"What did you do with it? You gave it to him. He hates you. You were supposed to give it to me. Where is it?" He was pleading. Their eyes met.

He stared imploringly at her as though she was the only thing he could see in the world. There was a roar like the ocean around her. He opened his mouth. A black moth came out, and another, and another. They gathered around her, dark, soft, fluttering, hundreds of them. Their wings stirred air against her skin. They clustered thickly on the wall and the ceiling and her dress. I am not seeing this, she thought. She batted furiously at them.

They dissipated like smoke. His face twisted with pain. It was so terrible that she reached for his hand. Hot, dry skin. She smelled stone and ice. A bruise on his arm was spreading like ink. He was shaking.

"Water," he said, and then there was blood. Bright red blood pouring out of his mouth over his chest, onto the floor, splashing her dress. His hand went limp. She jerked hers away and jumped back. His eyes rolled up. This was real. He fell forward, face landing in the blood.

Her throat closed with franticness. She could not breathe. Fear, black and relentless, filled her entirely as she clutched her neck. If she could have screamed she would have. Her chest was tight and painful. Sweat chilled her body. Her vision was a narrowing tunnel, and she was dizzy.

Someone pulled her away. Hands brought her down onto a bench. She leaned forward, head down. Her skin tingled. There was a damp cloth on her face and a cup of water in her hand. Beautiful clear glass, beautiful clear water. She drank deeply. When she looked up she saw a group of guards standing around the body. The blood glistened and seemed to move like sunlight on a rippling lake.

There was blood on her skirt. Blood from a man who had died delirious and hemorrhaging.

"Cut it off, cut it off!" she cried out, tearing futilely at the hem.

A guard—where had they all come from?—slashed at the cloth with a knife. "Don't touch the blood!" she said urgently. It seethed and shifted. "Burn it!"

He tossed away the cloth and said reassuringly, "It's all right, miss."

"It's not," she said, forcing herself to speak like an adult and not an eight-year-old. "It could carry poison or contagion. If you've touched it wash your hands now. Now. Send for the doctor."

The guards all stared at her. "Please," she said. "My father is a doctor. Blood infection is a horrible way to die." It certainly was not what he had died of, but they wouldn't know. She never should have said *poison*. It had slipped out before she had a chance to think.

There was another instance of silence that seemed to extend forever. Then the one closest to her said, "You wait here," and began to give orders to the others.

Exhausted, Tam closed her eyes and leaned back against the wall. If she was right about what it was she dared not tell them—they would panic. The royal doctor would know, he had to know. It was an instrument of war. She heard water splashing.

Blood. His skin had been so hot. Last night there had been rain, cool sweet-smelling rain, folding softly around everything. That was what to think about. Rain that made boots track mud on the palace floors, rain that drove the cats to prowl inside, rain that made the fires safe and pleasant. Not dark moths and blood.

The guard brought her a basin of fresh hot water and she plunged her hands in and held them as long as she could stand it. Her shoes were clean, and her stockings. She had been lucky. The poison could be taken in through the skin. She would burn the dress anyway.

Waiting, she watched the guards. With a great deal of efficiency they were keeping people out of the corridor. There might not be much to guard against, but they were well trained.

The doctor came fairly quickly. He had a kind face, with green eyes. He was younger than she expected, only forty or so. After a glance at the body he came to her side. She stood up. Her head had cleared entirely.

"The guards say you know what he died of," he said, obviously doubtful.

"Possibly," she said, mindful of listening ears. She looked down at her rent skirt. "Can we go somewhere else, please? I'd rather be away from him." Calm, giving no hint of the terror that had roiled her. She knew how to do this. It was not the first death she had seen, the first death she had described.

"Of course," said the doctor. He took her arm and led her into an adjacent room with a window looking out on the garden. It was papered in faint pink and gold and full of chairs and spindly-legged tables. It had a handsome tall clock and a still-life of peaches and pomegranates. The red seeds shone luminously on the canvas. No one would ever dare to die in this room; it was too decorous. He shut the door and looked hard at her.

"It might have been sickness," she said. She was unsure of whether she should tell him exactly what she feared. But it seemed too important to lie, or trust that he would find it out himself. "But I think it was blood-dust."

He raised his eyebrows. "How would you know a thing like that?"

She hesitated. "My father studied it."

"And who is your father to know himself?"

"A doctor. Hyrne Warin."

He looked at her with more interest. "What brings you here?"

"Summer court. Lady Cina invited me. She's married to my brother."

He gave a little grunt of acknowledgment, perhaps remembering the marriage, and went on. "What makes you think it was blood-dust?"

"The blood," she said. "He was entirely white, but he had started hemorrhaging beneath the skin. I expect you'll find the bruises. And he was delirious. He thought I was someone else. I think he was going into shock. Blood-dust is the only thing I know of that makes all those at once. Except for the red plague." Crisp, collected. She was not going to tell anyone how the man had looked at her, the raw need on his face. That she was going to remember the rest of her life.

He did not try to convince her she had not seen it. "I'll have to look under a glass," he said, "but I'll assume you're right for the moment. If it were red plague someone else would be dead already. Did any of the blood get on you?"

She gestured to the cut skirt. "Not on my skin."

"Did you wash?"

"Yes. And I told the guards not to touch it."

"Did you say what it was?"

"Of course not," she replied, somewhat indignantly. "I said it was sepsis or contagion. There had to be a reason for them to stay away that they would believe."

"You don't say a word to anyone, hear me?"

"I'm not a fool."

"I expect you're not. But I have to warn you anyway." He put one hand on the back of an elegant chair with an elaborately embroidered cushion. "There's no one else who will need to ask you, no one else you need to tell. I'll take care of that. Your work is to forget about it all."

"What if I'm wrong?"

"If you're wrong I'll let you know, but you still can't let loose you even suspected it. There aren't many people who know about blood-dust, and you keep it that way. You're lucky you have the right background; anyone else who knew what you know would be under arrest by now."

Tam had known it would not be prudent to speak her guess, but he was coming down on her as though it were a state secret. Perhaps it was. She let herself imagine what would happen if it were generally known that the Sarians had such a poison. "I understand," she said. She was still so very calm. "Who was he?"

"Cade. The likely heir to a very minor barony." He lifted his hand. "I must see to him. The guards will want to ask you some questions. Don't tell them anything about the blood-dust either. Not even if they ask directly. Wait here."

She nodded. There were no other options. Blood, moths, pain. It would have been better to go with Cina.

If he had been poisoned, had he been one of the men in the courtyard last night? Or had they been the poisoners? Why her, what made him die in her presence? It was nothing, all a tissue of spider-threads that reason would rip apart in seconds. Cade was dead and the mechanics of death would run their course. A funeral in a few days and then memory of him would fade away from all but the few who had actually loved him.

She waited. There was nothing in the room to occupy herself with. A few common sparrows picked at the ground in the garden, but nothing else moved. It began to rain again. She wanted to change her clothes. She would not think about the moths or the moving blood.

She was beginning to think they had forgotten about her and was working up the courage to go interrupt when a soldier came in. He was not a guard; he had to have some officer's rank, although he was too young for it to be very high. The glance he gave was followed by a stare, broken before it became rude.

He asked her a few ordinary questions, which she answered honestly. She expected him to go on and repeat the questions the doctor had asked her.

He did not. He said, "Did you know Lord Cade?"

"No."

"Had you ever seen him before?"

She thought about it. "If I have I don't remember. There are so many people here."

"Do you have any idea why he would be murdered?"

"How could I have an idea of that if I had no idea who he was?" she replied, perhaps too sarcastically. He stared at her in an unfriendly way, then continued.

"Do any of your friends know him?"

"I don't know." This was beginning to feel like an interrogation. "If there is any connection between me and Lord Cade other than the chance that I saw him die, I don't know it."

"You said he died of poison."

She folded her arms. "Blood poison. Sepsis. Or contagion. I explained this. I am a doctor's daughter. I have seen people die before. Sometimes the infection or disease is carried in the blood. It could be anything. Red plague, jungle fever. Do I need to find myself an advocate?"

The words *red plague* caught his attention. His eyes widened. "Red plague?"

"Probably not. But your doctor can decide that." She would scare him into leaving her alone.

He looked at her with rather more respect and said, "If it was murder and there is a trial you will have to testify. Don't leave without telling us. You can go on, then."

Not the polite dismissal it should have been, but she did not care. In her room she undressed and left the ruined clothing on the floor. She hurried into the bathroom, where she ran blessedly hot water and scrubbed her entire body. She washed her hands four times before they felt clean again.

She put on a clean dress and bundled up the other into a neat ball, washed her hands once more, then rang for a servant. A chambermaid or two was always about. She gave directions to burn the clothing, repeated it firmly to the astonished girl, then sat on the windowseat and thought. She left the window open even though it was chilly.

If the courtiers ever found out that she saw Cade die, no matter the cause, she would be surrounded by the horrified curious. She was certain the doctor would not talk. The guards might, but most of them did not even know her name. Probably it would all fade away, especially if Cade really was as unimportant as the doctor had made him seem. But it might be just as well to vanish somewhere for the rest of the morning.

Tam made her way to the library, chose a book, and settled herself in a comfortable chair in the corner by the tall windows. Rain left soft grey trickles on the glass and dimmed the garden beyond. The lit glowlamps—so many of them!—were set to a lower brightness, making the room feel cozy and warm. *Anyone else who knew what you know would be under arrest by now*. Her eyes traveled down the page but she read nothing. The book was a popular novel, replete with betrayal, ghosts, and a crumbling tower overlooking a black and rocky sea. She forced herself through two chapters, then gave up. If she was thinking so much about the Sarians, she might as well read about them.

She went back to the bookshelves. The library was well organized, but it took a while to find anything about Sarium. Even then, there were only a few books. One was titled *Beyond the Black Peaks*, which sounded promising. As she started to carefully remove it from the shelf, she was distracted by the one next to it. *Magicks and Alchymies of the Distant Easte*. There was a subtitle: *Being a Collection of the Barbarous Spells and Curses Practiced by the Eastern Peoples, With Special Attention to Charms and Potions of Love and of Hatred*. If anything merited the word *tome*, this did. It looked more likely to have something about blood-dust in it than the other book.

You fool, she thought as she carried the book to a table. If she was found reading it now, it would not look good. Better than before the murder, she told herself.

The table of contents was frustratingly detailed and disorganized.

Of the uses of henbane. A cure for warts. To renew a lost love. Phases of the moon and their influence on healing spells. Apparently the Sarians were as full of supernatural nonsense as the Caithenian peasants. She began turning pages. The type was small and cramped, and the pages were old and crumbling a bit. No one had read it for years and years. Even if there was a formula for blood-dust in it, it would be impossible to find without removing the book and reading for hours, which certainly had not happened recently. She sneezed.

That sufficiently tried her patience for her to return it to the shelf. Little flakes of paper clung to her dress. If she kept reading she was going to have to change her clothes again. Books were not the answer today. She would come back tomorrow if the rain kept up.

There was a large mosaic map of the Narrow Sea and the countries surrounding it on one wall. Tam stood in front of it and looked at the blue sea south of Caithen. Her father knew about the blood-dust because he had been in Sarium, and the doctor knew because the king's spies and scouts knew. But how had it come to Caithenor, to be slipped into the food or drink of an ordinary courtier? The reason he was killed did not puzzle her unduly; people had their secrets. He had crossed someone in love or money. A Sarian poison was a different mystery.

She touched Dele on the map. It was Caithen's only real port. There were small bays between it and the university city of Liden to the west. Liden saw some traffic, but not much. Farther on, where the Narrow Sea opened to the Great Sea, the Caithenian coast was rocky cliffs. On the Great Sea side, the western side, the cliffs grew steeper and more rugged the farther north one went. Village fishermen and smugglers were the only men to put in at those rocky beaches.

But Dele, Dele was a huge city, three times or more the size of Caithenor, with ships constantly coming in or heading out. It was all trade with Argondy and Mycene now that Illyria and Liddea were cut off by Tyrekh. Or rather, that was all the legal trade and travel. It would be no great problem to get a small amount of deadly poison in through the custom-houses and tariff-stops with so much traffic. Her brother had told her of the maddening noise and crowds at the wharves. And the corruption. Anyone with enough money could do as he wished.

For that matter, it would not have been so difficult to come in by horse. The border between Caithen and Argondy was guarded, but travel between the two countries had never been much restricted. There were always men who dealt with the enemy, they would find their ways.

It bothered her, though, blood-dust in Caithen. In the palace. Someone with power had it. Her father had told her it was extremely difficult to make and that Tyrekh kept tight control over all of it. It was not used for killing rats. Had it come from a chain of common criminals, or had it been brought directly from Sarium and placed in a Caithenian lord's hands? She told herself that it needn't be any kind of treachery. Buying Sarian poison did not make anyone less loyal to Caithen than drinking Illyrian wine did. Evil men always were on the watch for weapons.

She did not convince herself. Oh, Tam, she thought, why are you puzzling over this? It's not your affair.

It was certainly not the subject a young woman was supposed to think about, unless she was reading a novel like the one she had put down. Poisons, rivalries, and dark-robed sinister men were proper enough on the written page. If Cade had died in that sort of book it would have been because he stumbled on a dark and long-hidden secret, or drank from the forbidden flask. But what she considered now was politics, not fantasy. Not the province of a commoner, let alone a woman.

She smelled perfume. Sandalwood. It was too early in the day for such a scent. She turned quickly and saw Alina walking toward her. Alina wore a lilac-colored dress that would have made anyone else with her fair skin and dark hair look pale and ill. On her, it looked splendid. She was a handsome girl with large brown eyes and an excellent figure. She wore tight low-necked gowns that were perfectly fashionable and not too indecent; they shouted confidently, *Look at me!* And men did. Tam was partly scornful, partly amused, and, she admitted to herself, a little jealous.

Alina said, "Oh, Tam, Tam, I hoped to find you here. The most dreadful thing has happened."

"What?"

"Lord Cade is dead and they say it was poison," Alina replied breathlessly. She was young, only seventeen. Old enough to marry, but not old enough to know anything about death. Then Tam remembered that the girl's mother had died when she was a child, and she felt a little guilty for the thought.

She asked, "Poison? Who is Lord Cade?" The lie came smoothly.

"Nobody important, though he was rather handsome and rich. But it's causing a terrible commotion. There are guards everywhere. They may even search the rooms." Alina sounded more excited than concerned.

Tam thought a search unlikely. What would they expect to find? The poisoner would have more sense than to leave poison in his room. Or hers. Poison was said to be a woman's weapon. Of course they might have to make a show of it.

"Did you know him well?" Tam asked.

"Yes. I didn't care much for him. He was always showing off. What have you been looking at the map for? Don't say you are thinking of leaving already."

Sweetly said, but probably not meant at all. Tam replied, "Oh, no, I was just considering my brother's ships."

"Of course. Merchantmen, aren't they? How many does he have?"

"I have no idea," she answered. It was true, but not honest. "I can't keep track of them all, though I do know the difference between a sloop and a brig." Efan was nowhere near as wealthy as that implied, but it was none of Alina's business. "Should I be worried about Lord Cade's death?"

"No, no. But do come back with me, we girls should stick together."

Tam thought Alina chatty, vain, and dull, which was a deadly combination, and would rather not have come, but there was no graceful way of declining. She took one last look at the map and followed Alina out. In the halls they went side by side, Tam listening to Alina talking. She murmured occasional responses, meaningless questions.

The blood-smell was strong again in her nostrils and on her tongue. The story was a simple collapse in the hallway, no mention of blood spewing over a woman's skirt. The guards were well disciplined if that had not got out. Later, maybe. It was fortunate that she had been the only observer. If there had been more people, or a different person, the secret would not be kept. She hoped the maid did not say anything about the dress.

A few soldiers were in the wing, their height and weight and deep male voices contrasting sharply with the women in colorful soft dresses. They asked her name but did not stop her from entering her room. She closed the door and spent a moment smelling. No scent of metal or leather or man was in the air. She had brought few things with her, and they were all exactly as she had left them.

Thoughtfully, she walked to the window and looked out at the courtyard. *What did you do with it? You gave it to him.* Had he been sick enough to confuse her with Alina? Alina had thrown something down. Probably only a love letter, a lock of hair, some money to place a bet with. Not a pouch of poison. It was entirely unlikely that a girl from a small manor surrounded by farmlands would be able to come by Sarian blood-dust.

But why were the guards here at all? They had not searched her room, but they had to have a reason. To watch, to impress, to warn.

She needed to shut her mind off and think only of ordinary things. She picked up one of her own books.

She managed to keep reading until some time later when she heard a knock. It was a page with a message for her. She thanked him, took it, opened it. From the doctor. It said only, *You were right. Keep silence.* She tore it into pieces and tossed it on the embers of the fire. When she used the poker the edges curled up and the paper shriveled into ash. Memory did not work like that.

CHAPTER FOUR

C orin looked at the clock. "I don't have time to see him now," he said to his clerk. "Tell him to come back in a few hours after the council."

"He is unwontedly insistent, sir," said Teron. He was the perfect clerk: impassive, unsmiling, and ironic. Loyal to the bone.

He sighed. A lesser man he could ignore, but not the royal doctor. He pushed aside the paper he had been reading—inattentively, to be sure—and said, "Five minutes. No more." For a moment he thought longingly of the north, where there had not been so many people he had to accommodate. He would have liked to be on a straightforward Quest; Heroes did not spend hours signing things. He knew he would regret the thought when the war started.

When Berk came in, Corin said, "You're going to make me late for a council. This had better matter that much."

"It does." Without waiting to be asked, Berk sat down and leaned forward. "Lord Cade was poisoned this morning. With one of the most cruel and vicious poisons the Sarians have ever made. There's no question about it."

"How?" he asked, even as his mind was racing through the complications this presented.

"In his food or drink, most likely. He would have died an hour or so after. Unfortunately his dishes had already been cleared and washed by the time I got to them."

Corin leaned back and looked up at the ceiling. It was going to be a mess. "Why would anyone want to poison Cade?" he asked, thinking aloud. The man had no power or enemies; he was innocuous and unimportant, a hanger-on. He had no rival in love, property, or money. Dislikable to some, yes, but not to the point of murder. Cade was the sort of man people forgot about when he was not present.

Then Corin amended the thought. He had been away six weeks, anything could have happened. The man could have gone from being a follower, easily used, to a creditor, heavily owed, in one night at a gambling table. Or got himself so much in debt that he could never repay it.

Nor did Cade keep company only with the foppish innocent. He spent more time than was wise in the shadow of Baron Arnet, who was known to be in Hadon's pay. Cade could easily have learned something that necessitated his being gotten rid of.

Berk looked down and recrossed his legs. He was nervous about something. Corin said, "Which Sarian poison was it?"

"Blood-dust."

Despite himself, Corin exclaimed. Berk had not exaggerated when he called it cruel. Every organ in the victim's body failed, and there were massive hemorrhages. It was certain death, agonizing and swift but not swift enough. The poison looked like dust, could be dissolved in water, and had no taste or odor. A small pinch was lethal. "You're sure?"

"Oh yes. The death is distinctive and so is the blood under the glass. Whoever killed him wanted to be sure we knew it. It's not a poison of convenience." The slightly pedantic tone of voice told Corin that Berk was restraining impatience.

"We can't let this get out," he said. "Where would one get this poison?"

"From a Sarian," the doctor replied soberly. "And even that would be hard. It's far too difficult to come by for smugglers and thieves to bother about."

"Can it be derived?" he asked.

"Not without a fortune in chemical apparatuses and years of study. I couldn't do it with what I have here. None of your gentlemen who dabble in natural philosophy could."

That changed the picture. One did not use such a conspicuous poison without a reason when so many others would do as well. It was not murder born of ordinary enmity. They were meant to know that someone in the palace had ties to the Sarians. Or perhaps it was not meant for them at all, perhaps it was a message from one traitor to others. A punishment. What if Cade had been told to do something and got cold feet? If he had sold himself to the Sarians and then tried to back out, it would have been too dangerous to allow him to live. A political murder, not a personal one.

He cut off the speculation. "Do many people know?"

Berk said, "About the death, I am afraid so. It took time, and it happened in the corridors. Only one person besides soldiers actually saw him die, but plenty of people had a chance to see the body when they removed it. And the commander's got men asking questions already. The nature of the poison, only three people know and you and I are two of them."

Why had no one told him earlier? If Gerod's men were asking questions, Gerod should have talked to him already. The news must be all over the court by now.

"Who's the third? Gerod?"

"No." Berk seemed surprisingly awkward. "A woman. She saw Cade die—he got blood on her dress, nearly fell on top of her, the guards said. She won't talk."

Corin looked dubiously at him. It was unlike Berk to do something with a woman that would embarrass him. He had been happily and faithfully married for years. Perhaps he was protecting her. She would undergo an inquisition if other courtiers found out she had witnessed the dying. "Do I need to see her to make sure of that?"

"You might want to, she's damn fine-looking, but you don't need to."

"Why not? And why ever did you tell her?"

"I didn't," Berk said after a slight hesitation. "She told me. She was as calm as could be about it. She is the daughter of the one man in Caithen who knows all there is to know about Sarian medicines, poisons, and chemistries. Apparently he's taught her some things. I met him once, years ago, he's a very fine doctor and quite a scholar. He was offered an appointment in the Argondian court and turned it down. He could have had my place here if he'd wanted it. He's in the Academy."

It was an unbelievable chance. "You're sure she's who she says she is?"

"Yes. I checked and Gerod had her questioned. She has a perfectly good reason for being here; her brother married up. To Lady Cina. The odd part is having been the one Cade died in front of. She had no idea who he was. But she knew the poison, from how he died I expect. And had a good guess at what it signified. She wouldn't tell me anything in front of the guards."

That was almost too clever. But if she was the daughter of a man Berk respected, she might be that clever. If the man could have held royal posts here or in Argondy he had to be brilliant. And though Corin did not know Cina well—her low rank had kept her off the list of prospective brides—he knew she was no fool and would not have married into a family of fools. He had never made the mistake of thinking women were less capable of thought than men. He had only to look at his mother and sisters to see the fallacy in that idea.

"Would her father be useful?" he asked.

"I don't think so," Berk said. "I have the treatises. Do you anticipate more such deaths?"

That was pushing the limits even for Berk, but he decided to ignore the question. "Why haven't you told the commander yet?" He did not like Berk keeping that sort of fact from Gerod. It did explain why Gerod had not already come to Corin himself; he may have thought it a death of little moment if he knew of no tie to the Sarians.

Berk looked at him as though he had gone mad. "Do you expect me to pass on something with that kind of political implication to anyone without telling you first?"

Gerod, Berk, who was he going to suspect next of unreasonably hiding things from him? He had never been so wary and distrustful of men he had known for years. He felt like his father's dog, snarling at something familiar that had subtly changed.

He stood. "Tell Gerod about the poison," he said as Berk rose. He did not need to instruct the commander in what to do. "No one else. You'll have to be ready with some other poison for an explanation, something common. A sudden sickness would be even better."

"Even if that were true, people would believe it was poison. But I will cover it as I can."

"Do so," he said, more curtly than he usually would, and went unceremoniously past the doctor and out of the room.

❧

He was on time, barely, slipping into his chair seconds before he stood with the others for the arrival of his father. The king was very formally dressed. Corin was even more relieved he had not been late. He straightened the drape of his jacket and adjusted his demeanor. It would be all titles today with Aram looking like that. His own clothing felt confining after six weeks of soldier dress.

The old glass in the windows had slumped on itself, giving the grey sky a rippling and unfocused appearance. The council chamber was one of the oldest rooms in the palace, built centuries before the newer airier ones, with a heavy stone floor and plastered walls all in straight lines. The only relief from the whiteness of the walls was a few colored banners with no patterns or pictures on them. Aram liked it stark, without distractions or enticements. The brightness of the lamps did not shake the dim, close feeling of the room. Seana's husband had arrived; Simoun looked windblown, wet, and rather old. Corin felt a moment of pity for him, and then pity that he was pitied. Yes, it was time to be done with Seana.

There were a number of formalities and minor affairs to be got through. It was a full council, all seven dukes and the four High Lords and a number of trusted aides. Most people pretended successfully to pay attention. It was not a challenge to guess what anyone was thinking while this kind of business went on, though there was always someone to whom a small point mattered greatly. When he was younger he had wondered why his mother did not come to councils though she was entitled to. Now he understood completely. If he had Talia's privilege to speak to Aram only in quiet and comfort, he would do the same thing. He let his own mind wander.

The council table was very old, and although it was kept polished and sanded there were some scars that could not be erased: gouges where someone had angrily plunged a dagger into the wood, the various stains of long usage, uneven nicks and scuffs on the edges. The marks were as familiar to him as those on his own body. His gaze returned repeatedly to one long scratch in front of him. He began to wonder if the king intended to discuss the war at all. Other men were restraining their fidgeting rather less successfully. The room was hot and he would have liked to open a window, but he did not dare leave his seat. When Aram was being kingly and impressive, he had little tolerance for interruption.

Finally, however, after they had been going for about an hour, Aram said, calmly as ever, "And now, my lords, as some of you know, we have a larger problem. Tyrekh is invading Argondy at last." He held up a hand to keep them quiet and repeated much of what he had told Corin the previous night. No one was surprised—they had spent three years wondering when this would happen. He ended by saying, "This is all we know. I've sent out additional scouts and messengers, and the marshal has begun ordering our soldiers to the eastern border. We're also sending soldiers to the south coast to close the major ports. I'll let any of you who wish read the reports after we're done here, but you have the essentials."

"What is Tyrekh's troop strength?" asked Ellid. He was Aram's age, and by far the calmest and most reasonable of the dukes. Tai had married his nephew Ader, who was just as level-headed. Corin had always thought Tai would marry a rake, but she had surprised them all.

Coll, the Lord Marshal, said, "Fifty thousand invading Argondy and another two hundred thousand spread out behind him. There are reports of more bandit attacks in Caithen too, he may already have men here."

"How in the name of all that's holy did he get two hundred and fifty thousand men over the Black Peaks?"

Aram said, "He's had six years to do it. And those aren't all Sarians, he'll have added to his forces with captive men and mercenaries. We certainly had no way to stop it."

"A handful of dragons would have held those passes easily," said Ellid. It was a risky thing to say, implying as it did that Hadon was in the wrong. Word would get back to him from someone. Corin was sure they had all thought it at one time or another, though, and Ellid sounded more frustrated than disloyal.

"Tyrekh has his fire weapons," said Coll. "They may be able to shoot down a dragon."

The room was quiet as everyone considered weapons that could destroy dragons. Humans would not stand a chance. Corin thought several men looked a little green. He had never seen the weapons, but Joce had described one. It propelled small metal balls for yards, and the balls burst into inextinguishable greenfire where they landed. A few men so armed would be able to defeat all the palace guard.

Corin decided to change the subject. "Marshal," he said, "have we a way to sink the Argondian ships before the Sarians get hold of them?"

"We have a way, my lord. I don't know if we have time. Our best chance is to hope the Argondians think of it themselves."

"That's not good enough. We have to send men and messages."

"The Argondian coastline is nearly five hundred miles long and they have half as many ships. We haven't the men. Even if we could destroy all the naval vessels, there are merchant ships and fishing boats."

"We have to do what we can," Corin said. "The Sarians are no sailors, and you can't put several hundred soldiers on a fishing boat. If it's difficult enough they'll give up." Of course dragons could destroy the ships quite easily. He hoped no one thought of that. *The dragons are all in the north, spying on us.* That would stir them up right enough.

The door opened. The men all turned toward the sound; there was no one expected, and a guard was supposed to prevent such interruptions. The guard put his head in, and Corin, who knew him, could see that he was panicky. "Sir," he said, in a strangled sort of voice, "a dragonrider." It was not a place anyone would want to be, between a dragonrider and the king. Well, the lords had wished for dragons, now they had one.

"Let him in," Aram said.

The room was as quiet as it could be. The dragonrider's boots were loud on the floor. He did not have his helmet. He wore scuffed leather flying clothes, damp from the rain, and there was dark stubble on his cheeks and chin. His fingertips were stained a permanent yellowish-brown from sulfur. He had not removed his sword, which almost made Corin rise to his feet; Hadon used his riders as emissaries, but they were extraordinary swordsmen as well.

He came directly to Aram, bent his head cursorily, and held out a narrow package in red paper. That meant Hadon considered it crucial. Aram took it and said, "Is there a spoken?"

"No." He sounded almost scornful.

Corin felt the hostility around the table increase. No one liked the dragonriders—they were arrogant men who thought themselves well above the level of ordinary folk of any rank, and who had the standing of lords in the Mycenean court—but this one seemed particularly disrespectful. Corin did not look at his father's face as he unfolded the letter, but rather at his hands. They did not give anything away.

The king read quickly, then said, "There will be no written reply. Tell my liege that I hear him and obey him unchangingly. You may return to your master."

That was an insult, and Corin wondered if even his father could get away with it. The dragonrider scowled, then bent his head again stiffly, turned, and was gone.

Aram said, "Council is adjourned. We'll reconvene later. Prince Corin, a word."

His manner was steady. It was unlikely to fool anyone. Nothing broke up councils. If the news were good he would not be keeping it to himself. The council members stood up, the sound of their chairs pushing back loud and rough. Some of the men tried to linger. Corin said sharply, "If he wanted you, he'd say so. Go on." He herded them toward the door. No one objected. He said to the guard, "Keep everyone out," and shut the door hard before the guard could even acknowledge the command.

Furiously, Aram shoved the letter at him and said, "Read this."

Corin took it and sat. It was couched in formal language—Mycenean, of course—and included every one of the Emperor's titles. He skipped the verbiage with a sinking feeling and got to the meat of the message:

> *Our generals have taken your request for troops and are considering how best to fulfill it. You must be cognizant, however, that the time for Tyrekh's soldiers to cross Argondy may be considerably less than the time required for sufficient Mycenean soldiers to assist you to come north. We advise you to prepare defenses accordingly.*

> *In light of the dangers of the Sarians, we have taken the liberty of offering the hospitality and shelter of the court to the Princess Tai, and she has most graciously accepted.*

Corin felt his blood drain. His sister, his clever sister, with the strong quick hands that could fly over a piano, her brow furrowed as she played. His little sister whom he still called *mouse*. He said, "I will kill him." His voice shook with rage. His hand was on his knife hilt. He found himself standing.

"Sit down, Corin," Aram said, almost gently. He had regained his bearing. "You'll have your chance. We will get her out of there, don't worry."

"You don't believe him, do you?" he demanded. Tai would never go like that, she was a hostage. Hadon had turned on them.

"Of course not. But he's not going to kill her."

"Why do you think that?"

"If he kills her his other vassals will rise up against him, and he can't afford it. The Empire is cracking. And I've known the man for forty years. He bluffs."

"Tai's life is a hell of a thing to call it on. Are you—" He stopped before he said something unforgivable. Without looking at his father, he went to the window, stared out at the calming greyness. Aram said nothing. He took a few deep breaths. His father would not risk Tai. She was a splendid archer, with a fine draw and a sharp eye and the ability to be distracted by nothing. She would approach this the same way. He had to be that steady too. It did not escape him that he was still a young man, one who had been protected from loss and pain. If loss was coming, he had to face it instead of relying on the luxury of temper.

Sitting back down, he said, "I'm sorry. I'm ready."

"The first thing is not to let anyone know yet about it. I'll send to Ader, of course, we have to know what else happened. There's probably a messenger killing his horses to get here already, it shouldn't take long to find out."

"Will you tell Ellid?" Corin asked.

"I shall have to," Aram said. "He'll never forgive me if I don't. But no one outside the family. You'll have to pretend there is nothing the matter, can you?"

"Yes. What about Gerod?"

The king shook his head. "Not even him. If he knows he'll take some action that gives it away. All I will tell the lords is what Hadon said about the troops."

"Don't you trust them?" he asked, even as he tallied his own doubts. He was sure no one on the council would betray them to the Sarians, but he was less sure they would all stand fast against the Emperor. He was the overlord, after all, they would not even need to convince themselves they were not traitors.

"I don't trust them not to force me to do something stupid," Aram said.

"They'll know what it means about the troops as well as you and I do. Especially since—" He cut himself off.

"Since what?"

Reluctantly, he said, "Since you sent them all away. They know there's more to it."

"Leave that to me," Aram said. Corin reminded himself that his father had been king for more than three decades and knew his lords.

He was unable to be so calm himself, though. "Hadon can't expect us to believe this letter, why did he send it?"

"He may. Wouldn't you rather have her there than along the path of Tyrekh's soldiers? That's how he's thinking. He's quite correct about the time it takes to move troops. He may even be telling the truth."

"You can't mean that, not when he took her. Not when he's got his dragons watching us."

"Corin," Aram said, an edge to his tone.

"He doesn't even give us numbers," he said, frustrated.

"No. And I'll let the council chew over that as long as they want to. But he's not disclaiming suzerainty or ordering us to submit, so we have to act as though he is our lord. Listen, Corin, what happens to him if he sends a hundred thousand men here to hold off Tyrekh?"

"Kynos and Theron," he said immediately. He should have thought of them at once, but he hardly needed a lesson. Hadon's two sons were vicious, power-hungry, and getting impatient. Spies reported that they all three played each other double. That kept the power even, but if one of them gathered or lost an edge it would shift. If Hadon sent his best men north he would have no defenses against his sons. Three years ago, neither of them had any substantial backing. Now they both did.

"Exactly. Bad as he is, I'd rather have Hadon over me than either of those two."

"That won't make much difference if Tyrekh comes in. He's worse than any of them."

Aram said, "Yes. And if the cost of pushing back Tyrekh is having one of the princes as Emperor, I'll take it. But look where Hadon is. If he defends us, he is overthrown. If he cuts us loose, that might turn his other vassals against him. Once they see he doesn't honor his obligations they'll break away and he'll lose his power anyway. He's in a tight spot, he's stalling. There's not much we can do about it. But if we turn against him before he openly turns against us, we lose any chance of support. He may yet decide it's better to send soldiers here than have the rest of the Empire crash around him. I don't want to make his decision for him."

Corin stood up again and paced the length of the table and back. His father was right about the politics hemming the Emperor in. But something about it didn't fit. Why were the dragons surveying the north? And why on earth had he taken Tai? It was an entirely unnecessary provocation. What did he think to keep them from doing?

Another, grimmer, possibility occurred to him. "You don't suppose he's made some sort of deal with Tyrekh, do you? Hand us over to buy time?" It made a twisted sort of logic from where the Emperor stood. Give away the small country of little value to him while he built his army, and then swoop down on Tyrekh in three or four years and take possession of all the kingdoms Tyrekh held. It would increase the size of the Empire by half with very little work.

"I wouldn't put it past him," Aram said. "There'd be no point in taking her, though, if he had. If there's any dealing between Mycene and the Sarians, it's probably the princes."

That was an even more unpleasant thought. Corin wanted to kick something, hard. Instead he said, "So we kneel before him as we have and hope he's not the executioner. But what about her?"

"Well," said Aram, and halted. "The problem is one of timing. I have a sufficient number of men in Hadon's court who have some power or command to get her out of sight quickly. But if it happens too soon, he will decide to wash his hands of us immediately. Hostage-taking works two ways. He expects something of us. I want to know what it is."

"Wait a minute," Corin said. He knew there were spies in the Imperial Court, he had read the reports often enough. But courtiers were not going to be able to walk away with a hostage princess. Nor were they really trustworthy enough; anyone who spied for money could be bought by someone else. "You're not telling me that any of Hadon's lords would risk their position in the Empire to rescue her for us."

"No. I haven't managed that yet." Aram smiled ironically. "But it's not difficult to suborn soldiers who serve under a coward."

Soldiers. It wouldn't be foot soldiers either. "Who?"

"Alcias."

"Alcias?" Corin said, incredulous. The man was Hadon's second general. "What could you offer him that would make it worth it for him to abandon Hadon? He probably has more power than you." That was a rash thing to say, even for him, and he prepared himself for a reprimand.

Aram said, "*Suborn* may have been too strong a word. I haven't done anything to suggest that either he or I would turn against Hadon. But I have better spies, and he knows it, and he owes me. It's time to call it in."

"That is a dangerous game," Corin said. "How long have you been playing it?"

"Why do you think I haven't told you? Since we saw what Tyrekh was capable of."

"I don't need to be protected," he said fiercely. He rubbed his forehead. "You sound as if you have been expecting him to abandon us."

"Expecting, no," Aram said. "But I'm unsurprised. Men who seek power eventually overreach themselves, you know that. One always wants to have some leverage against them. If not against him, his sons."

Corin went to the window again. In this oldest part of the palace, the roofs were slate, streaky now with rain. The pigeons sat on the ridgepoles with their feathers ruffled to dry. In the courtyard immediately below him a message boy was hurrying across, the tails of his shirt billowing in the wind. A thought snatched at his mind and was gone before there were words to it.

He turned back to the king. "Do you think he really expects us to sit still and leave her there, Father?"

"I don't know," Aram said. "Perhaps he's testing our loyalty."

"Then he doesn't deserve it!"

"Of course not," said Aram. "Corin, I won't pretend to understand what he thinks or plans. But the fact remains that without Mycenean soldiers we haven't a chance against the Sarians. I would love to cut the chain between us and Mycene as much as you would. But not until the time is ripe."

"If he cuts it . . ."

"If he cuts it we fall to Tyrekh. It's an endgame either way. So all we can do is wait and hope that one of them makes a mistake."

He sighed. He nodded at his father.

Aram said, "Don't do anything rash. He may be after you, too. He knows how thick you are with her, taking her might be intended to bait you."

"Me? I'm not that kind of a fool."

"Don't count on Hadon knowing that," Aram replied. "You're young."

"His spies ought to know better," Corin said, affronted. He had shed his fecklessness years ago. He was not as unprovokable as his father, but he was hardly irresponsible.

"So they should. But watch yourself. There are probably already dogs circling here to see who falls first."

That made him think of Cade. "We've another problem," he said. "Lord Cade was poisoned this morning with blood-dust. Berk said it would be impossible to get without consorting with the Sarians. Although I suppose Hadon could come by it. Someone's been dealing with them, in any case. And if there's one traitor there's probably more."

"Well, that's a warning at the least," Aram said, grim. "Gerod is looking into it?"

"Yes, but I haven't spoken to him. I only found out just before the council. Do you want me to now?"

"I'll do it. Who else knows about the poison?"

"No one," Corin said automatically, before remembering the woman. He decided not to bother his father about it until there was a reason. Berk was generally reliable about people.

"Have you suspicions?"

"One always thinks of Arnet," Corin said. "Especially since Cade was a hanger-on of his. But I've no grounds for it. I wonder now if Hadon was involved, but we can't assume it wasn't connected to the Sarians." It was quite possible they were in the pincers of two empires. "Or the princes, if either one of them is leagued with Tyrekh."

"Odd that it happened the day after you came back," Aram said.

"The day after you set Joce to looking," Corin reminded him. "He may have stirred something up without even knowing it."

Aram swore softly. He turned his own head toward the windows. Corin went as quiet as he could, watching his father think. He thought there was more to it than ordinary worry. He wondered if Joce had reported the burns.

Then the king stood up. "I need to tell your mother." A pause. "Corin, I would rather not say this, but I must. War is not a time to toy with men's loyalties. Break it off with Seana."

A week ago, a month ago, he would have resented it. He said, "I have. You needn't worry." Already she seemed a part of his distant past.

"Good," Aram said. "I'm sending you out the rest of the day. Be in my receiving room in fifteen minutes in your riding leathers."

Corin could not help looking regretfully at the water on the windows, but he knew an order when he heard one. He nodded.

He arrived punctually for a change. The guards outside the door came to attention, and one of them said, "He's expecting you, sir." He pushed the door open and shut it behind him as quietly as he could, then halted. Once again his hand went to his knife hilt.

"No need, Corin," Aram said, notwithstanding the dragonrider standing beside him.

Corin's usual wariness at dragonriders was even stronger now, and he looked closely at the man. The rider returned an equally careful, inspecting look. Then he dropped formally to one knee and said, "My Lord Prince."

Well, I will never be surprised by anything again, Corin thought, staring. Dragonriders did not kneel for anyone, not even the Emperor.

The man cupped his hands, the sign of a Basilisk. *I obey him unchangingly. Return to your master.* There had been a code in that, and he should have seen it. Mark that one up as a loss. He gestured the man to rise and said to Aram, "I think I will stop playing cards against you."

"I'm sure you hold some cards to your chest equally well," Aram said calmly. Which was another one of his damnably effective tricks, to make you think he knew your secrets already. But Corin had experienced that enough times not to rise to it.

"Did the Emperor send you," he asked the rider, "or did you steal a dragon?"

"I volunteered," the rider said. "No one else wanted to bring that news. I'm a real dragonrider, my lord, that's not something one can pretend." He sounded Mycenean. Aram had to have placed him there years ago, when the man was fifteen or sixteen, all to have this opportunity now. It was a brilliant move, and one that would cost Aram his throne if Hadon ever found out. He could not have risked it with any man other than a Basilisk.

The king said, "I can tell you more later. Your sister is unhurt and well treated. We haven't much time. How would you like to ride a dragon?"

The leather clothes, which had been uncomfortably hot in the palace, were barely warm enough at this height, and even in gloves his fingertips were numb. He understood with his body now why it was that the highest peaks were snow-capped all year. But the chill was an inconvenience, nothing more, not when he was here, looking down at the tiny roads and houses, the curving rivers, the distant roundness of the horizon. He could see the wrinkles and folds of the land and the growing things in a hundred shades of green. The rainclouds lay behind them, slowly moving dark piles of wool. Ice crystals sparkled where rain on his jacket had frozen. The pleasure of this flying was more intense and stimulating than anything he had ever experienced. No wonder dragonriders were arrogant. How could they not pity and scorn the earthbound?

He could not speak to the rider; their helmets muffled their ears from the cold, and the noise of the wind would have torn away their words. It had all been planned before they set out, and he had nothing to do but trust in the dragon and the rider and look.

Everything was a marvel: the amazing silky hardness of the dragon's scales, the iridescence of its wing membranes, the swift steady flaps with which it flew. Its back was smooth and curved, no impediment to moving air. Strapped into a complicated harness behind the rider, Corin could not move much, but he was able to look down on either side. He had a spyglass, but it was queasy-making to look through when they were flying this fast, and what he saw with his naked eye was quite wondrous enough.

The only other time he had been close to a dragon had been at least ten years before, so he had been nervous while waiting to mount. The creature was so very big, and so very inhuman. Its sulfurous odor was not as terrible as he had expected. There was another acrid, musky scent with it. He could not see its muscles through its hide, but he felt them, flexing and contracting in a steady rhythm as it flew. Its body was hot, not unbearably so but evident. His legs were warm where they lay against it.

Kelvan, the rider, had warned Corin that four hours was long for a first flight, no matter how accustomed he was to days on horse. He did not believe it, but when Kelvan landed on a forested bluff overlooking a river after only two hours, he slipped off and discovered he could barely move. His entire back ached, his shoulders were stiff, and his thighs felt as though someone were pushing them apart with a ten-foot-long board. Looking at the dragon's back, he thought that was a good comparison. And now that they were on the ground, it was hot again. He loosened the laces of his vest, wincing.

"You'll take my word for it next time, won't you," said Kelvan with a grin. He was stocky, with short dark hair. Corin put him at thirty-five or so. "Stretch them out, or it will get worse. And have a hot bath and some wine tonight."

Worse? With a hand against the smooth bole of a silvery-grey tree while stretching his hamstrings, he realized he was about as isolated as he had ever been. They were in a clearing but with no roads for miles. The river below was white from water rushing over rocks, too distant to hear. The air smelled of forest and was tremendously, wonderfully quiet, disturbed only by the rustlings of small animals and the calls of a few birds. He could say or do anything here and no one would know.

Was that what Aram had wanted? There was a reason beyond pure pleasure that he had been taken away dragonback. For a quick, horrible instant he thought this was the beginning of exile; then he rejected that idea. His father would not send him off with no farewells and no preparations unless enemies were burning down the doors.

He had wanted to go west to Tai's home, to see her husband, but Aram had been firm against it. *If all else is well, there is nothing you need to do. If it is not we cannot risk Hadon knowing you were dragonback. If he finds out about Kelvan, we will never get her out.* Corin admitted the truth of that. Even so, he felt he was abandoning her.

The quiet was almost as blissful as the flight, and he did not want to break it. He would have been happy sitting a safe distance away and watching the play of light on the dragon's scales. But he thought he had to, and when he looked at Kelvan he was sure. The man's face had gone hard, determined about something, and he was watching Corin with an almost fierce intensity that had nothing of either humor or subservience about it.

He said, "My sister, have you spoken with her?"

Kelvan nodded. "I've seen her. I haven't spoken with her. She's treated as a guest, and she acts it. I think she's charming people more than Hadon wants."

"Good," Corin said savagely. "What's he up to? Why did he take her?"

Kelvan did not answer at once. A jay chattered at them. "I don't see Hadon often," he said slowly. "But when I did yesterday he did not look good. Healthy enough in the body, but I think there is something weighing down his self, eating it. I don't think he's desperate yet, but I would say for sure that he's afraid of something."

"Is he sane?"

"He's rational." Kelvan shrugged. "If he's mad, there's no sign yet."

"Is he weak?"

The rider did not answer. Corin did not push; the man knew Hadon much better than he did, and the question was unlikely to have a simple answer.

Finally Kelvan said, "I believe so, aye. If I may be frank, my lord?"

"Please."

"A bully on a throne is still a bully."

Four years ago Corin had gone to the Mycenean court to do homage for Caithen with his father. It was not his first time at the Emperor's court; he had been there almost every year since he could talk until he went to university. But this had been the first time that he too was required to do the rite rather than to watch it. He had walked the long path between assembled nobles and courtiers from the entrance of the ornate throne room to the throne itself, where he had knelt to swear the ritual oath, his hands between Hadon's. Afterward he had kissed the Imperial ring. Had it been only ceremony and tradition he would have thought nothing of it; but Hadon had given him a look that made him feel slavish and abased, and pointedly kept him on his knees longer than was necessary. The dragons carved on the arms of the throne looked down at him, mocking. The subsequent times had been no different. *Bully* was an apt word.

"What about Tyrekh?" he asked. "Is the Emperor going to leave us on our own?"

"I don't know. It's an ugly thing to do. If he does he'll lose the trust of many of his troops. And his vassals. And he can't afford that. But his sons are a real threat."

Corin did not bother to ask why Hadon had not executed or imprisoned them. That would only make the fractures greater.

He said, "Has he communicated with Tyrekh at all? Sent any dragons?"

"None. He's not selling you out, he's just pretending Tyrekh doesn't exist."

"Why is he watching the north?" he asked. "It is him, isn't it?"

"Aye. No one else controls the riders, I can assure you of that. I don't know why he's sent them there. It's not a desirable assignment, more a punishment duty, but with no reasons given and no man knowing what will put him in the next rotation. It's been months now that he's done it."

"When did they first go?"

"Nine weeks past."

Ten weeks ago Aram had decided to send Corin north. It had been another month before he left, but the plan had been well-known. "Are they still there?" If they had departed when he did, he would know they had been watching him.

But Kelvan said, "Aye, my lord, with no end in sight."

It meant something important, he was certain of that. But if Kelvan did not know, the answer was locked in Hadon's mind and might never come out. "Will the riders obey him even if he loses power?"

Kelvan spread his hands wide. "They're loyal the way most people are loyal. It's an easy thing to do. Show them something better and some of them will drift. But the dragons won't leave, and no rider will leave his dragon."

He wondered why the dragons would stay, but when he tried to frame a question the words evaporated in his mind and his tongue was stiff. Something did not want him to speak of the dragons, not even now with a dragonrider. He thought of the Dragon Valleys, which he had seen once from a distance, and cold crept through him. He had forgotten what mattered. It almost thrust him into panic.

He took a deep breath and shook it off. "And the soldiers, whom do they support? Does he have their loyalty in the same fashion?"

"I can't speak of the men, but most of the generals are jackasses with an overweening sense of pride."

"Which means?"

"Which means that they don't want to be embarrassed," said Kelvan. "And Hadon is on the verge of doing that. Shall I tell you what I told the king?"

"Yes," he said, thinking even as he spoke that it made no sense for Kelvan to tell the story twice. Aram should have waited until Corin could be present.

Which delay the king himself had created, setting the time for

Corin to appear. That had to mean he wanted to talk to the rider about something he did not want his son to hear. What was going on?

He let none of this show and listened quietly to the news from Mycene. By the time Kelvan was finished, Corin had a sharpened sense of the plotting and counterplotting, of where the Emperor might fail, above all of how fast things were moving to a point where Hadon would have to deal with his sons directly.

Yet none of it explained why Hadon had felt it necessary to take Tai, to watch the north.

Or why Aram had sent Corin a hundred miles away to hear it.

He listened. And when he had slotted everything away into the appropriate mental spaces, he looked directly at the rider and said, "Why did my father want me to come with you?"

Kelvan looked at him with a steady judging gaze. It was not the paralyzing stare of a Basilisk, only a man's assessment, but it was enough to keep Corin still. He had not been so appraised for years. He was certain that if he either flinched or defied it, the gate would slam down and he would never learn what the king intended.

Whatever Kelvan was looking for, apparently he found it. He said, "He wanted you to ride the dragon. That could not be done in Caithenor, since Hadon might learn of it."

He frowned. Kelvan wasn't making sense. "I mounted right there in front of the sentries."

"To ride it, not to be carried by it."

Coldness again, a touch of ice. Why? But that was to ask Aram. Then excitement pulsed through him as he understood what it meant. He was being offered something so impossible he had never even considered it. "What must I do?"

"Now? Come greet the dragon."

He caught his breath. Now suddenly seemed far too soon. But he went forward, stopping about ten feet from the dragon's head. It was so huge. Its eyes were closed. Kelvan squatted beside the dragon and stroked the scaly head.

The dragon opened its eyes. Kelvan beckoned. Corin forced

himself forward. He went to one knee slightly less than an arm's length from the dragon's wide nostrils and held out his hand. He was afraid, he would not deny it, but he would ignore it. He would not let it close around him. His hand was steady even though his heart was rapid. The dragon's eyes were like a cat's, yellow with a narrow pupil and flecked with green. He would not look into them. Its scales were bronze, with a red band around its neck, and its wings were red at the base, shading to bronze at the tips, glowing and iridescent. The sharpness of its claws was visible. It opened its mouth.

He knew without being told that this was the defining moment. He stayed kneeling, looking directly into that great red mouth with rows of white razor-edged teeth the length of his forefinger. The dragon's breath was hot and smelled of sulfur and molten iron and smoke and coal. Its tongue was forked like a snake's. His eyes watered from the heat and smell of the breath. But he kept himself still.

Slowly, lazily, the dragon closed its mouth again. It stared at him with one eye. Steam puffed briefly out of its nostrils, which almost made Corin lose his nerve. He kept his body taut, balancing with all the skill he had. The dragon closed its eye.

"Well done, my lord," said Kelvan, sounding pleased. "It takes most new riders weeks to do that."

"I don't have weeks," Corin said, standing. He backed away a few paces and felt the fear go out of him in a release that left him shaking a little. He took several deep breaths. "What next?"

"Next," Kelvan said thoughtfully. He took a step toward Corin. Corin blinked. The rider held Corin's knife in his hand, hilt extended to the prince.

He started, surprised, even alarmed. "How the hell did you do that?" It was not a power Corin had ever learned the wizards had. He took the knife back, a bit gingerly, and sheathed it.

"It's a dragon skill. Dragons do not live in time as we do, or in space. They extend through it. And when we ride them, they give us just a trace of that power."

He pondered it. Understanding lay on the very edges of his mind. The dragon seemed solid, animal, complete. It did not flicker or blur.

Then, for just an instant, he had a sense of a vast and icy darkness lying beyond the dragon. He shivered.

Enough. He had to be practical. "And all riders can do that?"

"I'm better than most," Kelvan said. "For other reasons. But we can all do it some. That's why we make good swordsmen. You aren't supposed to know that, by the way. I'm breaking faith."

"Does my father know?"

"Of course."

Corin was not sure how to take that. "Who says I'm not to know?" he asked, and heard a bit of truculence to his tone.

"The riders. No one is to know who is not a rider. If I were training you as an ordinary rider, I would leave it for you to discover on your own."

He was glad it had not been his father who made it a secret. "What about Hadon?"

"I would be very surprised if no one had told him. But we don't discuss it even among ourselves."

"He'd better hope his sons don't know."

"They may. But none of the three of them will ever ride a dragon, so it doesn't matter much. When you treat a dragon as a beast of burden, it gives you nothing."

Corin looked at the dragon. He wanted to touch it again, that incredible silkiness of scale and smooth muscle moving underneath. "How do you control it, then?"

"You have to learn to talk to it."

"Talk to it?" he echoed, feeling young and inexperienced.

Kelvan grinned. "You don't think you direct a dragon with knees and heels like a horse, do you? You make an agreement with a dragon."

"But how can a dragon hear commands with all the wind of flying?"

"The dragons speak with you mind to mind. That's how they speak with each other. And rider can speak to rider through them."

Corin briefly stared down at his feet. He did not know why that thought had never occurred to him. Well, perhaps he did know. He was not in the habit of thinking about dragons and their riders because they were the Emperor's servants, not his. It made him aware of how much he was transgressing.

"Come speak to it. Put your hand here; you have to be in contact."

The scales on the dragon's head were smaller and rounder than the scales on its body. When he put his hand on one it was as smooth as glass, with edges like a freshly sharpened sword, and warm to the touch.

Corin closed his eyes. For a while there was just the usual clamor of his mind. He stilled it, focused his thoughts on the dragon. It was images that came slowly to him then, not words: a darkness with a distant fire raging in it, a teapot lying in smoke-stained rubble, a black moth circling a candle. Colors, pulsing slowly. Brown, which was warmth, and green, which was pleasure. Grey for calm, blue for exultation, red for stubbornness. A bloodstained sword lying beside a crack in granite. A mountain, snow on its peak and sides, wind roaring around it, sending the snow into white sprays that glittered in the close-by sun. A man with eyes glittering like black stone who turned to ash. Braided garlic hanging from a rafter. A woman's hand with an apple in the palm, green and small and round. A small bronze pendulum swinging back and forth.

It stopped. He did not know what any of it meant, though it felt familiar. His breath was coming in short pants. He felt faint, dizzy, and bent over to keep the blood in his head. Kelvan had a hand on his arm, supporting him. Most men would have been afraid to touch him at all because he was the prince, let alone keep him from falling lest it injure his pride. Slowly the blackness cleared and he straightened.

"It's normal," Kelvan said, "but it means you've had enough. Don't push it."

"I didn't understand it."

"It takes time. Come, my lord, you'll be worn through, we should go back."

"When again?"

"I don't know," Kelvan answered, with that distant and inhuman look on his face. "Let me help you back on."

Even with the stretches he was stiffening already, so he did not refuse the aid, though, remembering Joce, he made sure not to touch Kelvan's bare skin. He would likely ache for days.

And then the crouching dragon sprang, dipped as it got its motion, and ascended, and Corin thought he would not exchange this for anything.

Flying back into the bright sun was difficult. They came to Caithenor when the sun above the clouds was getting low. The clouds were a pattern of shadows and color, reflected red and purple light. Then the descent, through thick fog, and there was the green patch that was the palace garden; he had not understood before how huge it truly was.

The dragon landed smoothly on the roof and folded its vast wings. Corin took his helmet and gloves off and tossed them to the ground, then began to fumble with the straps of the harness. The sentries had withdrawn to the farthest corners; few people wanted to get this close to a descending dragon.

He worked his way out and slid off. Pain surged briefly through his legs when his feet thudded against the roof. He leaned into the dragon for a bit, looked at how finely the scales lay over one another. Unexpected and pure, longing surged through him. To fly, to keep his body touching the beast's. He felt as though in the last few hours he had been more himself than he ever had.

Kelvan walked with him to the stairs down. At the top Corin said, "Thank you. For all of it."

"You are most welcome."

"Are you going on far tonight?" He could not keep a bit of envy from his voice.

"For hours yet. Dragons love to fly in the dark."

"Doesn't it need, well, fuel?"

Kelvan laughed. "Dragons eat once a week and are useless flyers for the first day afterward."

Corin wondered what dragons ate, then decided perhaps he did not really want to know. How did one say farewell to a dragonrider? "Fly well."

"Fly fast, fly well, and fly far," Kelvan said. "That is the proper way." He bowed. "Good evening, Prince."

Corin lingered until he could no longer see the dragon in the sky, then made his way down the stairs and to his rooms, where he had the recommended bath and wine before a late dinner. There was an ache in him, a terrible yearning to have the dragon in his mind once again, and he wished bitterly for a moment that he had never done it.

CHAPTER FIVE

❧

The library windows, three stories high and covering an entire wall, let in plenty of light even on a cloudy day. There were a few lamps on, but more for comfort than for need. The room was mostly deserted, and Corin found his favorite chair, in a corner near the windows with rows of shelves concealing him, and sat down with a stack of reports that had come in while he was north. Most of them would be routine, but he needed to catch up.

He liked the library and went there frequently when he wished to be undisturbed. The morning had been nothing but interruptions. It was not quite hiding—Teron knew where he was—but the extra effort of coming there deterred a large number of people. Those who did come in search of him came with softened footsteps and lowered voices. Even the angriest of men found it unseemly to argue in a library. The carpet was thick and sound-deadening, and the two floors of bookshelves that overlooked the reading area were usually quiet. Sometimes there would be noises, pages rustling, people speaking, a wheel on the lift or the cart creaking, but they were easily ignored. Rank, or at least ceremony, fell away here too; anyone could come in. Few besides courtiers did—many of the servants could not read, and only the nobles were permitted to take books out—but it happened.

He read the first few reports diligently and saw nothing unexpected. He began skimming. Half an hour later he had still not learned anything that made it worth his time. Corruption in the ports, a brewing land dispute in Pell, a turnpike robbery west of Caithenor. A fire in a country manor started by a lord's son too careless with his experiments. These things happened. Restless, he put the reports down and stared out the window. He was not sorry to have missed the reconvened council the night before. He wondered if there had been argument. Aram's power was by no means absolute, but he had a stronger will than nearly everyone on the council. There were so few options, though, that there could not have been much of a dissent in any case.

The plans had been put into effect; troops were moving south to Dele and east to Harin. The machinery of war had started, but it felt incomplete to him. Obscured. Things were awry, that was the word for it. Knocked off the axis of reason. Maybe Tyrekh really was a sorcerer.

He returned to reading. It was hard to keep his mind on it. He thought of his older sister. Mari was coming here. Would Hadon send a dragon to abduct her as well? The thought was worse because it called up the memory of dragon scale, of cold air, of the heat beneath him. When the dragon tipped in the air, the sun caught blindingly on the wings. Anger against his father spurted briefly through him. To ride an enemy's dragon was to be taunted. He pushed it away.

Again he had that urgent sense that there was something he was supposed to do. He felt tense, on guard. Some mistake he had made would land disastrously back in his lap. It was waiting. He scowled. Then he gave up. Too many other things needed attention for him to waste his time in fighting phantoms.

He made it through two more hours of tedium before yielding to the desire to stop. Even the spy reports from Mycene only repeated things he already knew. The stack of reports he had read—or looked at—was larger than the ones he had not. It would do. There were probably a dozen new matters waiting on his desk. He had to give some attention to the courtiers, too. Seana had come to see him that morning and he had told Teron to turn her away. He was going to have to talk to her but he had no time. He had no idea if Simoun had told her war was coming. She was no fool; if he hadn't told her, she would puzzle it out.

Dispirited, he gathered his papers and headed toward the door, walking rapidly past the high bookshelves. When he turned the corner at the end he collided hard with a woman coming the opposite direction. The book she was holding went flying, and she was about to go with it. He dropped the reports and caught her by the nearer arm before she fell.

"Are you all right?" he asked, silently cursing himself for his clumsiness.

"Yes. Thank you," she said, straightening. "I'm quite sorry." She raised her eyes to look at him, then froze. He knew he had been recognized, but he felt frozen himself. She was the shy woman he had glimpsed in the entrance hall, astoundingly beautiful. Without breaking eye contact, barely knowing he was doing it, he released her arm. She made a short curtsy and said, "Your Highness." She sounded embarrassed, and her face was flushed. He could not stop looking at her.

The reports he had dropped were scattered everywhere, and she went to her knees to pick them up. Quickly he came to his senses and squatted down beside her to gather them himself. Not only was it rude to let her do it, no one besides him should be reading them. That was not a mistake he wanted to have to admit to his father.

He made an untidy pile and reached for the last one, which was covering her book. Then his own gaze was stilled. The book had fallen open to an illustration of a Sarian warrior standing with a fire weapon at his shoulder. It was a careful engraving, beautifully inked, that showed the details of the weapon clearly.

He flipped the pages back to the title page, noticing as he did so that the other illustrations were equally well drawn. Some of them were of Sarian people and buildings, others careful sketches of elaborate machines with inset details of parts and precise measurements. *Beyond the Black Peaks. By A Traveler*. It was a history of Sarium, from nearly fifty years ago. On the facing page was a map. He stared at it. Of all the books in the library, why did she have that one? He looked at her, not knowing if he was more startled or suspicious, and their eyes locked again. Hers were deep lapis blue, sparkling and lively. Her black hair was glossy and full. He wanted to touch it.

Absently, he extended the book to her. "Here," he said. Their fingers brushed, stung. It was all he could do to keep from taking her entire hand.

"I'm sorry," she said once more. It sounded as though she were thinking something else entirely.

"It was my own fault," he said rotely. My God, those eyes.

She held out the papers she had gathered, and he added them to the pile he had made, still looking at her. They both stood up. He looked away from her at last and paged through the reports. "They're all here," he said, relieved.

"I didn't read any of them," she said.

She must have seen enough to know she shouldn't. "Of course not," he said. He would have said that even if he had watched her poring over them for an hour. He risked a look at the rest of her: slender and tall. Her hair reached nearly to her waist. Her figure was good—more than good—and her clothing conventionally modest. The adherence to fashion disappointed him. It looked very well on her, there was no denying that, but someone so striking should dress to match.

Then her face went full of mischief and she said, "Wouldn't it really be a much better idea to read that sort of thing somewhere private, Your Highness?"

He stared at her. He could not tell which of them was more surprised for her to have rebuked him like that. She hadn't meant to say it; that much was clear from the hand going up to cover her mouth in a vain attempt to withdraw the words. It made her even more beautiful.

Now she was about to apologize again. It was the last thing he wanted. "Who are you?" he asked to cut it off. "What's your name?"

She cast her eyes down. "Tam Warin, my lord."

Her first name was not Caithenian, but her last name was, a solid and unremarkable name, a commoner's. Her voice was cultured, clear, assured. She was no one's maid or paid companion, which meant she had to have a connection with someone of rank to be here.

"Why are you reading about Sarium?" he asked.

"The book was on the shelf, my lord," she answered demurely. It was another rebuke of sorts, and an undeniable one. He thought perhaps she was laughing at him behind that deferential manner. He would be a fool to countenance it.

"Fair enough," he said, then threw both pride and prudence to the winds. "Well, Tam Warin, will you have dinner with me? Don't answer now, think about it." He hurried away, before she could say no or he could change his mind.

❧

He practically fled to his study, said tersely to Teron, "No visitors," and shut the door. He felt about fourteen again. One look at those lapis eyes, so like the stone they even had the green-gold flecks, and he had utterly lost his mind. What in the world was he thinking, inviting a complete stranger to eat with him? There were women he had known for years who would start ordering their wedding clothes if he asked them that. But it was not just her eyes.

Somehow he made it through the rest of the afternoon. He had been coerced—ordered—into attending a dinner with two dozen or so other people, all of them young, none of them married, and he went with a mixture of relief at the distraction and irritation at the event. It reeked of matchmaking. It had the grace of excluding Seana, but he could not see the point of being there himself. All the women had been eliminated already as potential brides for one reason or another, and it was not the way to find a lover.

He was late, of course. When he arrived people were already clustered in small groups of threes and fours, filling the room with the hum of conversation. A few of them had mourning ribbons pinned to their shoulders. For Cade, he presumed. A hundred years ago a lord's death would have canceled the event. He kept looking, moving his eyes over the guests. Abruptly he realized what he was doing, trying to find that beautiful long black hair. She was a commoner, so she would not have been invited. Unreasonable disappointment cut him. He was in danger of acting like a moonstruck boy.

He sensed himself being watched and turned. She was young, pretty with a softness of the kind that had never appealed to him but did to many men, and had a look in her eye that could only be called an invitation. Her dress, an expensive embroidered pale rose silk, made no effort to conceal the bounty contained within. It was not hard to imagine removing it. There was no shyness in her face. He remembered her from the entrance hall the other day. Next to Tam, she had been. That was an unlikely combination. Tam would never wear such a gown, but if she did—he forced himself to stop.

He was joined shortly by Mattan, the Duke of Harin, who was only a few years older than himself. Mattan said, "You're looking well, Corin."

"That's unfortunate," he said sourly, and Mattan laughed.

Other people began to gather around them. Corin went through the motions automatically. A charming smile, a gallant kiss of a lady's hand, an artfully modulated laugh at a tired jest. Sometimes he wondered what would happen if he said something harsh or coarse or patently stupid. Would anyone dare to call him on it? Unlikely. Favor was the currency of a royal court. He understood that, but it went against him as well; he had to handle the courtiers as carefully as porcelain, lest he say or do something that upset the fine balance of the various factions. Soldiers were much easier to work with.

He missed Tai. She was always elegant and graceful, the perfect princess, during such affairs, and afterward she would share a bottle of wine with him and entertain him with wickedly acidic and accurate imitations of the guests. Neither of them had ever said a word of it to anyone else. Then he realized that she had probably confessed it to her husband. Sometimes he still forgot she was married. She would not have been here in any case.

He had not forgotten she was a captive. He kept the thought off his face and said politely to the woman he was talking to, "May I get you something more to drink?"

She dimpled and nodded, making her light brown curls bounce up and down. She had a slender neck and too much jewelry. "Thank you, my lord," she murmured.

When the bell rang for the meal, he found himself at the same table as the bold girl. She held her wineglass low, drawing eyes to her breasts when she was not speaking. He was not the only man who looked. Several other women were seated at the table, and he managed to flirt evenly with all of them, neither neglecting nor favoring a one. It was all restrained and as expected, and would give rise to no rumors. Well, no rumors beyond the usual ones.

After the sweet there was more standing and talking. As he inquired politely about the doings of yet another simpering lady, the falsity of it disgusted him. He was full of sharp restless energy. He needed to be doing. As soon as he courteously could, he broke off the conversation and sent for Bron.

The captain came mercifully quickly. Corin excused himself and went out. It was much cooler in the corridor. They moved a few feet from the door.

"Get six men ready for a ride," he said.

"It's pouring again."

He realized that he wanted something more than exercise. He wanted to make things move. "All the better. It will seem that much more urgent."

"I'm going to arrange backups if you're the bait," Bron said with a resigned expression that Corin knew well on his face. No doubt he was thinking to himself that this was one of the nights he would earn his pay. "Where are we going?"

He intended to give some sort of vague answer, but his voice became someone else's. "The Flats." His tongue felt heavy in his mouth. He made no effort to retract the words.

The door to the room opened as he spoke and a servant came out with a wheeled cart of dishes. Bron was silent, which meant that whatever he was about to say, it was not a simple, *Yes, sir.* As soon as the door was shut and the servant out of earshot he said, "My lord, you're crazy. I can't take you there at night, not if I have three dozen men."

Corin wondered with a trace of amusement what would happen if the courtiers heard that. Bron had said more blunt things in the past. He said, "I'm not going tavern-crawling. There's one man I want to see." The words came again in a patterning he had not meant. Whatever tangled and blocked his speech was stronger, speaking for him. He could resist it, change his mind, stammer into something else. He did not want to. The impulse had power, and he would never know what it was if he did not yield to it.

Bron said, "Don't tell me it's Liko. I thought you were done with him."

"He can still be useful." He realized something that gave reason to the impulse, that showed he had not gone mad himself. "If anyone knows about what killed Cade, it's him." Gerod had reported that morning on a discouraging lack of progress about the murder.

"Let Gerod do it, sir."

"No."

Bron made one last try. "Let me bring him here, or somewhere safer. It will do him good to be out in the wet, might get him clean."

He was right, it was a dangerous thing to do and Liko lived in squalor. Nevertheless, he would go. "That's missing the point. You heard me, Bron. Ten minutes." He kept his tone calm. His father had told him once, when he was very young, that the instant he had to angrily repeat an order, or win an argument by walking away, he had slipped.

Bron looked at him, clearly evaluating if he had pushed as far as he could, then said, "I need a little longer for the backups, sir."

"Fine. But don't dawdle."

By the time they reached the Flats, Corin thought he had perhaps let arrogance get the best of him. The rain was not torrential, but it was hard and steady. Paved and cobbled streets were slick, potholes masqueraded as puddles, the lamps could not dispel the gloom. The unpaved streets and alleys had become quagmires of sticky heavy mud. If the men were not thinking curses at him, the horses were.

In daytime the Flats was a busy loud area full of men loading and unloading barges from up- or downriver, piling goods onto carts to be taken to market or warehouses or wagons to go elsewhere, and laboring on the boats. The boats were not the immense oceangoing vessels that put in at Dele but smaller slower ships that fought the current with oars and noisy steam-paddles. The canal docks had everything that any waterfront did, sawyers and ropemakers and burly laborers, scrawny opportunistic cats, a square neat brick wharfmaster's house, blacksmiths and their hod carriers. There were plenty of illegal deals made, of course, but not at knifepoint. At night it was another story: the stevedores were gone, replaced by hired thugs guarding the boats and the goods, the taverns and brothels were full, and brawls were common and often large. The rain would quell some of the usual violence and roughness, but only some. Corin usually hated having an escort, though he had long ago conceded to it. It galled him sometimes, to be a man and still subject to the will of his father, but the policy on this had been laid out long ago. He remembered vividly a chastisement when he was fifteen or sixteen. *You can risk your own neck and I can't stop you,* Aram had said, *but I will stop you risking soldiers' lives for your own pleasure.* He had said, *It's a formality, I'll go alone*, and the king had for the first and only time in Corin's life struck him. It had not been hard, but the mere fact of it had shocked him into pained silence. *You are the prince. You are never alone. The men are not for you but for Caithen.* In the Flats it was a necessary precaution, not a formality. If he went alone he faced a good chance of a fight, not because he was the prince but because a solitary man was prey.

There were not many lights on the streets they went on. The buildings were cramped and shabby, the dirt streets narrow and dark. The rain had washed away some of the usual garbage and rot but reinvigorated the odors of what remained. Wet, skinny, miserable-looking women huddled in doorways. They did not call out to ply their trade; men on horseback probably terrified them. They no doubt expected the city watch to haul them off to prison. Here and there were dark heaps of rags that were actually men in stupors or illness. In the narrow spaces between buildings people had erected miserable little sheds covered with scavenged sheet metal. The rain beat loudly on it.

They were not going to the worst parts, where the buildings were falling apart, with holes in the roofs and no doors or shutters, the insides thick with filth and refuse. A man might die there and lie unburied on the street for days while the rats and the dogs and the crows worked at him. Many of the houses were abandoned, which had made them into gathering places for young men to rape women and kill one another. A few went up in fire every winter. Fire was the only thing that had a chance to cleanse the place, but it was always stopped lest it spread.

Every city had such places; it had been that way as long as there were cities. Humanity invariably sorted itself, and some people were the dregs. That knowledge did not make Corin any less ashamed that there was such a place in his city, on his watch. He kept such thoughts to himself. Nothing would divest him of authority sooner than to notice that the poor were people. Charity was women's work. He was glad of the rain, not only because it drove people in but because it prevented the men from talking to one another, saying things he did not want to hear.

He led them down to the wharf before going to Liko's. The black water, pocked with raindrops, lapped against the slimy pilings and stone walls of the quays. Boats rocked and creaked on their lines. Dull light from the lanterns on a few decks was the only illumination. The smiths had banked their fires and shut the doors. It was empty of people; even the mad, who walked disheveled and shouting in the streets, had taken cover from the rain. The birds and rats had all found refuge of some sort. It was still, lifeless. Across the water he saw only the darkness of the river bluffs.

He remembered a time when he had snuck out of his rooms at university and down to the Liden docks at night with a few other students. They went into a tavern, where he immediately discovered he was more fastidious than he had thought, and he slipped back out. A watchman confronted him while he sat at the end of a pier, legs dangling over the water. *You be careful, lad,* said the watchman. *If you fall in there's no one going to get you out.* He said, *I won't fall. I'm not cupshot.* The watchman lowered the lantern and asked, *Have you ever seen a drowned man?* Corin had to admit that he had not. He did not tell the man about the deaths he had seen in other forms. The watchman said, *There's no winning against water. Once you tire and slip under, you won't break free. All you will do is struggle and then die. Come step back.*

That had been before Tyrekh, when he still thought that nothing lay ahead of him except the same rule with a light hand over a placid country that his father had. Both of them had hardened since then.

He surveyed the docks carefully again. He was not sure what he was looking for. The water seemed menacing, the maw of some ravenous beast that would devour everything. It was ancient, cold, powerful. The boats were flimsy things that would break apart at the first surge. He imagined slipping after all, clutching helplessly at the slick wood of the pier and sliding on into the blackness, a cold weight bearing down on him, terror as his aching lungs gave up. He shuddered and turned his horse.

Liko's house was on a corner. It was the only one visible in any direction that had light coming out around the shutters and between the boards. There was not enough wind to move the cracked wooden sign hanging outside the door. Corin dismounted and rapped hard on the door with the handle of his knife. Bron and two other men were beside him, swords drawn.

The door opened and there was Liko, holding a candle that guttered fiercely in the draft. A few roaches scuttled into a darker corner. "Oh," he said. "You. Come in, but there's only room for three of you."

A skinny girl wearing only a thin dirty white shift was sitting on a wooden chair, the skirt hiked up to the middle of her thighs, her legs spread. The dark circles of her nipples were obvious through the fabric even in the dim light. She could not have been more than fifteen. Liko gave her a coin and said, "Get out, and keep your mouth shut." She got out. Bron and Alric did not sheathe their swords, and Corin did not ask them to.

There was an open flask on the table, but Liko did not appear to be drunk yet. It was hard to tell, but his eyes seemed clear. He was short, dirty, and gamy-smelling, with unwashed poorly cut brown hair and several weeks' worth of beard. His shirt was stained, and his pants were shiny at the knees and fraying at the ankles. He had been a well-off gentleman before he let the bottle take him. His family had petitioned successfully to have him cut off from the entail. Corin disliked him but did not underestimate him. He was clever, cunning even, and a survivor. He knew everything that happened in the district and in much of the rest of the city, and though he did not control it he knew who did. He made a living of sorts by selling useless medicines and even more useless advice to people more desperate than himself, and information to anyone who would pay for it. Corin tolerated his disrespect because he preferred it to groveling.

The room was not so much tiny as it was crowded. There were splintering crates stacked everywhere, a table, a bookshelf filled with dirty glass bottles and jars like an apothecary's, another bookshelf filled with a few books and many more yellowing pamphlets, ragged cloths draping broken chairs, and, unbelievably, a fortune-teller's glass ball. A few very old skulls, one missing its jaw, were on top of one of the bookshelves. It stank of urine and old vomit, cheap wine and vinegar. A sweet rottenness that was sulfur, and made him think of dragon. There was another smell too, something acrid. He looked around again and saw a distilling apparatus in one corner. That made this easier. It would give away far too much to ask directly about the blood-dust.

"Doing alchemy now, are you," he said, gesturing at the distiller. "Lead into gold? Love potions or poisons?"

"There's no alchemy in chemistry. Particulate matter cares nothing of the motions of the heavens. What people want, I supply." Liko spoke pompously, as though he were trying to sell his wares.

"What do they want these days?"

"A little of this, a little of that. Herbs don't cure everything." His eyes narrowed. "You don't think I sold what killed Lord Cade, do you?"

Right to the heart of the matter. Liko being who he was, it was not unreasonable for him to think he might be suspected of it. That was why Corin had come, after all. "Did you?"

"Not with knowledge of it. I'm not in the business of making poisons, whatever you may think. But I may have sold an ingredient or two." He waved broadly at the shelves. "One metal can act in many different ways depending on how it is combined. I can't answer for what other people do."

"What *do* you know about Cade's death?"

"I know only fleet-footed Rumor blazing among us. It's all the talk."

That had a good chance of being true. Few things would make more compelling gossip than murder in the palace. "What else does rumor say? Did he owe Akelon money?"

"Yes. But he was making payments. Akelon wouldn't have killed him, if that's what you're after. And no, I don't know where Cade got the money."

"Do you know who killed him?"

A hesitation. No doubt he was hoping to be paid first. "No."

Corin put a hand on his sword hilt and said softly, "You've heard something, or you guess something. Tell me."

Liko swallowed, then said, "I don't know who killed him. But he was down here too much even for a gambler. He must have crossed someone."

That settled one thing. Courtiers never came to this sort of place unless they had been caught in someone else's trap. They were paying debts or making illicit sales of their valuables to keep the blackmailers at bay. Cade hadn't been an accidental victim.

Corin asked, "What was he doing down here?" He wished the room were lighter.

"Watching. I never saw him talk to anyone. It was peculiar."

"Did you ever talk to him?"

Liko shook his head vigorously. "He came here once and wanted me to put him into a sleep-trance. He didn't make much sense. I don't think he really knew what he was talking about."

"Do you think he was mad?"

"No," Liko said after a brief hesitation. "Desperate, maybe."

"Well, did you do it?" Corin asked. He knew little of mesmerism, though it did not surprise him that Cade would practice it. It was a fad among the courtiers.

"No. I didn't want to be killed when he came to regret letting me hear whatever it was he wanted to find out. Or when it didn't work and he looked the fool. All mesmerism would tell him is what's in his own head."

That was prudent, although it was hard to imagine Cade as a killer. "Did he practice the occult?" That was a forbidden practice, not a fad, but a lord who would ask Liko to mesmerize him might well be lunatic enough to turn to the so-called dark forces for assistance.

"He hadn't the mind for any kind of science," Liko said contemptuously. "Not even the dubious ones."

"Conjury's not science."

"Tell that to someone who does it and he'll tell you the laws of magic are more complex than optics."

Corin grinned, remembering his university years and the tendentiousness of some of the scholars. Then he brought the conversation back to Cade. "Is he the only one who's been down recently?"

"The only one I've seen." Always the careful answer. "I don't know every retainer of every lord."

"And all he did was watch?"

"I think he wanted to see what was happening, that's all."

"Spying?"

Liko gave a half shrug. "How would I know?"

Corin did not say what he thought. He said, "And what is happening?"

Another hesitation. Longer this time. Corin let himself show some impatience in his movements.

Liko said, "There's people leaving. Laborers. Shoremen. Women." The way he said *women* made it clear he meant the whores, which was a bad sign. They were the first to come and the last to go anywhere.

Corin asked, "No work?"

Liko shook his head. "Plenty of work. They're scared."

"Of what?"

"Don't know." He reached for his flask.

With a quick grab, Corin took it from him. The man tensed, then slackened, obviously reminding himself whom he spoke with. Corin sniffed it. Cheap sweet wine. He tilted the flask and let some dribble out, dark like blood, onto the floor. The odor rose to his nostrils. It smelled more vile spilled than in the flask.

Liko said, "No more. Please."

"Then answer me." He let a few drops fall.

"The dead," Liko said with obvious reluctance. Corin wondered why. Perhaps he feared being accused of practicing the occult himself. Or just being taken for a fool. Anyone as well-off and educated as Liko had been knew that the dead stayed dead.

"What about the dead?"

"People say they're waiting. Opening doors that shouldn't be opened."

The phrase *opening doors* made Corin chill despite his own wealth and education. He put the wine back on the table but out of Liko's reach. Scornfully he said, "You don't mean that. People don't give up money because of ghosts." He was aware that he was also scolding himself.

Liko said, "You haven't heard these stories." He stopped abruptly.

"Go on, tell them to me."

"They say they look in the water and see the dead all pale and blind. Not bodies. There is a woman who comes up to you and touches your shoulder and you freeze like ice and she sucks the blood out of you while you stand there. Then she turns into a bird and flies away. At night there are cold spots you can't walk through and they herd you down to the water and the next thing you know it's morning and you smell like river water and your clothes are sopping. And sometimes you walk and turn and turn and you can't get anywhere, you keep coming to the same corner, or you're standing in a courtyard that's all white stone and nothing is alive and there's no way out. You come back somehow and your shoes are worn to shreds and you have scrapes and bruises all over your hands and arms."

It was more convincing than it should be. It rubbed at the edges of the blankness in his memory. There were drowned things in that water by the docks that would emerge white and swollen and blindly searching if they had the chance.

He glanced at Bron and Alric. Thankfully, neither of them looked persuaded. It reassured him. He said, "You know better, you're not a peasant. I wager there's not a person you've spoken to who can actually say any of it happened to him and not to the friend of a friend of a friend."

Liko shrugged again. "Of course it's false, but what's it matter what I think? That's what they think. So they go."

That was true. And useless. "What about Cade? Had he heard those stories?"

"Probably."

There was an answer in that somewhere, but it would not come to him. Nor was he sure of the question. Liko seemed just a bit too off-handed about it to be telling the truth. He decided not to push further in that direction. "If the dockworkers are leaving, what's happening to the cargo?"

And then, an additional nugget. "There are plenty of Myceneans, they don't seem to care."

It took effort to keep himself from swearing. That was bad. There were always a few Myceneans about, but not many. The ones who were poor enough to work as laborers were usually too poor to leave Mycene. If there were many, that had to be Hadon's doing too. He would give odds of ten to one that the Myceneans were the source of the stories, preparing a place for themselves to do whatever it was the Emperor—or his sons—wanted. Dragons in the north, spies in the capital. Hadon could be sending in soldiers to prepare a strike at Aram much worse than taking Tai hostage. But why, what was the threat?

At any rate, Cade had probably talked to the Myceneans even if Liko hadn't seen it. He had got himself in debt, turned spy for Tyrekh or Hadon, and then something had gone wrong. He became a weak link in someone else's chain.

Corin said, "Are there enough Myceneans to do the labor?"

"Yes."

He did not want to put Liko on the track of thinking that was important. He said, "Akelon is taking advantage of the situation, I presume." Akelon controlled the canals and docks and the other lawless pockets of the city, and had for more years than Corin had lived. He loaned money to young foolish gentlemen who had lost too much gambling, and they were in his power before they knew it. He was a king of thieves and had eluded capture so many times it was mythical. The watch was paid well so they would not be easily corrupted.

"Of course. So are the docking fee collectors."

In other words, the Crown. Corin let the jab pass. "Who else owes him?"

"Who doesn't?"

"Granted. But enough to really fear?"

"Brice, Ricard, Larron."

The names were not a surprise. They were young men who cared only about impressing young ladies and one another. Cade had been part of that set. They might be traitors with him. "If Akelon catches anyone else in his net I want to know. Anything else notable?"

"No."

He was lying, Corin was sure of it this time. He frowned. He was cold, and he pulled at one shoulder of his cloak. The candle flame flared high with the movement, brightening the room for an instant.

Liko stumbled backward, almost falling into the chair as though he had forgotten it. What the hell? Alric caught him hard about the arm and forced him to stand. With his foot he pulled back the chair. It fell over with a loud crash.

Corin took a step. The man shrank away from him. Alric moved his sword. Corin shook his head and motioned the guard back. "What just happened, Liko?" he asked softly.

"Nothing, my lord, I swear it."

"If your drinking has gotten bad enough to give you the rats, you're no use to me."

"It's not that bad." He held his arm out. It trembled no more than anyone's would.

"Then stop lying. Tell me what you saw."

Liko swallowed. "Just—the shadow. A trick of light. That's all. It startled me."

That was a lie too. Something had frightened the man, but he did not know what. A trick of the light. Corin had the uneasy feeling that it was something he had done himself, something he should have recognized. He glanced at Bron again for reassurance and was not reassured at all by the look of unease on the captain's face. Had Bron seen something too?

Then he put that thought aside, as he was well trained to do. The trick of the light had pushed whatever else Liko lied about deeper within him. There would be no quick way of getting it out now. It could be anything. Doubtless Liko had his own elaborate sets of plans that would be easily upset if Corin or his men poked around the docks too much. It seemed useless to press any further at the moment.

"Keep your eyes open. Someone besides Cade is putting his nose where it doesn't belong. He'll be down here eventually," he said. "And you had damn well better answer the questions of anyone else I send."

Liko made a bow that just escaped being mockery. Corin glared warningly at him and went out.

The rain seemed wonderfully cleansing. He spat. Without a word Bron handed him a flask. Water. "Thank you," he said, returning it.

"You got more out of him than I thought you would," Bron said.

In other circumstances Corin might have responded with a wry remark. This time all he said was, "It was adequate. Do you believe it?"

"Yes, sir, mostly. But I still don't trust him. He may be honest, but I don't think he's reliable."

Corin had one foot in the stirrup. He stopped. "Why not?"

"He's frightened. When people are frightened they make mistakes."

"You're right there," Corin said. He had thought he might be doing that very thing himself. He mounted and leaned over to address Bron. "Are you afraid of the other world, Bron?"

"You mean all that rubbish about the dead, sir? There's enough to worry about in this world. But—" He went silent.

"But what? Go ahead."

"It's the same kind of stories people were telling in the north. I don't like it."

"Nor I. Any guess as to why he didn't want to tell me?"

Bron shook his head, then said, "I think he believes it more than he's let on. Something's got to him."

"Sarians?" Corin asked.

"He knows better than that, even drunk."

That was a fair assessment. No, whatever Liko was afraid of, it was less tangible than a fire weapon. *Bad things are going to happen, Corin. Don't let them take you unaware.* He was convinced now that Aram had been talking about something besides war. Something that put a cold grip around his heart and held on while the world spun away into the dark. Something more suited to hexes and visions. *You'll need them later*, Joce said about the wizards. *Later* seemed to be approaching far too quickly. He should question Joce. Question his father, damn it. But when he tried to frame a question even here, the words would not come.

It was not worth thinking about in a downpour. He picked up the reins. His horse lifted its head. "What do you think of what he said about Cade?"

Bron didn't answer immediately. He mounted his own horse and looked around. He sidled his horse closer to Corin's and said in words hard to hear above the slap of rain, "Whatever Cade was doing smells worse than this place, sir."

Corin had already come to the same conclusion. "I'm afraid you're right," he said to Bron. "We've work to do." He kneed his horse into motion.

The rest of the evening unfolded before him: long discussions with his father, with Gerod, more bad news exchanged, piling tasks on everyone, and sometime well after midnight a cold, solitary bed. It didn't have to be, of course. Other women besides Seana would come quite happily to him. A prince need never be in want of lovers. That bold woman at dinner would require only a wink.

He thought of Tam and was stunned at how quickly the desire for her filled him. She seemed a decent, honorable woman. She would never come into his bed, so why was he taunting himself by pretending there was a chance at it? He should try to forget about her. She was too beautiful not to have formed an attachment to someone already. It was unreasonable to think she would break it for him, when he could give her nothing.

But now that he had called up the image of her, those eyes, he could not banish it. Hell. What was he getting himself into? Worse, what was he going to drag her into, through, that she did not deserve? Why did it matter to him what happened to her?

He swore aloud. No one heard.

❧

They were crossing a narrow street in a silent shop district when the attack happened. Riders came at them from either side. What he remembered most afterward were the splashes of water from the horses' hooves and the reflection of the streetlight on the wet blade of his sword. The guards went into a circle around him before it became obvious to everyone that it was at least two to one against, even with him, and that it was an ill-affordable luxury for him not to fight.

It was loud. The clang of sword blades, the grunts and breaths of the men, the whickers of the horses, the creaking wet leather, the rain. He had his hood back to see, and it was not long before the cloak itself became too hot as he sweated. Strike, parry, thrust, block, again and again. His wrist began to ache, although he was strong enough to keep his arm steady. There were two men against him, one on either side, the water running down their skin in little rivulets. He was taller, with a longer reach, and lither. He was also much the better rider, which was all that gave him the time to hold off both of them.

One of them leaned forward. Corin saw at once that it was too far. He lowered his point, then swung around in a half circle to the man's inside and caught him with a fast clean thrust to the heart before the man could reengage. The man slid forward and fell as Corin pulled the point free. He thwacked the horse with the flat of the blade to get it to move and ducked the other man's swing at the same time. He came up, swung himself, and clashed his blade against the other's, which did not waver.

Brute strength was not going to save him. He had to find some other way to win. He stopped resisting and used the second when the man rebalanced to step the horse back. They paused a moment, both breathing hard. Corin risked a quick look and saw that all the other men were occupied with one another. No one was coming either to his rescue or his opponent's. He wiped the water out of his eyes.

He kneed his horse forward and leaned over for a two-handed blow at his opponent's elbow. The man raised his sword quickly, but not quickly enough, and Corin cut neatly through cloth and muscle to the bone. The man's hand unclasped as the nerves and tendons let go, and blood fountained everywhere. He screamed, a terrible animal sound of pain. His sword fell, the hilt striking Corin's leg on its way to the ground, but the man, amazingly, stayed seated.

It would be murder to kill him, defenseless, though he would likely die of the wound. Corin watched from somewhere else as his sword rose and fell. At the last second he found the will to twist it so that the blow came with the flat. That was enough to knock the man from his horse. The horse ran without urging.

Corin wiped his eyes again and smelled the blood on his hands. He looked around him at the fighting. The fight was much more even in numbers now, which meant the guards had the advantage. He realized several more soldiers had come—Bron's backup.

Then one of the other men wheeled sharply around to face him. He went on the offensive, sword raised, and this time when the blades crashed against each other, his the harder, he felt a profound pleasure in knowing he was going to win.

It took all of three swift strokes before he had his sword at the man's neck, point pressing lightly into the skin. He felt light and quick and powerful. He did not remember ever having moved that fast before.

"Drop your weapon," he said. The man looked at him, then grimaced and pushed himself forward. The sword went in smoothly and neatly. Blood poured out his mouth and from his neck. He toppled. Corin pulled the blade out numbly before the man's weight took him down too. A man who would kill himself rather than face capture was a man who had a cause. Or a man who was afraid of what his own masters would do to him for having botched the job.

Bron was at his side. The fighting was over. "Are you hurt, sir?"

He had to save the speculation for later. "Not a bit. Anyone else?"

"I haven't checked yet, but it doesn't look like it. Nothing major, at least," Bron said. He sighed and swore. "What a bloody mess."

Corin nodded. His horse had its ears back and nostrils flared. He leaned forward and rubbed its head. "Send someone to get more men. I suppose they'll need a wagon, for the bodies. And I want to talk to whoever's got command duty at the nearest watchpost." He dismounted. "We need more light. Damn this rain."

As it turned out, two of the men had minor wounds. There were seventeen bodies on the street. Only five of the attackers' horses had not fled. Corin went with Bron from body to body. None of them had the height and the reddish hair of the Sarians. The man Corin had wounded was unconscious. Bron squatted beside him, felt for a pulse, looked at the wound and the blood. He forced open one of the man's eyes. "He's not going to make it," he said. He drew his knife. "You'd best step aside, sir."

He stood back and watched while Bron efficiently cut the man's throat. There was not much blood. The man must have been nearly dead already. They moved on.

The soldiers knew what to do and Corin left them to it. The carnage dismayed him. He could not help feeling that he had caused it. He had laid a trap in response to some impulse from outside himself. He should have resisted more. It was not much comfort to think that the deaths had all been on the other side; it might not be so next time. He was sure there would be a next time. He checked the horses: good stock, well trained, but nothing to identify them. The saddles and trappings could have been found in any saddlery.

The watch arrived first, then the soldiers. Corin was beginning to feel superfluous. The watch commander was slow and stolid and kept repeating that he had never seen anything like it. As soon as the men appeared Corin abandoned the watchman to the others and took Bron aside. A string of shops along one side had overhanging second stories and inset doors that protected them from the rain.

"Find anything?" he asked.

"No, sir. And I don't expect to either, not with them all dead." Bron glanced down, then looked back up and said, "Did you anticipate this?"

"No. I thought we might be followed, but not attacked."

"We could easily have lost," Bron said, somewhat grimly. "Don't keep things like that from me, not with matters as they are. I need more information if I'm going to do my job."

There was no good response to that, so he did not bother making one. Bron was in the right and they both knew it. He had not said anything to Bron about Hadon, but the captain had heard what Liko said. He could not keep his suspicions to himself now. He said, "They weren't mercenaries. If it turns out they were Mycenean, tell me or the king immediately. I don't care what I'm doing. And no one else."

"If the men guess?"

"Make it clear that if I find out anyone's been talking, even to another man here, about anything, I'll try him as a traitor." He whistled for his horse. "I've got to get back, Bron. How many men can you spare?"

"Ten, but let me pick them."

Corin nodded and mounted. "Do that now."

"Wait," Bron said. He put his hand on the horse's neck. "My lord, do you think they were trying to kill you or to take you?"

"Kill me," Corin said automatically, then really heard the question. Hadon had taken Tai, was he after him as well?

Unthinking, he raised his hand in the peasants' gesture and said, "I curse you, Hadon of Mycene."

He went colder than he had thought he ever could. The rainy street was suddenly heavy and full of hatred. A dragon screamed in his mind. He felt the curse leave him, cold and sharp as ice, lightless as a grave. Bron's face was full of fear.

CHAPTER SIX

⤕❦❧⤔

When Tam received the prince's note she held it a moment before unsealing it. Nothing on the outside distinguished the sender from the writers of the other messages that had been delivered, but she guessed. She had saved it for last; it could be anything. It was polite and somewhat formal, but it looked as though he had written it himself, and his signature was nothing more than his barely decipherable scrawl. He meant it, then. Tonight she could, if she wanted, sit across the table from the Crown Prince of Caithen himself.

Her first impulse was a childish excitement, which she pushed back. She supposed she might be the only woman in the kingdom who would consider turning down an invitation from Corin, but because she was so impetuous by nature she tried hard to do things deliberately, to have decided what to do instead of simply taking the first path. Especially with him; he had to be used to women chasing him, and she did not want to seem like she had come running at his call. She had more pride than that, for better or worse. On the other hand, she had gotten herself into this situation in the first place; it would be only right to play it out. She did not know what imp had made her saucy to him, but the imp needed to be paid.

Once the shock of the library had worn off yesterday, she had told herself that he meant nothing by it. When the *what if* thought rose up, she forced it away. She had distracted herself with games, conversations, an unusual chattiness that was remarked on several times. Now that it was real, she did not know what to do.

He could not marry her; that was not even a possibility to discuss. But if he could not marry her, then there was only one other likely reason for the invitation. If she said yes to the dinner, she was saying yes to much more. And that was the problem. Corin was said to be discreet, careful, and generous, but he was a man and no doubt wanted what men wanted of women. He had certainly looked at her that way. Lady Elwyn's son had looked at her that way too, but he had been considerably easier to disregard.

Pregnancy was easy enough to take care of. As a doctor's daughter she knew quite a bit about childbearing and its opposites. Nor would an affair with him damage her irreparably—since he was who he was, she would likely be exempt from the usual scorn heaped upon a man's mistress, at least in public. A future husband would not consider her used goods. No one would expect her to have rejected him; she simply did not know if she wanted to do it. The two or three times before that she had thought herself in love, with men who had courted her for months, she had not had any urge to take the man into her bed before she should, and had felt little regret when they drifted away before a proposal. She had no grounds for deciding if she cared enough for Corin; she could hardly say she knew him. Yesterday's incident did not qualify as conversation. It did not even qualify as flirting. What if he turned out to be arrogant, thoughtless, dull?

He had not looked like a prince, or at least had not been dressed like one, when she saw him for the first time in the entrance hall, and it did not even occur to her that it was Corin she looked at, although it was word of the prince's return that had brought her, caught in the wake of a flock of eager ladies, to the hall. His clothing had been very dirty, his brown hair lying every which way, and his chin unshaven for several days. He looked exactly like the soldiers with him. There had been a battered saddlebag slung over his shoulder. But she glimpsed his face, his shoulders, the way he walked, and thought, That is a man I would like to know better. He was very handsome. When his eyes touched on her face, she went shy like a girl and looked away while heat rose inside her. "Who is that?" she whispered to Alina. Alina turned a coy face to her and said, "Don't you know? That's the prince."

Her reaction had been pure sinking disappointment. Perhaps she should heed that, go to him because she had wanted him as a man first. When their fingers had brushed yesterday it had been like fire in her entire body. It had been nearly impossible to take her eyes off his face, especially with him looking back at her. Even remembering it brought the blood to her cheeks. She could still feel his hand on her arm, holding her up.

"Tam?"

She jumped. Jenet, who had rooms near hers, was standing in the open doorway. "Good morning," Tam said. She folded up the letter, thankful that it was so plain—had that been his intent?—and put it in a pocket.

Jenet said, "Is anything the matter?" It was curiosity and not concern that prompted the question, but it was said politely. Tam had quickly learned which questions were meant to be answered, and what the answers should be. If she responded patly, Jenet would obey the rules and stop prying. But of all the women on the floor Jenet was the one she liked the best, and it was briefly tempting to confide in her. She dared not say a word to Cina.

She compromised. "Not a thing, thank you. I am just wrestling with the eternal feminine dilemma of which dress to wear to dinner tonight." And that was the decision. For better or for worse, she would dine with him. All she had to do now was figure out how to get her answer to him as inconspicuously as possible.

"How formal is it to be?"

"That's where I can't decide. Formal but not too formal, handsome but not artificial."

"Of course," Jenet said. "One of those."

"One of those what?"

"Dinners. Where you're not sure how it will go, so you want to look your best without him thinking that you care too much. And you won't reveal the name of the gentleman yet, in case things go badly."

Tam laughed. "Does this happen often here?"

"Oh yes. Every unmarried woman I know has a dress for such occasions. Men aren't clear on what they want most of the time, so you have to have something ambiguous. Let's see what we can find in your things."

They spent more time than Tam had thought possible with her trying on dresses and Jenet commenting on them. She did not mind the time; it was raining again, and she needed a distraction. At last they selected something, and Tam sent Jenet on her way. That left only the problem of the acceptance.

She found plain paper of her own and wrote a brief formal reply. Then she went in search of one of the page boys who hung around everywhere like monkeys. They were not the common message boys who carried business between clerks or officials, but rather nobles' sons supposedly learning the niceties of court, which made them privy to potent gossip. It was hard to choose between a younger one who was less likely to question it and an older one who was more likely to keep his mouth shut if appropriately bribed.

She finally opted for the latter. "I want you to take this to Prince Corin," she said.

The boy looked her up and down and said, somewhat haughtily, "His Highness doesn't read letters from people he doesn't know."

She said sweetly, "He knows me," and unfolded his letter enough to show the signature, the simple name.

The boy looked at her again. She knew that she was perfectly decent, but it was obvious that he was trying to figure out how much respect she merited. The boy was surely old and wise enough in what he did to know about men, women, and what the prince wanted with whom. Perhaps she looked too respectable for a royal bedmate and he could not place her anywhere else. Perhaps he scorned her for being willing to go to the prince at all. Or was a note to Corin so very unusual and improper?

Even though the boy's inspection irked her she knew she had better not show it, or she would gain the reputation of a social climber who thought that being Corin's lover gave her royal status. Assuming of course that she did become his lover. But the boy owed her ordinary courtesy as a guest of the court.

She said, "I'm quite sure he will be pleased to receive this," and saw the calculation on his face. If the prince were pleased with the message he would be pleased with the messenger. Next time she would find a younger boy. A little application of the stick seemed appropriate. "I would hate to have to tell him there was a problem."

That did it. "I will take it right away," he said, and bowed.

That evening, half an hour past the appointed time, Tam pulled her shawl a bit more tightly around her. She had been sitting for a while, and the air was getting colder as night came on. Rain had been falling in dribs and drabs all day. A page—a polite one—had already come, "to offer His Highness's deepest apologies, but he will be late," and she was not sure how much longer she could bear the waiting. There was nothing to occupy herself with. She stood up; perhaps walking would warm her a bit, even if it was only back and forth across the hall. The shawl was a fine soft black velvet, edged with silk and patterned with flowers the precise color of her dress, which was an unadorned deep wine-colored gown with a low square neckline, slender waist, and full skirt. Her hair was up, but strands of it were already escaping the pins, and there was one tendril she kept having to sweep back over her ear. Her only jewelry was a simple gold necklace and gold earrings in the shape of a flower.

Her mood was swinging from excitement to anxiety, back and forth, making her fidgety. The hall was a marbled circle where several major passages intersected; there were stone benches and lush flowers and a fountain in the center. It had a high domed ceiling that she thought was lapis lazuli, with curving gold lines interwoven over the surface. The palace was a graceful and beautiful building, and she usually enjoyed looking at it, but not now. The lighting was the soft gold of the glowlamps, but even that she did not appreciate tonight.

Many people met one another here, because of its location, and there was nothing particularly unusual about one woman sitting alone in the early evening, waiting. She thought that was probably why Corin had chosen it, instead of having her escorted from her rooms. Occasionally someone walked through and glanced at her; for a short period a man across the room paced as he waited for someone himself. A cat sitting on the edge of the fountain looked at her as it dipped a paw into the water to drink. She petted it and was rewarded immediately with a loud purr before it jumped down and went about its own business. Mostly she was alone in the quiet. The clock had been striking the hour as she arrived; the half hour had just rung loudly in the empty hall.

It had been impossible to hide the fact that she was dining with someone from the other women in the wing, and she had not even tried. Two had offered to have their maids do her hair and face. Jenet was the only one who refrained from asking who the man was. Tam steadfastly refused to divulge the name of her Secret Lover. No one's guesses were close, and several were quite comical, but to all of them but one Tam just said calmly, "That's your guess." She outright and with vigor denied that it was Lady Elwyn's son, who was handsome enough but a braggart. When Tam had finally had as much as she could stand of Alina's twittering, she said, "Oh, he's just someone I met in the library," which was certainly true but also entirely misleading. The women were going to be insufferable when they found out—if they found out—and she was already trying to think up a stash of fibs. She knew she was jumping far ahead of events, and she rebuked herself.

Alina lingered annoyingly. Tam had resolved to be nice, and even when Alina made a remark clearly designed to elicit jealousy about how charming and flirtatious the prince had been at dinner the night before, Tam kept her mouth shut and smiling. It was just a thrust in the dark at all the women, not a snub directed at Tam, and Tam had no fear she had been discovered. Nor did she have any concern that Corin cared at all for the girl; a man who would invite the woman who mocked him to dinner would have no interest in a burr like Alina. Jenet had been to the same meal, and when Alina was not looking she rolled her eyes.

And then at last she heard footsteps and turned, and he was coming toward her. He too was well dressed but not overly formal, black trousers and a deep blue open-collared shirt, with no signs of rank or wealth beyond the cut and quality of the clothing. He was more handsome than she remembered. Her eyes went to him and her hands wanted to. She took a few steps, and they met beside the fountain. She made only a shallow curtsy; if he needed full-fledged ceremony he would have tossed her out of the library at once when she ran into him and out of the palace entirely when she was rude. The etiquette of the entire situation was amusingly thorny; no book of protocols would say how one greeted the heir to the throne after jibing at him the day before.

"Tam," he said. "If you will permit the informality. I'm sorry I made you wait so long. I only hope I'm worth it. You look far too lovely to be with such a lout." His voice was pleasing, strong without being gruff or deep. She had been too flustered to notice it the day before. His eyes were a cool blue that probably changed color with his mood.

"Flattery will get you everywhere, my lord," she said, hoping she sounded calmer than she felt, hoping he could not see the blood rising in her ears. Why had she put her hair completely up?

He took her hand and brushed his lips gently over it. Her skin tingled at the touch. "Corin," he said. "Please."

It made her feel suddenly shy at the same time that it sent heat to her stomach. She remembered a saying of her mother's: Be careful what you ask for, you might receive it. There was a look in his eyes that told her if she did not want him to court her, she had better say so immediately. He was still holding her hand. Properly, reluctantly, she withdrew it.

He said, "I've made you wait too long for dinner too. Come with me." He gestured her forward and stepped beside her. He was half a head or so taller than her, but he adjusted his stride to hers. Even though they were not touching, she was aware of his body close to hers, his easy strength and a gracefulness she was not used to seeing in men.

Feeling slightly awkward, she said, "May I ask where we're going?"

"Just the Terrace Room. If I hadn't been late we would have had a splendid view of the sunset, but otherwise it isn't particularly notable. It's simple and pleasant, that's all. You don't need to worry about any impropriety."

The reassurance was touching, because it seemed to come from a much younger, more innocent man. Her usual response would have been to banter, but he deserved better than that. "Thank you," she said, wondering if it meant she had mistaken his intentions in spite of everything else.

That question was answered almost immediately when they reached the stairs. They were wide, sweeping, very public stairs; two men were coming down, talking loudly about some other person they were unhappy with. Tam turned her head quickly away from them. Corin, entirely ignoring the men, took her arm in formal style to go upward; gentlemen did that on staircases. But he held her hand much longer than was necessary when he placed it on his forearm, and he looked at her with an intensity that seemed tremendously bold, especially in the presence of the other men. Oh yes, he was used to getting what he wanted. His shirt was silk and very soft. She was embarrassed to feel her heart quicken as happened in the dreadful novels that women like Alina adored. *(Dear Tam, you simply must read this, he rescues her from ever so many things.)* She dared not let herself fall in love.

He said her name, in the tone of someone who is repeating it. "I'm sorry," she said quickly, "I was thinking. It's one of my faults."

He made a sound that might have been suppressed laughter. "It's quite all right, I was saying something banal about the architecture."

"It's very different from home. Dalrinia is cramped and shabby and the streets are all gnarls, everything is old and falling apart. It's much more open here." Of course the palace was different from her home, what an idiotic thing to say. She was babbling. She shut her mouth firmly.

"There are plenty of miserable crowded areas in the city," he said. "There's a lot you haven't seen, and there are places you should never go alone. Don't let grandeur seduce you."

She thought there had been bitterness in his voice, and wondered at it. They were on the second flight of stairs now, and the lighting was dimmer, more shadowy. The marble was slick against the soles and heels of her shoes. No wonder women needed a man's arm. As soon as she had that thought she, predictably, stumbled.

Corin caught her exactly as he had in the library and held her up. "Careful," he said, when she was steady again. "You're starting to make this into a habit." His hand was still on her back.

"It's my shoes," she complained.

They both looked down at her foot in the thin black silk slipper. The throat was low, almost to her toes, and the skin on the top of her foot looked very white against the dark fabric. For a moment she felt exposed. Then it did not seem to belong to her but to some other woman. He was still looking at it too, and she glanced up quickly, meeting his unabashed eyes a second later. Neither of them said anything.

Another person's voice and clicking footsteps came hollowly up the stairwell. She adjusted her hand on his arm and took a step up. Stepping with her, he said lightly, "No one has killed themselves falling down these stairs yet. I would hate for you to be the first."

"That would be an unpleasant end to the evening," Tam said. "Well, I promise you I shall not run, not even when the clock strikes twelve. I wouldn't want you to have to try a shoe on the foot of every maiden in the kingdom."

"There are fewer of those than is commonly thought," he said, "it wouldn't take long."

"For shame to think that," she said, attempting to sound stern and failing entirely.

This time he did laugh. It was a nice laugh, not too loud. They went on in silence, a comfortable one. They had reached that comfort quickly, but then, she was sure that he had spent most of his life learning how to control the way people felt around him. When they left the stairs at the top of the second flight he properly lowered his arm. Guards there came to attention; the prince did not appear to notice. Tam, Tam, what are you doing? she thought.

They went down a marble hallway illuminated with glowlamps. Her reflection was a faint ripple of color on the marble. Arched doorways were spaced evenly on either side. Some of the rooms they opened onto were dark, but in others there were lights and voices, music. A piano echoed eerily from somewhere. A few guards stood here and there along the corridor.

Corin stopped in front of one of the arches and looked in. There was gaslight on in the small room on the other side, dim, and two guards standing near the entrance. They both came crisply to attention. Their gaze seemed to linger on Tam longer than on Corin. She felt nervous and looked down. What would they think of her, what stories would they tell?

Corin motioned her into the antechamber and then through a set of double doors on one wall. Within, she recognized it as a room that she had been shown briefly when she arrived. It was rectangular, with glass doors on the west, the garden side. The doors opened onto a long clay-tiled balcony with slender curved arches of pale green stone supporting the roof. Fountain water cascaded down at the southern end from an open terrace above. The golden wood of the floor was covered with thick green rugs; there were three small tables near the glass doors and other chairs and a sofa arranged decorously in the back. Cina had told her, somewhat cursorily, that it was open to anyone (by which she meant courtiers) and could be reserved for private gatherings, a popular use. Nothing about it suggested a lover's nook. It was neutral ground. If she reported having had dinner in the Terrace Room, no conclusions would be leaped to.

She glanced at him. He had been watching her, no doubt guessing what went through her mind. "Lucky for you it was available," she said drily.

He shut one of the double doors. "In fact I did have to boot someone," he said. "There will no doubt be great speculation about why, but I assure you the guards are sworn to secrecy and I am not known for trysting here."

Are we trysting? she thought, but she was too shy to speak it.

He said something to the guards outside, and they laughed. They liked him, she realized. That augured well of his character and their silence.

Corin brought the second door almost to a close, the perfect combination of privacy and propriety. The middle table was already set. A cart was beside it with covered dishes and carafes of water and wine. A servant standing near the cart, probably guarding it against hungry interlopers, bowed and slipped out the door on the other side of the room almost immediately. That door Corin latched.

He pulled a chair out for her, and she sat down. The plates were gold-rimmed with the royal crest in the center. She was not sure what was supposed to happen next and was about to speak when he began messing with the dishes, lids off, lids on, a stir here, a poke there. When he was satisfied with that it was the lamps, which he adjusted until there was a warm circle of light around the table but the remainder of the room faded into darkness. He lit several candles on the table. They flickered violently as he arranged them, flame leaping astonishingly high before it settled. He reminded Tam of a dog trying to make itself comfortable before curling up and going to sleep. Nervousness was about the last thing she had expected from him.

"And now wine?" he asked, finally sitting down. "Or are you in an abstaining mood?"

She held up her goblet and he splashed wine from one of the carafes into it. Expecting it to be excellent, Tam sipped. She was not disappointed. When she put the glass down, he placed his hand over hers, stroked it lightly with the edge of his thumb, then drew back. Something that could only be desire quickened in her belly.

Both of them turned out to be hungry, and they ate steadily without much talking, though their eyes met continually. She had been a bit afraid it might be something too rich for her stomach, but it was simple enough food: soft bread, soup, tender duck with sauce, fresh greens. He knew what he was doing in alluring her. That everything was so carefully planned did not bother her—even if he did it for every woman he wanted, it was much nicer than the usual clumsy overtures or unappealing directness most men in her experience had used.

She finished before he did and spent her time looking at him, tracing his face in her mind, marking how his hands lay on the table, gauging the breadth of his shoulders. He was not just handsome but assured without even being aware of his own confidence. He was entirely himself.

He finished and put the plates and tableware onto the cart, which he wheeled into a corner. The wine and water he left out. Tapping the carafe, he said, "More wine?"

"Not yet, thank you," she said. He had not drunk all his own. She thought it would be wise to match him.

"Have as much as you wish," he said, looking at both glasses. "I swear not to take advantage of you."

"I could say the same," she said, with a slyness she had not known she was capable of.

He smiled slightly. "If it were just you I would drink to abandon and let you do as you wished. But we could be interrupted any minute by some fool who can't wait until morning."

It had not even occurred to her that such might happen. "Isn't that the whole point of having guards?" she asked. "To keep out the fools?"

"Most of it," he said, looking into his glass. His hair had just a bit of curling unkemptness to it.

There was a heaviness in him that would pull them both down if she tried to pretend it was not there. Hesitantly, she laid two of her fingers across his hand, clenched on the stem of the wineglass. "You must be free sometimes," she said tentatively. She did not want to talk about any of that yet, it was too serious.

"Not with—" He broke off, sighed. He put his hand over hers. He said, "I need to ask you this. I'm sorry. Yesterday, the book you dropped, it was about Sarium. Why did you have it?"

It was not at all the sort of question she had anticipated. He had meant it when he asked in the library, then. He had been staring at her in such a way that she had not thought it mattered. Something must be happening, or he would not be asking.

I know what killed Lord Cade. She couldn't say that, not yet. If there was some present danger from the Sarians, she would learn when it was time for her to know. The shadows in the room looked like clumps of moths. Glistening moving blood. No.

Carefully, glad of a story to tell, she said, "My father was there, years ago. Before he married my mother, and again eight years past."

Corin interrupted. "Twice?"

"Yes."

"That's heroic."

"He doesn't think so," she said truly. His eyes had changed, to a clear green. She went on. "Just determined. He has told me things about it. When we first heard about Tyrekh. He said to me once that we should not call the Sarians barbarians. They're cruel, but clever, and they know many things we don't."

"A wise man, your father," he said, surprising her. "Go on." It was an encourager, not a command.

She tried to frame her next words unalarmingly. Telling him the whole truth of it was too complicated. "Some of the things my father told me were horrible, and I wished he hadn't told me. But once I had heard them, I couldn't forget them. There are many, many ways of being cruel."

"It's parasitic," he said. "The more you give it, the more it wants."

Tam looked at him. He was speaking out of experience. He was not all soft silk and fine wine, then. He must have seen or heard of wretched things. The courtiers were a flock of bright silly birds, and he was not part of them at all. He worked. It would have been very nice to kiss him, but she was not bold enough for that.

She said quickly, "So when I saw the book—I was bored, I was browsing—I had to read it, to know more."

"Of course."

"It's a fine library," she said, and could have kicked herself. That was worse than idiotic, it was presumptuous.

"It ought to be." She thought there was humor lurking in him. He shook his head as though he were shaking off water. "I don't need to put this on you, and I will do my best to put it off myself tonight. Let's start over. More wine?"

"Perhaps I will have some more," she said, sliding her glass to him. He refilled it and slid it back. She drank, then said his name, feeling the way her mouth shaped it. She had not really expected him to let her use it.

"What?" he responded.

"Nothing. I'm just trying it."

"Tam," he said, lengthening it slowly as she had done his. "It's an unusual name."

She had wondered how long it would take for that to come up. It always did. People usually tagged something onto that phrase— "for an unusual girl" or "It's pretty though" were the most common. She waited for him to say one of them.

He didn't.

"I think you are the first person I have met who didn't ask to hear the story of my name immediately," she said.

He moved his chair around the table until he was right beside her. Gently but with no tentativeness he lifted her hand and turned it over so its back lay in the palm of his own. "I want," he said, and kissed her fingertips, "to know every single thing about you. Including your name."

"Corin . . ." she said, hearing uncertainty she did not welcome in her voice.

He looked at her with a very serious face. "I'm not going to do anything you don't want me to," he said. He let her hand drop. "I didn't think we misunderstood each other, though."

"No," she said, "we haven't." She reached back down and locked her fingers with his. Just that simple touch roused her body more than any man ever had. She was in a fair way of needing to restrain herself. "But allow me a little bashfulness."

It would have been easy for him to make an ironic remark—after all, she had hardly been bashful in the library—but he said, "Then come sit beside me on the sofa, which is much more comfortable than these chairs, and we'll talk. Nothing more until you want it, Tam, I promise." He stood up and pulled gently at her.

She drained her wineglass in two quick swallows, then followed him across the room. They sat, and she settled herself so that she could see his face. That seemed safe enough. It was a very nice face.

Feeling shy again, she said, "I have no idea what to tell you. It would be much easier to tell you what I'm not."

"Negatives can reveal quite a bit," he said. "Go ahead." It was hard to tell if he was serious.

Tam took a deep breath and spoke, rapidly, almost nervously. He must know her background, she did not have to say anything about that. "I am not a poetess. Patient. Either brokenhearted or engaged. A good archer or rider. A spendthrift. A faithful correspondent. Uneducated. An older sister. Kind or a drunkard." She stopped. "Is that enough?"

"And which of those is a failing?" He refilled her glass. "I must say I am glad about the heartbreak and engagement." His face had a look on it she knew quite well from herself, politeness covering amusement. Well, if he laughed at her he laughed at her. She could always go home.

"Lack of kindness, I suppose," she said. "I am not a nice person."

He grinned, a splendid and amazing smile that made her want to do nothing but look at him. "Of course you're not. Most of us aren't. You try, though, don't you?"

"Yes. But sometimes it just slips out, like it did with you yesterday. I mock people."

"You were completely right," he said, sober again. "I deserved it. I'll wager you would not have said that to someone who was vulnerable, or who could not have known better. It's not unkindness to scorn pride."

"And you still like me?"

"Anyone who can't have his pride punctured once in a while is headed for disaster." He sounded like he meant it.

She said thoughtlessly, "You ought to teach that to some of the servants."

"What do you mean?"

"Nothing. I shouldn't have said it."

"If someone has been disrespectful to you, I want to know."

"It's nothing, Corin, really." He was clearly not going to let it go, though, so she told him about the page boy. "I'm sure he thought he was protecting you."

"Thirteen-year-old boys don't get to make decisions about who sees me. I do." He leaned over and kissed her quickly on the lips, drawing back before she even had a chance to respond. She shivered. Light as it had been, she could still feel it. She wanted him to do it again. "He was out of place, and I'll make sure he knows it."

It put her on the edge of a power she had not expected. "No," she said hastily. "It's not necessary."

"It's not the first time he's been complained of; he suffers from believing himself more important than he is. He knows better, or should." He kissed the back of her hand. "And an insult to you is an insult to me."

"But." If he took the effort about her that meant it was public. It was foolish to have hoped it wouldn't be, even for a little while.

"I can be subtle about it, Tam."

"I don't want to acquire a reputation as a shrew," she said.

"Of course not. Don't worry." He touched her hair.

They were silent for a while. It was surprisingly comfortable. She was tempted to slide closer to him. She said, "It's Liddean."

"What is?"

"My name. It's for one of my father's teachers."

"I think I want to meet your father," he said.

"No," she said at once. Then she realized he had said it solely to see her reaction. So he had an imp himself. Time to unleash hers a bit more. She said, "It's your turn. Tell me something about yourself. Something I don't already know."

"Oh God, do I have to? Anything you don't already know is going to be embarrassing. Let's see. My sister Tai came to visit me once at university, and of course no one thought a fifteen-year-old princess should go any of the places she wanted to go, so we dressed her as a boy and she came with me to the tavern. I wanted to make her a scholar, but she's too short, so she had to be Lord Somebody's son. Efric's, I think. We made him up."

"Did you get away with it?"

"That's not the response a perfect gentlewoman is supposed to make," he said, grinning. "Thank you for not scolding me."

"I never claimed to be one. Did it work?"

"Mostly. It was autumn, so she wore a cloak and hat and heeled boots and passed for a boy with no problems. But she didn't sound like one, so she had to keep silent, which she didn't much like. And she became bored rather quickly with male conversation. She told me it was all either pompous philosophizing or vulgar gutter-talk about women."

"I'm sure it was," said Tam, thinking that she wanted to meet Tai. "I'd like to do that and see what I hear."

Corin unabashedly looked her up and down and said, "It would be rather difficult for you to pass as a boy."

She blushed.

"I have to be up at dawn," Corin said at last. "We need to go."

They were sitting beside each other on the floor with their backs against the sofa. She would not have expected it of either of them. The wine was gone, but Tam felt extraordinarily sharp and clear, not drunk. He had not kissed her again. He kept looking at her, however, in a way that indicated he had no less interest than when the evening started, and he had not been shy about touching her hand or arm. The hours had passed very swiftly; there had been no shortage of things to tell or question or explore. She could have gone on all night. She liked him, which she had not anticipated. He was not at all the way she had imagined he would be.

"There's one thing I want to show you here before we leave," he said, going to the balcony. She followed him.

The last of the rain was gone, with a starry sky, vast and clear, and a stiff wind in its place. The moon was at the half and low in the west. Darkness stretched out below to either side and ahead in a broad expanse. In the distance there were little spots of light. As her eyes adjusted, she began to make out shapes, trees and shrubs and flower beds. The paths were lighter graceful lines, the ponds perfectly smooth blackness. Here and there something reflecting the moonlight glittered silver. Thin branches were whipping back and forth.

"It is more beautiful in the daytime, but not so bad in the dark, I think."

"It's tremendous," Tam replied. "All that black. But it isn't really black, if you look you can see lighter parts, shades of grey. Silver. Do you suppose there's anyone out there?"

"Unlikely. The ground is still far too wet for midnight trysts."

"How long will it be that way?" she asked, thinking she would like to take a walk the next day. Then she realized how the question probably sounded. "For walks, I mean."

He laughed. "The gardeners will put fresh gravel on the paths in the bad patches," he said. "If it's sunny there will be a crowd out there tomorrow. You should go wherever you wish."

"Nothing's off limits?"

"Nothing except the actual flower beds. I've nearly been strung up myself for walking across one. A trowel is a formidable weapon, and the gardeners don't give a damn who they're using it on."

"Really?"

"Really. Not even my father's dog is safe."

"I'll be good," she said. A particularly strong gust of wind blew hard against the skirt of her dress. It was cold, and she shivered.

"Here," he said, and moved behind her. He wrapped his arms around her and drew her back to him. His hands were folded across her stomach. She felt warm and enclosed. She shifted to be more sideways and tilted her head to look at him. Very slowly and deliberately he lowered his lips to hers.

Tam had been kissed before, if infrequently, and she thought she knew what to expect. But this was entirely different, not the nervous chaste press of lips together or the urgent wet fumbling that had been its predecessors. She thought, Experience is worth a great deal after all. Then she stopped thinking and just felt. Her whole body was responding to the sensation of her upper lip between his two, the brush of his tongue against her teeth. She pressed closer against him, brought her hands around his back. It was the most intimate thing she had ever done.

He took his time about it but finally stopped. "My God," he said. "I'm not sure that can be repeated." One of his fingers played absently with a loose strand of her hair. She felt hot.

"We can always try," she said.

"Yes, we can." He took her hand and led her back inside.

They looked at each other. Tam was surprised to feel no embarrassment. He was so beautiful. She wanted to feel his skin against hers, to take his shirt and slowly slide the buttons back through the holes, to place her lips on his round strong shoulder. It was his right hand that held hers, and she lifted it, kissed the palm very lightly, then brought the back of his hand to her cheek. For the first time in her life she could imagine lying with a man.

"I think," he said, "that was enough for this time." His eyes seemed darker, and the light fell in warm gold across his cheek.

It had not occurred to her that he would hold back. Words slipped out. "Are you sure?" She both wanted and did not want to sound full of desire. He could have done anything and she would not object.

"Tempt me not, fair lady," he replied. "I would rather leave you with disappointment than with regret."

She understood it, and at any other time would have thought that exactly what a man should do. This was different. Suddenly she had to know how he felt, be sure it did not mean he found her lacking. "But—Corin?"

"What, my lovely Tam?"

"There will be other times?"

"There will most assuredly be other times," he said, no hesitation or doubt in his voice. Then he sighed. "But I must warn you not to take absence as estrangement. Don't depend on me to entertain you. I want to be with you, but it may not be very often. I have more to do than preen my feathers." He kissed her hair.

"I know," she said. She decided to leave it there. They had

successfully circumvented power and obligation all evening, now was not the time to bring it up.

"You had better go to your bed so I can go to mine. Do I dare take you, or should I send an escort? You shouldn't go by yourself, not this late."

"I suppose an escort," she said. She had already been seen in his company on the stairs, but those men were not likely to know her. If Corin appeared anywhere near her room, the other women would all sense him immediately with their unerring instinct for a nearby male.

He nodded. "Bron can do it. Where did they put you?"

"On the fourth floor, in the Osstig wing."

"I can't imagine it suits you," he said, almost grimly.

An unexpected statement from him. "It doesn't. It's awful. I don't mean that I can't bear it, but the girls there, they are so silly and grasping and spiteful, all at the same time. They pretend to be nice to each other and then make plans behind each other's back. All they want is rich husbands, and the higher the rank the better. Most of them, I should be fair, they aren't all that bad."

"That is the whole point of having court," he said. "Forgive me, I should not have said that. But yes, I know the lot. Should I get you moved?"

He said it so casually, as though he could just snap his fingers and it would happen. Probably that really was the case. "Well, I certainly don't want you to show up there, they'd be all over you. But they knew I was seeing someone, they'll be waiting like vultures to pick me over. If I leave they will assume it's into his rooms."

"That could be arranged too," he said, grinning. "Oh, Tam, I'm teasing, don't be shocked. No one ever expects me to be anything but stone serious. I can find you something entirely proper if you want."

It was very tempting. There would be no way to explain it to Cina. "I think I'd better stay. For now, at least."

"I promise not to come in unannounced. But tell me when you change your mind. Word will get out, you know, this sort of thing always does."

"I know." If they wanted it to be a secret they would have to meet in a storeroom at midnight. "But we needn't encourage it. I'm not going to show you off. Corin, whom did you dispossess tonight? I want to have expected it when someone starts complaining."

"Dispossess? You mean the room? Baron Arnet. It was no great loss to him." He paused. She thought he looked tired, worried. He said, "Stay away from him, Tam. And his followers. They're vicious."

"Of course," she said, though she did not know who they were. She put her hand on his arm. "Have I a chance at one more kiss?"

"A very good chance," he said, and gave her a kiss even longer than the first one. It was different: she could taste the wine in his mouth, guess how his lips and tongue were going to move. She wanted him so badly. And he wanted her, that was apparent. She pushed her body harder against him.

It ended mutually. Tam took a few deep breaths. He laughed, put his arm around her shoulders, and said, "Time to get you back to the Hall of Deadly Sins."

They parted in the antechamber, the guard a discreet distance away. Tam was uncertain what to say. He leaned over, kissed her softly on the cheek, and said, "Sleep well, my darling."

She made the guard leave her at the entrance to the wing. When she went around the corner to her own hall, she saw Alina, Jenet, and Elyn sitting in the large open parlor at the other end of the corridor. That was to have been expected, although it was somewhat late even for them. They were drinking wine and had been through several bottles already, which was more unusual. The kiss felt as though it were blazing on her cheek.

Elyn came to meet her and said, "Oh do come, dearest Tam." She put her arm around Tam's waist. "We're celebrating, Jenet has had such a marvelous evening. Count Darrin, the young one who is so handsome, he's asked to escort her to the ball at week-end."

"The ball?" she asked stupidly. A moment later she remembered. Cina had told her on the first day. "Of course." She wondered why

Corin had said nothing. Was it because she had not committed to openness, or because he did not think it her place to dance with him in public? Was he already obligated to some other woman? The pang of apprehension she felt was strong enough to warn her that she was in more danger than she had supposed possible so soon. Firmly, she told herself not to make guesses about such things. He had other things on his mind, she had seen that and he had told her.

They had reached the others by this time, and Alina said, "You must be at the ball, Tam, you simply must. Everyone will be there. I suppose the prince will open now he's back."

Tam's lips pressed together harder, but she controlled herself otherwise. That was the second comment of the evening about Corin, was the girl going to be silly enough to try for him?

Elyn giggled and said, "Then it will start late."

Tam imagined what their faces would look like if she told them about her own Marvelous Evening. The smug pleasure she got just from thinking it shamed her a moment. Then she thought, They want me to play their damn game, I will play it, and they won't even know. He is who he is and I have the right to enjoy it. "I expect I will come," she said in her sweetest tone.

"With your gentleman of tonight?" Alina asked.

"Yes," Tam said, with just a note of coyness. "Dancing is the first step to falling in love, after all."

"It must have gone well. Tell us all about it, sweetheart. Is he witty?"

"Yes."

"And good-looking?"

"Very," she said, remembering the kisses. She felt color rise to her cheeks and hoped it was not noticed.

"And rich?"

"Absolutely."

"Oh, he must have lands, does he have good lands?"

"Tremendous amounts, thousands of acres."

Alina gave a little false excited clap and said, "Tell us who he is, do."

"It's a surprise."

Jenet, who was more sober than the others, said, "She's having you on, Alina. Don't be so thick-headed." It was easy to see why Darrin courted Jenet; she was pink and slender, golden-haired, round in all the right places. The neckline of all her dresses was exactly where it should be, neither a shade too high nor too low. Her income was probably comparable. She was twenty-two, but it was hard not to think of her as younger.

Alina continued, "Isn't there something little that you can share?"

"He has two legs and two eyes," she said, which brought a giggle from Jenet and a contemptuous look from Alina. He has wonderful hands. He has an amazing mouth. I wanted him to undress me. Oh, and a title, you didn't ask about that.

Elyn splashed wine into a glass. "Here, Tam. Give us a hint."

Tam took the glass but had no intention of drinking it. Even were it not likely to taste vile after what she had already drunk, she had had enough. She was feeling too giddy and reckless. It would be better to go to bed.

"Yes, do," said Alina. "What is the first letter of his name?"

There was no way she was going to answer that with the truth. But if she protested too strongly that would only draw attention to it. "First or last?"

"First," said Alina.

"Last," said Elyn.

"'M,'" she said. *My lord.* "I won't say more." She put down the wine, then turned her back to the others so she could use the window as a mirror to remove her hairpins. Her hair came easily down. She put the pins in her mouth for the moment. She wished she had done it earlier. It would have made her more comfortable, and Corin would have liked it. She wanted him to touch it, stroke it, wrap it around his hands.

"Where did your gentleman take you?" asked Alina, interrupting her reverie.

She felt herself closing up inside, defending. That was definitely prying of a sort she didn't want. Not so much the question itself, which was innocuous and predictable. But answering it at all, truthfully or not, would invite more questions. And then more.

"Nowhere special," she said around the pins. There were only a few left. She shook her hair out and ran her fingers through it a few times. It felt much better loose. She would have had to put it up again before she came back, it was completely scandalous to have it loose at night in the presence of a man. She took the pins out of her mouth and set them on the table beside her, and looked back at Alina. "Were you out yourself at all?"

"Oh no, just dinner with a few friends. Afterward there was a mesmerist. He was very entertaining." Alina paused. "We had to change plans rather at the last moment, or I should have asked you and your gentleman to join us."

That might have been one of those polite lies of society, or it might have been meant to cut. Tam could not tell. She thought she was beginning to see a streak of selfish cruelty beneath the chattiness. "And will one of them escort you to the ball?"

"Not at the moment," Alina said carelessly. "That leaves me free to dance with whomever I want. There are quite a lot of handsome men here."

"They aren't all rich," Elyn said.

"Wealth isn't everything," said Alina.

No, it's not, Tam thought, reassessing her. She was after power, and would try to find it in a man's bed. That was a more dangerous quest than for money. Eventually she would reach too high and be pushed down.

"It's a lot," said Elyn.

"It doesn't take anything particular to earn it these days," Alina said, which Tam was sure was a reference to her father and brother.

"You wouldn't say so if you didn't have it," Jenet said, surprising Tam. "Surely there's someone you hope to dance with, Alina."

"Nobody special."

That was definitely intended to cut. Tam wondered why. Alina could hardly be jealous of her about Corin now. Some other time she might have sparred back, but she was tired. She gathered up the hairpins and stood. "I really do need to go to bed, I've a touch of headache. Good night." Before any of them could say anything else, she walked away.

She lay in bed, wanting to sleep and unable to, wondering if her life had changed irrevocably or if this was just a dreamlike time that would pass by, wondering if she loved him already, wondering what she would do if she did. It was so entirely wrong. She had no expectations of anything lasting; in her experience, men were fickle creatures, falling in love with every fresh set of handsome eyes while expecting the women to be stalwarts of loyalty. It wasn't true of all of them, she knew that from her father's love of her mother, but it was true of all the rich young men she met. Why shouldn't this also be true of Corin, especially when he had only to raise a finger for any woman he wanted? But already she was hoping it was not so, that he was somehow different.

Like someone much younger, she thought, He kissed me! With that happy memory she rolled onto her side and went to sleep.

CHAPTER SEVEN

⚜

C orin bent over and signed the paper, then straightened. "There," he said to Teron. "That's the lot. And before noon, too. The messages can wait until after I've had a bit of a respite."

"I think you'd better see who they're from, sir, before you decide that," Teron replied in the tone that meant there was something potentially nasty waiting.

"Hand them over," Corin said resignedly. He was at his clerk's desk, not his own, because he had been unsuccessfully trying to leave for half an hour. He was late and hoped Tam had not given up on him. If anyone else came by with a request, any sort of request, he was going to have a tantrum. "But I'm not here. You can't see me." He went into as much shadow as he could to sort them.

One from his father. It couldn't be too important or he would have had it earlier. He unfolded it—it was not even sealed—and saw it was just a note from the king's clerk calling another council tomorrow morning. One with a woman's handwriting. Not Seana's, fortunately. There had been two yesterday, both of which he had ignored. They were polite, appropriate—she was not a woman to be vituperative or wheedling—but they still made him feel hunted. Half expecting it to be from her anyway, he opened the note and found only a dinner invitation from Ellid's wife for next week. He supposed he would have to go. A request for a meeting from Guye of Dele. Damn it. What did he want? He would have to see him, but he could put it off for a day or two.

He heard footsteps come by the door, pause, move on. He finished the stack and gave it back to Teron.

"Did I hear someone?" he asked.

Teron nodded. "Brice."

That would be one of Cade's friends, yapping about the death, wanting something done. There was nothing to do. Gerod had already cleared Brice of the murder itself. The commander had delivered a thorough report that morning, which amounted to *Cade was a fool and we still don't know who killed him*. Corin had suspicions aplenty, but that was not enough to hang a man.

"How'd you get him to go away?"

Teron drew his finger across his throat. "I'm sure there will be a written message soon," he said blandly.

"If he comes by again, send him to Gerod. I'll be back in an hour, but I'm not seeing anyone." There were exceptions to that, but Teron knew who they were. He had better add Tam to the group, though he doubted she would come. He had seen clearly that she was not going to take access to him for granted. It wasn't respect for rank but respect for work. She knew what work was.

He managed to make it into the garden without being stopped, and he relaxed some when he was outside. The air was warm, which felt pleasant after the perpetual coolness of the palace. It was palace etiquette that anyone walking alone in the garden should not be disturbed without a good reason, so he was reasonably certain of privacy, though the scope of "good reasons" was broad when it came to him. He walked quickly through the garden toward one of the small ponds.

A large willow tree beside the pond had a plain iron bench next to it, and he sat down. The water was clear and still. A few damsel-flies darted about in gleaming greens and blues. A larger one, with golden wings more than a foot long, rested on a small rock. Seeing a goldwing was supposed to bring some kind of luck. He thought sourly that he could use it. The drooping fronds of the willow moved lightly back and forth, scattering the overhead sun. A pair of ducks paddled across the pond toward the small island in the middle. It was neat and orderly, civilized, miles and miles away from Sarians with fire weapons and war-lights. Miles from Liko's wretched hovel and the stories that had got their claws into him.

He heard something on the path and looked. A suncock, trailing its red and gold feathers like flames. He stood up and shooed at it.

"Go away, pompous and vainglorious bird," he said. "Go on, go."
He waved his hands. It looked contemptuously at him, then saun-
tered back the way it had come.

"That's not very princely," someone said behind him. He jumped
despite himself, turned.

"They bite," he said succinctly. The expression on Tam's face told
him that the remark had been entirely intentional. "Your impudence
is going to get you into trouble some day."

"It's too late," she said. "It already has."

"I suppose so." There was no one around. He risked a quick kiss.
God, she was beautiful. Walking away from her last night had been
one of the hardest things he had ever done. They both knew what
was going to happen some time, even had there been no more than
a mild personal liking, but it was more than liking, much more. He
had never been so bewitched by any woman as he was by her. Before
they had even finished eating he had known he was hopelessly,
entirely, in love. It was selfish of him; he should not compromise
her honor by going any further even if she let him, or frustrate himself by courting where he could not wed. He did not have the will
to stop it. Tai had told him once that when he finally fell in love he
would fall hard, and how true a prediction that had been.

"I'm sorry I'm late," he said. "I kept getting interrupted. Come
sit." He held her hand and drew her onto the bench with him.

They spent a moment looking at each other, the first time in
outdoor light; her hair was less black and more brown where the
sun struck it than it was inside. It was down, with a narrow braid
in the center lying over the smooth fall. She looked younger. Her
dress was blue and very simple, but it suited her perfectly. The light
and shadows shifted on her with the movement of the leaves. "How
old are you?" he asked curiously. For all the hours they had talked
last night, there were so many things left to ask.

"Twenty." She moved closer to him.

Tai's age. "And no one has married you yet?" he asked, marveling
at his own good fortune. As he heard his voice, he realized it was a
terribly rude question.

"Afraid of my father," she said darkly. For a heartbeat he believed her.

Then he laughed. But there was nothing he could say in response that would not make it sound as if the thought of marriage had crossed his own mind, even if only to be rejected, and he could not do that. It would be cruel to imply, even in jest, that things were not as they stood. She knew the rules that bound them as well as he did, there had been nothing to discuss. She was entirely unsuitable.

"Of course I would never disobey him," she added.

"Really?" he asked slowly, ironically. "And what did he command?"

"Not to fall prey to any handsome young lords."

He could not tell if she was making it up. "You don't have to tell him. Besides, I'm not a lord."

"Now you're splitting hairs."

"I'm sure he would prefer me to the old ugly lecherous ones." He kissed her again, his tongue slowly and deeply probing her sweet mouth, his hand on her hip. She made no objections.

"Should I have done that?" he asked afterward, thinking too late that she might not want to be touched in public.

"I know how to say stop," she said. "Even to the likes of you."

"Oh? Let's see." A century or so later he realized they were rather too entangled for public view, even in a garden, and pulled away. He firmly removed her hand from his leg and his arm from her back. She smiled slyly and swung her head to straighten her hair. Neither of them said anything. Corin felt pleasantly transgressive as he had not for years. He had better be careful.

There was a nearby rose bush, and he drew his knife to cut one flower. It was white with a few yellow streaks. He trimmed the thorns off and worked it into her hair over her ear. "There," he said. "How was it when you went back last night? Were there vultures waiting for you?"

Something about it amused her. "Yes. I teased them and they didn't even notice. It's terrible of me to enjoy it, but I do."

"What did you say?" None of his palace lovers had ever been so scornful of the status seekers before. They had all been status seekers, for that matter. Tam was not the first commoner, but she was the first who had not come from old wealth and old land.

"I named no names but answered their questions with the truth," she said, "and they thought I was being coy and exaggerating. People don't expect truth much, do they?"

"They don't," he agreed, "which makes it powerful." He had watched his father use truth as a weapon, leaving his opponents staring into the sun they had professed faith in while certain it was not there. His father. Not just his father. The king. The subject they had avoided all last night. He had never been so self-conscious of it before. It wouldn't matter if he had no intent to have her as a lover for long, but it mattered with her. Everything mattered with her. He supposed he should get it over with, before she lost her chance to withdraw painlessly and privately.

"Do you care if my father knows?" he asked. "Or, I should say, do you care how he finds out? He will. And so will everyone else. If you're going to have second thoughts, best have them now. I would understand." Understand, yes. But it would hurt.

She seemed unsurprised by the question. "I'm not going to change my mind. It's not as though you sprung this on me. If it's a choice between you and rumor telling him, I'd rather it be you. Will he interfere?"

"I doubt it." The comment about Seana was the only thing Aram had said in the last seven years or so, even though Corin had not always made the best choice. Thinking about his father's approval made him feel very young again. When he was fourteen, Aram had said to him about women, *Don't get them with child, don't do anything they're unwilling to, and don't promise anything you can't give.* He wondered how well he was going to be able to keep to that last condition with Tam.

"What about the queen?"

It was harder to speak for his mother; arranging a marriage for him was her province, not his father's. But she knew that he would only accept a marriage of state if he was not constrained to it. Talia was nearly as practical as Bron. She had been a lucky royal bride—his father loved her—and she was aware that was unusual. "She knows I'm a man," he said. "Don't do anything scandalous and she will ignore it."

"Don't do anything scandalous! Corin, we already have."

"Outside of this," he said, grinning. "Although kissing is hardly a scandal. No drunken brawls, or gambling all night with criminals, or dancing in a fountain. Or telling everyone what they should do."

"In other words, stay in my place and be good."

It sounded harsh. It was, he supposed, the truth. He ran his hand through the ends of her hair, lifted a lock to his face to smell it. Lavender and mint, clean, sharp. He said, "Act with honor, and the rest of it will take care of itself. I don't mean a woman's honor, all modesty and politeness, though I know you have it. I mean bravery and truth and conviction."

She leaned her face against his shoulder. "There's not one man in a hundred who would say that of a woman."

And not one woman in a hundred who would say so to him. "I can afford to. I have enough power."

She sat so still and quietly that a butterfly lighted briefly on the flower in her hair. It was a deep fire-orange with red and yellow markings. It made him think of dragons. It hurt a little. He waited. He was good at waiting. A cricket chirped somewhere in the grass.

Her shoulders loosened, her face relaxed. "Thank you for not thinking I am a naïf."

He asked her something he had never asked anyone. "And do you think less of me for saying such a thing?"

She leaned forward and kissed his cheek. "No, Corin. Prince Corin. I know what I am getting with you."

"Are you getting what you want?"

"I want you." Another kiss, several of them, light and lightning on his skin. "I don't care about the rest."

He would never be able to explain to her the peculiar kind of ache her words roused in him. There had been other women who said that to him, but never with the honesty in their voices that was in hers. Regardless of the heat, he held her as tightly to him as he could until she said, "I can't breathe." When he released her, she tugged at her neckline and smoothed down her bodice. He let his eyes follow her hands. When he looked back up he knew she had been watching him.

He said hastily, "You know it's not separable, though. You get the whole package. Especially if we are in public."

"Such as the ball. Why didn't you tell me?"

"What ball?" he asked, bewildered.

For some reason that made her laugh. "The first ball of the season, of course. I'm told that you will open it. There was great excitement about being asked to dance beforetime."

He remembered vaguely about it now. He did not pay attention to such things and was usually reminded by Teron or the chamberlain the day before. His mother no longer submitted him to the indignity of telling him herself, as though he were a wayward boy. But he had to be there. Even with one sister a hostage and the other in flight, ignorant of her husband's fate. It was all the pretending he had said he would do.

She was staring at him.

"I forgot about it. I always do. Do you want me to take you?" he asked.

"I don't know, Corin. You look—is there something wrong?"

"Not about that. Not about you," he said. Probably he had already given too much away, but he could reassure her as to his feelings.

"Are you really offering?" she asked.

"Yes. Provided, of course, that you give me a dance."

"I'll give you the whole evening if you want. But everyone will think you have succumbed to my arts."

"Let them," he said recklessly. He stopped. The last thing he wanted anyone to think of Tam was that she had seduced him. He would not jeopardize her standing.

He said, "You must do what is proper for you. It's not my reputation at stake. I will ignore you entirely if that is best, though I must say that failure for me to notice so beautiful a woman would be equally remarked upon. I have been known to succumb easily." He would almost rather not see her at all than have only formal unfeeling words from her.

"If I'm as beautiful as all that my charms don't matter," she said. Carefully she touched his face. "There is no point in doing things halfway, if we are to dance together at all we might as well come together. I will take delivery of the whole package."

"Thank you," he said. He could not remember ever having cared about it before; balls had always been mildly pleasant but unimportant ways to pass time. What irony that this should happen now, when war approached.

"It will take some time to strike the balance. I don't want to embarrass you."

"You won't," he said. "I may have to ignore the jealous men, though."

"I am sure you will do it most amiably," she said.

"Dutifully, at least. And with no duels."

They went quiet for a bit. The sky was very blue and scattered with large white clouds. Damp smells from the rain lingered. The garden was a glory of red and purple and yellow flowers of all shades, and it was still early enough in summer that the tree leaves had not lost their green freshness and begun to dull. A handful of brightly dressed women and more somber men walked some distance away, well out of range of recognition or voice.

"Have a walk with me?" he asked.

"We'll be seen. I mean, you'll be seen. And interrupted. You need to wear a mask."

"I would if I thought I could get away with it."

Her face was suddenly serious. "You never get to play, do you?"

"Don't feel sorry for me, Tam." An idea, suggested by the masks, rose in him. "If you really want to throw all this off for a while, come with me to the fair."

"Now?" She sounded startled.

"No, not now. At night. No one will know it's us." He was seized with eagerness for the idea. He had gone to fairs many summers, not forsaking a chance to be wild and reckless. It would not be the same with a woman—he hoped he did not look awkward as he remembered too late some of the things he had done before—but he wanted to be with her outside the order and dignity of the palace and its grounds.

"Can you?" she asked.

"Yes." Bron would be furious, but he refused to let the attack of two nights ago confine him. Anyone who had gone to the lengths taken then to kill or capture him could find a way to do it here. He did not intend to hide his plans; the king could forbid it if he wished. But he wasn't going to let anyone else prevent him.

Tam was still considering it. He thought she was going to reject the idea, but when she spoke she looked impish. "All right," she said. "But you have to let me do anything I want."

"Anything?"

"Anything."

He grinned. "I'll trust to your basic decency," he said. "But if I don't get to say no, then you have to take my dares."

"Done," she said. "Shake hands on a bargain."

He complied, but instead of letting go of her hand after the shake pulled her to him. Her body relaxed into the curve of his arm and she leaned against him. There was no way she could know how much that simple tenderness softened him.

After a while she said, "Corin, what's happening? There's something going on, isn't there? Something big."

So clever, she was. He was so used to keeping secrets, to hiding things, that he could not shape any words. He swallowed, looked down, clasped and unclasped his hands. Then he met her eyes, and that released him.

"How do you know?"

"You didn't hide it very well last night," she answered.

Well, that was true enough. The war plans went on appropriately, but there were still too many unanswered questions. He would tell her what he could. "I'm not supposed to tell you. Not you especially, but anyone. But I can't imagine that most of it will stay secret much longer. The guessing must have already started. It will have to be announced in the next day or two. So I am not breaking too much of a confidence."

One of the ducks in the pond quacked at the other. They splashed water about, the droplets rising like molten silver in the bright sun.

"You don't need to break it to me."

"You deserve to know; you are going to have to put up with me," he said. He put one of his hands over hers and told her in a low voice about the imminent fall of Argondy to Tyrekh. He told her about Mari coming, but not Tai. That promise he had to keep. He should not tell her things the council did not know. He said nothing about the Emperor. Now that he had started, it was hard not to say it all. It felt very intimate. She listened intently, soberly, fully.

When he finished, she thought. He liked that about her. She brought his hand to her lips and kissed it, said, "Poor Corin, all this and I have you bothering about balls. You haven't told me half of it. This is why you wanted to know about me and the book, isn't it?"

"Yes. It was an odd thing in the circumstances."

He was relieved to see no blame on her face when she looked at him. She laced her fingers with his. "What I told you last night," she said, "it was true, but there was a bit more."

"What?" he asked apprehensively. He was unreasonably afraid she was about to tell him something that would force him to break with her.

"Lord Cade."

He had deliberately not tried to find out anything about her, but he had realized as soon as she spoke of her father that she was the woman Berk had talked to. He had decided then to wait and let her tell him. Softly, he said, "Go on."

She swallowed. The breeze moved shadows across her face. Her eyes were bright. She said, "I suppose you know this. I saw him die."

Though he had known, it was different to hear her say it. Thinking of Cade's blood and agony he felt as though she had been in danger herself. He gripped her hand. "Oh, Tam, I'm sorry."

"It was awful," she said. "His face—he was in such pain. All he wanted was for me—anyone—to end it. I stood there and watched. There was nothing I could do."

He knew that feeling. It never got any easier. Her face was steady and her mouth firm. Carefully, he leaned over and kissed her, not with passion but for strength. Her eyes closed. He wanted to tell her he loved her, but was afraid she would run.

She clenched his hand, her eyes still closed. "Corin," she said. Whispered.

"What?" he asked softly.

"It wasn't—I wasn't—there was something else. You'll think I'm mad." She was struggling.

He put his arms around her. He could not imagine what she might say, but nothing would drive him away from her. Her slender body was warm against him. "I've seen people who are mad," he said. "You aren't." He had no doubt of that.

"Before the blood—I can't say this."

"You don't need to."

"I must." She took a deep breath, then said in a low rapid voice, "I saw black moths come out of him. Out of his mouth. Hundreds of them."

He felt as though he had been thrown into a mountain lake, beautiful, placid, cold. It frightened him and it woke him with anticipation, excitement. Something was happening, changing. It was drawing him closer to whatever lay in the things he had forgotten. It was terrifying her. Gently, he kissed her forehead, her palm.

"It happened," he said. He had burned Joce, cursed Hadon. It was not born of charms and potions but of the deeper older power that had belonged once to the wizards. *There is a woman who comes up to you and touches your shoulder and you freeze like ice and she sucks the blood out of you while you stand there. Then she turns into a bird and flies away.*

He kept back a shudder. The light changed. It had an eerie, otherworldly quality to it, as though he looked through thick tinted glass. The sky was a deep blue, almost purple. The shadows were very dark. Once again he had the sensation that he was being watched.

With effort, he spoke, the words like sharp cracks. "I don't doubt it, doubt you."

"But how?" Her face was still strained, her body stiff. He saw that too through the strange light. He felt her stiffness, but it had no meaning for him. He was trapped. The willow fronds were carved on the face of the air. Light glowed around their edges. Tam's face was all contrasts, paper white and ink black, inhuman. Something ticked, a clock sound, over and over. Now, it said. Now.

A dog barked in the distance. That broke the spell. Ordinary sunlight shone on him. He could breathe again. The depth of his relief told him how frightened he had been.

"I don't know," he said, recovering. He could think about it later. "But let it be. You've said it, you can be done with it. Don't let it gnaw at you. Don't be ashamed." He was careful to keep back the habitual tones of command that wanted to come in to his voice.

"No one else saw them."

"No one else was brave enough," he said. "People are very good at not seeing things." Including himself.

That brought a silence. After a moment, her head still lowered, she said, "I wasn't going to tell anyone. Ever."

"It's not going to chase me off," he said. He looked for some way to lighten the mood without mockery. A pause, a moment of looking at her until she raised her head and met his eyes. "Tam," he said, nothing else, just her name.

"Yes," she said, answering something he had not asked. Then she drew away. She had passed the hard part, he saw it in the set of her shoulders.

She pushed her hair back and said, "I know what he died from."

He was good at setting things aside and working on practical issues, but it was rather disconcerting to see her do it. He realized he was probably going to underestimate her his entire life. "Berk told me you had guessed. He confirmed it?"

"Yes. That's why I had the book, to find out more."

"Did you learn anything?" he asked.

"Not really. You don't think I stayed there, do you? I ran away about as fast as you did, and I haven't dared go back."

She could not bring the book with her. That was absurd, he would write her out a pass. "Afraid of me?"

"Yes. I know it's foolish."

"I didn't go back either," he admitted.

"We wasted time," she said, a suggestiveness in her voice that he would never have anticipated. His body quickened.

"An entire day." There was still no one around. "Let me do something about that." He tipped her head back and kissed the hollow of her throat. She hooked a finger under the waistband of his trousers. He had never expected her to be so full of passion, as though she were starving for his touch. He was starving for hers. There was this soft smooth spot here, right above the neck of her dress, exquisitely kissable. Her breast was firm and soft. He tore himself away and sat on his hands.

She moved down the bench. "Am I safe here?"

"Not a bit. But I will endeavor to act more restrained."

"Don't inconvenience yourself on my account, my lord," she said. It had never been so lovely to be mocked. Then she said, "It's bad that it was blood-dust, isn't it?"

Berk had thought she knew the implications. "Do you understand what it means?"

"If someone here had blood-dust, he had to be dealing with the Sarians, or with other people who deal with the Sarians. And therefore he might be a traitor. Or she."

"Yes," he said. He wished he could tell her Hadon might be the source so she could put her mind fully to the puzzle.

"But why kill him? And why that way? It wasn't very secretive. Was it ordinary hate?"

"All we have now are guesses. But it worked, which is not a small thing. I expect there's plenty left for another victim or two if necessary." Such as himself. "It's not particularly hard to explain why he was killed. He may have been likely to confess something soon, or he had outlived his usefulness. He wasn't innocent." When Liko had said *desperate*, he had not been exaggerating; according to Gerod, Cade had been staggeringly in debt.

"How do you know?"

He supposed he was telling her far too much. But she had seen the death, she was owed an explanation. He wouldn't put it past her otherwise to try to solve the mystery on her own, which was unspeakably dangerous. He told her quickly what he had learned from Liko. He wanted to tell her about Liko's fear of him, the stories, the darkness in the water. But whatever blocked his tongue would not let him speak of those, not even to her, not even after her story of the moths.

So instead he told her about the attack. To his relief she did not become maudlin about it. He was beginning to realize that she disliked sentimentality almost as much as he did. He said nothing about the possibility that the attack was Hadon's or his sons' work too.

"There's something else," she said. "I don't know if it matters, but I think I'd better tell you anyway. It may be nothing."

"What?" he asked.

"The night you came back, the night it stormed, I woke up and couldn't sleep. So I went to the window and sat for a while. And I saw—there's a small ordinary courtyard below, with a walkway. I saw two men meet there, in the pouring rain, at three in the morning. One of the women in the wing threw something down to them. It didn't make any sense then. But I think it must fit into the rest of all this somehow. Cade died the next day."

"You don't know who they were, do you?" he asked without much hope.

"No. I assume one was a lord by his clothing. That was all I could see. I know the woman."

"We can watch her. Who?"

"Her name is Alina. Her father is a baron in Kariss."

Kariss. Farmland, but poor soil. It was not a wealthy county. He would have considered it an unlikely place for any intrigue except that it was also home to Arnet. He was not above seducing a neighbor's daughter and getting her to store poisons for him. Corin was more and more certain he was the murderer—none of Cade's acquaintances had any other discernible motive now that he was paying his debts, no Sarian connections of any sort had been discovered, and Arnet was the only one linked to Hadon—but he had no way to prove it. It was unlikely this would help either, but it was something.

"Thank you," he said.

"I think they mean to kill you," she said quietly.

"I expect so," he said. He had become used to that idea very quickly. "Nothing's going to happen here, Tam, there's no chance of it."

"But if there are traitors . . ."

"No one is unaware of that possibility, including me. Whatever happens will only have a chance of succeeding if it is entirely unexpected." He ate and drank nothing now that had not come straight from the kitchens. There were plenty of poisons besides blood-dust.

"Do you think war will come here?"

"Yes." He would have preferred to lie, but he owed her the truth. If he did not give it to her he would lose her.

"Even with—what about Mycene?"

Oh, how was he going to get around that one? He said truthfully, "We must plan for everything. It takes a long time to move a hundred thousand soldiers across an ocean. The Sarians are going to come through Argondy very fast." They had horses that were both swift and strong. "And Tyrekh's soldiers may have been sneaking in for months now. We've had reports of Sarian attacks."

"You'll have to leave, won't you?"

It was an unwelcome question, and unavoidable. "Eventually, yes. I will stay as long as I can, but my father is going to send me off sometime. He's made that plenty clear." Tam, Tam, she would need to be safe, he would give her a hundred soldiers if that was what it took. "What about you?" he asked. "Do you have friends outside of your city?"

She nibbled her lip, puzzling it out. "Yes," she said. "Why?"

"I'm going to have to send you home when the Sarians get too close, you see that, don't you?" She had to. She would not want to. "But I don't think they will leave Dalrinia alone. They want everything. You need to have some place to be if they decide to sack it."

That had not really occurred to her, he could tell from the tightening of her face. She held her hand out to him and he slid down to sit beside her. When he put his arm around her, she was rigid as could be.

"Let me help you," she said, her head down. "Let me come with you."

"I wish I could," he said. It hurt to even think of parting like that. "But you're not a soldier." He almost said she could help him by being some place where he knew she was safe, but he managed not to. It would infuriate her.

"I can endure hardship."

"It's not hardship, it's fighting. You don't know how to use a blade."

"It's the waiting, Corin, I can't bear it. If I have to go back to my parents' home and wait, and wait, and wait, I'll go mad."

He understood entirely. It would drive him mad too. But she was not a soldier. "That's most of what war is, waiting."

"I can help the doctors."

That was a suggestion hard to resist. There would be need of every person who could assist. But it was far, far too dangerous. Her father would have told her enough that she could imagine the things the Sarians did to women if she did not already know. "There's no way to keep you safe. I don't even know where I am going to be, I can't plan for you." If he said anything else he would stumble over his words into a quagmire of warning, threatening, persuading through fear.

She scowled. He didn't try to appease her or convince her. Finally she said, "Don't send me away any sooner than you have to. Please."

"I promise." He let himself touch her smooth soft hair. "Ah, Tam," he said, "I wish we could just find a quiet place." He thought perhaps she had the same restlessness he did, that quick wanting for things to change, to happen. Her eyes were a pale chilly blue instead of lapis, and they were challenging him. Gently, he leaned forward and kissed her eyelids.

"I know that," she said softly. "Do you think I don't know that what we have right now is grace? It's all right."

"It's not," he said, "but I won't belabor it since it's not changeable."

She kissed him. "Well, I would rather kiss you than spend whatever time we do have worrying." She pursed her lips.

He put his forefinger to them. She opened her mouth slightly, ran her tongue slowly around the tip of his finger, flicking the way a snake's would, burning his hand. He swallowed. She leaned toward him. He slipped her sleeve off her shoulder and kissed her skin. Her hand went to his thigh, right at the outer hip crease. Her eyes were closed. He tipped her back, noticing that her nipples had gone hard. If he pulled any more at her sleeve it might tear the seam; he didn't dare do it as much as he would like to. The dress fastened in the back, that was awkward. She slid her hand slowly across his abdomen. He wanted her as he had never wanted a woman.

Then both of them heard voices and jumped up guiltily. He could not see anyone, but they were obviously coming closer. His face had to be flaming.

"Go!" she said, pushing him on the chest. "You'll never get away if they see you."

He kissed her hard and raced quickly off, sure to take a path that doubled back so it was not apparent where he had come from. He heard a burst of laughter. His frustrated desire turned into exhilaration at his escape. As soon as he was far enough away he slowed down to a dignified walk. By the time he entered the palace he was entirely the proper prince.

CHAPTER EIGHT

⟨⟨⟨∘⟩⟩⟩

T am kept her eyes on the pond. She was still alert with desire. The voices were coming closer. When she looked around, she didn't see Corin, and she relaxed. It wasn't going to be a secret long, she could tell that already. She wanted him too much to waste time sneaking and hiding. Even thinking about wanting him made her body respond. She had had no idea she could feel like this. What if she had kissed him there in the library instead of freezing like a fool? He would have returned it, pressing her back against the shelves. And then—well, nothing, really, they were both too decent for that. At least she thought they were. Her imagination was ready to run forward, but she stopped it just as she heard her name.

It was Jenet, on the arm of a handsome man who must be Count Darrin. Alina was behind them, between two young men who appeared bored. She repressed a groan. Alina had already spent too much time prying and refusing to be gotten rid of in the first half of the morning. All three of the men glanced at Tam rather cursorily, and the glances turned into stares, shaken off later than was polite. It made her wonder if Corin had left some trace on her dress or skin. She remembered about the flower in her hair and reached up to remove it, but Jenet said, "Oh don't, it's lovely."

There followed a flurry of introductions (*Lady Cina's sister-in-law, you know; What an unusual name*), disclaimers of formality, and redundant comments about the pleasantness of finally having sun again. Tam would have preferred to stay while they went on, but when one of the bored young men offered her his arm and the count said, "And now we have our sixth," there was nothing to do but go along.

She did not have much to say to her young man, which presented no problem as he had plenty to say to her. At first she thought he was a boaster by nature, but she realized soon that he was trying to impress her. It was amusing. He was nice in his way. If he were set to hard honest work for a year or so to wear away all the veneers of wealth and leisure, there would be a real person when he finished. She wondered if younger sons still bought commissions in the military since Tyrekh had come west.

The walk turned into a luncheon and she resigned herself to staying with the group somewhat longer. The wine was good, though nowhere near what Corin had served her, and as the others admired it greatly, she gathered it was a privilege to drink. Count Darrin was in full display. When Tam's bored young man asked Darrin about the wine, he declared it the best the wine steward would let him have for an informal daytime meal.

"He did give me a morsel of news, though," Darrin said tantalizingly. Tam knew immediately what was coming. Oh God, she thought, please don't let me show anything.

Alina obliged him. "Tell us," she said.

"He decanted some of the best for the prince last night. The Illyrian red that is usually reserved for state dinners. From a wine merchant it would be five hundred crowns a bottle."

Tam sat back in shock. Her inability to stay calm went unnoticed as everyone else reacted with exclamations or whistles. She had drunk at least the value of a good horse last night. Five hundred crowns a bottle. Fifty marks. And he ordered the wine before he had even met her in the fountain hall. How could he have been sure she was worth such an extravagance? Not a word of it to her, it was not a brag. She wanted to go find him and ask him what it meant.

Tam's young man said, "I'd like to see the lady. It can't have been Seana, she's been gloomy since he returned."

Seana? Tam thought rapidly. The only Seana she knew of was the Duchess of Osstig. Married. Had Corin had something with her? It didn't matter, if he had he must have ended it for her to be gloomy. But why had he not told her?

The other man said, "So that's why Arnet had to cancel his gathering. I heard him complaining about it last night. It was very sudden.

His Highness wants the Terrace Room, find yourself someplace else."
He didn't sound very sympathetic to Arnet.

Tam worked at her food more elaborately than she needed to
with her fork. The pattern on her plate was a crimson dragon at the
center with its tail winding around the edge. It was a good thing she
had kept her mouth shut as much as she had about last night. Thank
God she had been prepared for some remark on it. She dared not
look at anyone.

"If you're going to serve that kind of wine to a lady, you aren't
going to do it in the Terrace Room. Especially not him. It must have
been something else there," said Tam's young man, Therry.

Jenet said, turning a little pink, "Maybe it was political." The men
all stared at her. Tam wished she could shake them.

After a pause, Darrin said with more thoughtfulness than Tam
had given him credit for, "That's possible. There's something going
on. Corin's hardly been seen since he got back, and the king canceled
a petition hearing yesterday. He never does that."

It was an interesting opening, and she would have liked to hear
more of what they thought, if they would deign to discuss it in front
of women. Not that she could say anything of what she knew. War.
It was still too remote and unreal for her to feel frightened, but she
had seen how it weighed upon Corin. She supposed he did not
show that side of himself freely.

As she was gathering her thoughts, Therry leaned over to her and
whispered, impolitely and not especially quietly, "If that's the case,
Corin's still free for Alina to chase."

Alina heard, as she was intended to, and glared at him. Rather
than striking back directly, she said with false concern, "How is your
gentleman, Tam? I didn't expect to see you in the garden alone. I
do hope nothing has happened between you."

It was an economical thrust, designed to make Therry jealous and
to humiliate Tam at the same time. It surprised her to be targeted
so overtly; what did Alina have against her? This was something
quite different from prying. It was far too rude for Alina to get away
with at the lunch table, even disguised as solicitousness.

"I beg your pardon," Tam said politely. She removed the flower from her hair and ran her fingers up and down the smooth stem, sniffed the blossom. "I must not have heard you correctly. Would you repeat yourself, please?"

Dead silence. Darrin, who was sitting at Tam's right, placed his hand over hers.

Alina was not up to the challenge. She wiped her mouth, put down her napkin, and stood up. "Please excuse me, I've just remembered something I must do," she said stiffly, and left.

"How stupid can you get?" Therry said.

Darrin lifted his hand. "You really shouldn't have said that about her, Therry," he chided.

"It was worth it," Therry said. "It got rid of her."

Jenet said, "She's in the same wing that Tam and I are. We can't get rid of her."

He had the grace to look embarrassed. "I'm sorry. I hope I haven't made things worse for you."

Jenet nodded an acceptance of the apology. Tam said, "Don't concern yourself. I can handle her." The last thing she wanted was for him to start trying to mend matters.

"I believe you can," he said admiringly. He added, "*Do* you have a gentleman?"

"Therry!" came the chorus, followed by laughter.

Tam joined in, but she remembered Corin's bitter comment about the court. All these games and feuds, just to get a little more power. None of it was unexpected, but it saddened her a little. As soon as she was seen with Corin, it was going to suck her in.

"I'm afraid I do, Therry," she said. "You're out of luck."

"She's keeping it completely secret, though," Jenet added.

"In this court, who could blame her?" said Therry. "But I must admit to being disappointed. You should prepare to fend off suitors, Tam."

"I can handle them too," she said, to more laughter. She could not keep herself from asking the next question. "Is Alina really chasing the prince?" Her voice was calm, unremarkable.

"Yes," said Darrin. "Or she would like to. She hasn't had much chance. Tried last winter for two weeks and he had no idea of it. Keeps her away from the rest of us, so no one is going to try to talk her out of it. No one will ever catch him, he avoids marriage like the plague. Would you like more wine?"

Jenet asked her to walk back to their rooms together. More out of curiosity than anything else, she agreed. Darrin kissed both their hands, holding Jenet's a touch longer. Tam wondered if he was that discreet in private. If they ever were in private. Jenet was sure to go to her marriage bed a maiden. Will I? Tam wondered. It seemed unlikely if things went on as they were. She was shocked at her own lack of shame.

Jenet said, "I'm sorry about Alina."

"She's not your responsibility."

"She is in a way. She's on her own, you know, her brothers are from her father's first marriage and twenty years older. Her mother died ten or eleven years ago, and she's no sisters or aunts. The only company she has is her maid."

Tam said, without sympathy, "You are kind to help her. But if she acts so rudely to everyone, it's no wonder she's alone."

"Well, she seems to have taken a particular dislike to you. I wish it weren't so."

"Forget about it," Tam said. "There are more terrible things in the world than being disliked by someone with no manners."

Jenet laughed, then said, "She's apt to try to steal your gentleman away, I'm afraid, simply for spite. She will never succeed, but you might be particularly discreet around her."

That could be a plain statement, or a subtle question. She was starting to fall into the game-playing already. Forthrightness was the only way around it. "Why do you think she wouldn't succeed?"

"You would not choose someone who could be interested in her. And even if you did, you're too beautiful for him to choose her. I'm sure that's why she's jealous."

"That's absurd," Tam said. She knew she was handsome enough, but so was Alina. And Alina was much more inviting.

"My dear Tam, you only had to give the signal and Darrin and the other men would have been on their knees to you."

"Bosh," Tam said. She did not want to discuss it anymore. "Thank you for the warning."

"When will you see him again?"

"I have no idea," she answered honestly. She kept herself from saying he was busy, because the busyness of most young men here was attending to the ladies. "We hardly know each other. I can't expect him to be giving me every minute of his day."

"You spent rather a long time with him last night."

"That was yesterday." If it was a hint, she was not going to go further. Was there nothing else to talk about besides men? At least they had not gotten around to discussing marriage yet, though Tam thought Jenet may have felt on uncertain ground there herself.

When they reached their rooms, a page was waiting for them. It was the boy who had been haughty the day before. He was much more deferential now. He handed her a message and said, "I'm to wait for a reply, please."

She cracked the plain wax and unfolded the letter while Jenet stood aside. Another paper inside had something that looked like an official seal at its bottom. She tucked it into a pocket while she read the letter. *Tonight at eight. You should eat first. There will be someone to escort you from the fountain hall. Be prepared for a lot of mud. Let me know if you need anything.* He had not signed it at all, but below the paragraph was another line, more hastily written. *If the boy is rude to you again I will make him act as a copyist for a month, and he knows it.* Below that, a third line, even more of a scrawl. *If you disobey your father, however, I will never tell.*

She laughed. The boy could probably not imagine a worse punishment. "Tell him I will," she said, refolding the letter.

He nodded and bobbed a short bow.

As soon as he was gone Jenet said, "How in the world did you get that boy to be polite?"

"Hmm?"

"He's arrogant to everyone."

"Then perhaps he was so to someone he should not have been," she said. "I haven't done anything." How easy it was to lie.

She took the other paper out of her pocket and held it carefully so Jenet could not see. It was indeed an official seal, beside a formal signature. It gave her all rights and privileges reserved to those of ducal rank. A full pass. She stared at it. He did not need to do this for her. It was a very very precious thing.

"Tam? Is something wrong?"

"Nothing," she said, clutching the pass. "Excuse me." She hurried into her room and shut the door.

First the wine and now this. From another man it might have been meant to urge her into bed, but she was sure that was not Corin's intent. She would not have needed any urging last night, and he knew it. No, this was a gift, pure and simple.

It was nearly dark when she put on her plainest skirt, blouse, and walking boots. The cloth was good, she would hate to ruin it, but she had nothing else. It was drab in the palace and would be too fine for the fair. She managed to leave the wing without being noticed. At the fountain hall, a soldier was waiting to escort her to "the private entrance," the same man who had brought her back the night before. He called her "my lady."

A cat trotted along behind them some of the way, tail straight, and followed when they went through a guarded arch with a velvet rope in front of it. Symbolic, of course, but she had no doubt the guards there meant business. It chilled her to realize she was in a part of the palace to which few people were admitted. The cat stopped at a narrow flight of ascending stairs and began to bathe itself, the licks loud in the stone hallway. There was nothing ornamental about the corridor this side of the rope. It was old and purely functional and had looked the same three hundred years ago. They passed several doors secured with heavy chains and a small, lonely looking guarded antechamber with a sculpted dragon on the lintel. Part of its tail was missing. It gave her a strange feeling of being in stasis, locked in place while the world went on by.

Corin was not there when they arrived at the entrance, but she did not wait long for him. He wore faded brown trousers and a coarse white shirt. His boots were worn and scuffed. No one would ever mistake him for a laborer, though; his hands were too clean, his back too straight. At a signal from him, one of several guards began to unlock the wooden door.

"Thank you, Bron," he said, extending his hand to Tam. "Ready, Tam?"

"Yes," she said, a bit nervously. It seemed very public, more public in a way than the fountain hall had been. She liked how he looked in the white shirt. Rakish, not entirely respectable.

He clasped his hand around hers and led her through the door, down a short flight of steps, and out another door into a small walled garden. A gravel path led to the main drive through a tall iron gate. On the drive was a very plain coach drawn by two very plain horses, with two very plain footmen in the back. They were broad-shouldered, and she thought they were actually soldiers, as was the driver. The inside of the coach was much more elegant and even had two glowlamps.

"First things first," he said when they were moving, sliding back and forth in the coach. It was better made than it looked from the outside, and it was not as bumpy a ride as Tam had expected. The leather seat was wide and well cushioned, and the floor was carpeted, softening the sounds of creaks and jolts. He put his mouth on her lips.

When they finally separated, they both realized his hand was on her bodice, the fabric between his palm and her breast suddenly feeling very thin indeed. It had happened briefly in the garden, but he had drawn back at once. She put one hand over his, pressing it closer. With his other hand he undid the top buttons of her shirt. She did not try to stop him. They looked at each other for a long time. She was hot and tense with wanting.

Slowly, wordlessly, he slid his hand inside her blouse and placed it on her breast. Her nipple hardened against his palm. He caressed her with thumb and forefinger. It was unbearably exquisite. He kissed her again while he tightened his grip. She shuddered in anticipation.

"I want you," she whispered. There. It was said.

"You have me," he said. Then, unbelievably, he began to do up her buttons.

"Corin!" she protested. It was completely backward, she was supposed to have complained when he started, not when he stopped. Her mother would be furious.

"Not here," he said. "Not in a coach."

She whispered his name. He put his arm around her and pulled her close.

Suddenly afraid, she said, "You won't hate me afterward, will you?"

"Hate you!" he said incredulously. "Why do you think I would hate you?"

"Because sometimes after men have a woman, they blame her for not staying chaste." She had heard them crying in her father's surgery too many times to think it unusual. "Seduce her, then call her a trollop."

"Tam, Tam, Tam," he said. After a pause in which she could almost hear him thinking, he said, "I know you are honorable. I know you are not the kind of woman who takes a man to bed an hour after she's met him. And if you make me wait five years for you I will."

She thought he would say more. When he didn't, she looked at him. He was watching her, not staring, and it wasn't lust on his face. He kissed her forehead.

"It's complicated," she said. It was so complicated she couldn't even figure out how to say it. She would have felt the same if he had been a brick mason, but neither of them could pretend he was not the prince. If he had been a brick mason she would and could have waited for marriage. She wondered if he understood that.

"I know," he said. It assured her.

"I won't make you wait five years," she said.

He laughed.

"You're far too perfect," she said.

"You haven't known me very long. But I hope you don't really think I would do that to anyone, let alone you."

"I don't," she said. Was he really worried? "I'm sorry, I panicked a little."

He stroked her hair. It made her feel safe. "Of course you did, you have a lot to lose. That's why we're not going to make love now. We have to do it properly."

"Properly!" That was absurd. Going to his bed was improper in so many ways.

She didn't have to look at him to know that he knew what she was thinking and it amused him. "Oh, stop it," she said. "I concede. Acquiesce. Bow to your greatness." She would have gone on, but he kissed her.

A particularly large pothole jolted them apart. Drawing the curtain aside briefly, Tam saw that they were still in the heart of the city. The coffee shops and alehouses were wide-open, the streetlamps lit; it was much brighter than she had expected. In Dalrinia any respectable shop closed by dusk. The sidewalks and streets were crowded with all sorts of people. The rain had gone, the air was warm, no one wanted to be inside.

She let the curtain drop and looked back at Corin. "Tell me about the fair," she said.

"Ah." There was an ordinary burlap bag beside him. She watched curiously as he opened it. He removed two silk cloaks, one colored peacock blue shifting to emerald green and one flame red shifting to black, and two masks.

"Not masks?" she said, feeling ridiculous. He held one up; his nostrils, mouth, and chin were exposed, but the rest of his face was covered with glistening black feathers fanning out from silver-trimmed eyeholes. Hers was a vivid yellow. "I thought you didn't want to be noticed."

"No one will, like this," he said. "These are unremarkable." He tossed her the blue cloak. "Stay close to me, things are apt to get wild as the night wears on. It's not entirely safe, you know. That's for daytime. There will be men behind us, but if we get separated you could wind up on your own."

"What if we do?" The thought made her a bit anxious.

"There's a guard tent near the center, make for there. Here." He reached into his pocket and removed something. It was like a coin, but thicker and made of a reddish bronze. It had an embossed eagle on one side and a crown on the other.

"Don't lose it," he said. "It's a courier token, it will make the soldiers take you seriously. It would give you credit with any merchant, too, but I count on you not to deplete the treasury."

The coach hit a large bump, and she dropped the token. He caught it quickly, without even looking, put it on her palm, and pressed her fingers closed around it.

"Aren't you being a bit too trusting giving this to me this soon?" she asked. "Even if I manage to hang on to it?"

"Never." He traced her lips with his finger. "If you couldn't be trusted with it you wouldn't take it. You might be sly and saucy but you're too proud to be a thief."

❧

Once at the fair, Tam saw immediately why Corin had called the costumes unremarkable. Many other people were in harlequin garb or spangled head to toe; there were hats a foot high and ribbons and bells dangling from collars and cuffs and belts; about half the crowd was masked, most of them fantastic or grotesque faces, half human, or animals, birds and cats and unicorns. The first row of stalls upon entering was crowded with costumes for sale for those who had not worn one excessive enough. A wolf's head mask in one stall caught her eye. It was strikingly real-looking, with up-pricked ears and a long toothy muzzle. Its glass eyes gleamed knowingly at her, not quite frightening but disturbing enough that she involuntarily looked back over her shoulder several times to see if it was watching.

Corin bought her little cups of wine, and she drank them without hesitation. There were fire-swallowers and fire-jugglers, acrobats and puppeteers, conjurers pulling swords out of bags, musicians of all sorts, fortune-tellers, vendors. They sold everything from cheap and gaudy jewelry to hot spiced meat to rare perfumes to trained mice and two-headed snakes. Music boxes played familiar folk tunes and popped open to reveal enameled mechanical monkeys hammering the strings. A man had set up a table for a chess-playing automaton and took wagers on the games. Many of the sellers were frauds and charlatans; at one stall a bird purported to be a phoenix was obviously a chicken with suncock feathers stuck to it, and at another the "magic stones" were plainly glass. It didn't matter. This was the fair, a world of lights and colors and frenetic movement. One came to exchange truth for illusion, to relinquish thought to fantasy.

Tam kept a tight hold on Corin's hand. There were so many people it was hard to walk quickly, and sometimes currents or knots of movement threatened to part them. She couldn't see any soldiers following them, though she had no difficulty picking out the ones among the crowd. Women wearing paint and jewels but very little else beckoned from corners or danced atop large wooden blocks, masked men naked to the waist wrestled each other or fenced behind ropes, pigs and goats roamed loose. Large brown bears competed for audiences with lifelike wax figures that bowed or danced. Children darted in and out through the crowd, their hands full of spun sugar candy or streamers or tinkling cymbals. It was very noisy, and the smoke from all the fires and torches obscured the clear and starry sky. The air was full of smells: food and fire and sweaty people, cinnamon and musky perfumes, damp mud, the sweetness of flower garlands and the yeasty scent of beer. Once someone jostled Tam, almost knocking her into a stall, and she lost her grip on Corin. Before she could even react he had hold of her again. She thought such a mass of people and sensations might disturb him, he who spent his life among people staying at a respectful distance, but he seemed to be reveling in it, urgent, almost frenzied. His hand was warm and his movement eager.

Some of the stalls were places to play games of skill or chance. Try your luck Try your skill See what you can win Play darts and win a prize for the young lady Can you guess where it is Today's your lucky day Try Try Try Win Win Win. At one the contest was of throwing knives at a moving bronze pendulum, and Tam said recklessly, "Try that one!"

She could not see his eyes well with the mask and the flaring light, but his lips curved mischievously and he put down his coin. The knives were small, and he shifted the handle carefully between his fingers until he apparently found the right balance. He watched the pendulum for a few passes, then threw. It was faster than Tam could see, and unerringly accurate. The gamester said, "Once is luck, you have two more throws." Corin hit twice more, just as easily, and, laughing, left the prize.

"You have a sharp eye," she said.

"My sister Tai is better. She hits anything she aims at, she could have done that from fifteen feet away." He stopped abruptly, as though thinking of something else. Then he took her hand and led her on.

They passed a stall with hundreds of glittering disks hanging on strings above hundreds of tiny candles lining the walls. Rainbows of light reflected everywhere. A heavy smell of incense drifted from the stall. A woman sitting on a stool was watching them. The woman said, "Tell your fortune, young mistress, young sir, come see come learn come try." It drew her irresistibly.

Tam looked at him. "Can I?"

"If you want." His mouth was serious; if he thought she was bowing to foolery he didn't show it. It would have no truth, she knew that, but she had never done it before.

The lights and the scents and the wine she had drunk made her float. She stumbled forward and let the woman take her hand and bring her down to sit cross-legged on a wool rug. Corin gave the woman a coin, then squeezed Tam's shoulder and stepped back.

She expected a glass ball or cards or palm-reading, maybe a throwing of the fortune-sticks or dice. Instead the woman took out four stoppered bottles of colored sand and opened them. She was a very old woman, shrunken, face wrinkled and hair white, but her black eyes were bright and sharp as a bird's and she moved quickly. She put a tarnished silver tray between herself and Tam and said, "Choose."

Tam pointed at the bottle of black sand, and the woman poured it into her hand and scattered it across the tray. Then the yellow and the red and the vivid blue. She said to Tam, "Now draw the lines."

Tam touched the sand and moved a finger through it in a circle. The sand separated into colors and followed her as though her finger were a magnet pulling iron filings. She felt too dreamy to be astonished. A spiral. Three short straight lines. Her hands moved on their own, knowing, and she breathed the incense and let them do it. A triangle of red, a half circle of black, a blue maze of squares. Mist floated across her eyes. She smelled stone and ice. Some place old, some place very distant. She had smelled it before. Cold air passed over her. She shivered and pulled her hand back from the tray.

The woman bent over it and stared, then swept her hands across a few inches above the surface. She began to chant. It was not in any language Tam knew. Heat burned between her shoulder blades, spreading down and outward, tingling her arms and legs. Little whirlwinds of sand scudded back and forth across the tray. The words hung, detached, meaningless. Images came to her. A moon bright over a black plain, curls of steam in a cave. A wolf howled from a high rock. Lightning flashed in a brassy sky over jagged black mountains. Wind blew across coals and sent sparks flying into the air. A roof beam with strings of braided garlic hanging from it. A mountain, jutting and crenellated like a fortress. A man whose eyes flashed silver, then turned to black stone.

The sand separated into its four colors. It flowed back into the bottles as the woman held them to it, one after the other. Time running backward. The tray gleamed. Watching herself from a great distance, Tam leaned forward and looked into the silver, suddenly bright. Her reflection rippled. It kept spreading. It was not her reflection at all, it was some color within the tray, iridescent. That too shifted and she was looking into a well of darkness. Here was a narrowing, a point where the emptiness cut through her world, but on the other side was an endless open space that swallowed light. A hole. A tunnel. Icy air stung her face. She heard a scratching on metal that set her teeth on edge. There was something old, old, old rousing itself, its hour come round.

She turned to look at Corin and saw that his eyes were a full flickering gold. Recoiling, she lost her balance and pitched forward. Her right hand hit the surface of the tray and went through as though breaking the surface of water. Corin clapped his hands over his ears as she pulled back in horror, a sharp scream coming from her mouth. Her hand was frozen and unfeeling.

The woman scuttled away. Corin grabbed Tam and pulled her up and out of the stall. The world sharpened and became crisper again. Her hand tingled with returning blood. She staggered a little and he caught her. There was a knife in his other hand. His mask was up. His eyes were ordinary, his face almost desperate.

"Corin?" She could call him that here, there were probably a hundred Corins in the crowd. Her fear was gone entirely, swept away by his need. It was not time to think about what had just happened to her.

"She hurt you," he said harshly.

"No." She could not tell him about his eyes.

"Your hand went through."

She shook her head. It felt like one burden too many to put on him. "I fell and bent my wrist. It may be sprained. That's all."

"Don't lie to me, Tam. I heard the noise of it. It cracked like ice. You told me about the moths."

She cradled her wrist. It hurt. The burning of her hand was almost unbearable, but she could not let him see it, she could not. There was a pressure in her chest. She had to draw a line, for his sake. "This was nothing, my lord."

It struck him. He sheathed the knife. "I'm sorry," he said unhappily.

She pressed into him, wondering if anyone else had ever seen him like that. "So am I," she said. "Can we forget about it? Please?"

"Of course." He kissed her. She no longer felt as though she were suffocating. His mood flashed into something else. "Come play." He twirled her cloak, then let it go.

Tam got hungry, and they ate meat served on skewers and licked the grease from their fingers. He bought her more wine, and she drank it quickly. He kissed her quite passionately, and she returned it the same way. When finally they broke it off several bystanders applauded.

A woman whose face was painted half green, half gold, called from a candlelit stall, "Love potions! Love charms! For men, for women! Come see, come buy!" Catching sight of them, she said, "Even lovers need my draughts! Come see, come buy!" The liquids inside the displayed flasks were brightly colored and almost shining like the candles. "Just a drop in his water and he'll please you all night. Or try this, it will make him crave you when you're absent. This one is for you, you'll have pleasure like you've never had, you'll fly. This makes you ten times as beautiful or him as handsome as can be. That one's for if he starts to stray, you may not need it now, but all men wander, you'll want it later."

Tam glanced at Corin at that, and he said gravely, "If you want to waste your money, feel free. A chain would be more secure."

"A golden one, no doubt," she said, and pulled him onward. Then she stood, transfixed. In an open space before them was a column of butterflies, red and gold like sparks, tiny and perfect. They fluttered in circles that moved up and down, rippling like a wave, color shifting like silk. It was the most beautiful thing she had ever seen. Both hands extended, she stepped forward, reaching, and the column broke and poured over her.

Butterflies no bigger than her thumbnail covered her entire body, their wings moving softly. She was afraid to move lest it disturb them. However this had happened, it was not to be questioned. Someone was playing a flute somewhere, a primitive wild melody that made her want to dance and leap, and she forced her feet to stay planted firmly and her breath to remain steady. She felt people watching but didn't turn her head. His movements slow and controlled, Corin stepped around to look at her, meet her eyes. They could have been the only people in the world at that moment. The red and gold flickering over her was her blood pulsing. Her body tingled with desire.

She took a step forward and the butterflies scattered, reformed themselves into a globe over her head. He mouthed her name and she flowed toward him, and when their fingers touched she was jolted with the intensity. Somehow there was space in the crowd, and he ran, and she ran with him. He matched his pace to hers and they sped through the marvels and sights of the fair, dragons only three inches long and the colors of gems, a hissing spotted wildcat, a man on stilts whose body was covered with inked pictures that moved and changed as his muscles flexed. They drank more wine and danced around a huge bonfire and skipped wildly into a maze. They turned randomly, without trying even to guess where they would go, and wound up alone in a small square room painted with bright and disorienting shapes and hung with irregularly shaped and spaced mirrors that threw their reflections back at them in fragments.

"Corin," she said, wanting him, and he pressed her against the wall, knocking down a mirror, and kissed her. One of his hands found its way under her shirt and up to her breasts, and she pushed herself into it, arching her back. She locked her hands behind his head. Her body knew what to do, and if they had not heard laughter and voices almost immediately things would have gone much further.

They worked their way out of the maze somehow and had more to eat and drink and raced toward the carousel, its cheerful music summoning them. The wooden animals seemed almost to be dancing and alive. They sat on two silver horses, side by side, and when the carousel began to turn Tam felt as though she were at the center of a stillness and the world was moving around her. The mirrored panels in the center of the carousel flashed and shifted with color and light. It made her giddy, delighted. They spun, round and round and round, the music clear and drowning out all other noise. The colors in the mirrors began to resolve into images: a crow, a waterfall, a castle, a bridge, a tree. A fire-red snake. Tam looked at Corin and saw with a shock that he had raised his mask and was staring at the mirrors with his body as tight and straight as a lance. The image now was a dragon, with teeth of silver and eyes of gold, its scales shimmering and irides-cent, brightness surrounding it. Steam was coming out its nostrils. It roared, and fire leaped out toward them, full of heat and sulfur, and the horses twitched and whinnied. It was muscle and skin and hair under Tam, not wood. She clutched the horse's mane and lay close against its back. Beyond the carousel was only darkness and silence, and the horses ran smoothly, effortlessly, over the pool of blackness beneath them. Corin's cloak was fluttering and moving with all the light and wildness of fire, and his head was illuminated with a golden light. Tam's own cloak had turned to blue flames, and when she lifted one hand she saw blue-green sparks flying from her fingertips. She gripped the mane again; it exploded into flame from her touch.

As quickly as it had come it ended, and she heard the music and saw the painted wood. Corin looked white and stricken. The carousel was slowing; she slipped down from her horse as soon as she could and took his hand. He dismounted slowly, and she brought his mask back from the top of his head to cover his face. She had no idea what she had seen, but even through the wine and remaining frenzy she knew he needed her strength far more than she needed his.

When the carousel was still she led him off and away, into the chaos and privacy of the crowd, and then behind a stall. For a long time he was quiet. She thought of the black moths, the twin to the butterflies, and rubbed her bare arms to warm them. He had accepted what she told him, she had to do the same.

At last he said, his voice as husky as a boy's, "What did you see?"

"The dragon came out of the mirror," she said.

He slumped, apparently with relief. "I thought I was going mad. It looked at me, Tam, it looked at me, it wanted something."

"It was an illusion, that's all." She had to settle him as she had after the fortune-telling. "I saw it too, you weren't imagining it."

"Perhaps," he said. He raised his mask again and reached out to lift hers. She thought maybe he intended to distract her with a kiss. "There are some more things I need to tell you about the war," he said. "But here is not the place. Let's go on. Unless you have had enough?"

"You have," she replied firmly. "Time to go back."

CHAPTER NINE

eige

Neither of them spoke on the coach ride. Tam pressed the token back into his hand and leaned against him. Corin put his arm around her, liking the warm feel of her body against his, but did not kiss her. He had gone cold inside the moment he saw the first picture in the mirror, and when the dragon reared at him and the horses galloped into darkness he had thought he would freeze entirely and break. Memory was coming back, memory of what had happened in the north, what had been done to him; the roaring dragon in the glass had unlocked his mind.

Riding, riding, he had been riding, and then the dragon came and put upon him a burden. *The Firekeepers have chosen you to free them from their slavery. You will forget this until the change is complete. When you remember it, then it will be time for you to begin your labor. The Firekeepers will watch, do not shirk it.*

The coach rattled along and he did not know what to do with the memory. Absently he touched Tam's hair. How could he tell her this? How could he not? There was no passion in him now, only an aching tenderness.

When they reached the palace and climbed the steps to the entrance, he discovered he did not want to go in. It was so strong that he stopped before reaching the door. Tam took a step forward, realized he was not following her, looked back.

"Corin?"

"I can't. I can't go in now." Terror was waiting inside, dark and tight and heavy. He had cursed Hadon and it had recoiled on him.

"You have to. You need to come in and warm up and rest."

Women, always trying to make things better, softer, suffocating. "No," he grated.

She held out her hand. He didn't take it. "Corin, you can't just stand there on the step all night. Come in."

"I can damn well do what I want," he said, and was pleased to hear her slight gasp of shock.

She turned around and went to speak to the guards. He knew what she was doing. It didn't matter. They could not make him move.

One of the guards came down and said, "Come, sir, the lady's right, it's past midnight."

Corin struck him. It was not a gentle blow. The guard swore, fell heavily, hit his head, went still.

After that came a confusion of lights and voices. He sat down and let them go. The man he had hit was breathing evenly, and when two other men came to pick the guard up he heard relief in their voices. No one touched him or spoke to him for a long time. When they did come he ignored them and they went away. There was a bright white-yellow star above. He watched it move slowly westward, out of sight.

He was shivering, but that didn't matter. He was filled with cold, tremendous and powerful cold, cold that would freeze the world around him and shatter it into tiny sparkling pieces, like diamonds, like stars. That was the unreal world, the illusion, the sorcery. What was real was here, in this purity of cold.

Something brushed against his cheek. He smelled death. He felt the presence of a thing older than the dragons, vicious, desperate. It was trapped. Its wings were beating hard as it tried to come through.

A man was talking to him. He did not look up. The darkness was on his back, ready to wrap itself around him, to stab his eyes and tighten his throat. What are you? he thought. He pushed against it. It shuddered and gave way.

Then a cloth was thrust against his face. He smelled the narcotic on it before he went limp.

When he woke it was early morning, the light still fresh, the air loud with birds singing their last songs before quieting for the day. His head hurt. But that was not as bad as the horrible rush of shame that accompanied his memory. What had he done? Tam, he thought, and heard it in the stillness of the room. He remembered swearing at her. At least he had not hit her. He swung his legs over the edge of the bed and leaned over them, face in his hands.

After a while he looked up. He was not in his own room; that would have been a distance to carry him. He recognized the place: a small side chamber off the entrance hall where messengers sometimes slept or rested while waiting to be sent off. It had no actual door, but a thick blue curtain hung across the doorway. A window looked over some bushes and a patch of grass. The bed was barely more than a cot. The only other furniture was a pair of unpainted and unvarnished wooden benches against two walls.

He still wore the clothes he had had on the evening before; his boots lay on the floor at the end of the bed, not even standing. They had put him down to sleep it off like any common drunk. He deserved it. But he had not been drunk.

His chin was scratchy, and he felt dirty and foul. Parts of his hair were sticking out. He stood up, steadied himself against sudden dizziness, then pulled the curtain aside.

The guard outside said apologetically but firmly, "You're to wait here, my lord. Orders."

That meant the king. Well, he could hardly expect that behavior to remain unreported. The guard probably had full authority to restrain him if it was called for. He was particularly tall and heavy. "Yes. Of course," he said. "I'd like a cup of coffee."

"I'll see what I can do, sir." Noncommittal.

It came quickly, though, by which he gathered he was not entirely in disgrace. He would not ask for anything else. It was hot and bitter, what he needed. He wondered how long he would be made to wait. Not too long, surely. He had responsibilities and had not done anything terrible enough to be divested of them. Or had he? He had struck a guard, and if the man had died from hitting his head that was murder.

He had drunk about half the coffee when the curtain slid open and Tam came through. He put the cup down at once and stood.

He felt hopeful at the fact that he was permitted to see her. She could even have been sent for. Then he thought of other reasons she might have come.

She had obviously had little sleep herself; her hair was pulled back but not brushed, and her face was pale and drawn. At least she had changed her clothes. They stared at each other a moment, both afraid to speak.

"Tam," he said. His voice was rough. "I'm sorry. I'm so sorry."

"Why did you do it, Corin? You weren't drunk."

How much easier it would be if he had been. "Either I'm going mad or the world is," he said, then stopped. He should not blame it on madness, he should admit he had made the choice to refuse to enter. Her eyes were dark, tearless, demanding. If he did this wrong he would lose her.

Looking at the floor, he gathered his courage, or perhaps it was humility. He faced her and said bluntly, "I was afraid. There was something utterly dreadful waiting inside. It smelled like death. I was the rabbit in the hawk's shadow. That's what I thought. If I came inside I was going to die, or worse." Her eyes told him nothing of what she thought or felt. He forced himself on. "I know it makes no sense. And I shouldn't have let the fear take me anyway. But it did. There was nothing else left. You don't have to tell me I failed." It stung more than anything ever had. When he was dying he would remember this.

"Does this—does this have something to do with what we saw last night?"

"What did you see?"

"The carousel horses, when we were on them, mine—" She paused, touched her hair. "Mine seemed to turn to flesh. We were riding over darkness and our cloaks had turned to fire."

He shivered. He had not thought she had been brought in so deeply as he had. The dragon in the glass, the leaping fire. So that had happened. And she, somehow, had seen it too. That was not a dream.

"Yes," he said. He should leave it there, make no excuses. He went on, not knowing if he was explaining or defying. "It brought me a memory. One I don't know what to do with."

For a few seconds longer she looked at him, her arms stiff by her sides. It was as though she were protecting something, or trying to be brave. She took an awkward step toward him. Tentatively, he extended his arms, and then she came quickly into his embrace, her sweet-smelling hair against his neck, her forehead against his shoulder.

They held each other hard. Relief was flooding him. This was the most important thing, this, her.

"You don't know how frightened I was last night," she said at last, in a small voice, speaking into his shoulder. "You became a different man right before my eyes. I knew you were in there, somewhere, but I didn't know how to get you out. I didn't want to make you do anything which you would not forgive yourself for later. It was like Cade again, all over, only worse."

"I don't know what's going to become of me," he said as calmly as he could. "But I will always come back to you, always."

"Did I do the right thing?" she whispered. "With the guards, I mean?"

How worried she sounded. She needed him to be steady. He took a deep breath and stepped into his familiar role. "Yes. Were they respectful to you?"

That brought a little laugh, and she pulled back to look at him. Her face had softened. "I wasn't even sure they'd let me in, dressed like that and it so late, but apparently word's got around. It was all 'my lady this' and 'my lady that' from the first."

"Good," he said fiercely. He couldn't marry her, and he certainly could not ask his father to give her rank just because he loved her, but he wanted it clear that did not matter. What she couldn't have by law she could have by fact.

She looked askance at him. "What would you expect? It's not for me, it's for you."

"Not last night it wasn't," he said. "You were making the decisions about me, if you'd told them to put me in a cell they would have."

"I was a convenient authority. Anyway, I wasn't the one who told the doctor to drug you."

"I wager you thought of it, though. Who did tell him?"

She hesitated, clearly regretting she had said anything about it.

She was not a person who hid her feelings well. It was part of what drew him to her; he was sick of artifice in all its forms. He saw her decide to go ahead.

"Your father. After he tried speaking to you and you did nothing."

Hell, hell, hell. He should have known. "He was there himself? Someone went and got him out of bed?"

"Yes. That one wasn't my idea. Well, what were they to do, Corin? No one knew what was wrong and you'd already been violent. There weren't any good options."

"You're right," he said. Take the prince by force or leave him on the steps like a madman, who would want responsibility for that decision? He might as well find out the worst. "I really made a bloody mess of things, didn't I. What about the man I hit? How badly did I hurt him?"

To his relief she answered promptly. "Mild concussion and some bruises. It could have been much worse."

"Thank God for that." He was still due for punishment, but at least he did not have murder on his conscience. "Did he talk to you? My father?"

"A little," she said, and turned red.

It was not at all the way he would have wanted them to meet. He hoped it had not been too hard for her. Aram would have been kind and courteous, he could be sure of that, but he was the king. "Oh, Tam, can you still possibly care for me after this?"

There was relief in her body too. She kissed him. "You taste like coffee," she murmured, and kissed him again. Her tongue moved slowly, maddeningly, across the roof of his mouth. There had never been anyone like her.

"You learn fast," he said, and she gave him one of her sly grins. "But you should go get some rest. Have you been up all night?"

"Most of it," she answered.

"You didn't lose your reputation, did you, being out so long?"

"Perhaps. No one saw me come back. They saw me get up, so I'm safe that way. I don't care, you needed me." A pause, then that twist to mischief that he loved. "I think I have a credible witness in your father."

"I don't deserve you," he said. He realized he was sliding the dress off her shoulder, and he made himself pull it up. She caught his hand and pulled it down to her breast. He kissed her, pushing her down to lie on the bed. She did not resist. Her hands were at his waist.

Then he heard a motion outside the curtain and footsteps. He pulled them both to a stand and jerked his chin toward the door.

By the time Aram entered they were standing a discreet distance apart. The king had the air of a man who had been up and about for some time, and Corin felt slightly less worried. Then Aram glanced at Tam. Corin's heart thudded.

She said, "He's all yours, my lord, have at him," bent her head, and backed away.

"No," Corin said. "Wait."

"Don't be silly," she said, and was gone. The curtain fell neatly into place behind her.

"She," Aram said, "is one of the most sensible persons I have ever met. Far more than you. You should listen to her."

"I know that, my lord," he replied with lowered eyes and a lighter spirit. That was high praise from his father.

"Do you want to tell me what you were thinking?"

He had heard those words before, many times, though not for years. Aram wanted an answer, too; admitting guilt and accepting punishment did not suffice. He had to go point by point through his own folly. The words made him feel like a boy, but he supposed that was how he had acted. He was long past the age of being chastised by his parents, but he still was not the equal of the king.

Without much hope of convincing Aram of anything, he said, "Do you remember when your dog attacked me, sir?"

"Yes."

"I know why now, sir."

"Why?"

"The dragons." He stumbled over the word.

His father said, not sternly, "Look at me, Corin." No title, which was a good sign.

He raised his eyes.

Aram said, "I have been expecting this for a long time."

"You have been expecting me to turn violent and act like a madman?"

The king's lips twitched. "Not exactly. Sit down, we have to talk. Briefly. I need you at the council in an hour, and not dressed like that."

Apparently he had been forgiven. He sat and picked up the coffee, still hot. Suddenly he was shaky.

Aram took a moment to settle himself, then said, "When you were very small, a few weeks at most, a dragonrider came with a birth-gift from Hadon. He looked at you for a long time, then looked up at me and said, *The dragons will choose him. Keep him warm.* That was all he would say. I had no idea what it meant—I still don't—but I knew you would step into that world sometime. I have been wondering if it was happening since you came back. If that was why the dragons were watching you."

He felt adrift, uncertain. "Why didn't you tell me?"

"What would be the use?" Aram asked. "So you could spend your time chewing over it incessantly, wondering why the dragons wanted you, when it would happen, all those questions? You didn't need to think about that. You needed to be an able and honorable man."

Grudgingly, Corin admitted the truth of that to himself. He would have worried over it like a loose tooth, grown angry when nothing happened.

"I could have told you in the past few years," Aram added. "But as you get older you'll find, if you don't already know, that the longer you don't talk about something the harder it is to break the silence."

"That's why you wanted me to ride the dragon. Why you put Kelvan there."

"It's one reason I put him there. Not the only one." He smiled ruefully. "As for the riding, I suppose I was trying to hurry things along, so we would know and be done with that part before war started. I might not have done it if I still trusted Hadon."

"I'm the reason for the war," Corin said flatly. "If you sent my dead body to Hadon, you would see Tyrekh fall almost immediately. Sarian troops would never make it through Argondy. He's not just abandoning us, he's using them to destroy me. You might as well kill me and save all the misery and blood."

He paused, prepared himself. "When I was north, a dragonrider came to me and said the dragons had chosen me to free them from their slavery and that they would give me their powers. Firekeepers, he called them. He said Hadon knew it already and was starting the war because of it. He made me drink something, which I think now was dragon blood. And he said I would forget it all until the change had finished. Sika knew. Last night—last night I remembered. Look." He extended his arm, palm upward. Fire danced above it, bending the air. He had known he could do it as he knew that he could close his eyes. "It was too much to bear last night." Even saying that was hard, more than he was ready to face.

"I see," Aram said, and Corin knew he did. He put down the cup, nearly empty, then once again put his face in his hands. His father did not touch him, which was the only thing that kept him steady.

After a bit he lowered his hands and said, "Now what?"

"You will make reparations to the man you hit out of your own funds. We'll forget about the rest of it."

"Yes, my lord," he said, rising. It was more generous than he deserved or expected.

Aram stood. "I want you to be careful, Corin. No more jaunts outside the grounds without a good reason and a dozen men. If you really are a target, he might do anything."

Rain, and men on horseback. Blood-dust. "I know. I will."

"A message came in about an hour ago. There are ten thousand Imperial troops on boats headed for Dele. I'm going to need you all day."

"Why is he only sending ten thousand troops?" Corin asked, puzzled. "That's not enough no matter whom he intends to fight, us or the Sarians."

"He'll occupy the city and claim it is defense against the Sarians. Then we'll have to decide whether to move against him or accept it. Either way we're damned, or would be if I weren't better at waiting. He'll make a mistake."

"Does he know yet that we don't trust him?"

"He must have known when Kelvan returned with no message." The king sighed. "No one has come from Tai's husband yet, which concerns me. I sent a man at dawn."

"Will you tell the lords about Tai now?"

"No. I think most of them have their doubts about Hadon's fidelity—they can see the same things you and I do—but I need the time. We can't confront him directly until she's free."

"So how are you going to convince them the ten thousand troops are enemies? They'll think he's keeping his promise to defend us."

"I don't need to convince them of anything now," Aram said. "We have our men going. If we decide to fight, they'll be there."

"You can't keep it secret forever, Father. Sooner or later they have to know for sure."

Aram smiled coldly. "Yes," he said, "but I'll make Hadon blink first."

Corin didn't like it. There was no reason for his apprehension. His father was right, their choices were few regardless of what the council knew. The marshal was aware and planning. Hadon lacked Aram's will. All the same, he was deeply uneasy. It was the same sense he had had since the north of slippage, error.

He had to be honest. "I don't think we should wait," he said. "I think we should move now. We're giving him too much time. There's no advantage in delay if he knows we don't trust him."

"What would you do? I can't get either his men or ours to Dele any faster."

The hard truth was that he had no answer to that. "I don't know," he admitted. "I've nothing rational to offer. It feels like a mistake, that's all. I should be going now, to do whatever it is the dragons want." If Aram asked him where he would go, he had no answer to that either.

"It's not time yet, Corin," Aram said. "The dragons have waited centuries, they can wait a few more days until we have your sister. Don't go rushing into this. You might trigger something else."

"I'm not rushing. I'm being pulled."

"You're a man, not a slave. Not even to the dragons. Wait. I need you yet."

So I'm your slave? he thought, and then was bitterly ashamed of himself. He knew better. He took a few deep breaths. He swallowed and spoke the most painful words he ever had. "You can't let Caithen fall just to save my life. Or hers."

He saw the grief on Aram's face. Then his father said softly, "It wouldn't work, Corin. Even if I gave you to him he wouldn't send the men we need. He has his own sons to fend off. I won't sacrifice my children for nothing."

And that was the truth of it. Hadon sent ten thousand troops because he had no more if he wanted to keep his throne. That was why he was using Tyrekh.

"Yes," he said. "Of course I'll wait."

"Thank you." The king put a hand lightly on Corin's forearm. He could not tell if it was for restraint or steadiness. "I don't know how you found her," Aram said, "but you would be a fool to lose her. Don't do anything stupid. Use your own judgment about what to tell her." He turned, looked back. "And for God's sake be on time this morning."

Corin was barely aware of leaving the room. He felt as though he had just been handed a grail.

❧

The low evening sun slanted across the table, reddening the white cloth and putting a glow on the glasses and plates. Corin poured wine for both of them, then sat down. He was acutely aware of the delicacy of the situation. This room was both softer and more sumptuous than the Terrace Room, and though the door was open and guarded with a busy corridor outside, he felt he was exposing Tam as much as he would have in his bedroom. There were soft burgundy and gold hangings on the walls, and a long low velvet-covered divan that he had no trouble imagining uses for. Her dress did not help matters; the cut was entirely respectable, but the shimmering gold of the silk brought out the blue of her eyes even more and warmed her skin tone. She looked soft and touchable and splendidly elegant all at once. Her hair was wound around her head in a sleek braid.

She sipped and said, "I don't merit the costly wine tonight?"

"How did you find out about that?"

"Apparently it made an impression on the wine steward."

He should have expected that. It probably had been one of the most scintillating pieces of gossip in months. "I'll cut out his tongue. I pushed my luck serving it to you once, I don't dare do it again for months. You'll have to be satisfied with the nectar of mere mortals."

She raised her cup to him and said, "I would drink swill if it was you serving it to me," and immediately reddened. He loved that about her. He lifted her hand and kissed it, then started as her foot caressed the side of his calf.

It was amazing. He knew she would not have been that forward with anyone else, perhaps not even if she'd been married to the man for ten years; she was perfectly decorous, and had all the manners of an accomplished young lady. None of that seemed to matter when it came to him. It made him think no less of her. He burned for her, and she for him, and it was as unstoppable as rain in spring.

Which did not mean he could not think about what the world saw, so here they were, with an open door and two guards doing duty as chaperones. Not even caring what was on his plate, he forked a mushroom and ate it, his eyes on her the entire time.

They talked in low voices. He had to force himself to be interesting; it had been a long day of talking over things and deciding very little. Once she fed him a bit of fruit directly from her fingers. He distracted himself with thoughts of tax rolls and salt measures. When they were done they left the table and she went immediately to the divan.

"Don't sit there," he said, biting his lip.

"Why not?"

"Because I can't stand it."

She leaned back on one elbow, reclining like an odalisque, then sat up and moved to a chair. His mouth was dry. He returned to the table, far enough away that she could not touch him, and drank hastily.

He finished the glass and poured himself another. He stared at it. Rich purple, almost black, but if he moved it into the light it would be clear as a gem. It was time. He admitted to himself that he did not want to tell Tam about the dragons, the memory, his father's story. Hadon's enmity. He did not want her to think him anything other than an ordinary man.

If he loved her, he owed her the truth, no matter how hard. He said, "I suppose the story about me making an ass of myself has spread everywhere by now."

"Actually it hasn't." He must have looked surprised, because she said, "It was late, there were only a few people who saw, and they were all soldiers. They aren't talking. You weren't drunk, Corin, it was obvious there was something wrong."

He swirled the wine in his glass. He imagined how it must have been for her to tell him about Cade's death. The moths. She had had that courage. She was the bravest person he knew. "I had better start with the north," he said. Then he told her almost everything there was left to tell, about the war, about Hadon, about himself. He told her what the dragonriders had said in the north and at his birth, about the cold and dark he had felt on the steps, about Liko, about the Myceneans at the docks. To his relief he no longer stumbled over words. He kept back only Tai's captivity. He kept his head down, face away from her, for most of it. She asked few questions.

He finished. She came over and bent to kiss his cheek. He gripped her hand hard.

"Corin," she said at last.

"What?"

"I'm still here."

It was almost unbearable. He stood up and put his arms around her. Neither of them moved or spoke. She kissed him. All their kisses had been different, and so was this one. Confident, but not enticing.

Finally she stepped back. "What happened after I left you this morning? Were you flayed alive?"

"Not at all." He had not had much opportunity to think about how to tell her. She would not want to hear it. "Did you tell my father anything about last night?"

She looked uncomfortable. "I shouldn't have said it, I couldn't help myself. I was too worried. He asked what happened to you and I told him you had seen the dragon in the mirror. He asked if I had and I said yes. That was all. Why?"

Not much, but enough. She probably did not even realize how fearless she had been to say those things. Aram would have, though.

"I think you softened him up," he said.

"I did?" Her tone was truly surprised.

"He was much kinder than I deserved, which has to have been for your sake, not mine."

"That's ridiculous."

"You kept your head, Tam, instead of falling to pieces. He respects that."

She fidgeted with a decorative button on her skirt. He realized she wasn't going to say anything else about it. "Should you have told me everything you did?" she asked.

"Yes," he said. "I need your thoughts."

"You want me to feel useful."

"Trusted."

"I know you trust me, Corin," she said. She walked to the window. The light of the sun made her dress shine and showed the soft hairs escaping from the braid. "You have shown that abundantly. This is different. It's not my place to advise you."

It struck him in the heart. He went to her. "Tam," he said. "Tam Warin. Look at me."

Slowly, reluctantly, she turned. He put his hand on her cheek. "Your place is with me as long as you want it. Entirely."

"How can I tell you what to do? You can't make me privy to state secrets."

"I can."

"Your father . . ."

If he gave her the bald truth, exactly what Aram had said, it would be too much for her. She was confident and strong and not fooled by pomp, but she respected power. Carefully, gently, he kissed her. "He said I could tell you whatever I wished, Tam. I'm not spilling things I should not be spilling. I'm not asking you to do anything you shouldn't."

"He trusts you not to be fooled by my wiles?"

It was jokingly said, but he heard the worry behind it. "Tam," he said. "It's not that he trusts me not to be fooled, but that he trusts you not to be fooling me. Don't doubt you have his favor. He told me not to lose you, do you understand?"

She stepped back, her hand over her mouth. "I can't—Corin, what does that mean?"

"It means what we want it to mean," he said softly. Except for the one unalterable condition.

Tears sprang to her eyes. They glistened. He wanted to touch her but she had to come through this herself. She swallowed. Then, as he had seen her do before, she drew herself together.

"In that case I want the better wine," she said.

"You little devil," he said, relieved. If she had to make a jest of it to keep her footing, he didn't mind. It was better than running. How hard it must be for her to push her way through the thickets of the court only to find herself in the center of them with him.

He took her hand. "Will you walk with me?"

"Where?" she asked.

To my bedroom, he thought. "About."

"The garden?"

She sounded anxious. It would be the most public he had been with her. He knew he was challenging her.

"No," he said. "I'm not that much of a fool. The only woman here I could walk alone with in the garden after dark is my mother. And the insects can be bad this time of year. But I can show you the palace. Bring you to the places no visitor is allowed. I warn you though that most of them are dull and look like one another. Say no if you don't want to, Tam, we can stay here. But I haven't the time to take you anywhere in town."

She thought about it, then raised her eyes to his. She said firmly, "Show me the interesting places, and tell me all the sordid stories. I should change my shoes. Where will you wait for me?"

He admired her resolve. "The fountain hall," he said, "but I'll have to hide in a corner so no one traps me."

He was intercepted by a messenger who told him Mari was not far out of town and her husband only two days behind her. It was the first decent news in days and made him almost cheerful. At the fountain hall he made sure a large plant was between himself and the sight line of anyone casually walking through, and he talked to one of the guards for good measure.

It seemed hours before Tam came. "I'm sorry," she said before he could remark on it, "it's impossible to get away from them. Just when you've said something to one person another comes along and you have to repeat it."

"I probably deserve to have to wait," he said. He kissed her hand. "Are you ready?"

She nodded. "Lead on, Your Highness."

That meant she was happy. They made their way quickly and correctly, not touching, through the wide corridors, which seemed to be extraordinarily full of people. Tam maintained a formal dignity he had not suspected in her, coolly ignoring everything but him. There was so much of her he still did not know. She was full of contradictions and complexity.

The men who saw her were not. They stared, no matter their rank. Eyes were quickly averted when they saw him. Briefly, it amused him; he was not used to being second place. Then he realized he was going to have to find a way to make it clear she was to be respected, not coveted. He had to step carefully with it. If he gave her something it could not be allowed to seem return for being in his bed. That meant he had to make sure she did not come into it. It took work to not show frustration.

He remembered walking to the Terrace Room that first night with her, hoping desperately no one would come out of a room and see them. It could have happened at any moment, but he had got them into the antechamber and shut the door to the hallway before it did.

Bron, who had far better things to do than stand guard outside a room while Corin cultivated a woman's affections, had only poorly concealed his irritation when being told to do so. Then he had seen her and straightened more than he did for Corin, his own display feathers going up before he recalled himself. Corin still did not understand how she had been free of other attachments.

He showed her the council chamber, the king's private library, the map room, his mother's receiving room, the ceremonial armory. But they were both soon bored, and it was not long before, despite his better sense, they went out one of the garden doors. They stepped onto a broad flagstoned area with a few trees inset and a flower bed bordering the other side. A path ran parallel to the building in either direction. Early white stars shone in the clear sky. Bats darted everywhere, feasting on insects. In the garden, frogs and crickets competed loudly with one another. He heard voices but did not see anyone.

"My God," said Tam, "you didn't say anything about the noise. How big are those frogs?"

"Tiny. Half the length of my thumb. Sometimes they get inside and can be heard for yards and yards down a hallway. When you get close to them they get quiet, they're hell to catch. I speak from experience."

"You brought them in, didn't you?"

"A few of them," he admitted. "But really, they are quite adventurous on their own. Which way?"

"You decide. I don't know where to go."

Resolutely he turned away from the enticing darkness of the garden. He spent an hour leading her about between the buildings, into small grassy courtyards, under covered walkways, in and out of narrow doors, past the kitchens with their smells of meat and spice and woodsmoke, through the kitchen garden with rosemary strong in the air, across the sundial court where he had been tutored endlessly in geometry. He made certain not to take her any place a lady should not go. They were seen now and then by servants and guards but by few courtiers. Some places were very dark and quiet, causing them to tiptoe into the shadows and take much too long to come out, while others were splashed with light and full of sounds from inside: voices, music, clashing metal, crockery, water. There was no area he did not know, but watching her discover them was almost as stimulating as exploring had been when he was very young. He had been given free range then, and he took it. It was years since he had gone places where his duties did not take him; the boy who had wanted to know what everything was and how everything worked was long grown.

The night cooled, and Tam grew chilled. Corin put his arm around her and walked her back in through one of the garden doors. It happened to be the one that led to the more formal areas of the palace; it was the door through which a foreign dignitary would be taken to view the gardens or to walk for a careful, term-setting conversation with the king. The rooms nearby were mostly used for state affairs and were dark and empty tonight. There were several guards along the hall but no other people. The hallway lights were low.

Tam shivered. He felt her body trembling under his arm. It was highly improper to touch her so, but he was the prince, damn it, custom could go to hell. "What is it?" he asked, keeping his voice low.

"It's a little spooky," she said. "All this emptiness."

He understood what she meant. Many times he had walked back to his own rooms after some business kept him in his study for hours, and even those familiar and well-traveled hallways felt cold and slightly eerie in that midnight quiet. Here, where everything was designed to impress rather than to be useful, it seemed even more inhuman.

They walked by the high golden doors that were one of the four public entrances to the throne room. He thought absently of the bare splendor within, the elaborate roof beams and gorgeous wall hangings and all the space for standing with not a place to hide. There had been a dragon seal on the floor once, but the Myceneans had destroyed it. It was an old room, restored and enlarged several times over the centuries, first built when war was far more present, when power meant naked force and domination. He knew that his family ruled because his forebears had been stronger and luckier and more cunning than their rivals. Strength and luck and cunning were nothing to shrug at, and he did not underestimate what they had done. But kings no longer had to be warlords, they had to be gamesters. Even more so since Mycene took the dragons.

"Do you want to see?" he asked, since they were there.

"Can we?"

At first he thought it was a naïve question, as though she had forgotten who he was. Then he realized that she knew he was rule-bound too and did not know what the rules were. Even with all the things he had told her, she did not know the customs of this place. She was not a courtier.

He stopped to touch her face. "Yes," he said softly. When Mari came he would put them together.

She considered it, then shook her head. "No. Not now, in the dark."

He was not about to force her. "A cat got in once," he said as they walked on, "and took a nap on the throne."

"No."

"Yes."

"What happened?"

"What could happen? It was a cat. It got out before anyone could catch it and the rober spent half an hour picking cat hairs off the cushions."

She laughed. They were passing an unlit hallway that he knew was never used, and he gave in to temptation. He turned into it. She followed him to the end, down the stairwell to the landing. It was dark.

"Where does this go?" she whispered.

"Nowhere. The storeroom below was rebuilt years ago and the door is blocked off. No one is coming." He stroked her neck and slipped a finger under her collar. Her skin was amazingly soft and smooth.

She made a noise that was neither a word nor a sigh. He took it as permission to go ahead and pushed both sleeves off her shoulders.

The dress was snug and would not go down without being unhooked, so he gave up on that. She stroked his arms and left her hands lightly on his wrists. He kissed her bare skin feverishly.

Then they heard voices and both froze. There was just enough light from the main corridor for him to see a glint in her eyes. He touched a finger to her lips for silence. She licked it, arousing him more. Her hands came down to his thighs. After a few seconds he realized they weren't stopping. He swallowed and firmly lifted her hands back to his shoulders.

The voices moved on. She said in his ear, "Don't you want to?"

"Are you mad? Of course I do. But not here," he said, although his resistance was almost gone.

"Then continue the tour," she murmured, her tone suggesting it was rather a different tour that she had in mind.

"You are a witch."

"Maybe."

"If you keep teasing me like this I'm going to have to go find some other woman to keep myself sane," he said. It was not entirely a jest.

"Who says I'm teasing?"

He took her up to the roof. It was a long ascent, and she was sweating and winded by the time they reached the top. That should slow her down some. The stone still radiated heat from the day. There were no seats up here, nothing but the flat stone and the guardhouse at one end and the coop for the message birds at the other. The moon was overhead, not at the full yet but bright enough to see by. He led her to the western wall so they could look out, over the blackness of the garden, the lights of the city, the river curving through the hills and fields beyond. They were high up, a good fifty feet or more above the other levels of the palace; if it had been a clear day they could have seen for miles. At night the kingdom had no edge.

The air that had felt too cold while they walked the grounds was welcome after the exertion of their climb. The rushing of the fountains and waterfalls everywhere made a pleasant noise. He had heard that sound all his life. When he was a boy, he had come up here on the nights that were too hot to sleep and sat, back against the wall, legs extended, listening to the water, watching the fireflies. Sometimes there would be a storm coming, far to the west, a pile of clouds and orange flickers of lightning while the wind picked up. Now no one came up except the sentries and the birdkeepers.

And dragons. Dragons with their gleaming claws and iridescent wings. Dragons with their enthralling eyes. Dragons who were the Emperor's captives. Dragons whose silky scales would have been blue and shining in the moonlight.

"Corin?"

He brought himself back to the present. She never shortened his name, he liked that. "Yes?"

"I've been thinking," she said.

"About what?"

"Dragons."

It had caught up to her. He wondered if she would understand how beautiful they were. "What about them?" he asked, holding back other questions with an effort. He was prepared for her to decide to leave him. It was difficult enough to be the companion of a prince, let alone one who had been given a mission. Why had they chosen him instead of some peasant or poet?

"What holds them?"

That, however, he had not expected. He had underestimated her again. He shook his head slightly, scolding himself, and said, "I have no idea." It made him realize how little he had to go on. Kelvan might know, but Kelvan was a thousand miles away.

"The dragons—what do you *want*?"

It was an impossible question. It tugged him. "I want to ride," he answered softly, remembering wind and shining scales and a river far below. Remembering the dragon's eyes and the images whose meaning he had almost known. "It was bliss."

Her face was ageless, wise. "And the rest of it? They gave you a task—a command. They gave you power. Are you afraid?"

He could not remember if anyone had ever asked him such a

thing. In another woman it would have been charmingly innocent, in her it was a challenge. Not to be brave, but to be truthful.

"I was," he said. He thought about it some more. "Now, I don't know. I'm not trembling in my boots. I don't fear the dragons. I will do this thing, Tam, whatever it takes. But it will make everything different. I can't know how until it happens."

"Must you do it?"

Must. "I'm not being compelled," he said, and knew it for the truth. "I could turn my back, refuse. I don't know that I could live with myself afterward, though."

"How will you start? With a war on, doesn't your father need you here?"

"I had this very conversation with him this morning," he said. It came out more harshly than he had expected. "No wonder he likes you, you're more like him than I am."

"Corin!"

"I'm sorry," he said. He could not admit, even to her, how helpless he felt.

There was an awkward silence, the first between them. Before he could break it she shifted and said, eyes averted, "Corin, I lied to you."

For a moment the world went still. "When?" he asked over the coldness in his gut. He knew about the little fibs where she held back what she was feeling, everyone did that. But this must be something important.

"At the fair, the fortune-teller's stall. I couldn't burden you. I think I already knew something was going to happen. Your eyes had changed. They were dragon eyes. My hand—it did go through that tray. You didn't imagine it. It was cold, very very cold." She paused. He reached out and briefly rubbed her shoulder, comforting them both. He was glad it had been no greater lie. "It was an opening. I don't know how I did it, or even if I did it, or if it was done to me."

She stopped. He had the sense that she wanted to say something else. He waited. He hoped she did not fear his anger. When she did not speak, he said softly, "You did right not to tell me. I would not have known what to do with it then. I had to remember things first."

They were silent again, but this time it was comfortable. He saw the dark swoop of a hunting owl over the garden. He reached for her hand and held it warm against his. He thought he could feel the blood moving.

After a while she spoke. "There's more, love."

Love. She could not mean it, not yet, not so soon. He could not help hoping. "What?"

"The thing on the steps, the dark thing, I felt it too when I made the opening. It was waiting. What is it?"

He remembered that sweetly rotten smell of death. "I don't know," he said. The poor people in the north would know. Liko would know. It had been watching him for years. God, he could not let it get at Tam. He had no idea how to stop it. He wanted to clutch her to him and hold her safe.

Instead he spoke. "Tam, whatever's happening to me, call it my doom if you will, I'm sucking you in too. You're not going to be able to get out. I don't know if I can protect you." He could not bear to tell her she should go.

"You're not doing it. I saw the moths. I think maybe it's like looking at water under a lens, it's full of living things, moving, in their own world, and they're there even when we can't see them, they've been there all along and only in the last two centuries have we learned to see."

The rightness of what she said was like a force. A difference in seeing. The world itself was unchanged. He did not have to change to meet it, only had to shift his gaze. Hope blossomed in him. "You are a marvel," he said. He kissed her.

She returned it fully, eagerly. "Another?" He gave it to her, slowly, tasting everything. Her hand was on his hip. He pressed closer. Now her fingers were under his waistband sliding toward the center, telling him to yield.

He drew back. "I can't let you," he said. He wanted her so much it hurt, but he could not allow this. "You have to be free to marry someone worthy of you. If we go on you can't go back."

"Then what do you want from me, Corin? What else is there?

You said last night we would." He could not tell if she was more hurt or angered.

"I never should have started this," he said. Every word was a blow. "I've put you in an impossible place." He bit the inside of his lip.

"I have my own will," she said. "Do you think I haven't thought about this? There's going to be a war. This may be all the time we have."

"Tam," he said, aching. "Don't you see?"

"Of course I do. I don't care. You haven't with other women, why do you now?"

"Because I love you," he said. He had thought the words a hundred times already, but it felt strange to finally have said them. "I didn't love them."

"So the one woman you love is the one you won't make love to?"

"Don't," he said harshly. "Don't."

She did not rise to the anger. Instead she took his hands, gripping them hard, and stared at him. He could not see the blueness of her eyes, but he felt the force of the gaze. "No one ever gives you anything," she said.

"What do you mean?" he asked, startled.

"It's all due to you. Earned or owed or traded for. You don't know what to do with something without ties. Let me give you this, my love, please."

It hit him in a place he had not even known was tender. She was the only person who had ever found it. And he had to put her aside. He did not have the strength—or cruelty—to do so. He returned the grip on her hands and bent his head toward hers. "Tam," he whispered. "Are you truly sure?"

"Completely." She gave him a kiss that left no room for doubt.

He ripped his mouth away and said, "Come with me?"

She said nothing but gave him that sly smile. They made their way down the steps and through miraculously empty hallways and stairwells. If he had seen a single other person he would have sent her back to her rooms. He could do nothing about the guards outside his door, but they knew better than to breathe a word.

He built up the fire in the bedroom, then turned to her. She unlaced his vest and helped him slip his shirt over his head. She touched his chest and shoulders and back and wrists, first with her fingers and next with her mouth, delicate butterfly kisses that seared his skin. She brought his hand up to the soft firmness of her breast.

Somehow he moved away enough to reach the hooks on her gown and undo them, one by one, all the way to her hips. He slid the dress off her; it fell to the floor in a soft rustle of silk that could have been the flames. He drew down her undergarments and felt her tremble when he ran his hands down the insides of her smooth thighs. She fumbled at his belt. Soon he too was naked, both of them glowing red-gold from the hot light. Shadows flickered across her perfect body. He took her breasts in his hands, and she pushed her hips against him, and he could have entered her then if he wanted to.

Instead he brought her down on the bed and kissed and touched her everywhere. Her response was sweet and far less timid than he would have expected from a virgin. And virgin she was, even had he not known he would have able to tell from her little movements of surprise, her momentary uncertainties about how to shift her legs or arms, a tentativeness in how she touched him. She did not know yet what she liked any more than he did. He nibbled one of her nipples, kissed her hip, ran his fingers along the silky folds between her legs. He found the spot that made her shiver with pleasure, then saw the fear of it on her face, and came up to kiss her and comfort her, and slowly her hand came down to his thigh, and he pushed into her before either of them expected it, hard, drawing a short cry from her. Then her hips came up and thrust against him. Her eyes screwed up and her mouth opened in sudden ecstasy. She groaned, and he could contain himself no longer, and everything was white exploding light and then he was falling, falling.

When he came up she was lying on her side, propped on one arm, looking at him. Her hair was sweat-dampened and her skin glistened in the firelight.

"Are you back?" she asked.

"Did I hurt you?" he answered.

"Yes, but it was worth it. There wasn't much blood."

"I'm sorry," he said. "I tried not to. It will be better next time." He sat up and pulled her into a light embrace. "My lovely love, you honored me."

"Was it—did you—?" She stopped.

"You are splendid," he said simply. He kissed her shoulder, put his hands softly on her breasts, cupped them until her nipples hardened. He slid his palms down her sides to her hips, her buttocks, her thighs. "I want every inch of you."

She kissed him and stayed in his arms a bit longer. Then she got up and began to pat herself dry with the edge of the sheet. There was determination in her movements.

"What are you doing?" he asked.

"I can't spend the night, Corin," she said, reaching for her undergarments. "If I leave now I can be in my bed at a time that is halfway decent. It's not that late."

"Stay," he said, but weakly.

She didn't deign to answer that. He got up and helped her dress, brought her a damp cloth to wash her face. She dabbed at the roots of her hair as well and put her braid back up. He put on his own clothes. She took his hand. "When will I see you next?"

"Tomorrow morning, early? In the Sun Room? I won't have time for anything else."

They made the arrangements, and he assigned one of the guards to take her back through the private passages. He kissed her on the forehead in full view of them. "I love you," he said, and let her go.

CHAPTER TEN

⮜❧⮞

T am arrived first, on time, and told one of the servants the prince was coming. That gained her a secluded table by a window and food almost immediately upon it. The table was set with the dragon plates. She realized now that whatever else they were, they were a shout of defiance to the Empire. Once she began to notice dragons, it seemed that they were everywhere. The bread was so fresh it was hot to the touch. The sun was bright, gold on the grass outside and the stone tiles within. It was a much more pleasant place than it had been when she was with Cina. She sipped her tea quietly, looking at the sunny courtyard.

She had always been rather scornful of people who let their lives fall to pieces because of a lover, but now she understood it better. It was hard to keep herself calm and within the limits of decorum even the next morning. He loved her. Last night she had made it into her room when it was still early enough for other women to be up; she had even played a short game of cards. No one knew except the guards that she had been in Corin's bed that night. It was a tremendous, wonderful, splendid secret.

It, or some of it, was not a secret she could keep much longer— the ball that evening would ensure that—but she had to be calm and assured, not silly-giddy about it. She certainly had to behave properly as long as possible. She had not yet decided what to do about her sister-in-law, who would write to her brother immediately, and her brother would write her parents, and her father would come after her at once. He would not doubt her honor, he would simply think she was acting far beyond her place. It was ironic that Corin's father was apparently far less concerned than her father would be. Of course if Corin abandoned her she might be ruined, whereas if she abandoned Corin it would leave no stain on him.

The night before last, when Corin stood defiantly on the steps, she had known something was wrong before he swore at her. She said to one of the guards, *He's not drunk. I can't persuade him to come.* She had no confidence that the man would do anything, especially not when she looked like a farmwife, but he had said, *I'll get him, my lady,* startling her. Then Corin struck the man and knocked him down with a crack on the head that could be heard from where she stood, and the guards looked at one another, and someone said, *Fetch his captain,* and she realized it was herself. Her heart was full of dread. The man who came was the same one who had escorted her to Corin's side earlier that evening, and from the Terrace Room the night before, and she was chilled to realize it had been no mere soldier he had asked to do it. The captain, Bron his name was, went down to speak to the prince but got no more response than anyone else had. He came back and drew her aside. *If he won't speak to me and he won't speak to you, my lady, then we have two choices besides force: leave him there or wake the king.* He was looking at her, waiting for her answer. The doctor was in a corner, tending the injured man. Corin stared outward like a statue. He couldn't be left there, he couldn't. *Then get the king,* she said, looking anxiously for a cloak to cover her muddy skirt while her stomach went painfully tight.

Some time later, Bron came back with Aram in his wake and a black dog following. Tam hoped desperately Bron had already explained things to him. The king went straight down the steps to look at his son. He got nothing from Corin either. The dog stayed at the top, its ears laid back, its tail swishing. Occasionally it whined. Its hackles were up partway. Aram watched Corin for a while.

Finally he came up and walked directly to her. The dog was at his side but no longer fierce. The king was dressed plainly and did not seem to have been rudely roused from sleep. That other Tam she didn't know curtsied and said, *Your Majesty.* He looked at her. It was Corin's face and not Corin's face, older, darker, a different shape to the eyes and chin, but that same intensity of expression. He said, rather more gently than she thought he would, *What did he do to himself at the fair?* She answered, without thinking, *He saw a dragon in a mirror, my lord.* With that unchanging gaze Aram said, *Did you?* She could only manage a *Yes.* Not accusingly, he said, *Why have you stayed?* and she said, *What should I do, crawl into a corner and cry? I won't abandon him.* Then she remembered she was speaking to the king, but it was too late to take back the words. Before she could apologize, back away, he smiled a little and said, *It's hardly abandonment to leave him to his men.* She said, *If they push or pull him too hard, something will break, my lord.* He put his hands on her shoulders. *What do you suggest we do about him?* he asked. The dog nuzzled at her hand with its warm wet nose. Its approval mattered. She remembered her father standing over men writhing in pain, women in agony with labor, and said, *Vitriol ether and a few drops of camphor.* It could hardly be the answer the king anticipated. Aram looked at her for another long moment and said, *He's going to need you.* Then he went to speak with the doctor.

The doctor glanced up at her. She remembered him speaking to her after Cade died. What might he be thinking now, to see her with the prince?

She watched nervously as one of the guards went down to drug Corin. No one interfered when she followed them into the guardroom. They slung him on the low bed. There was no chair, so she knelt beside him, arms on the bed. Tiredness began crawling over her. She did not know how long she had been doing this, watching, waiting for the drugged sleep to turn into ordinary rest, when she was tapped on the shoulder. She looked up and saw Aram offering her a cup of tea. By then she was too weary to react. *Don't let yourself get stiff,* he said. He gestured toward the bench. *Come sit here. I don't expect you'll go to bed if even I tell you to, will you?*

She said, *Someone has to watch, my lord. Until the drug runs out.* She was too tired to realize he had probably already heard it from the doctor. *Why?* he asked, and she said, *In case it was too much. It might stop his heart.* She remembered her father saying those very words to her in his surgery. Aram said, *There is nothing anyone can do about a stopped heart,* and she said, *If you watch you can make sure it doesn't stop. There are signs. Blue lips, slow pulse, cold hands.* It made her think to check Corin's pulse, which she did. Steady and strong. It was hard to put his hand down again.

Something was in the cup besides tea. Not enough to go to her head, but enough to make her muscles loosen and some of her anxiousness retreat. Aram sat beside her and asked her a few questions, then slipped into silence. Finally Corin inhaled deeply, stirred, turned from his back to his side, and she knew he was in normal sleep. She put the empty teacup down. Her arms and hands were shaking. Aram stood up. She rose quickly, but not before he could take her hands and help her. *He's fine. You've done very well. Now go to bed. Do you want to be told when he wakes up?* She nodded. He put his hand under her elbow and escorted her out. A guard drew the thick curtain closed behind them. Quite unexpectedly the king asked, *How did you meet him?* and her imp got hold of her. *It reflects rather badly on him, my lord, I think you had better get him to tell you. I want him to still like me.* Then she began the all-too-familiar clap of hand over mouth, but he laughed and sent her off with a light push on the back. A soldier walked with her all the way to her room.

It was obvious now that Aram had known why she stayed but wanted to see what she said. He had no doubt judged her quickly and accurately. That was his business. Afterward he would have found out everything about her. And he had approved, even liked her.

Although perhaps the only thing that mattered to him was that she had seen the dragon too. She felt suddenly like a child, standing on tiptoes to peer over a wall and watch things she did not understand. Aram must know a thousand things that she did not. She buttered a slice of bread and nearly tore it with nervousness before she could calm herself again.

When Corin finally came in she could tell at once; the conversations at the other tables went quiet for a breath. She was glad she did not know anyone.

She rose politely, doing her best to pretend no one was watching.

Equally politely, he kissed her hand. "My lady," he said, a touch of playfulness in his eyes.

"My lord," she said, bobbing her head, and they looked conspiratorially at each other as they sat. It was probably obvious to everyone that it was a sham.

For a few moments they ate without speaking, just looking at each other. The cheese was salty and hard, the red grapes were sweet and firm. Tam broke the silence by saying, "What have you got to do today?"

"More of the same as yesterday," he answered. He impaled a slice of pear with his fork. "Coaxing and convincing. Unfortunately I have to do it to people besides you." He was dressed more formally than she had usually seen him, with a closed-collared shirt and a jacket over it. It suited him but made her less confident of her place. Which was not what she wanted at the moment.

"There will be plenty of pretty women at the ball who would like it," she said.

"Damn the ball!" he said, and she laughed, then looked around to see if it had been heard.

"Should I plan to just stay in my room and lacquer my fingernails instead?" she asked.

"Of course not. I promised to bring you and I will. Besides, my mother would kill me if I didn't open it for her. I told her to find me a suitable partner, I don't want to be bothered with looking. I'm sorry it can't be you."

"I'm not," Tam said fervently. She was glad she didn't have to persuade him of that. "All those people staring, waiting for one missed step and wondering if there's any significance to your choice."

"That's going to happen anyway."

"Not the same as it would for the first dance."

"Why ever do they care so much?"

"Don't be an innocent," she said, keeping her voice low. It would hardly do to chide him in public. "You know perfectly well that women want power as much as men, and that is what a ball is about. It's going to be guessed at all day."

He put his hand over hers. When she looked into his eyes, she saw they were more green than blue today. "Don't ever stop telling me what you think," he said. At first she thought he was teasing her, then realized he was serious. "Not enough people do," he said. "They tell me what they think I think, which is downright useless. And half the time insulting."

It was hard, looking at him, not to think of the ways he had touched her the night before, the way his body had felt against hers. It would be so easy to let everything else go. She refilled her teacup. It was black tea tinged with jasmine, something that was supposed to be a favored drink of Mycene. She had added the herbs she needed, not without a sharp pang of regret.

"I'm afraid I have nothing to do myself," she said.

"Perhaps you should come and watch the court."

"I can't imagine anything more dull."

"Come now, Tam, don't you want to see me in all my glory?"

She made a face at him. "I can wait until the ball for that."

"Oh, we're back to the ball, are we? What about you? Have you a gaudy enough gown?"

"Every fashionable woman travels with at least three ball gowns, even if she is going to spend the night in a smithy," she said. Then, running over in her mind the gown she intended to wear, she saw a problem. "I'll need help dressing."

"I can take care of that," he said, grinning.

"Behave yourself, my lord. But truly, can you find a maid? Otherwise I will have to ask Cina, and whoever she sends will ask all sorts of questions I don't want to answer. It'll be no use telling her it's not her affair; it's a bad idea to have someone do your hair if she's angry with you."

He touched his chin. "Like being shaved by a barber with a grudge. Yes, I can see that. Dear heart, you can have an entire bevy of household servants if you want."

"One maid will do."

"Then you shall have it." He hesitated. "You realize this means I will be talking to my mother, don't you? You can't put off meeting her much longer."

Her appetite vanished. It was worse than meeting the king. But there didn't seem much of an alternative. "Why would she want that? I haven't any political value." She knew she was being disingenuous, but it was easier than truth.

"Certainly you do," he said. "But that's not what she would be interested in this time. She wants to see you because I love you, that's all. What about Cina? Will she make trouble for you?"

She hadn't wanted to think about that either, and certainly not to inflict it upon Corin. Reluctantly, she said, "I don't know what to do about her; when she finds out about you she will bring my father upon me like a fury."

"I thought he was a reasonable man."

"He is. And he expects me to be reasonable too. And that does not include falling in love with the one man in the kingdom I can't marry."

"Love isn't reasonable," he said. "Don't borrow trouble, Tam. If he comes I'll talk to him. I can be persuasive."

"He can be stubborn," she said, which made him laugh.

"And Cina, should I leave her to you or speak to her myself?" he asked.

"Leave her to me," she answered with a sigh. "It would be cheating for me to hide behind you."

"You, my love, are a remarkable woman." He reached toward her hand, then withdrew.

She did not want to be praised at the moment. It would be too hard to resist touching him. "You didn't show me the kitchen," she said, looking at the food. "Beneath your dignity?"

"I didn't take you into the boiler-houses either," he said. "I'm not allowed in the kitchen. No one is who doesn't belong there. It's noisy and hot. You wouldn't like it."

"Don't tell me you never snuck in and stole some food."

"The last time I did that I was twelve. I got caught and was made to wash dishes for an hour. I learned my lesson."

"*You* washed dishes?" she asked incredulously. "Who dared to tell you to do that?"

"It was my mother's orders," he said. "She is a great believer that the punishment should fit the crime."

"That wouldn't happen now, though, would it?"

"That wouldn't happen now," he said. "I can go in and interfere however I like. But the less I tell other people what to do the better. There's enough work without it."

"I know that," she replied. "But . . ." Her voice trailed off. She drank more tea.

"You didn't expect me to think of command that way, did you?" This time he did touch her, his finger searing her cheek. Her breath caught. She stared at him. For an instant they were entirely alone. She wanted him. He brought his hand down from her face.

She realized with a sudden sharp pang that her father would like Corin for his practicality. He would still haul her away.

"You just thought something sad," he said, his voice low.

She shook her head. "It's nothing."

After a pause, he said lightly, "I can take you to the kitchen if you really want it. But I wager you can't cook any better than I can."

"Can you cook at all?"

"Over a campfire. Does that count?"

"It's more than I can do," she admitted. She knew how to plan a meal within a budget, knew what was needed in what measures for many things, but the shopping and preparing were left to the cook. "On the other hand, I do know how to mix medicines."

"Well, then, you're not any more useless than I am," he said.

"Women are always more useful than men," she said, teasing back. Her imp took over, though it left her with enough discretion to whisper. "There's only one thing men care about, after all."

He raised his eyebrows at her. "I beg your pardon. Just who was so determined last evening?"

If she kept on she would dig herself into a very deep hole. "Never mind," she said, and blushed.

He was about to say something, but they both heard footsteps. It was a page with a sealed message for the prince. Tam watched

Corin read it. His face barely changed. He refolded it and slid it to her. The boy looked startled.

"If you can't hide surprise better than that you'll never be a good courtier," Corin said. Tam was sure he was deliberately not hiding his own impatience. "Go." He waved the boy away.

Tam waited until they were alone to read. It was abrupt. *Vielle has fallen. We must act now.* The capital of Argondy. Only the king would have written to him so. It had been a public gesture of trust to give her that message regardless of what it said. No wonder the boy had been startled.

She gave it back and said, "What does it mean will happen?" It did not seem real.

He picked the seal off and began to fold the paper into smaller and smaller squares. "I don't know yet," he said. "For you, maybe nothing. Don't go anywhere I can't find you. I will tell you as soon as I can." He drained his cup and set it down with a decisive motion. "Don't get up." He stood.

I love you, she thought at him.

His face softened. He leaned over and kissed her firmly and improperly on the lips. "Don't worry," he said.

She stayed a while longer, watching the movement of the sun on the grass, nibbling at the food. When she finished she wiped her face with the napkin until it had to be immaculate and made sure there were no crumbs on her dress before she stood. As soon as she left the room the gossip would spread like pox, she had never had to be more perfect. She would not subject herself to this for any other person.

The comb was only wood, but it was quite beautiful, glossy and reddish and finely grained. The handle was inset with a filigree of a running horse in gold. "When did he give you this?" Tam asked.

"Yesterday," Jenet answered.

"It will be a ring next."

"Do you really think so?"

"Yes. You have pretty hair, he must be desperate to touch it. Thus a comb."

Jenet looked happy, then said despairingly, "But sometimes he's so dull. How could I marry a man I couldn't talk to? I don't have to love my husband, but he shouldn't bore me. If I married him I should have to have ever so many scandalous affairs."

Jenet could not possibly mean the last sentence, she was far too proper, but Tam heard a real fear behind it. "Well, what have you tried to talk to him about?"

They were in Jenet's sitting room, all pale green and silver. Tam had a book with her, her place marked with the pass. The window was on the garden side of the palace, and birds were singing outside even though it was early afternoon and hot. They were drinking a sweet pink juice that had been iced; moisture was beading on the silver cups. Tam did not expect much of the answer; she remembered Darrin's tendency toward pompousness.

"Oh, he goes on at length about his land and his art collection and hunting. He has his county to administer, but he never talks about that. I imagine he thinks I would be bored or wouldn't understand. Every so often he asks me something about myself and then pays no attention to the answer. It's not so bad when we're alone, but that hardly ever happens."

"That doesn't sound promising," Tam admitted.

"I know," Jenet said, and lapsed into a glum silence.

"Suppose he's quite interesting in, well, other ways," Tam suggested slyly, to see what would happen. Then she remembered the night before and felt herself blush.

Jenet turned slightly pinker and covered her mouth, coughed. Although they were completely alone, she whispered, "He seems to, um, have potential."

"Is it a good enough match for him to be serious?"

"Yes."

"Then you shouldn't encourage him if you don't want to marry him," Tam said.

"I know. But aren't they all like that? How do you pick one over the other in the end?"

"Well, if you want to marry a rich man with a title you have to expect he will be most interested in himself. You have the leisure of falling in love afterward."

"Oh, Tam, don't say things like that, it's so melancholic."

"Who are his friends? Are they any better?" If they were all like the two bored young men she had met, there was not much hope in them either.

"A few. But none of them are half so good-looking."

"Can't you complain to one of them and see if Darrin gets the message? He may just be trying to impress you, you know."

"No," Jenet said. "Even if it were proper, I'm too bashful. I expect you could if you were in my place, you're much bolder."

"Perhaps I shall. I will dance with him and tell him everything he's doing wrong."

"No! Don't! You're not serious, are you?"

"Not unless you want me to be," Tam said, laughing. "It wouldn't likely do any good anyway, Jenet, he wouldn't listen to me. You'll just have to get him alone and be very interesting yourself. I'm sure he is trying his best for you."

"I hope so." She leaned forward and said, "And yourself? Are things quite all right between you and your own gentleman?"

"Quite," said Tam, thinking what an understatement it was. "He had some business to attend to this afternoon."

"He will be back for the ball, though?"

"Yes, though I may have to go down before him to watch the opening. Men always take longer than they think they will getting ready." She was becoming an experienced liar.

"That they do," said Jenet. She refilled their cups. "You're radiantly happy, you know. He must care for you tremendously."

Water bubbled outside somewhere. No one would ever think a war was coming. Tam had heard nothing further from Corin, which would worry her if she allowed herself to think too much on it.

"Is a ball at court much different from an ordinary ball?" she asked.

"The dances are the same," Jenet said. "And so are the rules. But it's grander. With Princess Tai not here it's anyone's guess who will be the darling of the ball."

Not me, Tam thought. She did not say it. Once she was seen with Corin her friendship would be worth cultivating. She thought of backing out. They had been seen last night in the halls, this morning in the Sun Room, but not by people who knew her name. After tonight everyone would know. She could not refuse to dance with other men lest she be seen either as haughtily proud or touchingly besotted. He had to know that. She remembered his hands on her last night and quickly sipped her drink.

Jenet said, "You're beautiful enough it could be you, you know."

"I hope not," Tam said, startled. "Perhaps I had better wear a sack."

"It wouldn't suit your coloring," Jenet said with a straight face.

Tam stared at her until she cracked and began to giggle. Tam said, "I didn't know you could be that droll. Does Darrin?"

"No."

"Show him. That will make him notice you. If he really loves you he will like it."

"You don't mean that."

"Of course I do. Then you'll find out if he wants you or just your property."

Jenet looked down. She had not said anything when Elyn darted in and said, "Beware, Alina's on her way to talk to you. Hello, Tam, I don't think you can run either."

As quickly as that she had moved from outside to inside, from stranger to conspirator. Alina was the common enemy. Had Jenet and Elyn always disliked her, or had there been a shift of allegiances?

But there was no way to escape Alina now. Jenet said, "Do join us, Elyn," and brought two more cups over to the low marble-topped table.

"That's killing the messenger, Jenet," said Tam, which brought a polite false gasp from Jenet and an impolite stifled laugh from Elyn.

Elyn sat down and adjusted her dress. "Are you getting ready for tonight yet, my dears?"

They spoke together, stopped. Before either of them could speak clearly again, Alina appeared. "My goodness, Elyn, you needn't have been in—" She saw Tam and stopped midsentence. "Tam, dear," she said, coming forward to peck her cheek. "How nice to see you." This despite having insinuated the night before that Tam's gentleman must be poor if he could offer nothing but a walk. (*There are some smaller theaters, you know, where one needn't pay as much.*) "I thought perhaps you were abandoning us forever last evening."

Tam said, "Oh, not at all." She resisted the impulse to give an explanation for anything or to rise to the suggestion of impropriety. She would try to be polite. "That's a lovely necklace you're wearing, is it new?"

It was in fact pretty, if ordinary—a delicate gold chain set with an occasional round diamond. A pendant with a very large diamond at the end hung several inches down. Quite the show of wealth. "Oh yes," Alina said, her hand coming up to touch the necklace. There was an incongruous bruise on the underside of her wrist. "It was a gift."

"From an admirer?"

Jenet nudged Tam as if to say, *Don't get her started*, but it was too late. "Yes. I do believe he is quite fond of me."

"I'm sure with very good reason," Tam said, unable to resist taking a page from Corin's book and sweeping her eyes up and down Alina's snug satin dress. Alina did not blush, if she even noticed. "Will he be escorting you tonight?"

"Yes. And yourself?"

Her good intentions disintegrated. "Your friend can hardly take both of us, I am afraid I will have to settle for someone lesser."

"Quite," said Alina coldly. She faced the others. "Jenet, may I ask your maid to do my hair? After she's done yours, of course? Mine just can't do the style I want for the ball without it going crooked."

"Certainly," Jenet said, sounding not at all certain.

"It must be dreadful to have a maid you can't rely on," Tam said. She knew it was a mistake to say it as the words came out.

"I can rely on her for most things. It's certainly better than having no maid at all."

"I won't argue your experience on that point," Tam said. She was going to have to leave before something worse rolled off her tongue.

Elyn hastily filled Alina's cup and said, "Who's to open the ball with the prince, do you know?" A harmless enough question and a reasonable change of subject. Tam prepared herself.

"I've no idea," Jenet said, sounding bored. "What did you ever do about your shoes, Elyn?"

Elyn refused to be distracted. "He breakfasted with someone in the Sun Room this morning. Not Seana, everyone knows it's over but her."

Tam wished Elyn would be quiet. Sooner or later she was going to say something Tam didn't want to hear. It wouldn't even necessarily be about Corin; Elyn was the sort of person who delighted in recounting the embarrassments of others.

"Who?" asked Alina.

"My friend didn't know her. And of course he couldn't describe her, he's a man. Apparently Corin is quite smitten. My friend said he kissed her right there."

Tam expected to see anger or jealousy or maybe even hurt on Alina's face. Instead, the expression that flickered across before it was covered by unconcern was fear. It puzzled her so much that she did not even have to suppress her own reaction to Elyn's statement.

She stood up as Elyn said, "They didn't come together, though." The room was getting stuffy with four people in it. She opened the window a few inches wider to let in more breeze, warm though it was, and leaned out briefly before returning to her seat.

Elyn said, "Are you going to be exclusive to your friend, Alina, or will you dance with others?"

"That will depend on who asks me," Alina answered with her too-bright smile. "And yourself?"

"Oh goodness, what's the fun in dancing with just one man?" She sighed. "The best dancers aren't always the best-looking. I may have to toss a coin. What about you, Tam? Are you going to try to keep your secret by dancing with a dozen different men?"

"That's an excellent idea," Tam said. "Will you line them up for me?"

Elyn and Jenet both laughed, and Jenet said, "Which dress will you wear?"

"The blue one, with the seed pearl trim," she answered, thankful for an innocuous topic. She reached for her drink.

"Rose is much more fashionable this year," remarked Alina. "As a color, not in hair." Tam nearly knocked over the cup with suppressing her laughter.

"Rose doesn't match my eyes," she said. She saw a page at the door. The boy could not have picked a better time.

His message was for Jenet. She turned color as she read it. "He wants a private interview after the first dance," she said when she was done.

"Lucky girl," Elyn said, embracing her.

They were still exclaiming about it when a soldier appeared at the door. He was dressed in a formal uniform, not the usual plain attire of the men on duty. Everyone went unnaturally silent. Tam hoped fervently that he would not single her out. But if he was not bringing a message from Corin for her, it could only be something worse.

He said, "My ladies, His Majesty commands you to the Great Hall at once to hear him speak." He bowed and departed before any of them replied.

Tam did not join in the rush of speculation that followed. She knew what it was about. *Vielle has fallen.* The war was going to be declared. She picked up her book.

"Oh," said Alina, "that's yours. Are commoners allowed to take things out now? I hadn't heard."

Jenet and Elyn went silent. Tam said, "You're hanging by a thread, Alina, don't push me any further. Thank you for the hospitality, Jenet." She stalked out.

Tam was still seething when she reached the Great Hall. It was already full and getting fuller. Not just with courtiers, either—there were servants and clerks and various officials packed together in the back. The doors were flung wide-open, letting air move. There seemed to be guards everywhere. The ceiling shone with iridescence that moved across the surface like oil on water. The floor and lower part of the walls were a handsome pale marble, the upper part of the walls pearly gold paint. Banners, bright and forceful, hung from the balcony. On the floor underneath it the eagle crest of the royal house had been worked in tile. It was not a room for casual chitchat. She wondered how old it was.

She did not see anyone she knew, although there were faces she recognized. On the balcony above a number of soldiers were standing very alertly. Bron was among them. He raised his hand ever so slightly, gesturing her toward the nearest door, then stepped back out of her sight. She went to the door and stood as inconspicuously out of the way as possible, not too close to the guards. Cina came in from the opposite side but was talking to someone and did not appear to see Tam.

A few minutes later a page came by and quickly, without lingering, put a message into her hand. It was as discreet as it could be, she supposed.

The message was not in Corin's hand, but the words were his. *You needn't stay. But if you do, come to the robing room afterward.* It had an obviously hasty seal on it. In case a guard wanted to send her away, no doubt. Or keep her from leaving.

She looked around and saw that Cina had spotted her. She acknowledged her with a small nod. Too many people stood between them for either to make her way easily to the other. But it meant she could not very well walk out. Cina would want to talk to her afterward, she would have to explain about that too. Word had to have made it to Cina by now that Tam was seeing somebody. Well, perhaps it didn't matter if she found out here instead of at the ball. It would save a scene. She sighed too audibly.

People were talking to one another in low voices; the seriousness of what was happening had permeated them. She was near the front, only a few rows of people ahead of her, and the presence of the guards at the door had thinned the space. No one wanted to be close to an armed man. She could see the balcony perfectly.

Bron caught her eye again. He was, she realized, observing the people near her very acutely. Guarding her. She would have liked to draw back into the crowd and watch with ordinary anonymity, but she was quite certain she was not supposed to. It could hardly be done inconspicuously now. She was standing close to the coronation portrait of Aram; when she looked at it this time, she saw innocence. Corin looked much more like the Aram she had met than he did like that young man who had been crowned.

At last, when Tam was beginning to seriously consider taking Corin's offer and leaving regardless of what Cina thought, a deep bell was gonged. Feet stopped shuffling, voices quieted. Tam did not want to see what came next, to watch Corin be formal and powerful. Oh, you fool, she thought to herself.

The ritual caught her anyway. She stared upward as everyone else did when the Lord Marshal was announced, the prince, the queen, the king. Talia stayed back. Tam heard someone mutter, "Not an engagement, then." The queen wore a formal and ornate dark red gown. Both Corin and his father were robed but Corin was bareheaded. Aram was not. Instead of the heavily jeweled helmetlike affair that was a state crown he wore something simpler, closer to a coronet. It conveyed the gravity of the situation quite as well.

Tam let Aram's words roll over her without listening much. She heard enough to realize he spoke only of the Sarians with not a word about the Emperor. It was an omission that she understood, since Corin had told her that Hadon almost certainly wanted him dead, but it made her tense. She did not need Corin to know that without Mycene they were doomed. Nor could she be the only one there to realize that. *What about Hadon?* would be the first question on the lips of many. She was glad she would not have to answer that. It was not the only thing he was not saying, either.

Most people were listening with quiet respect. Not much fear, which was a good thing. The glow and movement of light on the ceiling shifted and responded to Aram's voice. She wondered if it was something he could control at will, choosing when to shadow his words and when to bare them to brightness. The people around her did not seem at all aware of it.

She compared this king with the one she had seen two nights ago. He was more untouchable here; she would have controlled her imp and never dared to say the things she did if he had been like this then. If she had seen him like this first, she might have controlled her imp better around Corin as well. It was a far cry from the man who had given her a cup of tea and clapped her on the back. She shivered a little, realizing the extent of that familiarity. And trust.

Twice her eyes met Corin's. Neither of them held it. Both times she was intensely aware that he wanted her with him. He seemed as calm and poised as his father, sober but confident of victory. It was very well acted. The second time she saw the flame and shadow around him, the dragon shape, heat and light. They had possession of him. She shifted uneasily.

Pain seized her, sharp and sudden, as though her whole body had been ripped open, and then was gone, lightning-fast. Sweat stood out on her brow, and her hands had gone white. Her mouth tasted metallic, like blood. She wiped her forehead and watched the color returning to her fingers. In some other world there had been an arrow, or an earthquake, or a spell, and the course of events diverged irrevocably from now. Black moths, colored sand. A cold dark thing trying to get out. Wings flapped, claws scratched. Urgency that was not quite panic filled her, and she looked up at Aram, imploring him to finish soon. Their eyes met but he gave no outward sign of having seen her and continued speaking.

When the king ended his gaze swept the room evenly. He turned. It was over.

People were moving around. Cina left through another door. Tam stepped into the corridor and showed the note and seal to a guard. He gave her directions.

Even so, it took her a few minutes and she hoped she was not too late. The guards at the door to the robing room scrutinized both her and the seal much more carefully, and one took the note in while she waited. She decided it was an opportunity to practice looking dignified. The guard returned shortly, gave her back the note, and admitted her.

Corin was waiting. His robe was off, and he looked like himself again. To Tam's relief, Aram was already gone. Then she saw the queen. Her stomach sank.

Corin held out his hand. Tam was tempted to hit him, but she took his hand instead. He squeezed it, smiled at her, and led her to the queen. She wasn't just the queen, she was his mother, damn it, it would be impossible to please her.

Now is not the time to fall apart, Tam thought. Corin let go of her and stepped back. When Talia met her eyes, she curtsied and said in a blessedly steady voice, "Your Majesty."

"Tam Warin," the queen said. Her eyes were the same shape and color as Corin's, though her hair was fair. She was a few inches shorter than Tam. She said, in a quite ordinary tone, "I've heard quite a bit about you."

"Oh no," Tam said, before she could stop herself.

"All of it favorable, I might add."

"Thank you, my lady."

"The king is not easily impressed."

"I would hope he isn't," Tam said. Was she never going to learn?

Talia laughed. Then, seriously, she said, "You were in the audience. How was the speech received?"

This was a test. There would be no punishment if she failed, but Corin would be disappointed. She would not look at him for support, she would not. She straightened and said, choosing her words precisely, "I think the danger is well understood, but no one is terrified. But tomorrow, after people have had a chance to think it over and they really see the urgency, there are going to be a lot of questions."

"About what?"

She remembered going with her father to treat people after fire tore through half a block of houses. The people who were uninjured sat on the street, staring numbly into the ruins of their homes, their lives forever altered. She said, "Most of them will be the usual questions. Where do we go, what do we do." She hesitated, gambled. "But then they will start wondering why we are in this alone. And what else is there that they haven't been told."

Talia nodded. "If you start to hear enough of those, let us know. Any of us, even Aram." She looked past Tam to Corin. It was as though they were continuing a conversation they had started earlier. Then she said, "I won't impose on my son's patience any longer. But I do hope to speak with you again soon."

"Whenever you wish, my lady," Tam said.

"May I give you a piece of advice about the ball tonight?"

"Of course."

"Drink plenty of water. It will help." She walked past Tam, said to Corin, "Don't be late," and left the room.

As soon as the door was shut, Tam turned on Corin and said, with more irritation than she meant in her voice, "You should have warned me." It was better than she had expected, but all she could think of was what she should have done.

"If I had warned you, you would have worried."

Sometimes she hated it when he was right. "Did I pass?"

"Of course you did, love," he said. "She likes you."

"How can you tell?"

"She used my father's name, not his title." He drew her in and put his arms around her. His body felt good against hers. Passion roused in her, then settled. A faint smell of metal clung to him from the cloth of gold. It made her think of dragons. She wished she and Corin could vanish.

"Corin," she said, "something happened, or didn't."

"What do you mean?" He was plainly thinking of something else.

"It was not here. I don't know." She had no words to describe what she had sensed while Aram spoke. There was a badness somewhere. She should not distract him from thinking about the war with her imaginings. "Why didn't you cancel the ball?"

"There's nothing we can do, Tam, they may as well have their last pleasure. It will be different after the Sarians cross the border." He kissed her. Then he added, somewhat grimly, "And you're right.

Once they start asking questions, nothing will get done. I need them to be distracted a while longer."

There it was, the hard side of him. She was going to have to get used to it.

"How much time is there?"

"Two or three weeks if the Sarians come by foot. Much less if they ride. We aren't going to keep people here, but I don't want them to panic. They can start leaving tomorrow, peacefully. Except for the ones who would go east."

"What about me?"

"I won't send you away sooner than I have to. But when it's time, you need to go." He touched her cheek. "Tam, things are going to change for you after tonight. Especially with a declared war. Are you sure you want me to come with you?"

"Things already have changed," she said. "What difference does the war make?"

"It's going to drag you in. A thousand people are going to want to know if you know my secrets. Some will be curious, some will be spies. If I am with you during a war, they will know you are not a passing fancy. They may even try to get through you to my father. It could be horrible. I don't want you to endure that needlessly."

The apprehension in her belly told her it could easily lead to a quarrel if she answered thoughtlessly now. "Is it better for you if we keep things as they are?"

"It doesn't weigh to one side or the other for me," he said. "My duties won't change. But I don't want you to be between me and all the arrows coming. There will be a lot."

"I can manage," she said. Alina's jealousy seemed petty and far away now. But with a pang she realized how little time they had actually had together. "You've been in a rush all day, Corin, is it going to be better tomorrow?"

"Unlikely. Why?"

"You've told me what's happened, but we haven't really talked about it. Or how it plays out. I can take the questions and the gossip and the prying, but I might make a disastrous mistake if I don't know more. I don't know whom to trust or not. You can't just keep warning me away from people."

"I'll find you the time for that somehow. You deserve it. You need it." He kissed her lightly. "I have to go," he said. "I'll come get you a little before time."

Time can trap you, she thought, wind around things as transparent as glass and strong as steel and before you know it you're caught. Nothing moves. It mattered terribly but was unchangeable.

She watched him walk away with a straight back and rapid pace. She suspected he was already thinking of something else. She wanted to run after him, to warn him of danger, but he knew as much as she did. She could do nothing but stay wary herself.

CHAPTER ELEVEN

⁓⁕⁓

am had eaten a light dinner when the maid arrived, with a quick curtsy and a statement that "Her Majesty would like me to help you with anything you need, my lady." Tam's experiences with someone dressing her in the past had been with foolish-seeming girls who chattered and gossiped endlessly, asking questions and never waiting for an answer, while they pulled strings and curled hair with efficient graceless force. This woman was young but otherwise entirely different; her voice was more educated, and her attention was absolute. She had brought scented soaps for Tam to use in bathing, stones to scrub off rough skin on her feet and hands, and handsome and strong hairpins. She adjusted stays and laces with such skill that Tam, who had worn the gown before, was stunned to see how differently she wore it now. The neckline was trimmed with a stiff and heavy brocaded silk that had chafed her skin in the past; the maid's adjustments revealed that it was meant to stand up instead of lying flat, moving subtly with her breath to suggest fullness across the breasts. When the maid had finished with Tam's hair there might have been two score pins in it, but Tam could not feel any of them, and her hair looked glossy and alive. Troublesome strands that could not be pinned up were curled to the perfect balance between girlishness and enticement. The maid reddened Tam's lips and rouged her cheeks (*Just a little, m'lady, you do have nice color already*), lined her eyes at the outer corners, and added a little powder to the lids that was invisible when on but which changed the shape of her eyes to something more almond. When the maid held up the looking-glass, Tam saw a stranger, beautifully soft with a suggestion of alluring knowledge.

"He's not going to recognize me," she said, feeling both slightly foolish and delighted.

"He's not going to be able to keep his eyes off you," said the maid. "Nor will the other gentlemen, if I may say so."

"You're a magician."

"There's other girls I could work on for hours who I could never get to look like this," she said wryly. "And they couldn't wear a dress that simple at all."

Tam liked the gown and was glad that it was good enough. It was a shimmering sapphire-blue silk woven with contrasting threads to make it look gold when the light struck it a certain way. There were no crystals or lace trim. It had off-the-shoulder sleeves, a bodice and waist embroidered in thread of the same color, and a sweeping skirt cut at an angle to the weave, making the shifting colors of the silk a contrast to the darker-seeming bodice. The hems were all edged with seed pearls. It was light and comfortable, for a gown.

She made sure her shoes were not too slick-soled or high-heeled for dancing, then thanked the maid and settled down to wait. It was close to time, but she was afraid to move much, lest something wrinkle or fall irreparably. For a while the hallway outside was loud with the voices of other women moving about, laughing. Briefly she considered joining them, but she thought she would be too easily rattled if she saw Alina. Jenet and the impending proposal could have the stage.

Fortunately for her nerves, she did not wait long before a boy appeared and told her Corin was ready. She followed him out of the wing, passing several waiting gentlemen, who stared, to a small side chamber not far away.

"My God. Look at you." He came forward and kissed her, quite lightly, obviously wanting to avoid smearing the lip color. "I have something for you. And it's a loan, not a gift, so don't get all prideful and refuse to wear it."

It was a diamond necklace, each stone as clear and colorless and sparkling as a diamond could be. She stood still while he clasped it around her neck.

"I'm really allowed to wear this?" she asked. "It's not a royal heirloom reserved for state occasions?"

"It's not," he said. "It was a gift to my sister Mari from a suitor she later rejected. He refused to take it back. My sisters and mother pass it back and forth between them. Mother suggested you wear it."

"I take it I passed highly," she said. "Are you ready? I thought you would be longer coming."

"I'm going to shock everyone by being early," he said. "Unless you want to vanish with me into an empty room and keep me there long enough to preserve my reputation? They can't start without me." His forefinger slipped under the edge of her gown.

She pulled it out. "You have to wait, my lord," she said primly. "Who are you going to open with?"

He took her arm as they left the room. "Should I leave you guessing? You still have time to place a few bets. Not you, don't worry. You should dance with whomever you wish."

"Tell me. Then I won't hate her at once."

"I thought you didn't want to open."

"I don't. That doesn't mean I want someone else to. It's all right, Corin, I'm not really going to hate anyone." She squeezed his arm.

"Well, in this case I most certainly don't want you to. It couldn't be better," he said. "Mari arrived late this afternoon. I'll dance with her, and no woman can feel that I've passed her over for some more beautiful potential bride."

"But wasn't she—isn't she—her husband—"

He understood. "She told me it was better than sitting alone and thinking. He's not far behind her."

"You're sure?" She did not think she could dance with anyone, even her brother, if she were in that situation, wondering where her husband was, when he would come, if he was safe.

"It was her idea."

She felt more grateful than she should have at the thought that no one would wonder if he meant anything by his choice. It sent a signal that he did not want to honor any woman there, but it could not offend them or provoke them to come second place to his sister. "You should do that for every ball," she said. "Keep yourself away from the battlefield."

"You do have little faith in your own fair sex. Where did you acquire this belief that all women are armed to the tooth against each other?"

"They aren't, all the time. But when the stakes are high enough they are, and how could the stakes be higher than here? Don't tell me you don't know that."

"I've taken myself out of the game," he said, a bit fiercely. "There's only you."

Oh, love, she thought, the game goes on, I can't drop out that easily and neither can you. "Who is Seana?" It slipped out, a childish question, one that should have turned to ash with what he had just said. She was ashamed of herself.

"A mistake," he said.

"Why?"

"For several reasons. She came to me the night I returned from the north, and I sent her away. Don't be jealous."

"I'm not," she said, though it was not entirely true. He was done with the woman, it was obvious, but she envied the past. "Why didn't you tell me?" To her relief, her tone was only mildly curious.

"I suppose I assumed you knew. Most everyone does. They probably know I sent her away, too. It's nothing you should concern yourself with, she isn't the type to be vengeful. If she's there tonight she'll be civilized. I'm not proud of it, but there's no reason it needs to dog either of us. It's over." He pressed her hand.

Tam glanced around. They were alone. She stopped him long enough to kiss him. Then she had to find a handkerchief to wipe the color off his lips, and he had to dab at the skin around her mouth. The suggestion of an empty room was tempting, but she was afraid that if she said it neither of them would stop the other, which really should not happen. She realized, surprised, that she was happy.

When they came to a flight of steps beside a balcony, he paused. Below, many men and women, colorful and elegant, were walking across a wide hall. She could have spent time just watching from above. Somewhere close musicians were tuning their instruments. "The entrance to the ballroom is through there," he said, gesturing downward.

She took a step forward, stopped. "I don't even know what I am to call you."

"You've already made 'Highness' into a parody," he said drily. "What's left? 'Your Gracelessness'?"

She blushed.

"Don't worry," he said, kissing her forehead. "It would matter if it were politics or diplomacy or a High Court. It's not, it's a ball." He made an amused sort of noise. "You should be able to entertain yourself highly while they try to figure out what to call you. Do be nice about it, though, will you?"

"I'll try," she said. "This sort of thing always makes me devilish, I don't know why."

"Because you get bored with people less clever than yourself, which is most everybody," he said. "I will do my best not to abandon you to them too much. The first dance, clearly, and I will certainly be ambushed several times by politickers. But that should be it."

"You wouldn't know what to do with yourself if you had nothing but pleasure to think of."

"You're right," he said. "It's an irremediable character defect. Come, let's go in."

The ballroom was splendidly lit, very crowded, and insufferably hot. Tam had a moment of unreasoning panic, fear that she might get lost or sucked away. She gripped Corin's hand and felt her palm sweating. It was hard to breathe. She understood Talia's advice about drinking plenty of water. The sound of voices was a loud roar. She tried to ignore the people looking at them and hoped there was no one she knew.

"Here," he said, almost pushing her into a cushioned chair against the wall. "Sit. It should be better soon, it always crowds up by the entrance at the beginning. When music starts people thin out. I have to go find Mari, will you be all right here? Do you want to come with me? Should I find you a partner?"

"I'll stay here," she said, with a forced smile. "Until you come. I'll be fine, it was just so hot there." He squeezed her hand, then disappeared into the press of dark-clothed men and wide-skirted ladies. It was only a ball, she had been to balls before.

It could not have been more than a minute before a young and fairly good-looking man appeared beside her. "Are you unaccompanied, my lady? Might I have the honor of the first dance?"

"I'm sorry, sir," she said, and felt the impishness begin to rise. "I am already engaged, my partner has just had to step away."

"A later one then?"

"Perhaps. If you might ask me then?"

"Of course, of course." He kissed her hand, bowed, and walked away.

One.

The next man was average-looking, blond, about forty, not fat yet but headed inexorably there. He wore a heavy ring on his right hand that suggested considerable wealth. He bowed before speaking and said, "I would be most delighted if I might have the honor of your company as the ball begins, my lady." He sounded powerful; his voice had the inflections of high rank.

"I regretfully must decline, my lord," she said, "as I have already been engaged for the first three dances."

"I will take the fourth," he said, in the tone of one who is used to receiving what he demands. She had never heard Corin use that voice, not even to servants. It riled her.

"I'm afraid that will not be possible, your lordship," she said. She shouldn't, she shouldn't. But the words would not stay back. "I've just decided to give it to the first gentleman who asks me courteously."

His face darkened, and he turned stiffly away. Several men standing nearby laughed.

Two.

It was another minute or so before the third one appeared. He was so young and awkward that she felt sorry for him, and refused as gently as she could.

The fourth man was Therry, who was clearly expecting to be turned down but said it never hurt to ask. She spoke briefly with him, then sent him on his way. He joined Darrin and Jenet farther down the hall. Jenet gave Tam a rueful smile, shrugging her shoulders. It could not have been clearer that she had told him not to bother. Tam wondered if Jenet had already seen her with Corin. Likely not.

The fifth one was more clever, which was all that saved him from a snapped reply; she wanted to be left alone by now. She should have gone with Corin, he could have found an innocuous partner for her. If only the music would start.

This man was handsome and obviously of high rank, but his tone was friendly and not arrogant as he said, "May I inquire as to your intentions for the sixth dance, my lady?"

"The *sixth*?"

"You have been turning away all who asked for your company, my lady. Including His Grace the Duke of Dele, who has probably not been rejected for years. I therefore assume that I would also be rejected for the first few dances, for whatever the reason. But you might not yet be engaged for the sixth one."

"Well . . ." she said, even as she was thinking in a panic that she had insulted the Duke of Dele, which could cause trouble for Corin. On the other hand, this man seemed to approve of it. And other men had laughed, perhaps the duke had no real power here. She knew from her brother that he had no real power in Dele either.

Carefully, she said, "I do not have the honor of knowing your lordship by face. May I in turn inquire as to whom I would be dancing with?"

"Or rejecting? Mattan of Harin."

Another duke. But considerably more polite. She said, "Sir, the truth is that I am engaged for the entire evening. But I will happily give you a dance in spite of this if you will help me fend off any other askers."

He laughed. "Done. If I just sit down . . ."

"I think that would help a great deal."

"And your partner, why has he left you here to myself and the other wolves? Do not tell me he has been such a cad as to abandon you."

"I don't believe he expected there to be quite so many," she said honestly.

"He must be young. A beautiful face that has not been seen before is to men as a candle-flame to moths," he said.

For just an instant she remembered the darkness fluttering out of Cade's mouth. Her skin pricked. But she could not think about such things now. It was the ball, and a duke was waiting for her to introduce herself. Mattan had probably made the comment a dozen times to other women, and she thought cynically that it was the diamond necklace that really drew the men. Best to disillusion him at once.

She said, "I hope they would not be too disappointed to learn a face is all I have to give them, my lord, whether they are wolves or moths. I've no title at all."

"That need not be a concern at a mere ball," he said. He took her hand and kissed it, his dark eyes sparkling. Damn. "You do have a name?"

"Tam Warin, my lord." She said it with downcast eyes. She had trapped herself by her own request, but she could perhaps be less interesting. She hoped Corin would not see. Why had she come for the first dance at all?

"Tam. Liddean, isn't it?"

"Indeed, sir." A sustained measure of music finally came.

"I hate to see you sitting here alone for the first dance."

"In truth, my lord, as this is my first ball here, I very much wish to watch. There are so many people I do not know yet. Perhaps you will tell me who is who." Then her tongue betrayed her again. "Unless there is a lady who might think you a cad for abandoning her?"

"I don't have a chance with you, do I?" he said cheerfully.

"Not a bit," Tam said, relieved. There was no displeasure or seriousness on his face.

"He's a lucky man. Well, if I can't charm you I can at least entertain you. But I have to warn you that I don't know all the current scandals."

And then there was a real swell of music, and the talking quieted, and the people standing found chairs or leaned out of the way against the wall. The ball had begun.

It was beautiful in its way, the perfect circles each couple made as they traveled the larger circle, and the colorful wide sweeping circles of the skirts. The lights were low and golden, the music rich and resonant. Corin was a good dancer, and she would have enjoyed watching him if she had not even known him. His sister was better, but he kept up with her. They looked very much alike. Mari, much to Tam's self-righteous pleasure, wore a deep green gown without the slightest hint of rose. She was tall also, though fair-haired. Corin kept his attention focused on his sister and did not look in Tam's direction at all.

Mattan turned out to be a useful companion, as he knew who almost everybody was. If he did not know all the current scandals he certainly knew many of the old ones, and he could be delightfully caustic. Now that he had stopped seducing her, she found that she liked him. He pointed out an attractive red-haired woman dancing with a much older man, smiling falsely. "There's a scandal in the making," he said. "Duke Simoun and his wife Seana. Now that she's been dropped by His Highness, she's going to have to look elsewhere, and she's not going to find anyone else who can get around the duke so well."

"Dropped?" she asked, knowing she should not. She was afraid of hearing something that would taint Corin for her, even if she did not believe it.

"With a crash. There's Corin now, with his sister. He's getting slipperier every year."

Tam changed the subject somehow, then looked for other people she knew. Cina, having an absent husband, was sitting on the other side of the room speaking with several other women. The young married women whose husbands were not present would dance later, with very carefully selected partners. Jenet and Darrin were dancing with each other as though they were the only people in the room. They both looked very young. Alina was dancing with a dark-haired, thin-faced, handsome man, who had his hand lower on her waist than he should have.

He turned his head. Tam met his eyes. They burned into her. He hits her, she thought. She looked away quickly. "Who is that?" she asked Mattan.

He frowned. "Arnet. A girl that young should avoid him. I hope she has a friend to warn her. He's only a baron, but he has plenty of power."

Corin had warned her against him, but he had been vague. Seeing him, she had no need for the warning. She hoped he would not remember her. Alina would point her out, though, there was no chance of being ignored. "Why should she stay away from him?"

"He'll use her until he's bored, then cast her off with nothing. There's four girls I can think of without even trying who made much poorer marriages than they should have because they let him have them first."

She wondered how much "letting" was involved, but she was not about to argue such things with him now. Alina, that fool, would play right into his hands. That kind of girl always did; she had seen enough of them begging her father for help. Then it occurred to her that Alina might know exactly what she was doing. She looked again at Arnet and tried to imagine him in a rainy courtyard at night. Perhaps. He was tall enough. She would have to see him walk.

She could not discuss that with Mattan, though. "What if she made that mistake with some other man?"

"If he was a proper lover, no one would ever know. And even if it came out, he'd only need to pay for her to go abroad for a year in high style, and by the time she came back it would all have been 'forgotten.' That's not Arnet's way. He's cruel to his tenants, too."

That would be why Corin had called him vicious. It did not reassure her.

Mattan added, "His wife was found hanged a few years back. He killed her one way or the other, and everyone knows it. If she really did commit suicide, he drove her to it. Is that girl a friend of yours?"

"Not a friend, only an acquaintance I don't much care for. But I don't wish her harm."

"Someone else will have to charm her away from him," he remarked. "She'd probably end up with a broken heart, but that will have to happen sometime, won't it."

"I'd advise you not to try it yourself, my lord," she said. "You'd tire of her in about two minutes and it would take much longer to shake her off."

"Pity," he said. "She's got quite a nice figure."

Was that all men thought about? With Alina, however, that was all she wanted them to think about.

When the dance ended, Corin was somewhere at the top of the room. She stood up. It felt too conspicuous to wait for him. "If you will excuse me, my lord," she said. "I have enjoyed our conversation."

"I as well," he said. "If your gentleman does turn out a cad, I should like to be the first to tell him so."

The floor was crowded enough that she was afraid the next dance would begin before she reached him. But when she had finally curtsied and smiled and excused her way through, it had not.

He was talking to someone, and she watched a moment, enjoying looking at him when he was not aware of her. There was what she expected was a usual cluster of men around him, wineglasses in their hands, their voices confident and loud. All the worry she had felt earlier came rushing back.

He turned, saw her. His face lit up like a boy's, and he passed his glass off to another man without even looking at him. She felt a surge of love. When they met he moved her expertly into the dance circle; the music started before they had time to say more than a few commonplace things to each other.

They were observed. It made her nervous and she missed a step. He said, "Don't mind them."

"How did you know?"

"Because they're always there. Like flies, circling, buzzing close when they get a chance. Difficult to swat."

She took some time to answer, said, "That sounds a lot like a whine, Corin."

"I suppose it was." He did not sound repentant. But after a few more beats he said, seriously, "You're right. I will do better." Then he smiled at her, that soft sweet smile of his, and she found herself melting.

She was careful not to stare too long into his eyes, that was too intimate for public. His hand was firm and warm against her back. He did not say much, just looked at her.

"You know," she said, "I loved you from the moment I saw you, before I even knew who you were."

"When was that?"

"When you came back from the north. You were very muddy. I thought you were a soldier."

"How long was it before you were disillusioned?"

"Seconds. I was disappointed."

"You aren't now, are you?" he asked. "If you prefer me muddy I can oblige."

"That won't be necessary," she said, smiling, laughing, full of wanting. They touched each other but were so far apart in the formal positions.

Corin said, "Do you like Mattan?"

"I didn't know you saw."

"I notice most things," he said, and there was something quite serious about it. His eyes must be busy constantly, so he was not caught by surprise, so he could adjust to the smallest changes before others did. It seemed a hard way to live.

"He made himself very agreeable," she said. "I liked him. But I don't know if I would trust him with anything I cared much about. He seemed impulsive."

"I have that feeling too. But in all fairness to him, he's never given me reason for it. He's got his province well in hand and prosperous. His villagers like him, and so do his barons, which is not an easy combination to achieve." His eyes reminded her that war was on its way. And Harin would take the first blows.

"He's clever. I promised him a dance." She told of their bargain.

He said, "You realize he got the better of you, don't you?"

"How so?"

"He would have stayed talking to you and keeping the others away even if you hadn't said you would dance. The art of power, my love, is making people give you something for nothing and think they are being rewarded in the process. He's quite good at it."

It sounded very cold. She remembered again that she had seen only the gentler side of him.

"And you haven't learned yet how much power you have," he added. "You are so astonishingly beautiful that he would easily have given you something for nothing."

"I'm not going to manipulate people like that!"

"No. You're direct and forthright. You would rather win with logic than anything else. But if you stay with me, people will try to manipulate you, and you have to be able to defend yourself. You're going to have to behave in ways you don't like, Tam."

She knew he was right. That was what he meant about her having political value. It would have been better to stay hidden. They were already past the freedom of just loving. "You don't mind about it, do you?" she asked uncertainly.

"About the dance? No. And if I did, it wouldn't signify. I'm not your master, Tam. You make your own choices. I don't need to be jealous." He smiled his own most sly smile and said, "Besides, I'll enjoy watching you."

"I'm sure you won't be the only one," she said, and saw that her dig had been quite as effective as his. "You can't monopolize me, you know."

"I can and I will," he said, still grinning. "What's the use of rank and power if not for that? You haven't made any other bad bargains, have you?"

"No." Then she remembered. "Worse. Oh, Corin, I made an awful mistake. I was rude to the Duke of Dele."

"You were rude to the Duke of Dele." His tone gave no hint as to whether he was angry.

"I didn't know he was the duke, I do have more sense than that."

"But you did mean to be rude, no doubt?"

"I couldn't help it. I very politely told him that I was engaged for the first three dances, and he demanded the fourth. So I said I had decided to give it to a gentleman."

He stifled a laugh. "Did anyone else hear?"

"A number of people, I think."

"When that gets around you are going to be the most popular person at court," he said. "He's an arrogant bastard who needs to be taken down every so often. But Tam, despite that, you have to be more careful."

"I know," she said, looking down. It was a well-deserved rebuke. "What should I do?"

"Don't worry about it at this point. You can give him a polite and proper and sincere apology tomorrow after he's had time to cool off. Just don't do it again."

"I won't," she promised. "Is he going to think you put me up to it?"

"I doubt it. He knows me well enough to know I don't work that way. When you talk to him, be careful not to make excuses or blame a wayward tongue. As soon as you start explaining yourself he has you in his power. Just apologize."

"I can't give myself airs," she said. "He outranks me."

"Not now he doesn't," he said. "Not in society. You needn't be arrogant, Tam, but keep your dignity."

"What dignity?" she asked.

He grinned. "Don't try to tell me you have no dignity. Or pride. I know you better than that." He lifted his hand partway off her back, then brought it back down, obviously recollecting the formality. "That doesn't mean you can't enjoy yourself, even here."

She nodded. Best to let it go. "You dance well."

"You're better," he said.

"It's my cloven hooves," she replied. He laughed and spun her into the outer circle, where the couples moved more rapidly, and by the time it had ended they were both breathing hard. Tam felt nervously at her hair, but it all seemed to be in place.

They danced the next two, more slowly, talking less, looking more. She saw Elyn, who gave her a most unladylike gesture of success, and Cina, well composed. Seana watched with a thoughtful face. Tam made herself meet the duchess's eyes. There was no overt hostility in them.

After the dance ended Corin said, "You've done three rounds, you should sit down. I'll bring you a drink." They were beside a guarded entrance, and he made a sign with his hand, quick, unobtrusive.

Her feet were indeed beginning to hurt, so she sat and hoped to be left alone. But there was an empty chair next to her, and he had not been gone more than a few seconds before it was filled by Cina.

Cina looked around, then said in a low but intense voice, "What are you doing, Tam? You're going to disgrace both of us."

"Then many of the women in this room are also disgraceful. I'm not doing anything I should not be doing."

"That is not so, as you well know. It's wholly improper. And imprudent. You're being taken advantage of."

"So I'm a fool and he's a selfish knave?" She restrained herself from saying what Corin would think of that; it would only make things worse.

"No," Cina said patiently. "But you're young, Tam, you're not acquainted with the ways of the world. Or with the ways of the court. You're beautiful, of course he wants you. That means you have to be all the more careful. One dance is enough. Three is far too many. If this continues I shall have to tell Efan."

Tam had had this conversation so many times in her head that she had no trouble controlling her temper. "Cina, I know you are trying to do your duty by me, and for me. And I grant that with any other man you would be right. But not this time."

"If you don't stop people will think he means to take you to bed after the ball, you don't have a chance at anything else. Give it up before you're ruined."

It's too late for that, she thought. Fortunately it stayed behind her lips. "Cina, please. Leave it for tonight and let him talk to you tomorrow. You can write to my brother after that if you still need to." She had hoped not to have to involve Corin. It was hardly fair to Cina, who was only doing as she had promised she would, and it was a burden on him. But she did not know what other choice she had.

"Why ever would he talk to me? I don't hold him accountable for flirting."

"Because it's not flirting. I've dined with him several times already."

"Tam, how far has this gone?"

She should tell her what Aram had said. It was too difficult. "Far enough to know he's not going to seduce me and leave me. He's been scrupulous."

"You're very sure of yourself."

"I'm very sure of him."

Cina looked at her, hard. "Did he give you that necklace? It's not paste, is it?"

"It's a loan," Tam said. She could not keep herself from continuing. "From the queen."

"The *queen*?"

"Yes. She offered it."

Cina was not a person who fidgeted, put her hands out of place, showed nervousness of any sort. She did not do anything of the kind now. Her face was still, composed. She said, "Tam, be careful. Love can be a will-o'-the-wisp for the best of men. You've no future with him. I'll give you one day. If I'm not satisfied with what I hear by this time tomorrow, I will write to Efan, or send you home. You aren't a fool, but you're doing a very foolish thing." She stood up.

Tam hardly heard what came after Cina said her brother's name. Instead her mind was full with a sudden image of a Mycenean ship docking in the dark night and soldiers descending the ramps, swords out. Lantern light broke and reformed on the waves. She was sure it was true. It would have frightened her if she had not been so concerned for Efan. "Cina, wait," she said hastily, rising.

"What else is there?"

"Write to him now. Tell him to leave Dele." She realized she was holding her wrist. Nothing hurt, but her body remembered the tray at the fair.

Cina stepped closer and lowered her voice. Tam had to lean in to hear it over the music and talk. "What do you mean?"

"Please. It's the war. It will come there, he has to get out." *Ten thousand soldiers sailing for Dele.* When Corin told her that last night it had slipped by, one detail in a much larger story. Now it had lodged itself in her mind forever.

"The king didn't say—" Cina stopped. "You know something else."

"Yes."

"Have you lost your mind, both of you? Even if he's telling, you should not be listening."

At another time Tam might have laughed. "No. I'll explain everything tomorrow, I promise, or he will. It's all right that I know. Just tell Efan to leave. Please."

"And how am I supposed to post anything this time of night?"

Tam was sure Corin could arrange it, but she also could not imagine using a royal messenger for her own purposes. And certainly not if part of the letter was telling Efan to come and whisk Tam away home before she did something indecent. Then she realized she should think more of her brother's safety than her own pride. "I'll get it sent as soon as you write it," she said. "Say whatever you must about me, but convince him to leave."

Cina gave her another long hard look. "I don't want you to ask any more favors of him. I'll post it in the morning. What I said about one day still stands."

Tam nodded. She would tell Corin anyway, and if there was any real danger he would take care of it. It was not worth arguing over. She had no intention of losing to Cina, but there was no point in having the battle here. Cina knew it too, and smiled cordially at her. There must be no sign of a row. They exchanged sisterly kisses on the cheek. Tam expected Cina to step on her foot, but she did not. The parting was the very model of amity.

Another dance had started when Corin finally reappeared with wine, a rare clear greenish-gold. "I'm sorry," he said, "I was waylaid several times. I hope it's adequate, it's the best that's up there. Will you give me the next one?"

"No, you have to buy it."

"Can I pay you later?"

She laughed. "There will be interest owing on that."

"I have plenty of interest," he said, with a look that came perilously close to a leer. "May I also ask you to pretend to be lovestruck?"

"It would make for livelier gossip if you are lovestruck and I am cold," she said. "But I'd rather bore them." They clinked glasses together. It was good wine, headier than she was used to. "I talked to Cina. Or, I should say, she talked to me."

"With what result?"

"She threatened to send me home if I don't break it off by tomorrow evening. I'm only here at her behest, I have to do what she says if I want to stay within my family. Which I do. I'm afraid I said you would talk to her."

"Of course. And nicely, I promise. Tomorrow."

"Corin—my brother—is Dele safe?"

"For now. Does he have the wit to know when to get out or will he be as stubborn as you?"

"Probably stubborn." She was anxious, but she did not want to tell him about the vision, if that was what it was, here.

"I'm hardly going to command him out with force, but I will be sure he knows all he ought. Do—" He broke off. At first she thought he had decided not to say something, then realized he had gone alert, tense as a hunting dog waiting to be loosed.

She watched the dance. Jenet was still with Darrin, her fair hair darkened at the brow with sweat. They had better set the wedding date soon from the looks of them. Tam put her hand lightly on Corin's wrist, and he looked at her, his face focusing with a swiftness that was almost frightening.

"Do noble marriages still need to be approved?" she asked.

"Yes, though they always are. Why?"

"Darrin and Jenet, there—he was going to propose tonight."

"They look happy with each other," he said. "They're both handsome enough. Is there a problem?"

"He bores her."

"Ah," Corin said. "Do you think it's incurable?"

"Not if it's caught early," she answered, thinking she sounded like her father. "But she's far too shy to tell him. I don't know if he can figure it out himself."

"Well, that's certainly no reason to deny the wedding. But I can try to enlighten him now if you'd like."

"You wouldn't."

"Why not? A little royal advice never hurt a man."

"On marriage, from *you*?"

"There is that," he said, laughing. "I concede I lack qualifications there. Maybe it will be up to you to put some backbone in her." He finished his wine and set the glass down, pulled her up. "I see Mattan. Let's go give him his dance and be done with it." He took Tam's arm in the precisely correct manner and led her to the duke's side.

"I understand a dance is owed you, Mattan," he said.

"I believe that was the agreement," Mattan answered.

The men looked at each other. Tam was afraid they might actually row. Then Corin said, "Enjoy yourselves," and dropped her arm. She handed him her glass.

When they could talk under the cover of the music, Mattan said, "I see now why I didn't rate. Well, you were certainly tactful about it."

"There is no easy way to tell a man that he doesn't dance well enough," she said.

A silent measure. He said, "You almost had me believing that was the reason. You're very good."

"No," she said, considering it. She wanted to speak seriously to him. "It's easy to fool people who don't know you, and even easier when they are thinking about themselves. They don't really listen. No one here actually cares very much what I say, so they take it for granted it's true. I'm sorry, I don't mean you, my lord." She should just sew her lips together.

"And how, Tam—I may still call you Tam, mayn't I—how does a woman as young and ladylike as you become acquainted with that very worldly knowledge? It is not part of making an accomplished woman that I ever heard of."

"It is the most necessary part. If a woman said what she really thought or felt, men would scatter in all directions."

"And what do women really think of men?"

Which was not what she had meant. But she would leave it there. "That they are vain, thoughtless, giddy creatures who need someone to take care of them."

He laughed. "I take your point."

"Will you believe me when I say I didn't mean to deceive you?"

"I should have guessed," he said. "When the most beautiful woman in the room is turning away even dukes and the prince is dancing with his sister, there are no other likely explanations. I hope I said nothing to offend you."

"Nothing."

"Thank goodness for that. But I think I will take no more chances and concentrate on dancing for a while."

"It never hurts to improve," she said.

He was in fact a good dancer, though he faltered once near the end, recovering before she lost the beat, and she enjoyed it. When the music stopped, they were far up the floor from where they had begun, and he walked her back to Corin's side. Corin put his arm around her. It felt tender, not possessive. The publicness of it surprised her.

Mattan said simply, "Thank you." He looked at Corin, hesitated, spoke in a quiet rushed voice. "Corin, 'ware Arnet. He was watching my lady."

Corin's arm tightened about her. "Is there more?" She could tell that he was forcing himself to be calm.

"No, my lord." Mattan took Tam's hand and kissed it, then made an almost formal bow. To Corin, not to her. Tam was abruptly aware of how much power Corin had.

Corin nodded tightly, a dismissal. He turned. "Come outside a moment with me, love," he said. He was still strained.

She followed him through a room filled with food-laden tables and out a door onto a balcony. There were other people on it. They all moved away, leaving them one end. Below in the courtyard a couple was arguing. The word "again" came clearly up. The night air was cool. Moonlight silvered the wall opposite them.

He leaned his forehead against hers. In a more ordinary voice, he said, "I've been a fool. You were right this afternoon to remind me that you don't know who to trust. I should not have come with you. I have made you enemies. They will do everything they can to use you against me."

It seemed absurd. She knew he meant it, but she could not imagine what could happen. She leaned into him. He kissed her hair, but it was absent. Plainly he was thinking about something else.

"What could they do?" she asked.

"I don't know. Nothing direct. They're all under watch." He put his hands on the railing and looked upward. His hands were still but not clenched. He leaned closer to her and said, "Arnet likely killed Cade. We'll never be able to prove it, though, not without someone else pointing a very convincing finger. But he's quite dangerous. And if he's watching you, he is planning something to Hadon's benefit."

"I think he's the man I saw in the courtyard," she said. "I couldn't swear to it, though." Even if she could, it would only prove Alina had dropped something.

"I doubt you'll need to," he said. "It's the woman we need. Perhaps I'll have her questioned." His tone was unconvinced.

"She's terrified of him," Tam said, remembering Alina's face that afternoon. "He hurts her. Can't you arrest him as a spy?"

"For taking pay from my own liege lord?"

She felt naïve. For all that Corin had told her, she did not think as he did. Below them, the young man of the couple swore and walked away; the woman stood with her hands to her face, her shoulders shaking. Corin said, abruptly, "Tell me what my father said to you that night."

It startled her. He was wanting a certainty she could not give him. "He said you were going to need me."

"I do," he said. "Tam, be careful. Please."

"I promise," she said.

He said nothing for a while. The ballroom was a roar of mingled noises behind them. She smelled honeysuckle. At last he spoke. "You mustn't tell anyone this. I need your word. It's the only thing you don't know yet."

What could it be? "I won't."

"Hadon holds Tai hostage. He took her six days ago."

She felt sick. He had been carrying the weight of his sister's captivity all this time. No wonder he was worried about her. She put her hand on his arm. It was rigid.

He said, the most despairing she had ever heard him, "I'm trapped here, Tam. Helpless. The dragons want me, but I can't do anything while Hadon has my sister."

There it was, the knot between his ordinary life and the world he had been thrust into. The rules had changed. She said, "Talk to the dragons. Tell them that delays you."

"What can they do? If they could free Tai they would not be bound themselves."

"You don't know that. You don't know what binds them. You don't know what power they have. You don't know what power you have. You need to learn what they gave you, and you need to find out what they still can give you. You're going to kill yourself if you try to do this alone." She did not know where the words came from, what part of her could have any insight about dragons. But she knew he had to hear them.

He looked anguished. She wondered if it was too big a burden. Then his shoulders set. He had made some decision.

She reached for his hand. "I would like some water, can we go back in?"

He nodded. When they stepped back into the ballroom it seemed hot and bright. He beckoned to a servant and sent the man for water, then found a chair for Tam. He did not sit himself. He said very little, even after the water came and she had her fill. His eyes kept moving, and his body was taut.

"Corin."

"What?"

"If you don't settle down people are going to think you're angry with me."

"I'm sorry," he said. He reached down and laced his fingers with hers. "I hope I'm not spoiling it for you."

"What are you worried about?" she asked.

"I don't even know," he said.

She touched his forearm. "You're about to explode, you need to move about or do something. I can take care of myself."

He shifted from one foot to the other. "I hate to leave you alone. Something bad is going to happen. I can feel it coming."

Nothing stirred in her. No dust or darkness or black wings. Then certainty struck. She shook her head. "It already did," she said. She felt cold despite the heat of the room and resisted the impulse to fold her arms across her chest. "This afternoon. While your father was speaking."

"I wish I'd listened to you then."

"There was nothing to be done." She tried to think of someone else he trusted who could calm him. She stood up. "Can I meet your sister?"

"I should have done that already," he said. "I'm a boor."

"Mattan said cad."

"He did, did he?" Abruptly he pulled her to him and kissed her. It was no light touch of lips, it was as full a kiss as any he had ever given her. She resisted a bit—it was far too public a place for such a kiss—then gave in. Cina would skin her alive. Her body roused.

When he broke it off she found that her hand was on his chest. Hastily she brought it down. "How much longer must we stay?" she whispered.

"We can't leave together," he said. "I just ruined your reputation enough. You should probably slap me."

"If I were going to do that I would have had to do it when you started," she said. She was glad he seemed to be recovering a sense of humor. "You can't come to my room, and I'm certainly not going to go wait alone in yours. What are we going to do?"

"Not tonight, Tam," he said. "Not when everyone is watching us. If you go alone to your maidenly bed, then they know you matter. I'm not known for restraint, showing it with you will raise your standing."

"To what?"

"To what it should be for the woman I love."

Her mouth dried up. What was he suggesting? Certain she was about to say the wrong thing, she said, "That won't work for long."

"It doesn't have to." The next dance had started, and he caught her hands, swept her into the circle.

"What are you doing?" she asked, though she was enjoying it.

"This is the fastest way to the top of the room. I intend to perform my social duty."

"And then stand there drinking with the other men? Why aren't they dancing?"

"You're welcome to try to convince them. They might dance with you. You're lively enough. It's damn boring having to listen to women prattle about nothing."

"I'm aware of that," she said. "But what do you expect them to talk about if they can't go to university or take part in commerce or politics? It's damn boring sitting around sewing."

She was not sure what to expect for a response. "You," he said, and broke all rules of the dance to kiss her, "are not someone I ever want to argue against in public, because you will slice me into tiny pieces before I even know it. However did you get this way?"

"I'm not inbred nobility," she said.

He burst into laughter and lost the rhythm of the dance. She stumbled, and he drew her out of the circle into the watchers. She was about to ask him how he had got that way himself when she saw something that stopped her voice entirely. Words seemed stuck in her throat. She pushed them out. "Corin, look. Your sister."

He looked. The humor died in him instantly. He said, almost snapped, "Sit down." Then he hurried away, barely restraining himself from a run. Tam walked backward, still watching him, knowing it was something bad. She turned her head briefly enough to find an empty chair and sat down without paying any attention to what she did. She felt as though she were about to watch someone step off a cliff and could not make herself heard or seen in trying to stop it. The ache that had begun in her when he told her about Tai deepened painfully.

The uniformed man talking to Mari had to be someone of importance. The princess stood with her head down and her hands made into fists, obviously trying not to cry. Corin reached her, touched her. She fell into his arms. He spoke briefly to the man, then moved toward a small door in the back, one arm still around his sister. He did not look back toward Tam at all.

Other people were watching now. The dance had come almost to a stop. The important-looking man came and spoke to the musicians, who started playing something lively, though at first it seemed wooden and a bit off-key. Tam sat still, unsure what to do, unsure what had happened.

Someone sat down beside her. She looked, feeling angry, and saw Jenet. It touched her.

"Can I help?" Jenet asked quietly, sincerely.

"I don't know. I don't know what's wrong." She sounded frantic to herself, and she took several deep breaths. "It can't be anything too terrible since they want the ball to continue. Who's the man?"

"Gerod. The guard commander."

"My God," she whispered. What had happened? It couldn't be that anything had happened to Aram, he would have come to Corin first. If it had been a matter of Mari's children, someone else would have come. But there had to be some danger involved. Danger that had hurt Mari. Danger that made Corin forget all about his worry for Tam.

"No wonder you kept quiet," Jenet said. "I don't think anyone guessed. He does like you, doesn't he?"

"Yes," Tam said absently. Her stomach was clutching. She forced herself to look at Jenet and saw the ruby ring on the woman's hand. She said all the appropriate phrases, hardly hearing them, and Jenet replied with the same automatic correctness.

The commander was looking at her. "I think I need to go," she said, standing. Her feet took her toward him. When he saw her coming he moved to meet her.

"My lady," Gerod said, tightly formal, "His Highness would like you to come with me."

"Of course," she said. It was rote. There were a hundred eyes watching, more. She refused to give them anything that would shame either her or Corin. She found Cina. Her face was white. She must have realized that Tam was right about Efan. Tam thought a reassurance at her, then turned to Gerod.

She was as stately as could be while she walked out beside the commander, but as soon as the door was shut she slumped a bit. The commander tactfully ignored it.

He took her not to Corin's rooms, but to what seemed to be a sort of family sitting room somewhat of a distance away and down a different hall. Inside, she drew back, uncomfortable, noticing only that there were quite a lot of people present and knowing she was not one of them. Then Corin was with her, and he put his arms around her as though she had been in some great danger.

"Thank you, Gerod," he said. "Tam, let's step into the hall where it's quieter." He gripped her hand.

But he did not say anything for a while. She thought he was in pain, but if so he was very good at hiding it and she could not be sure. The grip on her hand had loosened, but nothing else about him had. His face was hard, carved. The corridor was well lit, but even so it seemed eerie to her, very white and shiny with marble, gas lamps flickering like marshlight.

"Do you remember what I told you about my sister's husband Ves?" he asked abruptly.

A little thud of knowledge dropping into her. "Something's happened, hasn't it?" And it had Mari weeping, it had to be bad.

"Yes, not just to him." A pause that stretched into waiting. "I'm just going to say this, love, there's no way to make it anything but cruel. While we were in the ballroom, a dragon landed. I felt it, I should have gone up then. The rider dropped two bodies on the roof and left before the sentries could do anything. And they were . . ."

"One of them was Mari's husband."

He did not bother to affirm it. "The other was my sister Tai's husband. Both of them, Tam, both of them. They were not easy deaths."

God. It was too terrible for her to even feel pain about it. It was entirely unreal. She imagined it, the roof where she had kissed Corin in the darkness, the soft air, the dragon bearing down with its bloody load.

He said, "Hadon didn't need to hurt Tai this way too."

"It's—Corin, it's evil," she whispered, staring up at him, squeezing his fingers between hers. She had seen malice a few times before, but this, this was beyond malice.

"It is. I am going to kill him for it." His hand itself seemed to get cold as he spoke. It was not a threat, it was a vow. There was no room left in him for anything of mercy or forgiveness, not to Hadon, not to himself.

"Oh, my love," she said, aching for him, knowing he was going to drive himself until it was finished. He was so stiff and straight that she knew she could not ease him.

He swallowed, said roughly, "You see what this means for you, don't you?"

It was unexpected, and took a second for her to understand. "I can't possibly be in that kind of danger. I'm not worth that much."

"This—this thing he did, Tam, it's not any kind of war. It's meant to hurt. After tonight all Hadon's spies at court will know I love you. That's all he needs. Ves and Ader weren't killed because of who they were, they were killed because of who my sisters are." His voice was flat, cold, inarguable. "He wants to hurt me especially."

She touched the necklace. If the man who had given it to Mari had married her, he would be dead now. "What will we do?" she asked, feeling him slipping irretrievably away from her.

"Don't talk to anyone tomorrow except Cina any more than you have to for courtesy. Anyone. And you need guards."

Guards. She hated the entire idea. "Am I trapped inside? Don't make fear for me into a prison, don't, it will kill me, ruin me."

"No. If they're any good, which they will be, you will hardly notice."

That was a relief, if a small one.

He said, "You should go somewhere they can't find you."

"I won't be sent away, Corin, I won't."

"I knew you would say that," he said, softening a bit. He put his fingertips lightly on her cheek. "Not yet, Tam, we will trust to the palace guard for now. But you're going to have to hide eventually. Probably soon. I no longer think Hadon would not kill a woman.

You won't be the only one gone to ground. There's already a bird sent to the garrison in Dele to get your brother out. I was an utter fool." Gently, he touched her forehead with one finger, brought it down to the side of one eye. "You're so very beautiful," he said.

It almost broke her. Staring at the marble on the other side of the hallway, she said dully, "What now, I mean tonight?"

"My father wants words with you."

"Now?"

"Yes. Come on."

She did not want to. She had no choice. She nodded and followed him back in, hand in hand.

Very quickly—she was not quite sure how it happened—she was alone in a small side chamber with the king. It was dimly lit by a single glowlamp, with no windows, and furnished only with two uncushioned wooden chairs. Aram did not sit. The walls were plain unplastered stone. It intimidated her a bit. She wished Corin could be with her.

There was nothing forceful in his voice, though, when he asked, "How much has Corin told you?"

"He says it is everything, my lord."

"Did he tell you about Tai?" His daughter. One could not have guessed from his tone.

"A little while ago," she answered. "Very briefly."

"And the dragons?"

"Yes," she said faintly. Corin had said his father knew. He had told her what Aram said about the rider at his birth. But admitting to Aram that she knew made a bond between her and the king. They both knew this about Corin, and Aram had to know Corin would not have told such to a woman he did not love. It was like saying she carried his child.

The king said, "The wisest thing for you to do would be to pack your trunk and be out of here at first light tomorrow."

Greatly daring, she said, "Is that an order, sir?"

"No. At least, not yet. But are you sure you understand the risk you take in staying?"

"Yes."

He looked at her for a long intent moment. He said, "I believe you do. There are some things I need to tell you, then."

She nodded. It suddenly seemed unreal. She wanted to spin time backward, an hour, a day, a week. How far back would she have to go to make a change that mattered? If she had gone into town with Cina that day she would not have seen Cade die, and none of what passed would have happened. For want of a nail. It would not have changed what Hadon did tonight, though.

"The first you probably know already. Be careful whom you trust. Man or woman."

"Yes," she said, not without sadness.

"Most people here will mean you no harm, but don't rely on that. You have good instincts. Listen to them."

She wondered what made him so sure of that but said, "I will."

"If you need me, come. I will be sure my clerk and guards know to admit you."

"I don't—my lord, I don't deserve that. I'm not . . ." Her voice trailed off. He knew what she was, there was nothing to tell him. "You're trusting me on very little."

"Your face doesn't hide much, my dear," he replied. "You were tested that night. I saw how you watched him."

It was an extraordinarily intimate thing to say. She looked down.

He gave her time for several breaths. Then he said, in a soft and relentless voice that pulled her eyes to his, "Tam."

"Sir."

"The second thing I would ask that you not tell Corin."

That was an order. "Of course not," she said.

"You can't go with him. None of us can. But he's going to drive himself hard until he does leave, especially now that this has happened. Try to temper it. And if you think he's going to break, tell me."

Her eyes stung and blurred. Embarrassed, she dashed the tears away, but it was a moment before she could look at him again. "What else?" she whispered.

He ran his fingers through his hair in a gesture that was Corin's. "You have wit and courage, Tam. Use it." It was about the last thing she expected from him. Men did not say things like that to women, nor kings to commoners. It was the kind of command one gave to an adviser or trusted friend.

But what did she really know about kings anyway? Aram was as he was, whether or not it matched Tam's expectations. He wasn't going to let her complain or whine about her inadequacies. Whatever he wanted of her, it was not servility. She heard her answers. Yes, of course, I will. She was more than that.

In the next room a clock chimed midnight. She straightened and looked squarely at him. "What are you going to do about what's happened?"

"I can't even begin to know," he said. His voice was still calm, but this time she could tell it did not match his feelings. That shook her. She realized she had to tell him more. Maybe Corin had, maybe he already knew. But she owed it to him. He had admitted uncertainty to her. He knew about the dragons, he would listen.

Awkwardly, she said, "I've had a sense—I've felt—there's a fraying in the world somewhere. I don't know what it is."

He stared at her for a long time. "You don't know yet how much power you have, do you?"

It startled her. "What do you mean?"

"You See things."

Startlement became fear. "I don't," she said, her voice suddenly hoarse. The boats sailing to Dele called her liar.

He put a hand on her shoulder. That was power, to touch so freely. It steadied her, though, as it was intended to. He said, "You told me you saw the dragon in the mirror. No one without power could have seen that. Who knows where it came from. Perhaps it has been in your family's bloodlines for centuries, perhaps it is a random stroke of fate. It is not unnatural, nor to be feared."

"Are you saying I am a wizard?" It was bizarre, even mad, though it was impossible to think such a thing of Aram.

"No. Just a Seer. There are more forces in the world than we know yet."

Wind. Fire. Fluttering moths. Time. She had told Corin more or less the same thing.

He walked over to the glowlamp and touched something on it to make it brighter, then turned back to her. "You need not use it," he said. "No one will think less of you. But if you don't use it, it should be because you choose not to, not because you can't. Don't hide from yourself."

He had put a burden on her with one breath and lifted it with the next. "And if I choose to?"

"I don't know what will happen. And I will make no suggestions."

"Is this what you want from me against Hadon?"

"Want?" he said softly. "It has nothing to do with what I want or need. It's not a matter of duty, Tam, it is for yourself alone."

She was quiet. Murmured voices came through the wood of the door. She knew that Aram was capable of waiting much longer than she was. She should not hold him so, not tonight, not now when war had been declared with blood and agony.

"I need to think," she said.

"Of course. But whatever you do, be careful," he said. "There are things more powerful than you. You don't know what you might disturb."

It brought all the urgency she had felt that afternoon rushing back. She said, "Corin's felt it, my lord. Something waiting for him. It's already roused."

"He has?"

"Yes. That's why he didn't come in that night. It wasn't just the dragons." She hoped she was not betraying him, but the king had to know.

Aram sighed, said grimly, "Thank you."

"I think it wants out."

Suddenly he seemed haggard. "I expect you're right," he said. "There may be nothing to do about it. Have you felt it too?"

She could not speak. She nodded.

"If it comes after you, either of you, run. Don't try to fight it."

"I won't. And I'll be careful," she said, wishing absurdly that she could somehow reassure him.

"I can't ask for more," he said. "Now, there are a few practical matters. Can you ride?"

"Adequately."

"Improve. I'll have a teacher found. And you'll need to learn to defend yourself. You may have to leave somewhere in a hurry. Wear trousers."

Trousers. That simple word brought the reality of war to her.

"What else?" she asked.

"Talia will have to put you somewhere else. You'll sleep up here, in Tai's room, tonight."

But, she thought. She saw a faintly amused expression on his face that told her she had said it. She felt very young.

He said, "It will be easier to guard. Everything else can wait until morning."

It was a dismissal. She bent her head. He opened the door and gestured for her to precede him. She obeyed.

It seemed as though everyone in the room was watching them, waiting for the king. Corin stood next to his sister, who was straight and tearless and very pale. Bron had come. Aram shut the door behind himself and faced her. He spoke in a low voice. "Try to rest. Corin will be up all night, he'll need you clear-headed tomorrow."

She nodded. "My lord."

Then, to her utter astonishment, he leaned down and kissed her forehead. "Sleep well," he said. He turned his back to her and stepped toward a grey-haired man she did not know. She thought with a sudden sadness of her own father. There was no going back now. What Aram had told her changed everything.

≈≈≈

CHAPTER TWELVE

A t dawn Corin walked down the steps from the palace entrance and stood on the grass in the cool blue shadows of the eastern wall. His body and mind were both restless. He had not even tried to go to bed. He had not changed his clothing, though he had discarded the formal jacket. There was still a chill to the air, but it had no bite. It would probably be a hot day. The sky above was flooded with early light. He looked back at the palace and saw the red glow of the sun on the tower tops. Not far away he heard a wheelbarrow on cobblestones. A rooster crowed. He smelled bread baking. An ordinary morning. Behind him the guards, twice as many as usual, stood alert on the steps.

It had been a tumultuous night, fragmented and inconclusive and unsettled. Little bits of conversation flickered through his mind. *I'll be all right, Corin, truly I will,* said his sister with red-rimmed eyes. Aram, looking wearier than Corin had ever seen him, said, *I should have let you go dragonback to look.* Himself, speaking to the dukes whom he had been sent like a page boy to gather from the ball: *My gracious lords, His Majesty commands you to an immediate council. He wishes to tell you why himself.* He found Cina and told her far more than he had intended to. She said, *Forgive me, my lord, but you can't marry her.* The stark immovable fact. *What do you need?* Aram asked. He answered, *I don't even know.* He was going blindly into a locked darkness that nothing had prepared him for. He had thought of how little pain he had suffered; now it was coming, barbed and entangling.

More words floated up from his crowded memory. *Sometimes you walk and turn and turn and you can't get anywhere, you keep coming to the same corner, or you're standing in a courtyard that's all white stone and nothing is alive and there's no way out.* Liko had seen the dragon in his shadow somehow, he was sure of that. And afterward Corin had sent off the curse that was as cold and deathlike as whatever waited for him hidden in the darkness.

Opening doors that shouldn't be opened, he thought. That was what Cade had been trying to do. That was why he had wanted to be put into trance. He had hoped to find something in that cold world. Had he been murdered because he failed or because he succeeded? Hadon would know. He imagined the Emperor, withered with fear into something inhuman that clawed at life.

God, how much easier it had been when everything was politics. Damn the dragons. Damn Hadon. He clenched his fists. He did not know enough, not anywhere near enough. He was not trained to combat specters.

Free the dragons. From what? What hold did the Empire have on them?

He thought of Mycene, the lush green valleys, the terraced fields on the mountainside. The Emperor's palace, with its splendid views and grand staircases and gilt ceilings. Distant dragons sparkling in the sunlight. Lizards and cats and snakes lying in the sun. The jungle at night, dark and thick and moving and alive. Monkeys screeching. The south end of the capital, more squalid than any place in Caithenor. It too was noisy with shrieks, human sounds of anger and pain and despair. Was he to go there?

Frustrated, he pushed thoughts out of his mind and stood a moment in stillness. Slowly he became aware of the ground beneath him, the cool dampness under the dried soil, the small burrows of animals, the clay, the bedrock. It was his land. It was an immense and sleeping dragon, curled around an ember of fire. It was the home of the peasants' corn goddess and the lord of the dead. It wanted him. There was power in it, spreading everywhere like some vast circulatory system. He felt its hum in his bones.

He turned. He was wasting time. As he went back up the stairs, he once more had the feeling that he was being watched. He looked east again. The few clouds above the horizon were limned with gold, splendid. He made up his mind.

❧

Bron argued fiercely with him, but yielded after he snapped, "Take two dozen men and hit him over the head if you must, but I want him here." Corin could not remember the last time he had lost his temper with the captain. He went to bed for an hour and felt more tired when he roused from a thick dreamless sleep. He bathed and dressed carefully. It was still early by courtier standards, especially the morning after a ball, and as much as he wanted to see Tam he thought he would let her sleep. She was going to need it to hold up to the world today.

He went to his study. He would have liked to tell Teron to keep everybody out, but there was no justification for it. The work he was to do had no meaning in the imminence of war. He might as well be interrupted. As word got out—Aram was revealing what had happened and had doubled the guard—he would be faced by panicked people seeking assurance or advice or money. Cina had been relatively calm about it, saying only, *I shall have to take her home.* Most courtiers did not have her poise. He had said to her, *She has chosen to stay and the king allows it. He regards her highly,* which had rattled her a bit. She had gathered herself together and said, *I had better stay to help her through things, then,* paused, added, *I will not interfere where His Majesty has permitted, but please, my lord, be careful of her. She is still quite young yet.* He answered, *I know. I will.* For a moment they looked at each other, man and woman only, full of the same fear.

It was about an hour later when Teron put his head in at the door and breathed loudly until Corin looked up, hoping to hear that Bron was back. "The Duchess of Osstig, my lord," he said tonelessly.

Oh hell. Seana. He should have expected it. "Send her in. And see that we are not disturbed."

She closed the door quietly. They looked at each other. How had he ever thought her beautiful? She sat down and said, "I have no intention of being difficult, Corin. I just want to know the truth."

"We're done," he said. "It's not negotiable."

"Will you tell me why?"

He could not be angry now. "It was never a good idea, you know that. And with a war on, it's impossible. How much loyalty do you think I can get from a man who knows I'm in his wife's bed?"

Her hands were neatly folded in her lap. She rubbed one thumb deliberately against the other, then said evenly, "That's all quite true, but don't you think you could have found the decency to tell me before parading some common woman around?"

"Apparently I couldn't," he said, as composed as she, though he was bridling within. "I'm sorry it happened that way, and I grant that you have a right to be angry, but there's nothing I can do about it now. She has nothing to do with you, it would be the same without her."

"I expected better of you," she said.

As well she might have. "I can tell you again that I am sorry, but that won't change anything. You can comfort yourself with the knowledge that your husband is the better man."

She drew in a sharp breath. He heard the cruelty in what he had said and wished he could pull it back, but that too was done and unchangeable.

"She—"

"She and I are not under discussion, Seana, and never will be. You and I are. Or were, I have nothing else to say."

"Corin—"

It was perhaps the importuning tone in her voice that snapped him. No longer caring if he hurt her, he said harshly, "Seana, both my sisters' husbands were brutally murdered yesterday. Do you think I have either the time or the desire to listen to you beg for something you can't have? Count yourself lucky I don't love you, or you might be dead with them."

There was a very long silence. Then she stood up, cool as could be, and said, "I understand. I said I would not be difficult, and I won't." She stepped backward to the door, put her hand on it. She curtsied. "Your Highness."

She or, more likely, Teron, closed the door again. Corin stared at it without thinking anything. He swore a few times, clenched his teeth, and then bent again over his desk.

Time passed in splinters and fragments. He spoke to visitors without really hearing what either he or they said. His mind kept dancing around, thoughts of his sisters, of Sarians, of dragons, of Tam, constantly intruding. He had been excused from seeing the bodies with a suggestion that was really a command—Aram said it had shaken even Gerod—and his imagination insisted on filling that gap. At last he stood up and stalked to the window and thrust it fully open. He smelled newly mown grass.

I have to leave, he thought. His jaw was tight, his shoulders tensed. I have to leave now.

He closed his eyes and leaned his head briefly against the cool wall, then went back to his chair and resumed working.

He could concentrate no better than he had, and he was just about to go to the gardens in an attempt to clear his mind when he heard footsteps rapidly approaching the door. Teron said something, but the door opened without even a perfunctory tap for courtesy.

It was Tam. Her face was pale. Before he could be surprised that she had entered so he saw Joce standing behind her, giving Teron his iciest stare. That could only be his father's command; it was something he never would have dared to ask for. He felt immensely relieved.

"What happened?" he asked, taking her hands. Someone shut the door.

She pressed briefly against him. He imagined he could feel her pulse beating.

Then she stepped back and looked directly at him. "Alina's dead."

It took him a moment to place the name. "Did you find her?" he asked.

"No," she said. "Her maid did. I heard her scream and went to help. I was prepared for something horrible. She hanged herself." She was calm, the doctor's daughter who had seen death many times.

He hoped she did not feel the need to pretend strength in front of him.

He touched her face. "Gentle, love. Are you all right?"

"Yes. Just sad. She didn't deserve that. She left a note. It said—it said—" Her eyes closed briefly and her mouth set, as though she were about to be sick. She went on. "It said, 'Arnet killed Cade. He was in the way. I helped. I'm sorry.'"

Corin wanted to be relieved that the mystery was solved, but knowing Arnet he could not be. It seemed unlikely that the baron would have written a message accusing himself, though. He said, "Are you sure she did it?"

"Unless he has the power to lock a window from the outside four stories up or slip by all the guards entirely, she did it. I saw her alive fifteen minutes ago. I would still set the death at his feet, though. He's responsible."

"He's probably cleared out by now, I doubt we'll catch him," Corin said. "Why do you suppose she did it? Pangs of conscience?"

"I think fear. Perhaps of him. There was a bruise on her wrist yesterday that looked like he had held her, and I found another on her shoulder just now. Or she may have been afraid of getting caught. You might not have noticed, Corin, but it feels like a war camp or a prison out there. Soldiers are everywhere."

"Good. And speaking of that, why were you in that wing at all? I thought you were moved."

"I had a few things to get still. They put me in the wing next to yours. It's much too grand. And it's going to be lonely, no one's going to find me there."

"That's the idea," he said. Those rooms were reserved for only very high-ranking guests and were much more sumptuous than she was entitled to. That too had to have been his father's doing. What was he thinking? When Aram had kissed Tam's forehead last night, Corin had been as stunned as the rest of them. It was beyond courtesy.

"I'd rather take my chances with a crowd," she said. "It has one advantage, though."

"What's that?"

"No one will know if I sleep with you."

"We can't," he said.

It hurt her. "Why not?" she asked stiffly.

"It's too great a risk now that they know about you. If there were to be a child—"

"There won't be," she said with certainty. "I am not my father's daughter for nothing."

It relieved him, yet saddened him too. He did not want to have his heir born out of some loveless obligation.

"They don't know that. They would try to find you and kill you to end the line," he said. "Even if they had already killed me."

"I can choose my risks," she said. "We've had this argument already, remember?"

He found it suddenly very hard to speak. He kissed her lips, remembering that very first kiss, the taste of Illyrian wine and cold wind and curiosity. "I'll send you home with a dozen bottles of the best wine," he said. "No point in leaving it for the Sarians."

"Don't change the subject," she said. She kissed him passionately.

He put his arms around her and pressed her close but said nothing. It was brutally unfair that Tai and Mari had lost this. How could he trust anyone else to keep her safe? He had to. He had to go. He lifted her soft hair with his hand and let it spill down the side of his arm like water. He could not even ask her to wait for him. She deserved better.

"Well?" she asked softly.

"You can come," he said. He felt closed in, pressed upon by too many other presences. She ran her hand down his back, and suddenly he wanted her more than he could endure. He forced himself to step away.

"What's the matter?" she asked.

"Nothing beyond what you know of. Nothing to do with you," he said.

There was a silence. She looked around the room. It was the first time she had been there, and he wondered how it matched her expectations. He remembered looking down at her yesterday from the balcony—had it only been yesterday?—and being aware, as he was supposed to be, of the gulf between them. He didn't want her to feel that here.

"Sit down," he said. "Not in that chair, it's uncomfortable."

"Intentionally?" she asked with a trace of wryness that reassured him.

"It keeps people from staying too long."

She smiled at him, a shadow of her usual grin, but did not sit. He watched her clasp and unclasp her hands, several times. Her fingers were slim and elegant and beautiful.

At last she looked up. Her face was white. "Your father—your father says I have power."

That threw him. Not so much the power, whatever it was—she had seen the moths and the dragon in the carousel—but that his father would know. It was such a secret thing. "What did he say?"

"He said I'm a Seer. And that it's a natural force we do not understand. He was very calm about it."

"He always is."

"But what—how could he tell?"

"I don't know," he said. He thought of the wizards, hidden away in their tiny mountain enclave. He had gone twice, once when he turned eighteen and was told the secret and a second time a few years later. Aram had gone more often. Perhaps he had learned the signs of power.

But Tam was no wizard. She could not even carry it in her blood from some distant ancestor; any child got of the two races was barren. It must be a wild thing, springing into being of its own accord. The thought that she might not be able to bear children flittered treacherously across his mind. He pushed it away.

"Tam," he said, "don't let my father get under your skin. He has a full bag of tricks and he can't help using them. There's enough to worry about without adding him."

She pointed at the door. "What about him? Joce. I don't need an assassin to watch over me. Don't try to tell me he's an ordinary soldier."

"If Joce had been with my sister, she never would have been taken," he said bitterly.

She came to him. They put their arms around each other. Neither spoke for a long time.

At last she said, "If it will help you for me to go, I will."

"Oh, Tam." He knew what that meant to her.

Teron's chair scraped on the other side of the door. Corin took a deep breath. "Let's decide later," he said. "We're about to be interrupted."

A knock. "Come," he called.

The door opened. Liko stumbled in, followed by Bron. Corin thought Bron had probably given him a push. The scent of soap clung to him. His hair was clean, and his clothing was new.

He opened his mouth to ask Tam to leave. He did not want Liko to know anything about her. What came out was, "Stay here, my lady. Captain, bring Joce in, please, and shut the door."

She looked startled. He knew it was the dragons moving through him. He whispered into her ear, "Sit down, love, and watch," then took his own seat. He turned it to face Liko, who stood sullenly with Bron and Joce flanking him.

He looked at Bron. "Any trouble?"

"Nothing to speak of, sir."

"Good. Liko."

The man mumbled something that might have been an acknowledgment.

Corin said pleasantly, "I've no time for games. Don't make me ask you anything twice. I want you to tell me everything you didn't the last time about Lord Cade."

Liko said nothing. Finally Bron stepped closer. Then Liko spoke. "He spent a lot of time talking to the Myceneans, and he had Imperial coinage."

"What else?"

"You won't believe me. It was absurd, even for him."

"Let me be the judge of that."

Liko still looked sullen and defiant. He said, "He wanted me to put him into trance so that he could get instruction from the Emperor. He said Hadon would not write it or use a messenger, but that they could speak together in the dark place. Obviously I refused."

"Did he find anyone else?"

"I've no idea. I told you before that he would have killed me if I went along with it and found out what was in his mind. Not that there was much in it."

Corin remembered how Liko had hesitated before telling him the stories of the docks. He pushed. "You believed him, didn't you, Liko?"

"Of course not, my lord." His voice was faster than usual, his face a little flushed.

"You believed him and you were afraid of what might happen. Afraid of what he might do, what Hadon might do. You aren't entirely a charlatan, are you? Have you got some power?"

Silence. Bron moved restlessly. Liko mumbled, "Cade had no power, nor have I. No one does. The wizards are all dead."

"Then what would have been the harm?"

"He was speaking treason!"

"That's not what stopped you, though. You could have turned him in for a nice sum. Why didn't you mesmerize him?"

The man stared at him. Clearly he thought he was being trapped or made a joke of.

Corin said, "I don't hold the truth against anyone. Even if it seems absurd."

Liko looked down, then said almost inaudibly, "He meant to go into the dark place to talk to Hadon. I don't know what it is, but it's real. He knew that too. Putting someone in trance is like water on a road, it goes to the ruts that are already there. I didn't want to risk it if someone else had already let him through."

"How would Cade have been let in in the first place if no one has power? Or were you lying about that too?"

"It's—" He broke off and thought. His eyelids fluttered rapidly. He made another false start, then said, "Sorcery works that much, if one has the will and the strength. Not many do."

Corin interrupted. "You do."

Liko made a small, mocking bow. "I did." Once. Before. A long time ago.

"How does it work?"

"The spells, the rituals, they focus the mind, that's what opens it. It doesn't matter what color candle you burn or where you burn it or how the planets are aligned, it's the attention to the flame that counts. Trance is the same."

"You might as well call that power," Corin said. He did not want to think about the implications at the moment. "Cade had no power, he had to use someone. Who would it have been if not you?"

Liko shrugged. "I don't know. He didn't come back."

It was no use asking him if he thought Cade had found his way in. He would have nothing to say on that count either. Corin shifted focus. "The dark place, can anyone be brought there?"

Liko looked uneasy. Corin suspected he knew where this was going. "If they want to, my lord. But both men have to really will it, and the one has to have the strength. It's not going to happen by accident at a dinner party."

"Could you have brought him through if you wanted to?"

"Perhaps. I haven't tried for years. There's a reason that place is separate, I don't want to open something I can't shut. It's a bad place. And if anything in there gets a chance to come out it's not going to stop to thank whoever released it. Devour him, more likely."

Wise man. He remembered the trapped thing, clawing at him, hungering. Cade might have realized he would be a victim and tried to back out, or simply failed in his attempts to speak with Hadon, but by then he knew too much. The pieces clicked neatly into place. Tyrekh advanced, Tai was kidnapped, Corin came home—things were moving, and Cade became a liability. A little Sarian poison put Cade away and shifted the gaze eastward, and other plans were made. Arnet was not foolish enough to risk himself in the dark place just to speak to Hadon, if he even had needed to. Corin knew he should be that sensible.

But the dragons had touched him. Him and Tam both.

Must you do it? Tam had asked. *Must* was a hard word. He did not believe in destiny or fate. He had the choice. He should do his duty by his country and not go haring off on a fool's quest he would likely fail in for the sake of the dragons. If he did free the dragons, Mycene would fracture and leave Caithen to be even more firmly gripped by Tyrekh. He could not let that happen either. There was nothing to be gained at all by following the path the dragons laid before him.

He had vowed to not even glance at Tam so as not to draw Liko's attention to her, but he could not help himself. She was looking at him. Understanding flashed between them. He stood on the brink, and her hand was in his, not to pull him back but to leap with him if that was what he chose.

He faced Liko again and committed himself. "Mesmerize me."

Bron said, "My lord!" at the same time Liko said, "What!"

"You heard me," Corin said. He shot Bron a glance that he knew would quell him. He would hear about it later, but the captain would not challenge him now.

Liko said carefully, "You want me to put you into trance."

"Yes."

"I can mesmerize you. There's no certainty anything else will happen."

Corin shrugged. "Attempts fail. But one must try."

"What warrants my freedom if something goes wrong?" Liko asked.

"Is there a risk?"

"My lord knows where his own mind might lead him better than I do."

A few centuries ago such disrespect would have earned him a summary beheading. But it was true. Corin said, "You have three witnesses."

"All loyal to you."

He heard Tam try to keep back an exclamation. He said, "You don't want me to hold you in contempt. Do it." He was not doing well today at getting what he wanted diplomatically. He hardly cared.

Liko had the wisdom not to say anything else. There was a cord tied around his neck. He slid it over his head, revealing an attached shiny agate pebble. He stepped closer to Corin and stopped with a courtier's instinct for what was too near.

In the most serious voice Corin had ever heard from him, he said, "Watch the stone." He began to swing it gently back and forth. "Sleep," he said. Corin followed the movement of the stone, let the rhythmic words drift over him. His eyes grew heavy. Darkness fell.

Someone was shaking him. He jerked into awareness and saw Bron beside him, looking worried. The captain dropped his hand. Tam was next to him, grinning. He hoped Liko could not see her face.

"What happened?" he asked.

"You were too tired," Tam said. "You fell asleep."

"Well," he said, and laughed. "So much for that." He could still choose to forgo the dragons' path.

Tam leaned forward. "Let me do it."

He went serious at once. "Tam," he said in a voice too low for the others to hear, "you don't know what might happen."

"Neither did you. I'm the one who's already been there," she whispered.

Even so, he was frightened for her. He gave up on pretending she did not matter and said, "You've just been through a shock."

"A word, my lord," said Joce. Everyone looked at him.

He would know. Corin beckoned. Bron and Tam moved aside without being asked. Joce bent over and said into Corin's ear, "I can watch them both. She's strong enough."

That was some safety. It was not enough. But someone had to See, and she had done it. She had done it with enough clarity for his father to know.

"Does he have power?" he whispered back.

"I don't think so. He'll ride her wake."

"Is there risk?"

"There's always risk, sir. But I don't think much."

He glanced at Tam. She was no more going to back down than he would. He said, "He thinks you've recovered. Do you?"

"I'm not afraid of ghosts," she replied.

He wondered if she knew this was a turning point. Their eyes met. She gave him a sweet smile that almost made his heart break with fear of losing her. She knew.

He stood up. She took his place. He noticed how very blue her eyes were, how perfect the line of her neck. Brave one, he thought at her. He waited until Joce was standing behind Liko to say, "Go ahead."

Liko looked nervously at him, then began to swing the stone. His hand shook a little. Tam slipped into trance quickly and smoothly. Her eyes were closed, her face peaceful.

"Who are you?" Liko asked.

She spoke, her voice pitched normally but very even. "Tam Warin."

"How old are you?"

"Twenty."

"Where were you tranced?"

"In the palace in Caithenor."

"Who was with you?"

"Prince Corin, his captain, a guard. You."

Liko looked up at Corin. "All's well, my lord," he said. Behind him, Joce nodded slightly, confirming.

"Go on," Corin said.

Liko looked back at Tam. "Are you there now?"

"No," she said.

"Where are you?"

"Someplace dark."

"What can you see?"

"Nothing but darkness."

"Is it a building?"

She said nothing at first. Her face screwed up a little. Then she said slowly, "No. It smells like stone. Somewhere outside. I think maybe it's a cave, or the bottom of a canyon. The walls are so high, so dark. It's night, maybe, but I don't see stars."

Chills ran along Corin's back and arms. The Dragon Valleys. He looked up at Joce again, who made a hand-sign. *Nothing wrong.*

He wanted desperately to touch Tam but knew he could not if this was to proceed. Bron was tensed like a hunting cat.

"Are you alone?"

She did not answer for a long time. Finally she said, "I think so."

Corin exhaled slowly. He had not realized he was holding his breath. He had to remind himself that she was here, in this room, safe.

"Can you hear anything?"

Tam shifted on the chair. "There's wind," she said. "It's blowing very hard, I can hear it whistling. Nothing else." Then a long pause. Her face wrinkled with concentration again. "No, wait. There is a different noise. A scrape. Something scratching. It's like metal on metal, it hurts my ears. Piano. Someone is playing the piano. The air is moving around me. It's cold."

He did not need to see Joce step forward to know that meant trouble. Instantly Corin said, "Bring her back."

Liko snapped his fingers. She sat bolt upright. Her eyes sprang open. "Corin," she said urgently, "the dragons. The roof. Now. Run."

"Tam?"

"I'm all right. Go, hurry. It's Tai."

This was what would free her. He said over his shoulder to Joce, "Question him some more, then let him go," and ran. He heard Bron stop to say something to Teron but ignored it. The captain would catch up to him.

The stairs on the last two levels were steep and narrow and not well lit, and he was forced to go more slowly. Bron was just a few steps behind. They made enough noise with their coming that the men in the guardroom at the top were ready and attentive, not slouching and talking the way they would be again as soon as he was well gone. Roof-watch was a tedious and mostly unnecessary duty. Last night it hadn't been. There were two men stationed here and two at the other end. He ordered Bron to send them all down a level.

It was still morning, but heat rose from the stones around him.

Sun blazed on the pale granite and made him squint. There was no wind. In the west a line of greyness might have been gathering clouds or might only have been heat haze. He hoped a storm would break the heat. The air felt heavy.

The spot where dragons came, when they did, was quite noticeable. The stone had been scored by claws and darkened with fire and ash. It glittered from thousands—millions—of bits of crushed dragon scales that could not be seen alone but had accumulated and compressed over the centuries. The blood left last night had been scrubbed off, and the unnaturally clean stone was brighter than that around it. He shielded his eyes with his hand.

Electricity crackled along his skin, raising the hairs on his arms. Everything went silent. He thought it had been quiet before, but now he knew what silence was. The light changed into that heavy tinted stillness he had seen once before in the garden. He walked toward the dragon stones, not even hearing his footfalls. Bron stepped toward him; Corin waved him back, a dread that he had gone deaf growing in his gut. If everything else had been still and motionless that would have been easier to accept than this sudden total quiet.

He knelt beside the stones. In the strange light he saw the bloodstains that were forever part of the stone now. Heartsick for his sisters, he touched one of the stones. It seemed to yield. He flattened his hands beside him and leaned forward, looking. The stones began to ripple with light.

It quickened and silvered, until it was as shiny and bright as new-minted plate. The ripples continued, iridescent, like oil on sunlit water. Like a dragon's wing. He could hear them, the faintest hums, in his head and not his ears. He was no musician, but Tai was, and she had tried to tell him how she could hear the notes before she played them. Now he understood.

The sounds increased in volume until he could make out distinct hums and whistles and clicks. Like birdcalls, but more complicated and within the mind. The dragons were talking to one another, but he did not understand the language to speak back, to ask.

Images. He tried to make images, but he could not keep them

from dissolving into one another. He stared at the shining stone, listened to the whistles. His sister's face would not stay fixed in his mind. *I need her to be safe.* He was mired in words.

Carefully, very very carefully, he put one fingertip on the stone again. He felt it ready to give beneath him, to open up and swallow him whole. The sounds shifted, were clearer, sharper, more distinct. They seemed straighter and less wobbly, as though he had been hearing them through a distorting liquid that was gone. The dragons were aware of him. Some of the sounds were directed to him.

You wanted me, he thought. *I am here. You wanted me. I am here.*

Over and over, until they had no meaning for him, he did not know who was *you* or *I* or *am* or *here,* they were just a rhythm of sounds, a beat like surf. His body was absent. Fire roared. He was at a still point, and the world and time spun around him, streaks of light and motion.

Blackness spread, and he thought he looked down a passageway or a well, a curving endless darkness. It was bitter cold. *I could step through,* he thought, though he did not know where he would go.

No, said the dragons. *It is not for you.*

His breast thrummed with the force of their words.

A memory. Tai played an elaborate, lively, beautiful melody, and he stood leaning over the edge of the piano, listening, knowing he had heard it before and unable to say where. She looked at him and saw that he was puzzled, and she sang a few words, so softly he had to listen several times to understand them. When he did—*Oh, the barrels are full, let's set them to roll*—he began to laugh so hard he could not stop. He sank onto the piano bench beside her. She finished a chord triumphantly and started laughing herself. It was a common and crude drinking song, one that became more and more vulgar verse by verse until it dissolved into incomprehensible thieves' cant, and she had dressed it up and beautified it so that it could be sent out into the highest society. *I didn't know you knew that,* he said to her. *Guards have their uses,* she said. She began to play again, this time in a minor key and very slowly, with low notes. *Now it's a dirge,* she said. *I think I prefer the other version, Corin, shall I make that one your coronation march?* He said, *If you will play the dirge at my wedding,* and she elbowed him off the bench, flexed her fingers, and started something else.

"My lord!" Bron shouted, and he lost his balance, fell, as darkness rushed over him with the force of a waterfall, stinging, pressing him to the ground, filling his nose, his eyes, his ears, his mouth, and then came the dragon sounds again. He reached toward them, desperately. Please.

She was there, in the darkness, hand extended to him. He got to his feet and reached for her. Ice crystals glittered on his arm. He could not feel her hand, though he saw it clasped in his. He pulled.

He got his arm out, saw her wrist, her face. She was almost through.

Then something tugged at her, jerking him forward into the darkness. He pulled but his arm was cold, his face was cold. He tried to shout her name and felt ice forming on his lips and in his nose. Her fingers slipped out of his grasp. He lunged for her and was blocked. He heard her cry out, but it was very distant.

He tumbled backward onto the roof, landing with a painful jolt, and the darkness vanished. There was no Tai. The ice on his lashes melted and ran into his eyes. His face tingled. He sat up, felt light-headed at first but steadied. His fingertips were stinging. Oh God, he thought, please let her have made it back to Mycene. Damn you, dragons, damn you. Whatever Hadon might do now was not as bad as what waited in the darkness.

He tried to rub some life into his white cold hand. Bron knelt beside him and rubbed it methodically between his own until Corin shook it free, feeling the blood moving again.

Only then did they look at each other. "What did you see?" Corin asked.

"A dragon. A black dragon. It came and was gone like that. It was cold." He was obviously shaken.

"They move faster than our eyes can see," Corin said. "That's all."

"Yes, sir." The captain did not sound convinced. But he probably would not want to pry too deeply. There were things men preferred not to know.

Corin stood up. He thought that he smelled fire. He knew what uncontrolled fire looked like, long smears of brownish-grey along the sky, pillars of smoke seeming as substantial as stone. Nothing. The sky was clear. He went to the wall and stared down at the garden. Yesterday it would have been full of gaily dressed people. Now the only color among the different greens was the flower beds.

He longed for Tam. She was going to have to wait. It was time to go and report failure to his father.

It was dark when he finally went to his rooms. He sent one of the guards to let Tam know he was free, then shut the door and sank tiredly into a chair. Aram was sending his mother and sister off tomorrow, someplace he would not reveal. Bron was to go with them; when Corin went, he would go alone. Corin wanted Tam to go too, but he knew she would be happier at home, and safe enough with Joce. He had seen her briefly at midday, long enough to tell her what had happened, but no more.

Tam took longer than he expected to come. When she did come in, she smelled of the stables. She wore a knife in a plain leather sheath, as well as trousers and a peasant-style shirt that was too big for her. She had her hair in two girlish braids and looked about fifteen.

"What," he said, "have you been doing?"

"Making friends with a horse. That is your father's fault. Should I go bathe?"

The trousers showed the shape of her buttocks, hips, and legs as no skirt ever could. There was a lovely curve at the top of her thigh. "You can bathe here," he said. "But your boots go in the hall. Sit down. Have you eaten?"

"Yes," she said. "Riding isn't the only thing I've been learning. Look." She handed him the knife. He drew it and looked at the blade. It was light for his hand, the sort he had carried when he was a dozen years younger. The steel was good, not the very best Cylician but much better than the blades worn by most men.

"Is someone teaching you?"

She struck a pose. The position of her arm brought her breasts forward temptingly. "Joce," she said.

"Good." He was not sure he would have trusted any other man to do it, not when she looked like that.

She flopped into a chair. He knelt and pulled her boots off. She wiggled her feet. He resisted temptation, took the boots out into the hall, gave a few orders to the guards. There was a curtained alcove farther down the hall where Joce could sleep. When he shut the door he bolted it. Then he went to the bathroom and began to fill the marble tub.

Tam came in. There was still a scent of hay and sweat about her, but that was almost pleasant. "I don't have anything to change into," she said.

He stood behind her and cupped her breasts. "You can wear something of mine," he said. He ran his hands down her sides and then back up under the shirt. He kissed her neck. "Silk, velvet, the finest royal robes." He squeezed her nipples.

She turned around and kissed him for a very long time. "I love you," she said. She leaned over and felt the water. "Now go away."

Reluctantly he went out, shutting both the bathroom door and the bedroom door behind him, and looked for something to do in the sitting room. He paced. He picked up books, turned pages, put them down. He swept the hearth clear of ashes three times.

He was on the verge of opening the door and talking to the guards when he heard the bedroom door open. Her feet were soundless on the carpet. He turned.

Her hair was down, damp and shining. She wore a dark red silk robe of his. It was too long for her, the sleeves falling past her wrists and the hem trailing on the floor. She had belted it tightly, but it gapped at the top. It clung to her body at waist and hips. Her legs were shadows in the robe. Her breasts were loosely covered, undefined, tantalizing fullness. He had never seen anyone so beautiful.

She put her arms around his neck. She smelled different now, yet familiar. He puzzled over it, then realized it was the soap. She had used his, not her own. He gave silent thanks that he had not been in the habit of keeping lavender soaps and rose creams and other such womanly things in his own bathroom for his lovers that would have made him think of someone else. He put his hands on her hips.

She kissed his chin. He wished he had shaved.

"Tam," he whispered.

"Corin." She was so confident. He did not know where she got it, she who blushed when looked at. Her fingers were at his placket, unbuttoning his shirt.

He reached down to untie the robe, but she shook her head, so he contented himself with running his hands along the silk, feeling her body underneath. She finished with his shirt and pulled it off, kissed his collarbone. "I love your shoulders," she said.

Then she slipped away and went to the bedroom door, leaned seductively against the frame. He turned off the glowlamps, leaving only a candle for light. He picked it up to carry into the bedroom. He had barely put it down when she was coiled around him.

"You are like a hungry cat," he said.

"I am hungry."

"Do as you wish," he said. How was she so sensual, so knowing, when she had been a virgin two nights ago? "We have all the time in the world."

"I think you need to show me what there is to do," she murmured.

"With pleasure."

"Isn't that the point?" she asked, and he burst out laughing. She was grinning too. He could not remember ever having had such amusement in the midst of lovemaking. Other women had always been a little cautious, a little deferential, even in the fullness of passion. He supposed he had made them so.

"Behind you, my love," he said, "is a most useful tool in the conjugation of the sexes. It is called a bed."

She looked demurely at the floor. "What do you do with it?"

He started to speak, then stopped. "Tam, I don't want to hurt you," he said.

"I just spent three hours on a horse," she said. "I don't think you can do anything that hurts more."

She wasn't going to be able to walk tomorrow. "Don't let me," he said. "There are plenty of possibilities. Now, I believe I was about to tell you of a bed."

"So you were."

"Sit down." This time when he tried to untie the robe she did not stop him.

A dog was barking, loudly and repeatedly. Corin sat up slowly, puzzled even through his drowsiness; there should be no dog here. Beside him Tam was asleep on her side, turned toward the wall. It sounded like his father's dog. And as soon as he had that thought, he was awake and tense, fear cold in his belly. He could feel the dragons heavy in the air, approaching. He blazed the candles into light without thinking.

He dressed rapidly in riding leathers and shook Tam. "Wake up." While she was still making her way up from sleep he looked for her clothing. It lay discarded in the bathroom. He grabbed it and went hastily back to the bedroom.

She was sitting, the blanket clutched in her hands. "Corin?" She sounded scared. "Corin, what is it?"

"Get dressed," he said, tossing the clothes at her. He found some loose coins and swept them into a money pouch. He never carried much, but it should be enough for her. A cloak for each of them. His gloves and knife. His sword. Her knife.

She was dressed. She fumbled with the knife belt but had it on soon enough, awkward but secure. He put his sword on while she pinned the cloak. There were people running in the halls, he could hear them. She looked small and lost and fierce.

He gave her the money. "We have to run."

"What's happening?"

"The dragons," he said. "Hadon is sending them against us." He took her hand and pulled her toward the bedroom door.

"My boots," she said.

"They're outside."

They were out of the bedroom by now, a few paces from the door to the hallway. Someone pounded on it from the other side. He slid the bolt free and jerked the door open.

There were three guards and Joce. The barking dog was loud and coming closer. Tam's boots, freshly cleaned and polished, stood in the hall. She picked them up and tightened her grip on his hand.

He ran with her to the entrance hall to the wing. Mari was already there, looking haggard, holding the baby. Bron carried her small son, who was still deeply asleep with his head against the captain's shoulder, and the nurse had an armful of blankets. A dragon was landing on the roof, its hum insistent. It was calling him.

Tam sat on a bench to put her boots on. He saw her hands shaking. A short staircase went to the upper level of the royal apartments, and several soldiers were coming down it. Aram was behind them, one hand gripping Sika's lead, Talia on his other side.

Corin looked at Tam. She stood up. Everything had happened so fast, already he had only snatches in his memory. He wished time would stop so he could hold this moment forever.

"You're leaving," she said.

"Yes."

"What should I do?"

"Go home. Be careful."

She flung her arms around him. He had nothing to give her but exile. He tipped her head back and kissed her. The grief was beginning in his throat.

"I love you," he said around it. The forbidden words rose to his lips. He did not push them back. "Marry me."

"I love you," she said, hardly more than a whisper. "I will."

He kissed her again. When he looked up, Mari was standing beside him with her betrothal ring in the palm of her hand. "For now," she said.

He slid the ring on Tam's finger. His father was next to him. Aram said, "Do you mean it, both of you?"

"Yes," said Corin. Tam nodded. A single tear was sliding down her cheek. He could see her forcing the others back.

"This may be my last official act," Aram said. "Clasp hands. Do you, Corin, take this woman, Tam, to be your lawful wedded wife?"

"I do."

"Do you, Tam, take this man, Corin, to be your lawful wedded husband?"

"I do."

"Thou art wed. Now go, Corin, get out of here, now."

He looked at her. I will come for you, he thought. He did not say it. *Don't make promises you can't keep.* He kissed her one last time, then ran. He heard the king command the guards not to follow. Up the steps, the hallway, the next steps, the roof. The dragon.

Kelvan was standing midway between the dragon and the stairs. "My lord!" he called, his voice sharp and rich all at once.

On the dragon now, the straps, the helmet. The crouch and leap, the loud wingbeats. The surge of joy at flying, quickly tamped down. Below, the city was darkness blotched with fire, and there seemed to be dragons circling everywhere, fire falling from them in hissing rushing showers of white light and sparks. Kelvan was flying up, and west, the ground rapidly falling away, the fires diminishing to tiny glowing embers. It was getting very cold.

Kelvan twisted in his seat and made a gesture that seemed to indicate safety. Corin slumped as the driving fear rushed out of him. Below was a vast and sweeping plain of darkness, the fallen kingdom.

CHAPTER THIRTEEN

T am stood quiet and still as Corin raced out of sight. She had no thoughts, no feelings, not even a sense of herself. Then the moment cracked. The baby was whimpering. *Go home*, he had said, but she had no idea how to do that.

Aram had given the dog's lead to Talia, who was rubbing its ears. The king was speaking to Joce. They were talking about her, Tam was certain of that, but it did not matter. She knew she should say something to Mari, but if she spoke at all she was going to completely fall apart. So she waited.

The men came to her. Aram put his hands on her shoulders. She looked numbly at him, and the intensity of his gaze pulled her into presence. She bent her head, and that other Tam said calmly, "My lord."

"Go with Joce," he said. "Be safe. This isn't the end."

Joce was beckoning. She went. Two guards followed.

It was all movement again, not running but quick paces, many glances behind. Down many short flights of stairs, through an old and heavy door, into a narrow and ill-lit corridor that seemed to go on forever. Doors opened from it on the left but not the right, which was only plain unplastered stone. Their feet were loud and echoing, except for Joce, who was quiet even in boots. She was afraid to say anything, and no one else spoke.

And then, finally, another flight of steps, up this time. They were old and crooked and an ugly mottled yellowish-grey. The door at the stairs' top opened into a stone guardroom, several men alert within. Each of the three other walls also had a door set into it, all with new and heavy bolts and shiny hinges. The one on the left was open, more steps descending into darkness. She moved toward it.

"Not that way," Joce said. He caught her by the hand and pulled her to the door opposite the one they had come in. She followed him out into the night.

Not darkness: there was a reddish-orange light everywhere, and thick stinging smoke. Bits of ash drifted through the air. When she looked up, she saw more fire pouring down, and she could hear the keening screams of the dragons, like a hunting hawk's but so much louder and harsher. The hair on her body stood up, and her skin pimpled.

Joce was still pulling her. The guards had not come. She jerked her hand free and caught up to him. They were going toward the stables. He started to run as soon as she was with him, and she ran as well. He did not outpace her as they crossed a stone courtyard to the stable gate.

When they reached it he looked around. "I'll bring out the horses," he said. "Wait. If anything happens, yell." It was a quick commanding voice that would have brought resentment boiling up if she had been elsewhere. As it was, she leaned against the gate, clutching it tightly, wishing she had something else to think about.

It was impossible to ignore the fire. The city would be burned to nothing within hours. The palace still stood, massive, stone, unshakable. But there were lights in many windows, and fearful voices. Her eyes were burning miserably from the smoke. The flames compelled her. She took a step forward. Cina was in there, and Jenet.

"No," said Joce from behind her, startling her. He was leading the horses out, the ungirthed saddles sliding on their blankets. He had a water flask slung over his shoulder.

"Cina—we can't leave her," she said urgently.

"The king sent men," he said. "There's nothing you or I can do better."

She shook her head, acknowledging the truth of it, and went to help him with the saddles. They had to get out quickly. There was no one to linger for. If Corin was out on a dragon, he was miles away. Joce helped her up, mounted himself, said, "Stay beside me or behind me. We're making for the North Road, if we get separated keep going." Then he put his heels to his horse.

I don't know how to get to the North Road, she thought.

They took the usual track from the stables to the gates of the grounds. Amazingly, two guards were still standing at their entrance post. Joce pulled up sharply, said, "The prince got out. The king was on his way. Make sure the people know that, know they're not dead."

They were able to gallop through the streets surrounding the palace, which were wide and well maintained. Most of the large buildings were dark, and there were few other people on the streets or outside at all.

A dragon screamed. Tam's horse put back its ears but did not stop or rear. There was a sound like a crack, and then a hiss, and then brightness; a mansion half a block behind them had gone up in flames. Tam peered over her shoulder and saw a tree black against the orange, its leaves waving in the fire's wind. Already the air was hotter. It frightened her; she kicked the horse forward until she was right beside Joce, and then they both went faster.

But all too soon they were in narrower and more crowded streets, thick with people fleeing in all directions like ants whose nest had been disturbed. Most were on foot, some were on horse or even in a coach. Tam tried to stay beside Joce, but several times he had to reach over and pull at the reins himself to keep them together. The horses were not panicking, but she was having difficulty controlling hers; it had been trained for a better rider. The buildings were all dark against the reddish-orange dusky sky.

They came to a street so crowded that they had to walk the horses. In the eerie glow the faces did not look human; they were masks, or paintings, or they belonged to some other kind of creature altogether. They all had the same numb expression, they all looked alike in mute disbelief. Tam supposed her own face was like that. Joce's was not; his was hard and dangerous. She knew that he had been a spy among the Sarians, and it was easy now to see that he had probably done it very well. If Corin had not so obviously trusted him she would be fleeing from him too.

Joce turned abruptly into a narrow alley. The houses were high and cramped together, looking like cracked and fissured canyon walls in the strange light. If one of them caught, she and Joce would go up like tinder immediately. Her throat was too dry to swallow. Her eyes were starting to swell shut from the smoke.

The alley opened onto a curving narrow street with few people. They mounted again. Joce turned left, then halted at the sound of a roar and a crash as a stone house collapsed into rubble ahead of him, blocking the way. Tam watched for a moment, stunned by the immensity of it. Dust clouds billowed up orangely. When she turned to the right, she saw several sheets of fire licking at one another and the nearby buildings. They were trapped.

Frantic, she stared in every direction. The horse's ears were flat against its head and it was breathing fast. There, between those two buildings, a dark passage. She kicked the beast forward. To her surprise Joce did not try to stop her. The passage was very narrow—she could have touched the walls on either side if she had extended her arms—and the horse went carefully. They came out in a square with houses on three sides and a lane on the fourth. Streetlights shone along it. The horse went that way without urging.

After that time passed in jerks and starts. She went from one corner to the next without noticing anything in between. Then, finally, they came unharmed onto an empty street that was lined with warehouses on either side. On the right, the road went slowly and straightly downhill, probably to the river. Joce looked at her, then turned left and took them uphill. The horses trotted with what seemed to be relief. The hill was long and high but not steep. When they reached the top Joce halted and passed the water flask to her.

Tam took one drink, judiciously, then said through thick cracked lips, "Where are we?" Her throat was raw.

"Drink all you want, my lady, there will be more."

She wondered how, but had two more long swallows. The water was still slightly cool, and it was the most wonderful thing she had ever had. She returned the flask to him. He took only a short swallow.

"We can rest a bit more," he said. "We're only a mile from Northgate. We're almost through."

The wind was picking up, and when she looked west she saw light flashing along the sky. She wondered if dragons could fly in a storm, if the wind would spread the fires everywhere before rain could put them out, if she would be out of the city before it struck.

There was a very low and distant rumble of thunder, and she realized she had not heard a dragon cry for a while.

She rubbed her face tiredly. "Let's go."

The warehouse district was large and empty. The few people they saw scurried out of their way. It was dark; there were no fires here, and no streetlights. The buildings loomed against the orange glow of the sky. As they rode, the clop of the horses' hooves on the empty street began to seem louder and louder, and then even menacing. Tam shivered.

Warehouses gave way to empty shops. They turned. She saw the pale arch of Northgate not far ahead of them. And then she saw the green-white brightness of the light behind it, and the long shadows of armed men, and the scattered bodies on the street.

She turned the horse before she realized it, and so did Joce. He led her at a gallop through a maze of streets. She kept looking over her shoulder to see if they were being followed. This was much worse than running from fire. Her hands were slippery with fear-sweat on the reins. She remembered things her father had told her about heads on stakes, women raped with knives.

The cobbles became dirt, the buildings were smaller. The rain started. Still there was no sign of pursuit, and it was hard to think of anything but the storm. Wind flung stinging raindrops against her skin and whipped the puddles into rippling seas. The air was still full of the acrid scent of smoke. A lightning bolt that would have whitened the air on an ordinary day made it into bright blinding mist. Corin's cloak was a plain dark wool, suitable for cool mornings or windy evenings, but it was no protection in the downpour. She kept her face lowered and let the horse follow Joce's.

Eventually the houses and shops thinned and then gave way to open ground. It was very dark. But by the time the storm moved off, she thought it was becoming lighter. She realized that they were back on a main road. The field birds began to sing in the trees and hedges. The darkness slowly faded into grey and then into the land's own colors. The sky was clear. Water caught in spiderwebs glimmered.

They stopped. Tam looked at her legs and noticed as though they belonged to another person that they were trembling. The soaked pants were clinging to her. She released her grip on the horse and let her feet be looser in the stirrups. Her back hurt, she was still wet through, there was a light breeze that was making her cold. On one side of the road was a field, the green shoots only a few inches high in the dark soil. On the other side, between the road and a line of old thick dark trees, was a meadow, its grasses bent over with their own wet heaviness. A few rabbits were sitting up, watching the riders. A hill covered with trees rose behind the meadow.

Joce turned his horse. The rabbits scattered. Tam followed him. Caithenor was back there, a cloud of heavy brown smoke still hanging over it. Their view of the city itself was cut off by the gentle rolls of the land and by distance. Tam wanted to see the palace, tall on its hill, but could not make out even that, only the smoke. She was very tired.

"We got out," she said. Her voice was thin and trembly.

"We got out. I don't think they saw us at all."

"Who were they?"

"Sarians," he said. "Or Myceneans with Sarian weapons."

Tam had known that. Otherwise she would not have asked. "They got here too fast. Even with dragons."

"Yes. I'm afraid Hadon's betrayal was much deeper and older than we thought."

Tam nodded. It didn't seem to matter. She took a deep breath and sat up straight. "What now?"

"There's a village up ahead, a few miles. Can you ride that far, my lady?"

"I'll have to," she said. "But I'm no lady now, or where we're going. Call me by my name."

"As you say. But in that case you will need a different pin for your cloak."

She had put the cloak on without examining it. Now she saw that the design was the crowned eagle of the royal house. She hoped she had not gone off with Corin's only royal brooch, leaving him as undecorated as any commoner. Well, nothing could be done about it. She wondered if Aram had noticed.

Suddenly it struck her as funny, and she laughed. There was an edge of panic in the laughter, and she stopped immediately. At least she still had that much control. She looked down at her hand for the first time. The ring fit well. The band was an engraved gold, the stone a large emerald. It was obviously a betrothal ring, one that had been given to Mari by her husband, who was dead now. And Mari had given it to Corin to give to her. She was married to him.

She wept soundlessly, not trying to stop it, and Joce did not try to comfort her. After a few minutes she was done. I won't cry again, she thought. "I'm ready."

The sun was well up when they reached the village. They stopped at an inn, to rest and water the horses. Joce left Tam in the common room, where she waited nervously until he returned with a sack of food for them and clothes for her. She took them into a room to change. The shirt was too large, and the pants too long, and both were stained and worn, but they were clean and dry. She rolled up sleeves and trouser legs, tightened the rope belt, and found Joce readying the horses. They set off again, carrying their breakfast.

Twice in the morning they saw a circling dragon shining high up against the blue sky. Otherwise there was no evidence of war.

They took the country roads, not the main highway, avoiding towns. Fields and pastures and woodland-covered hillsides, goats and streams and ancient oaks. Here and there a shrine with a bit of food, some feathers, a woven hex. Villages that were only a few huts on rutted roads with dogs yelping and children staring, fascinated. It became a blur for Tam. Whenever she thought of Corin she raised her head and stared along the line of road as far as she could see, and after a while the thoughts vanished in the warmth of sun on her bare forearms and the breeze bending the grasses on the verge.

By midday it was quite hot. They stopped to rest on a tree-shaded riverbank, not far below a mill. They could hear the mill working and the water roaring through it, though they could not see it for the trees. After they ate, Tam sat motionless in the lassitude of heat and watched the sunlight twining through the branches. Even the birds were still.

She was thinking it was time to go when she heard the shrill cry of a dragon, close. She shuddered. The horses stomped nervously. Quick as a cat Joce was squatting beside her, one hand on her shoulder. His skin was fever-hot.

She squirmed and looked at him. He raised a finger to his lips and then released her. He rose lightly and went to the horses, caught each one's reins in a hand. They were trembling and sweating, ears back and nostrils flared, but they stayed under his control.

Tam felt it then, the dragon presence, searching. It was a cold sharp needle in her mind. They won't hurt me, she thought. They won't hurt me. Not if they want Corin to help them. But she could not help remembering the things the dragons had done under Hadon's command. Bodies on a roof, fire in the sky. If they were slaves she was not safe.

She stared at the ripples on the water, the sun glancing off in silver, and emptied her mind of everything else. Images came to her. Black lava flows. The stone was rough and full of pocks. A waterfall spilling down a tall mountainside, and a river with a scattering of huts beside it. A throne with dragons carved on the arms. A blood-stained sword lying on granite. A man whose skin was the waxy white of death and whose lips and fingernails had turned blue, with steam curling around him. A black moth, circling a candle flame.

The dragon was speaking to her, but she did not understand it. They had done it once before, telling her they meant to free Tai, but she had only understood because she was already in their space. She thought of colored sand on a silver tray and wondered if they had spoken to her then as well. It made her shiver.

The pain in her mind vanished. The dragon cried again, higher and farther away. It was leaving. Joce released the horses, which bent to grazing as if nothing had happened. He looked at her and she was frozen by his gaze. It was gone in less than a second. He had to have some sort of power, not just knowledge of it. It was strange how readily she accepted that now. Aram had known, which was why he had put them together. She wondered if Joce knew about the dragons and Corin's task.

She stood and asked the question she had been trying not to think. "What if the king didn't get out?"

"That we will hear news of. I am certain he did, though. There were plans in place. Better you know nothing of them."

"But if he didn't . . ."

"If he is dead, you are the queen," he said. "And nowhere will be safe. We will probably have to hide in the Fells. It will be hard."

You are the queen. The food she had just eaten felt heavy in her stomach. What had she done? "They'll come looking for me," she said.

"I am afraid so."

"Can we go through the woods and fields?"

"Not on horse. I would prefer not to turn loose the horses until we must, they are too useful."

"They're too good," she said. "No one will recognize me if we walk. I'll cut my hair."

"They will be watching your home," he said. "We can't go there."

"My parents—" she said, frantic. If Cina had not escaped, or Jenet, or others, they could have been tortured to tell everything they knew about Tam. Alina might have talked before she died. When Tam opened the door, Alina's black blind face had been in front of her, swinging slightly. The rope squeaked as it moved against the bar. One of her shoes dragged on the floor, scraping. She felt sick.

Neither spoke. Tam wondered if Joce was waiting for her to give him an order. A coldness moved across her skin, like wind. Nothing stirred in the leaves. She swallowed.

"The dragon," she said. "It spoke to me. I didn't understand it."

He did not respond to that either. His face was not its usual unreadable mask. He seemed troubled, perplexed. It was uncharacteristic of him. He took a step toward her. Suddenly she was frightened. Did he mean to leave her, or to force her with him?

He took her left hand and kissed Mari's ring, gently released it.

His skin was still hot. His face smoothed. "My lady," he said. "I need to tell you something so you can choose well. But I am breaking my word to several people, including the king. It is rightly he who should tell you, not I. Can I have your promise of silence?"

"Does Corin know?" She did not want to keep secrets from him.

"Yes."

"Then tell me, and I will keep confidence."

"I can get you into Dalrinia unseen. Even into your home."

"With power."

"Yes, my lady."

"What kind of power, Joce?"

"Wizardry," he said.

Tam understood things then. His hot skin, his silver eyes, his freezing gaze. The stories said wizard-power was within, not power that one reached for. She understood too what a terrible secret it was.

"But I'm not one," she said hesitantly.

"No."

"Did you tell the king I had it?"

He shook his head. "I had no knowledge of you earlier than you had of me. My lord has no power either, but he has made enough study of it to see it when it chances to awake."

It was almost too much. She said, "What do I do?"

He took what seemed years to give her an answer. "You have to know your power," he said at last. "I can teach you that through the knife."

"Then do it." She realized it was her first command. She took a deep breath and drew her knife.

He said, "First stillness. Turn your blade up and watch it. Hold with both hands if you must. You have to be the blade."

She obeyed. The knife was straight and silver. The sharpness of the edges gleamed in the sun. She stared. Time slipped away into nothingness. Elbows bent, she held the knife still and upright, a line between her hands and the sky. Her legs were a line too, pinning her feet to the earth. She was utterly still and the rest of the world moved around her. The knife was radiance. She had not thought that light had weight. But everything did. Souls were moths and love was butterflies. The true world was out there, where the carousel horses had run, and if she raised the knife she would pierce through the shell surrounding her and enter it again. Her breath was slow and even. Silver light spilled down her arms like water. It had felt much like this when Liko put her into trance.

"Stillness, and speed. Swing the knife."

A crow cawed in one of the trees. It echoed in her head. It would speak words to her if she let it. She moved her arm in the motions he had taught her. She was surprised at how much easier it seemed; the weight of the knife balanced her. Quiet, like the standing had been. She swung her arm out once more and felt that connection, the light going through her. Once more, over and over.

"Enough," he finally said. He sounded pleased. She was surprised at the disappointment in her. It felt extraordinarily natural, the knife a part of her body. She had not wanted to stop. He must have sensed that, because he said, "Don't try the knife practice alone. You'll wear yourself out or get into a bad habit."

"Yes. All right." She sheathed the blade and looked at the river again. The water moved slowly and steadily, covered with green reflections and light-tipped ripples.

In Illyria there was a place called the Lake of the Dead. She had been to it years ago, before Tyrekh, when she and her brother accompanied her father on the first part of his second trip to Sarium. The story was that there had been a town there once, centuries ago, and then rains came, and then an earthquake. The quake shook the weakened earth and threw rocks down into the flooded river, damming it. The waters rose and filled the valley, drowning the people and buildings. On certain moonlit nights the town was said to stir again, the fully fleshed dead moving through the water as if it were air. It was a beautiful place, with high wooded hills on either side and water the deepest blue Tam had ever seen. There were no dead, she knew that, but it was, or had been, a gateway. She saw that now with astonishing clarity. Memories of power lingered and became stories.

There was power in Caithenor. Lines spreading and branching

like roots, some frail tendrils and some thick knots that would sprout again like witch-grass if you broke them. It was a knot under the palace. That was what had enabled her to See, and Aram to see her.

Black moths. Corin on the steps, staring inhumanly outward. Aram's hands on her shoulders. Horses riding over blackness, the scrape of claws and rush of wings. The crow cawed again. She found it, a darkness in the thick shadows of a tree's branches. Hidden in the sunlight. She could do that.

"Even if it's safe, I can't risk something happening to my parents. I'm going to have to go back to Caithenor," she said.

"We dare not. It's very dangerous," Joce said. "As much from random acts as from anyone looking for you. There's no safe place to hide, not with Sarians there. We need to go to Pell. It's large. You will be well hidden. I can find the king's agents."

Agents. He meant spies. If they were loyal she would be safe.

"Not back to Caithenor yet," she said. "We'll let things settle a little. Find barns and clearings and root cellars to hide. I'll practice. But if you have the power to sneak me home unseen, even where they will be waiting for me, I trust you have the power to slip us back into Caithenor unnoticed when they have stopped searching."

He looked at her for a very long time. If he refused there was nothing she could do about it; it would be both stupid and useless to run away from him.

"Why?" he asked.

She told him the only truth she had. "In Caithenor I am stronger."

He was silent again. She could not read the expression on his face. Finally he said, "God help me if anything happens to you and I live to tell about it, but we'll go back. And on our way and when we are there you will do exactly as I say."

"Agreed," she said. It was a fair bargain.

He held the horse for her to mount. When she looked down at him he said, "His Highness could not have chosen better."

She flushed. He pretended not to notice.

CHAPTER FOURTEEN

❧

An eerie blue light flickered along the ridgetops. Sometimes it flashed brightly, bleaching exposed granite into something as stark and lifeless as a full moon. The ribbon of waterfall cascading down the cliffs at the eastern end of the valley caught the light and threw it back so that the mountain seemed to be splitting. The sky was black and starry in the east, but the wind was blowing hard and cold. Clouds were piling rapidly over the sea.

"What is it?" Corin asked. He had been in the wizards' valley before, but he had never seen such a light.

"Something is trying to get in," said Kelvan.

"Soldiers?"

"Perhaps. Would you have me check?"

Corin shook his head. "No." He trusted the valley's defenses to hold. But if he had in fact been traced there somehow—it seemed impossible—he had to leave. Flee once more. He had a brief image of being pushed farther and farther north until he was alone on a plain of ice at the top of the world. Dragon cold come to meet him. He rubbed his right hand and arm reflexively.

Tai had made it back alive and was now locked in lavish but well-guarded apartments. Kelvan said there was no longer any pretense that she was a guest. It was the attempt to rescue her that had unleashed the attack on Caithenor. In his bitterest moments Corin blamed himself for that too. He had precipitated battle before they were ready. Aram had had things in hand, he never should have interfered. Even if he had brought her through, Hadon would have sent forth his dragons. Corin had no idea if anyone in Mycene could have seen what happened, but Hadon had known, and that was enough.

By speaking through the dragons to a rider he trusted, Kelvan had learned that Tyrekh himself had come in to Caithenor on dragonback the day after they fled; there had been an agreement of some sort after all. Sarians had come in rapidly on horse. The foot soldiers, who must have been slipping in for months, were mostly Mycenean, but there were some Sarians among them. Mycenean or Sarian, many had fire weapons, as did the riders. Kelvan himself had a war-light. Hadon had equipped his men well. Corin knew his father was not dead or captured, but nothing more about Aram. Kelvan had obtained the names of some of the dead. Too many of them were men and women Corin would miss, including Ellid and the marshal, Coll. He had received the news of the discovery of Arnet's body floating in the river, a knife in its back, with a most unprincely satisfaction. He tried not to think about Tam.

"Is it possible Hadon knows about this valley?" he asked.

"Not unless someone managed to find out from my dragon," Kelvan said. "I haven't come back that often, and I've never been followed. No one has any reason to come this far north, and Hadon wouldn't want to send anyone. It's too close."

"To the Dragon Valleys." They lay eastward, on the other side of several ridges of higher mountains. "I thought the dragons couldn't go back."

"They can't. I tried once and the dragon nearly lost its mind. I was sicker than I've ever been. I thought it would throw me. But he's not going to take chances."

So they should be safe from any of Hadon's riders. Corin did not find that as reassuring as it should have been, since something was trying to get in. The valley was part of a huge swath of Crown lands, wild and lordless, and it was not unlikely that someone would consider the lands a place to search. But it was twelve difficult days from Caithenor by horse. He could not possibly have been tracked by Mycenean soldiers yet.

Wind whipped his cloak against him. The slow dark river was white-capped with the force of the wind pushing against the current. At its mouth, where it met the tide, the water foamed and bubbled. "We'd better get back inside," he said. "It's going to be hell when this breaks."

"I think we need to go see Rois. She may know what it is."

"This late?" It was past midnight. Kelvan had roused him when the lights started, and they went to the riverside, away from the trees that sheltered the cottage, so that they could see. It had been a peaceful place until then. Corin could have stood there in the daytime and watched the reeds and small waterfowl and sunlight for far too long. Even with learning to ride the dragon and losing repeatedly to Kelvan at swordplay, he had too much empty time. No papers to read, no soldiers to train with, no courtiers to placate. He felt inexcusably idle. He still had no idea how to set the dragons free. Not that he dared to do anything yet, while Hadon held Tai. He was learning rider skills fast—everything from understanding dragonspeech to staying strapped in while the dragon turned sideways to checking for scalemites—but such speed was of little use until his sister was freed.

"No one sleeps when that happens," Kelvan said. He gestured broadly at the blue light. "We won't be the first ones there."

"So it's happened before? It might not have anything to do with us?"

"Aye."

There was no more conviction in Kelvan's tone than Corin felt himself. Things were moving, and he was at the fulcrum. He glanced over his shoulder, up the hill. There were no lights on in any of the houses. Huts, really. But Kelvan would know. "Let's go, then," he said. The track was rough and would be difficult in the dark, even worse if it rained. Kelvan refused to use the Sarian light in the valley, and Corin understood him. It would have been a kind of desecration.

They walked past the bulk of the resting dragon. It was dark and still, as undisturbed by the wind as a rock. Corin had to restrain himself from extending his mind to it. The temptation was constant. But it would be too easy to lose himself entirely in dragonthought. He was not supposed to be able to speak to the dragon without touching it, but he could. It was one of the powers they had given him. It would be the hardest to let go of. His senses had sharpened, hearing and sight both, and he was gaining a rider's quickness. He did not care much about those things; it was the speech that seduced him, the images and the words and hums, the dragon presence that extended across time and space beyond the tiny bit of dragon he could see.

That should have extended, he corrected himself. They were tethered to the Empire now.

The path was uneven and gullied, switching back and forth along the hill. Above it the forest was thick and impenetrable, until it gave way to the towering cliffs. Branches were creaking in the wind. It was almost frightening in its wildness. He had given up wearing his sword—there was no need here—but not his knife. He touched the handle for reassurance. The ordinary world was only an outer layer in this valley. Beneath it seeped the old powers and magics of the wizards, quiet and noiseless but ready to leak through into what he so foolishly called *real*. The huts changed their appearance sometimes. It would not have surprised him if the forest moved or the trees spoke.

It was only the dragon power that allowed him to see such things. Six months ago it would have been an ordinary village to his eyes. Poor and powerless.

Rois's hut was about halfway up the hill. As they drew closer he could see the dance of firelight through the cracks in the shutters. He heard low voices before they opened the door.

It was crowded. There was a momentary silence when they entered, a quick assessment of danger. It did not offend him. Caution ran deep in these people. That was why they were still alive. They all knew who he was—it was the only way Kelvan could have brought him at all—but that did not make them less wary of outsiders. Four days was not nearly long enough to earn their trust.

The cottage floor was well-worn wood covered with faded and stained woven rugs. Pots and braids of garlic hung from the rafters. There was something familiar and even soothing about the orderly twists of the garlic stems, and he realized he had seen them before in dragonspeech. It was reassuring to think that the dragons had expected him to come here. The sleeping area was only a loft above the lower room. It could have been any peasant's hut in Caithen, except that the wood was too well planed and joined, the wall above the fireplace too clean of smoke, the hinges on the door too well made. He had a sudden sharp memory of standing in this room with his father. It had seemed as stately as Aram's receiving room, and the king had not looked out of place. Corin had felt out of place himself, somehow smaller and rather stupid. He straightened. He could not afford to feel that way now.

Rois was standing by the fire. She was an old woman, slight, with white hair that hung in a dark-tipped braid nearly to her ankles. He had spoken to her once before, briefly, insubstantially. It had been sufficient for him to know she was at least his match in wits and far surpassed him in wisdom. Her eyes met his and he sensed she had been waiting for him. He suspected Kelvan had known as much. He walked forward alone to join her.

Despite the noise and closeness of the people, there was a quiet space for them. He was as sure as he had ever been of anything that they could not be overheard. A plain wooden stool was to one side of the hearth; as he approached, Rois sank down onto it. He stood in front of her, feeling as though he were about to undergo an examination from a tutor.

She spoke. "Sit down so I can see your face, lad."

Lad! There was nothing but the floor. It was stone here by the hearth. He sat and crossed his legs. She leaned forward and put her thin dry hands on his cheeks. Power seared through him. He jerked back. His breath was coming fast.

She dropped her hands and looked at him. He could not see the silver of her eyes, but he knew it was there. She said, "You are very like your father, Corin."

It was the first time anyone in the village had used his name. It startled him. "Not so much as you think." He wondered how well she knew Aram, to be able to say such a thing.

"More than you know." She straightened. "What is she like, your wife?"

Wife. He was not used to that either. He had told Kelvan only the barest details but was not surprised they had been passed on. It mattered to the villagers who would be queen. Who had his heart in her hand.

"Strong," he said. "Fierce and just and gentle all at once." He paused, made himself meet her eyes. "She is a Seer. Neither of us understands it." Though they had had no time to speak of it.

"It happens," Rois said. "Usually nothing wakes it. We were the same race in the beginning, you know."

He had not known that. But of course they must have been. He nodded. "I fear for her," he said. Kelvan had said that the garrison in Dalrinia had surrendered without bloodshed, which reassured him a little. Of Tam herself he had heard nothing. If she had been captured it would have been trumpeted. But he could not keep from imagining her lying dead in a pasture somewhere. He knew what happened to refugee women.

"Joce will keep her safe."

"Is that a prophecy?"

"We have helped protect you all your life. The shield extends to those you love."

"The Basilisks."

"And others. I was there at your birth. Your mother's maid, a stablehand, a gardener. The people no one ever sees."

"Tam sees them," he said, missing her for that as well.

"You are a fortunate man," she said.

He did not feel fortunate. But there was no point in self-pity. He shifted and looked at the fire. Watching the light, he said, "Am I pursued here?"

"Perhaps. You won't be found. The barrier won't fall."

He felt dwarfed by the power behind her words. He said, "You don't need the king to keep you hidden. Safe. You are far stronger here than an army of ten thousand. Why do you give up your children as servants?"

"Do you ask that question of your other subjects?"

Neatly turned, and that meant he would not get an answer. The wood was fragrant. He forced himself to breathe deeply and loosen his shoulders. The fire's roar and crackle would drown out his thoughts if he let it. It would be so easy to just give up. A bit of wood fell off the end of one of the logs in a shower of golden sparks the color of dragon eyes.

Still watching the flame, he said, "How much has Kelvan told you about the dragons?"

"He said that they have set you the task of freeing them."

"Yes. And I don't know how."

"You know more than you think you do. They've given you the answer," she said. "You simply have to remember it."

That sounded impossible. He clenched his teeth. "What do you know about them?" he asked, a touch of accusation in his voice.

She looked evenly at him. "There is a story that it was wizards who led the Myceneans into the Dragon Valleys. They thought they would be the dragonriders. The wizards took the dragons' fire, but instead the fire killed the wizards, and the Myceneans murdered the ones who were left. It may not be true. It is true that our power began to wane at that time. But I have no special knowledge of dragons."

It only increased his frustration. He could hardly shake a better answer from her, though. He scuffed at the stone with his boot.

His skin tingled sharply, stopped. The room had gone quiet and tense. He was not the only one who had felt something, then. A man near the south window opened the shutters. The blue light flared blindingly. Something dark, wind-tossed, was flung through the window and landed hard on the floor. A bird. Stone-dead, with a broken neck. Its feathers had already lost their luster. The people closest backed away.

Corin stood. He felt sick with fear for Rois, for the villagers. "I can't let this go on," he said. "I'll leave the valley now. Whatever's trying to get in, it's me it's after. I think it's more than soldiers."

"What?" she asked sharply.

"I don't know. It's there in the dark place, the cold place. It stinks of death. Perhaps it guards whatever holds the dragons, perhaps Hadon means to turn it loose on me. It's terrible. And it's desperate. If that's what's out there, if it's free, it may be powerful enough to get through the barrier."

"No," Rois said. "If it were that powerful it already would have. But if it is waiting for you, you must not leave the valley, you will draw it down upon you. I do not need to know what it is to know that anything from the dark place is cruel and in love with pain."

"I'll have to leave the valley to free the dragons."

"Yes. But don't go until you are ready. It is not worth the risk."

He looked at the other people in the cottage. The power of all these wizards in one place must shine like a beacon to any creature that had the eyes to see it. Kelvan had his arm around a pretty, dark-haired woman whose face was laid against his shoulder. It made Corin feel lonely.

Rois said his name. It brought his attention back to her. He said, "The risk to me, or some other risk?"

"The risk to you. You are needed, and not just by dragons."

He had nothing to say. He was the prince. For all he knew he might be the king now. His life was not his to risk casually, dragons notwithstanding. Hadon probably knew that, knew he would be paralyzed by duty. Once Seana had told him he had too much conscience to be king, and he had laughed and told her she was the proof he had no conscience at all, but he knew that he did. Hadon was not hindered by such things.

He watched the light on Rois's cheek. She put her hands in her lap and he saw that they were smooth and straight, not the hands of an old woman. When she was young she must have been beautiful. Then she shifted, and it was gone. Her skin was thin over sharp knuckles. Her face was wrinkled. She looked at him and he guessed that she knew what he had been thinking.

A blast of cold air tore through the room, extinguishing the fire. Rois leaned forward and passed her hand over the wood. Flame sprang up. He had that power too. But he would not use it here in the wizards' valley.

She drew her hand back from the flames and pulled them with her like thread off a spinning wheel. One strand, another, and another. They lay on the air, fluttering, color shifting like opals. She began to weave them together around her fingers, cat's cradle of fire. He watched, fascinated, caught. Without looking at him, she said, "I do not know if dragons are political creatures. I do not know if they care what you are. But you have to remember it."

"I'm not in danger of forgetting," he said bitterly.

She stopped the weaving and turned, offered him the net of flame.

Tai had done this with yarns when she was young. He had never learned the moves. It was something more than idle entertainment for Rois, of that he was certain. A spell, a warding, a prophecy.

She brought her hands together and the flames winked out. "Your lady wife, does she know what's roused?"

His lady wife. He imagined Tam's response to that. "No," he said, stopped. He had run to the roof before he knew everything she saw in trance. They had not spoken of it further in the scant time they had had. That last night, they had tried to shut the world out entirely. "I don't know. She might. She would have told me, but there was no time."

"Does she know how dangerous it is?"

"She knows," he said, remembering how she had tried to tell him the afternoon before the ball. "That may not stop her. She is brave. And very stubborn." If something led her into that place, she would go, heedless of risk, determined.

"Joce can protect her against that too if it comes to it."

Strong blue light flashed through the room again. Everything went momentarily two-dimensional. He remembered the battle with the Sarians at the inn, the way the war-lights had flickered, the white paint on their faces. He should have known then that he would go into exile.

He looked at Rois. Her eyes were sharply silver. "I need help," he said quietly, a declaration, a fact. He would not bargain for it, nor would he demand it. If none was forthcoming he would carry on the best he could.

She was silent for what seemed hours. He expected her to tell him that she could not or would not give him anything. He resisted the urge to look around.

"I can help you," she said finally. "But it's not my help you need. Anything I give to you will only postpone what must happen."

He knew what she meant. But he wasn't ready to think it yet.

Wind blew him and Kelvan roughly about. They crashed into each other more than once. Corin barely kept himself from twisting an ankle on the uneven ground. When blue light flashed he saw the forest above tossing like the sea. The clouds tore along the sky. His eyes watered and his face was raw and cold from the force of the gale.

They reached their own cottage and hurried in. The floor was made of wood, with dips in it from years of treading in the same place. Kelvan got the fire going and they bent in front of it, warming their hands. It hardly seemed summer. The wind shrieked around a corner. It was easy to imagine voices in it. He would have worn a charm around his neck if he had had one.

He felt Kelvan watching him. He looked up. The rider was standing to the side, attentive, forceful. He remembered that as a rider Kelvan had significant power of his own in the Mycenean court. Four days was not long enough for him to know Kelvan well either. He trusted him entirely, but he could not predict what he might do or say.

Kelvan said, "Did she give you anything?"

"No. As soon as I've warmed up I'm going back to bed. We can make plans in the morning." He fell silent. It was not an adequate response, but there was nothing else. He realized that he had gone to Rois like a child, expecting an answer, a magic wand, a dire sword. Disappointment was flattening his mood, damn fool that he was.

Something made a noise on the roof, and he looked up sharply. It was not repeated. A branch, probably, or a shingle blown loose. It had not had the dull thudding sound of the dead bird.

When he turned back the firelight had thickened. He looked at the soot-blackened stones of the chimney and thought that if he extended a hand to touch them they would recede ever farther into a place he could not approach. He was certain that behind him there was only darkness. The room was a stage set, Kelvan a wax figure.

Then Kelvan spoke, his voice formal. Corin nearly jumped at the sound. "My lord."

"Yes?"

"Should I gather the riders?"

"Not now," he said after a moment's thought. He suspected Kelvan was as restless as he was, wanting to act. "But decide which of them you can trust, we'll need them later."

He was still cold but suddenly he could not stand to be in the presence of anyone else. He went into his own tiny room and shut the door firmly, lighting the candle with a quick mental flick. A straw pallet, not even a bed, covered with worn and scratchy wool blankets. One window, missing a shutter, and a piece of cloth nailed over the gap. It was rippling now in the wind. The candle was greasy and shapeless and burned smokily. It cast unsteady shadows. There was nothing to shield it from the draft. He pulled the remaining shutter closed to do its best to keep out the wind.

He left his cloak on and moved the candle on the floor nearer to the pallet. He sat down carefully. Sleep would be a long time coming, he would not even try yet. His mind was more unquiet than his body. He stretched out his legs and remembered that first night with Tam, sitting on the floor, watching her face, doing everything he could to restrain himself. She had to be safe, she had to.

Outside there was a roar and a wail and a bang. His head jerked up. The shutter crashed into the room. On the wall underneath the open window, black shadows were creeping over the sill, latticing themselves, tangling. Branches, bones. He could not move. He watched, too numb with disbelief for fear, as they thickened and extended. They covered the wall like leafless vines. He had never seen anything so dark, not even the dragon space. They left the wall and moved toward him across the floor, making a faint rasping sound. He could have wrapped his hands around them. They could wrap themselves around his hands. They groped and slithered like blind thorned snakes.

He scrambled backward and jostled the candle. Hot tallow splashed on the back of his left hand, burning painfully. This was real. Now the fear rushed over him, worse than any nightmare he had ever had.

He remembered absurdly the fairy tale of the sleeping princess and the briars, growing for a hundred years to cover the castle and all within it. At birth the princess had been cursed to die by the bad fairy, and the good fairy changed it into sleep. They had done this to him too, he was sure of it. O dragons, he thought helplessly. The thorns were made of iron and sharply hooked. Their rasp sounded like a creature scratching at a door. He felt as though he had fallen into a pit. Darkness rushing up to meet him, his heart in his throat, his head whirling with dizziness. The blackness advanced. It was merciless and absolute.

Instinct or training or the dragons moved him. He grabbed the candle and held it up to the shadows. Begone! he thought. He said it aloud, commanding, while he reached to the mind of the dragon outside. The flame flared up so brightly he closed his eyes.

When he opened them again the shadows were gone and the room was ordinary. The wind was still blowing hard, but it no longer frightened him.

For a while he sat, trying to make sense of what had happened. Heat-sweat cooled on his skin. Firelight from the other room seeped under the door and around the edges. He rubbed the tallow-burn on his hand, which hurt. Then he went to inspect the damage.

The shutter had been wrenched off at its hinges, but the wood was still intact. There was no chance of rehanging it now. He lifted the cloth and stuck it back on its nails. There was a good-sized rip where it had been torn away, but it held. He felt it between his finger and thumb. It was coarse, a thick weave with little prickles where stem or seed of some plant had not been carded out.

He was sure the shadowthings had not been hallucination or vision. Things had been roused. Rois, for all her power and knowledge, was not going to give him counsel. He was in too deep for what she knew and remembered.

You're going to kill yourself if you try to do this alone, Tam had said. He let the cloth fall and went back into the other room to talk to Kelvan.

CHAPTER FIFTEEN

❧

T he Sarian language was full of short words and hard sounds. In the last hour Tam had become far more familiar with it than she had ever expected to. One of her legs had gone numb from being motionless so long. She was hiding close enough to the stream that the rushing water would cover any noise she made in moving, but that would not help if the soldiers saw movement in the brush on a windless night. Joce was a dozen feet or so away from her, completely quiet. She knew where he was and she still couldn't see him.

It was not the first time they had been forced to hide in the brush. She was briar-scratched, insect-bitten, and sunburned. They had abandoned the horses days ago, leaving them in a pasture whose owner would either swoon with his good fortune or go running to the sheriff to avoid being taken as a horse thief. But this was the longest time they had been hidden. The Sarians were searching far more extensively than was justified by the size of the small one-room cote. The war-lights cast hard shadows over the clearing and tangled the shadows in the trees.

It had occurred to Tam several times that perhaps she and Joce were not the targets of the search. Perhaps the Sarians were looking for a magic ring or a lost love letter. Something smaller and more important than a prince's wife. Or, more likely, they were playing wait-it-out. There were four of them, heavily armed. They had swept their war-lights through the bushes and up and down the trees. Only Joce's ability to hide them with illusion those few seconds the light had been on them had kept them from discovery. Her skin had tingled when he did it.

She was not even frightened anymore, just bored and uncomfortable. And hungry. She was always hungry, it seemed. They moved and slept, moved and slept, and ate when they could, which was not often. She had been practicing with her power, practicing that slide into stillness and quiet, and that made her hungrier. It was not starvation, she knew what starvation was and this was not even close, but she was losing weight.

Finally the Sarians gave up. They took their horses, huge and unbelievably fast beasts, and went back west along the path from the cote. Tam heard the gallop of hooves through the ground for a long time after they reached the road.

She waited for Joce to call. The first time they hid she had come out as soon as she thought the danger was gone. He had been very angry with her.

The bushes rustled as he moved. "It's safe," he said. She crawled out slowly. Her leg burned as it woke up.

She lay on her back and flexed her leg while looking up at the tree branches and a strip of clear sky. A small reddish star was directly overhead.

"What was that about?" she asked.

"They knew we were here."

"How? They didn't have dogs."

"We must have been seen on the road. We passed a few people."

Tam remembered them. A boy of about twelve, a woman carrying a baby, a tinker with a skinny donkey and an empty cart. All of them had looked afraid. None of them would have lied to an armed man, especially not a Sarian. She hoped whoever had told had not been killed. She had seen too many bodies in the past few days to think it was a realistic hope.

They had circled Caithenor slowly over the past week and were now five or six miles to the south, on the Dele road. They saw Mycenean soldiers frequently, Sarians less often. They passed the smoking shells of farmhouses that appeared to have been burned for the fun of it, torched fields, slaughtered cattle. Dragons constantly crossed the sky. None of them had tried to reach her mind again.

She drew her knife and felt the edge. Had it not been for the war, it would have been a pleasant night. The air was mild. Owls hooted occasionally. The moon was up by now, blotching the ground with silver where it showed through the trees. The frogs were noisy.

Lying on the earth, Tam felt power underneath it. It was strong here, stronger than other places she had been outside the city. She could not possibly say how she knew. She felt it as distinctly as she felt sun or moisture or cold air on her skin. If she had the time to lie peacefully on it, it would seep into her. But she did not have the time. She had not learned yet how to draw from it. She wondered if it had something to do with how long the Sarians had searched.

Joce said, "If those soldiers are going back to the palace, we may soon have a bigger problem on our hands."

Back to the palace threw her into vision, as phrases sometimes did. A row of bodies dangled from the balcony in the Great Hall, turning a little with the air. It was too dark to see faces. War-lights blazed green-white at the gates. A Sarian rode up. He was bare-chested, and the light gleamed greenly on the rings in his nipples. His face was painted white. A body lay casually over the back of his horse. A pack of barking dogs raced toward him. He tossed the body down to them and rode on toward the stables.

Tam pulled out. If there had been any food in her stomach she would have vomited. She sat up. The sudden movement startled an animal in the bushes. She said, urgent, "Where does it come from, Joce? How do I make it stop?"

As though he were speaking to a restless horse, he said, "Easy now. Wherever you just went, you came back. It will take experience to close it faster, that's all."

"But what is it? What is my power?"

"Whatever you have, my lady, is not what I have. The powers that are left to the wizards are powers that serve for hiding and escape. You See through those things. You may eventually be able to Change things as you See them."

You don't know yet how much power you have, Aram had said. She shivered. She saw a darkness pass quickly over the sky and knew it was a dragon.

"What about the dragons?" she asked.

"I know nothing about dragons."

She sighed and returned her knife to its sheath. "What did you mean by *bigger problem*?"

"I wouldn't be surprised if they return with reinforcements. They seemed to have a good sense that we were there."

"We should go back into the city where it will be easier to hide."

"I agree," he said.

For once. She managed not to say it.

He said, "We'll go back in tomorrow if we can. And once we are there, I will find a place where you can hide safely and I will go learn what is happening."

"Is there such a place?"

"A few."

That was all she was going to get. She wished suddenly, painfully, for Corin. She said, "Are we sleeping outside or in the cote?"

"It smells better outside," he said.

Joce made a small fire. Tam went to the stream and washed her face and hands. They wrapped up in their cloaks and lay down. That was how it had been for days. Her hair was filthy. She listened for hoofbeats, but the earth stayed silent.

❧

Mycenean soldiers lined the Dele Road where it met the Southern Ring Road. It was a hot day. The road was paved, and Tam could feel the heat of the stone through her boots. She kept her head down and let Joce put his arm around her with hand lower on her buttocks than any well-bred lady would ever countenance. His touch was so cool and impersonal it might as well have been glass. She was sweating with nervousness as well as heat.

"Your sword—they'll see it," she whispered.

"No," he said.

Her skin tingled under her knife sheath. Illusion, she thought.

They were not stopped. Just two tired country lovers coming to see what the city could give them now. She supposed the guards would spend much more time scrutinizing anyone of her description who was trying to leave.

The city streets were mostly empty. The air was stifling. The smell of smoke, burned wood and burned flesh, still hung over everything. They walked through an area that had not been touched by fire, but the doors and windows of the houses were shut. Already it had that desolate air of a place abandoned. The few shops they saw stood with open doors and ransacked goods. Some buildings had been defaced with crudely scrawled obscenities. A thin dog approached, then slunk quickly away when Joce touched his sword. Grey ash coated the bricks of the buildings and the tree leaves.

They stopped in an empty public park to stand in the shade of a large oak. The fountain was not running. Birds wandered about and flitted from bush to bush, looking for scraps of food that no longer existed. Tam wiped the sweat from her face with the edge of her hand. Joce handed her the water flask.

"What next?" she asked, after a long drink.

"I know where I want to take you," he said. "It will take some time to get there."

"What if it's no good?"

"Then we'll try the next place." He went abruptly taut. "There's someone close. Come," he whispered. He reached for her hand.

They walked quickly out of the park. On the way they passed the body of a hanged man dangling from a tree branch. It was recent enough that he did not smell yet. His shirt was ruined silk and his feet were bare. They were soft. He had been rich.

When they were on the shadeless streets they stayed in the center, well away from any places someone might slip out of. Joce did not let go of her.

It was not long before they came to a burned area. Fire-blackened buildings stood with empty window frames and sagging roofs. Many were gone entirely, just a pile of shattered bricks and twisted bits of metal left. Seeing them, Tam thought of contorted insects or spiders. Stone buildings had survived better than brick, but the insides were empty caverns of ash. Dragons making a dragon-land. Here and there a building that the fire had skipped stood pristine amid the rubble.

"What are we running from?" Tam asked after a while.

"It was either soldiers or looters, I did not want to find out which."

She nodded. The destruction was making her feel numb. The heat haze and the grey ash and the black char made everything seem colorless.

Block after block it was the same. Single walls standing in the midst of piles of fallen stone. Blackened timbers leaning drunkenly against one another. Dusty lumps of glass made from fragments that had fused together with heat. Steel tankards jumbled together beside the staveless hoops of beer barrels. A grimy porcelain teapot that had survived, its bold Liddean pattern still bright. Rain had mudded down the ash and now it was thick and stiff where it had settled. Some parts of the streets looked like riverbeds, swirled and drifted with current. Leafless charred trees rose desolate from the plain of ash. Her boots acquired a thin coat of ash, and her throat was dry.

Other buildings were standing in the distance, and when Tam raised her head she could see the tallest towers of the palace. She wondered what it was like inside. A husk, a deserted place of haunts, or a prison, full of rats and fear and suffering. Mycenean soldiers were said to be honorable and well disciplined but if the Sarians were there it would be hell, especially for the women. Better to have burned. She thought of Cina and felt sick.

Once shadow flickered over them with a smell of sulfur, and she looked up to see a dragon swooping low. It was close enough that she could make out the rider on its back. She clenched her fists and looked away. She waited for a stab of pain in her mind, but none came.

Slowly they drew nearer to the edge of the devastation. They passed houses and shops that were singed but intact, and then they came into another area that fire had not touched. It had once been a fashionable shopping district. Now the stores were boarded against looters, and the vendors sitting cross-legged on the bare street were selling flour and onions and dried beans.

Tam was thirsty, and they stopped in the shade of a tall building that still gleamed silver with sun. She drank deeply. As she was returning the flask to Joce, four Sarian soldiers walked by. They seemed immense. All of them had swords and knives, and two of them had bows, with black-feathered arrows. She froze.

"Look down," Joce hissed as he took the flask. She obeyed. A dragon cried overhead. This time the pain spiked through her. She thought Corin's name.

Joce took her hand again and pulled her softly to a walk. The soldiers had passed.

She was jumpy after that. Real fear set in. The dragon had found her, what if it told its rider? She kept herself from looking over her shoulder time after time, but her eyes scanned rapidly from side to side ahead of her. Joce let go of her but stayed very close.

They walked at least another hour, along narrow tree-lined streets past modest houses. It was an older part of Caithenor, with smaller buildings and mismatched stonework. They saw no one. The fear slowly ebbed out of Tam, and so did her strength. She was trying to get up the courage to ask Joce to rest when he said, "Here we are."

They were on a street that had probably been still and quiet even before the war. There were houses on one side, built close together and right against the cobbles, all with a general air of mustiness. On the opposite side was a large brick building next to an old stable. The stable doors were padlocked with a heavy chain in good enough condition to mean it had not been abandoned before the dragons came. There was moss on the roof, and the wood was weathered.

He pointed to a nearby elm with large spreading branches. "Wait there. I need to be sure it's safe. I might be some time, but I will be able to hear you if you shout."

Tam nodded. She did not like the idea of being out of his sight at all, but she knew there might be more risks inside. She retreated nervously to the shade of the tree.

Joce crossed the street and went around the corner of the large building. Momentary panic rose when he went out of sight. Then she got hold of herself. Her legs were aching, and she gave up appearances and sat down at the edge of the street. The air was humid. Nothing moved or made a noise, not even animals. The leaves had lost their spring freshness and seemed to droop a little.

The stone in the shade was pleasantly cool, but heat rose from the surrounding cobbles.

Tam felt power here, even stronger than on the road to Dele. A dragon screamed overhead. Her hand went to her knife hilt. It passed, with no pain, no visions. Heavy silence settled back over the street.

She was getting drowsy with heat and inactivity when Joce came back. His shadow was long. She stood up hastily. He led her to a small door opening from an alley on the other side of the building. He did not seem to have forced the lock. Across the alley was a low brick windowless warehouse.

He pushed the door open and she followed him into a large dim room. There were slatted windows high up, and her eyes adjusted quickly. It was, or had been, a theater. Not an elegant one whose stage hosted the most famous of actors, only tiered rows of benches surrounding a slightly raised platform on three sides. Pigeons were roosting in the rafters. Bird dung and feathers splotched the floor here and there. There was not much dust. She did not smell mold or garbage or other waste anywhere. Its disuse was recent.

"Backstage?" she asked.

"A corridor and two dressing rooms. I startled a cat, who seems to be doing an excellent job keeping the vermin out."

"Pity it can't get the pigeons," she said. "It's a good place, Joce, thank you. How did you know about it?"

"Followed someone to it a few years ago. It was just a hunch that it might be vacant now. No one is going to look for you in a forgotten theater. I checked the stable and the warehouse, too, they're just as empty. We should eat."

They made a meager meal of dried dates and stale bread washed down with water. When they were finished Joce briefly showed her the rest of the theater, marking the other two doors and the windows in the back. He found a small lantern and lit it for her. He said, "I'll be gone a few hours. I'll bring back more food. You should be able to hear anyone coming. If it's not me, run, don't hide. Keep your knife ready, and don't go to sleep."

"How will I know it's you?"

"You will," he said. His eyes were silvery.

"Where are you going?"

"To find three or four people, if I can."

She locked the door behind him and went to the stage area, where she sat in the center with her legs folded and her knife drawn. She put the lantern to the side. The air was warm but not hot. The wood of the platform was unvarnished, but well smoothed with wear. The pigeons began fluttering about again. The cat appeared, a lean muscular beast with large paws and a smooth black coat. It sat beside her. When she reached to touch it, it backed away, so she put her hands in her lap.

It was, she realized, the first time she had been alone since they fled the palace. The few times that Joce had not been at her side his place had been taken by the nervous waiting for him to return. But he thought she was safe here. Perhaps he had enchanted her, or placed a spell on the building, or it was he in the form of a cat.

All of which were absurd, and not worth thinking over. Not even with all the other things that had happened.

If they had made it to Dalrinia she would have been home for several days now. What would she have told her parents? Probably nothing. She looked at the ring on her hand. Corin's cloak and its telltale pin were stowed away with a change of clothing in her pack. In Dalrinia she would have hidden the ring too, to avoid her mother asking questions, and then there would have been no sign that anything had happened to her besides flight from a burning palace.

And if Myceneans came looking for her? They might have searched her parents' home already. If she were there she would have to surrender herself to protect her parents.

And then they would use her against Corin.

Stop it, she said to herself. There was no point in wasting time or energy in thinking about possibilities that would not happen. Myceneans might already have swooped down on her parents and told them she was the prince's lover, but she wasn't there and they wouldn't find her, and if they came after her here she would run. If she was captured, Joce would rescue her, the abducted princess saved by the loyal knight.

It occurred to her then that she was not worrying about the future but was grieving the things she had lost.

As time wore on, she decided to explore the theater more thoroughly. There was a square in the stage that looked like a trapdoor, but with no latch. She found the stairs and went below. A door opened into a room with metal cables extending to pulleys at the ceiling, and she realized the square was actually a small lift. The room was dank and chilly. She raised the lantern and saw movement as creatures hurried out of the light. They were not large enough to be rats. The floor was stone. There was no bolt on either side of the door; the room would work neither as a hiding place nor as a trap.

She went back up and into the dressing rooms. Costumes spilled out of chests and lay scattered on the wooden floor. In each room there was a large mirror mounted on the wall and a table and stool in front of it. The tables were piled haphazardly with face paints and hairpins and cheap jewelry. At one of them a red silk scarf embroidered with a golden pattern of interlocked straight lines was hanging over the edge of the mirror. It had been expensive by the look of it. Tam fingered the soft fabric. It caught on the rough spots of her fingers. It seemed wrong to leave something so beautiful for looters. She folded it up and put it in her pocket. She would make good to the actress if she ever got the chance.

She wiped the dust from her hands onto her pants and returned to the stage. The cat had disappeared. She drew her knife again and laid it on the floor in front of her. She put her forefinger on the hilt and reached for power.

It came hard and sharp with a flash of light from the knife blade. She was momentarily blinded. When the afterbrightness faded from her eyes, she saw that the knife was still glowing with a faint blue-silvery light. She reached toward it and watched as the light collected in her hand and spilled over like water. It invited her in. She considered, decided not to. Not yet.

❦

Joce returned before it was fully dark. While they ate, he told her what he had seen. Mycenean or Sarian soldiers everywhere that mattered, the docks, the main thoroughfares, the watch stations. Disease had not begun to spread yet; the water was still good and the Myceneans had been burning the bodies. Looting and wanton destruction had been got under control by means of merciless executions.

But, he said, and, But, she echoed, no one knew who commanded the soldiers. Some said it was Tyrekh himself. Others said it was one of the Mycenean generals. Several lords were known dead. The rest might never have existed. The soldiers had taken away anyone who asked them anything the first few days, and now no one asked. Trade went on uneasily, few words exchanged. No one would say the king's name. Women hardly went out at all; too many had disappeared early on. It was a silent city, huddled fearfully into its hole like some small beast.

Tam said, feeling low, "We shouldn't have come. I don't know what I was thinking. We can't just hide forever."

"People can do anything in war," he said.

She supposed it was true. "But we can't win this war. It will just go on, until it seems normal to be occupied."

"We'll win."

"How can you be so sure?" Corin had never had such confidence.

"Mycenean soldiers will not tolerate the Sarians. The Myceneans are vainglorious, but more or less honorable and civilized."

"There are more Sarians."

"Not in the long run," he said. "The farther west Tyrekh extends, the thinner his forces become. And Tyrekh made a mistake. He gave his weapons to the Myceneans. Here." He held out an apple, green and small and round.

Tam bit into it. It was crisp and sour. She contemplated his words, then said, "But who's going to get rid of the Myceneans?" She wished she had been able to read more politics. She was not very well educated to be a prince's wife.

"They'll miss Mycene. They won't like winter. Occupation is tedious. They will either go home or become Caithenian despite themselves." He folded thick bread around a lump of cheese. "And Hadon will likely have to recall them anyway. The Empire won't last another generation."

"Why?"

"It's become too corrupt to sustain itself. When the other vassal kingdoms see what happened in Caithenor, they will act before it happens to them."

"If that happens too soon we'll be left to the Sarians," she said.

"The king has made—" He hesitated, then went on. "Arrangements with a Mycenean general. He can stall things if he has to."

That was probably something he was not sure she should know. She asked anyway. "Why would he do it if Aram's dead? There's no benefit to him." She knew enough about bargaining to be certain of that.

"The king isn't dead."

"You can't be sure."

"When I went out I made contact with someone. He had reliable word the king is safe. The general will have heard the same."

"But—" She stopped. There was no point in arguing. Even if Joce was wrong, neither of them could do anything about it. And she wanted him to be right, why was she trying to talk him out of it? Because you're contrary by nature, Tam, she said to herself. She said aloud, "Damn it."

He laughed and began wrapping up the food.

Before she settled down to sleep, Tam stepped back outside to breathe clean air. Bats were darting in the twilight. Drawn by the lantern light behind her, a moth fluttered onto the door frame. It shocked her into stillness. Then she saw that it was a small dun-colored moth, quite ordinary, no death omen. Her skin prickled anyway with recall of the wings fluttering against her.

She woke slowly and groggily to Joce shaking her. She sat up stiffly. "What is it? How long have I slept?"

"Not long, barely more than an hour. But someone's coming."

She did not bother to ask him how he knew. "Who?"

"Soldiers, I think. They're doing a sweep."

A flash of vision, white-painted faces reflecting the green of war-lights. They carried unsheathed swords with edges glinting in the light. One carried a garrotte loosely in his hand. They were close.

"There's nowhere to hide," she said, trying to be calm.

"No. We need to run again."

"Are they looking for us?"

"I don't know," he said, standing and offering her a hand to rise. He had the water flask slung over his shoulder and his sword out. "It may be routine, but it doesn't matter, they'll take us either way."

They went out the side door to the unpaved alleyway. Joce locked the door behind them. The sky was clear and starry. The moon was not up yet. The air was cooler than it had been but still full of summer warmth.

"Run," said Joce.

She did, her boots coming down hard on the packed dirt. Her body was full of sudden strength. Fences and walls on either side of her, stable doors, startled cats. Her blood pulsed. Her legs burned. Sweat ran into her eyes and down her body. Strands of hair flew into her face. Joce was behind her, running smoothly and quietly.

She ran until she could barely breathe. She stopped and leaned against a wall, gasping. Her sides ached. Her shirt and pants were clinging uncomfortably to her. She was afraid, but it was a thing she knew rather than felt. Her throat was sore and her lungs hurt. She bent over and put her hands on her knees. She tried to speak and was racked with coughs.

Joce put a hand on her back and the pressure in her lungs eased. She straightened, wiped her face with a sweaty forearm. Her hair was sticking to her neck.

A dog barked somewhere distant. Joce dropped to the ground, laid his ear against the earth, then leaped to his feet. His eyes flickered silver. "Hounds," he said. She knew what they were: the

Mycenean bloodhounds used by thief trackers and slave catchers. He cupped his hands. "Over this wall."

She put her foot in his hands. He pushed her up with astonishing speed and grace. She pulled herself on top of the wall, twisted, and lowered down feet first. He was beside her in seconds.

They were in a garden. They slunk along the wall, around the stable, crushing soft grass underfoot. Honeysuckle bloomed some- where, tossing her in memory back to the night of the ball. They went over the wall at the front of the house, across the street, past unclimbable pointed iron fences, came to another wall.

He boosted her up again but said, "Don't go over." It was about a foot wide. He took her hand and led her along it. Tam stared at the back of his head. She was walking too quickly for comfort with darkness and a fall on either side of her, but she knew it was not fast enough for him. There were too many things to be afraid of now. She was exhausted. Corin, she thought.

Joce led her along a maze of walls and a few times over the roofs of small outbuildings. They had to scramble down and back up to cross the alleys. The walls ended and they returned to the streets. The houses became smaller and closer, the streets narrower. Trees and lawns vanished. There should have been noises on a fine night like this, people talking, cats hissing, a baby crying through an open window. Everything was still and silent. There were no gas lamps lit along the streets, and the houses were dark and lifeless.

Joce stopped. The houses here were built right next to one another and against the street, there was no getting between or around them. No trees to climb. Cellar doors, if there were any, would all be in the back.

Tam started to speak, but Joce hushed her fiercely. He seemed to be listening to something. Then she felt dragonpain in her mind.

She looked up and saw it descending. Huge, blocking out the stars, the wings vast. She smelled sulfur. Her heart raced. Foolishly, desperately, she drew her knife. The dragon's talons were probably longer than the blade.

It landed and the rider dismounted. The wings folded partly but not completely and were all angles and lines against the sky. She could not tell what color the dragon was, although she could see a different shade of darkness at its neck. The mouth was closed.

She tried to find the stillness. If she could only speak to the creature.

Joce stepped in front of her, his sword unsheathed. She knew she should run, try to hide from the rider at least, but it seemed so futile to run from a dragon. The panic had dropped away and her mind was clear now, fear-sharpened.

The men advanced toward each other. The rider had not drawn a blade. Joce and the rider spoke simultaneously, the words blurring so she could not hear them, each with a questioning tone. Joce sheathed his sword. They knew each other. For a faithless frightened instant she thought she had been betrayed.

Then Joce said, "It's all right, my lady, we're safe." *Safe* was not a word she would have used near a dragon. Tentatively she approached him. Her body was still ready to flee.

The rider bowed and said, "The prince has sent me for you."

"Which prince?" she asked, suspicious. She could not see his face.

"Prince Corin," said the rider. "He said you might not believe it, so I am to tell you that he is sorry he could not bring any of the Illyrian red."

That had to be him. If he were a captive he would have said something that warned her. This was the rider who had taken Corin. She dropped the knife and stumbled into Joce with relief as her legs went loose. He supported her.

The rider said, "It's a long flight, and we'll stop several times. You'll need warmer clothing, my lady, let me get it for you." He went back to the dragon.

Tam looked at Joce. "Is this the right thing?"

"Yes," he said. "Not only the right thing, but the best thing."

"What will you do?"

"Find my way back into the palace and kill Tyrekh."

For a moment she was speechless. "You aren't jesting."

"Not a bit."

"How will you get in?"

"Illusion. Trickery. Deceit."

"You'll be killed."

"Probably. But I won't fail." He took her hand and kissed Mari's ring, then picked up her knife. "Come, my lady, you need to leave."

He kept himself between her and the dragon's head, which she was glad of. It was so much bigger than she had expected. She avoided looking at it. The rider gave her two thick woolen shirts, which were far too large and far too hot. The sleeves of one fell past her fingertips. She started to roll them up, but the rider said, "No, my lady, it will keep your hands warm."

Both men helped her up onto the dragon. The rider tightened straps about her. It made her nervous again. There is nothing to fear, she thought, but her hands were sweating. Joce seemed puny.

She did not know what to say to him. She settled on, "Thank you."

He bent his head briefly, then walked backward away from the dragon. He gave the head and front legs a wide berth. There was something strangely reassuring at seeing him wary of the dragon. It reminded her that not everything had changed.

The rider sat behind her, then gave her a helmet. "I won't be able to hear you," he said. "If you need something, use your arms to get my attention. I will hold on to you if it's windy or you start to fall asleep. Don't worry, the dragon won't let you fall."

Tam nodded and put the helmet on. It was too big too, but when she piled her loose hair on top of her head it fit well enough that she could secure the buckle under her chin. What am I doing? she thought. The dragon scales were black in the darkness. They were as smooth as Corin had described. Her legs were warming.

Joce was farther down the street. She waved a hand to him and saw him wave one in return. She jumped a little when the rider put his arm around her waist. The dragon's posture changed. She felt its muscles tense. Her own body tightened in response. Then it leaped.

CHAPTER SIXTEEN

The approaching dragon intruded upon Corin's dreams. He dressed rapidly and hurried outside. The mountains were black against a rosy sky. The dragon was high up, a small spark of red where the sun hit it above the peaks. He lost sight of it as it fell below the level of the sun. Then he saw it again, large and dark and getting closer. By the time it landed a thin crescent of gold was showing above the eastern ridgeline.

He was at the dragon's side before Tam slipped off. For the first time he paid no attention at all to the dragon. She was thin and pale and exhausted-looking. When she unbuckled the helmet and let it fall, her hair tumbled down her back in a rat's nest of tangles.

She said, "Never ever again," and fell heavily against him.

He put his arms around her and said, "What happened?"

Kelvan said, "We got tossed about a bit."

"He's lying. It was a lot. I was sick three times," she mumbled.

Corin had had his own share of stomach-lurching dizziness and terrifying vertigo while dragonback. He knew what she was talking about. She was still able to walk, it must have been smooth most of the time.

He led her into the hut. She pulled off several layers of clothing and washed her face. She drank a great deal of water. Then she went into his room and dropped onto the bed. "Corin," she said hoarsely.

He took her boots off and put the blankets over her. It was still very dim in the room. He kissed her. She returned it, but without much vigor. "Go to sleep," he said. "I'll be here when you wake up." He kissed her forehead and went quietly out of the room.

It was nearly noon when Tam emerged. He was outside, making useless notes to himself in the dirt with a twig and scuffing them out with his feet. She called his name. He hurried to her.

This time the kiss was full and long and everything it should be. Corin wanted to make love to her right there in the tall sunlit grass. He could tell she was not ready yet, so he kept his hands in the proper place. They sat under a tree and looked at each other a very long time.

She broke the silence by saying, "I must look ghastly."

"You do. But you're still beautiful."

"Flatterer."

"I'm allowed to flatter you. I'm your husband." How very odd the word sounded in his mouth.

"I defy you to praise my tresses."

"I will help you work the snarls out, will that do instead?"

She said, "Yes. But be careful."

"I will. Turn around. Sit close so I don't pull."

It was maddening to be so close to her and touching only her hair. But the knots came out more easily than he expected. He worked steadily, kissing her neck when he had the opportunity.

Her first question surprised him. "Are we really married?" she asked. "Legally?"

"Yes. There are formalities to go through—you should have been titled first, for one thing, and the council of lords should have approved—but the king can make a marriage. There were certainly sufficient witnesses. There's no law against me marrying a commoner. It's just not ever done."

"So it's a valid marriage, but do I have rank?"

"Not technically. But my love, if we win the war the formalities will be observed. We'll probably have to get married again. If we lose it won't matter."

"Why did he do it?"

Corin had thought that one through more than a few times. When he was feeling bitter he supposed that Aram was trying to legitimate any child that had been conceived so the line would continue; when he could be logical, he knew that there was no good political reason for it. Much better to have stayed unwed so that there was a chance he could be used as a bargaining chip if necessary. There were no opportunities left now for a marital alliance with some other Mycenean state.

"I don't know," he said. "He likes you, but he doesn't do things out of sentimentality. Especially not under those circumstances."

"He didn't seem surprised," she said.

He had been too caught up in the chaos of fleeing to pay attention to anyone but her. "No," he admitted, remembering other things that had been done for her. The necklace, Joce, the room near his, the permission to tell her everything. "When you see him next, you can ask him."

"Joce was certain he was still alive," she said. "He told me so yesterday. He said he had heard it reliably."

"Then we can rely on it," he said, feeling a weight lift. He had not been privy to his father's plans for hiding, but he knew how intricate the web of spies was. If he had not been sent to the dragons, he would have been in a large city somewhere, giving his own orders to his father's agents. But here he was instead, with the dragons and the wizards.

"Tam," he asked, "did Joce tell you who he was?"

She turned her head to look at him. Her face had more color in it. Her eyes were bright. "He said he used wizardry. That was all. I didn't ask him anything else."

"I need to tell you then," he said. "There are only a few more tangles, let me get them first."

He worked them out, then she faced him again. Her body was swallowed up in the large shapeless shirt. He ran his finger down the outside of it from her breastbone to her waist and was pleased to see it define her figure better. She made a little noise of satisfaction and moved closer to him. He slipped his hand under her shirt but kept it on her back.

"This is very secret," he said. "If we were anywhere else, I wouldn't tell you at all without my father's permission. Joce is not the only wizard. So is Kelvan. As are the people of this village."

"Ah," she said softly. "Of course. That's why he could be trusted not to go over to Hadon."

He had somehow forgotten how quick her mind was. He stood up and helped her to her feet. He gestured to the huts farther up the hill. "There is no place you could be safer," he said. "Nowhere. There is no getting into this valley without a wizard. But that's all it is. A shelter. They can't end the war or free the dragons. The dragons are still my task."

"Yes," she murmured. He was not sure it was in response to what he had said. He watched her take in the valley, the river, the sea. Her face was still. The power in the valley might be visible to her in some way.

She ran her fingers through her hair, winced. "You missed one," she said, sweeping a lock over her shoulder and beginning to disentangle it. "Corin, you didn't bring me here just to keep me safe. You changed your mind, and it wasn't just because we got married. What do you need of me?"

There was no reason to deny it. "I don't know yet. Advice, mostly, I think. The afternoon before the ball, you said to me that we hadn't really talked about what had happened, and then more things happened. God, I don't even know where you've been the past week, what you've been through. We need a very long talk before we decide anything." It had been an endless three days after Kelvan left to look for her. All Corin knew from the rider was that he had found her with Joce on a street in Caithenor.

"I haven't breakfasted," she said. "Can we eat while we talk? And then can I have a bath, if such a thing is possible here?"

"Yes, to both," he said. "Let me get food, and we can sit on the riverbank like a pair of merry lovers. I'm afraid I haven't got a lute."

"Would I want to hear you sing?"

"Probably not."

They found a shaded spot where the ground was firm. A white heron stalked its prey in the shallows. It looked dragonlike itself when its beak darted downward into the water. High above, a pair of hawks circled lazily in the bright sky.

There was fresh bread, goat cheese, venison, and blackberries. The plate was unglazed earthenware, but when Tam picked up the cutlery she raised her eyebrows at him. "This was made to last," she said.

"The village is not as poor as it looks," he said. "The Crown provides."

"How do things get over the mountains?"

"With difficulty, on mules. Mostly it comes by ship."

"How many wizards are there?"

"Here, maybe five hundred," he said. "In the rest of Caithen, a few dozen. They are dying out, there's no new blood."

"How lonely it must be." She reached across the basket and briefly put her hand in his. It seemed as though it had been years since anybody touched him. "Well, my Corin, my prince, what are we going to do?"

He wanted to put the facts on the table first. "Tell me what happened to you."

"Very little. We made it out of the city and then skirted it, bit by bit. We slept on the ground. We went back in yesterday."

"Why? That was your idea, wasn't it?"

"Yes. Joce took some convincing." She smiled. Then her expression went as sober as he had ever seen it. "He said he was going back into the palace to kill Tyrekh. He'll do it, won't he?"

"Yes. And it's better than even odds that he makes it out alive."

"Are there other wizards in Caithenor?"

"There were a handful. But none so good with the knife. And none who know the Sarians as well as he does. He would never have left you, but I expect he had well-laid plans for assassinating Tyrekh if the chance arose. But Tam, it was foolish to go there."

"It seemed the right thing to do," she said. She put her plate in the basket and her chin in her hands. "They would have found me if I'd gone home. And there's power there, I thought I should be close to power. Joce has been teaching me. It seemed a better place to learn."

"Was it?"

"We weren't there long enough," she said. She hesitated. "It was bad, Corin. It's still a city, but it's wounded."

"How bad?" he asked, dreading the answer. He had heard Kelvan's reports of what he saw and what the riders saw, but that was not the same thing.

"I don't really know what it was like before this," she said. "There's a lot burned, but not so much as I had expected. It can be rebuilt. That's not the real wound. It's occupied. Everyone is afraid. No one comes out. Joce said that no one dares to speak of your father because those who did early on disappeared. I think Joce found out a lot he didn't tell me."

"He should have told you everything," Corin said, irritated. Joce had no right to keep things from her now.

"He didn't have much time," she said. "I don't really want to know the details of the executions. We were running again last night. And we certainly didn't expect someone to show up on a dragon and take me to you. How did Kelvan find us, for that matter?"

He had asked the rider the same thing. "As I understand it," he said, "the dragon smelled you."

"*Smelled* me? Like a dog?"

"In principle. I don't think the dragon's actually smelling. But you were with me before I left, so it had your trace on me, and you had my cloak, so it had mine on you. It took a while to find the track, though."

"Where is it now?"

"Eating."

"Eating?" Her face blanched. "Eating what?"

He grinned. "Not people. Deer, mountain goats, a wild pig. There is plenty of game. Then it will sleep like a baby that's full of milk and wake up tomorrow."

"I don't want to think about the scat," she said.

"Unspeakable. But the dragons burn it up." If someone had told him two months ago that he would be in exile talking about dragon droppings with a commoner who was his wife, he would have had the person shut away as a lunatic. Even more so if he'd been told he would be happy.

They had eaten everything themselves. He lay back on the grass. She moved over and lifted his head into her lap. He closed his eyes. Her lips brushed his forehead.

"What shall we talk about first?" she asked.

Nothing, he thought. He sighed and ticked things off on his fingers. "The war. The dragons. Hadon. Your power. Me, I suppose. Is there anything else?"

"That's plenty," she said. "Corin, how did the Emperor know to target you? Really *know*?"

It stopped him. It was the other side of the unanswered question of what held the dragons. There had been a shift in the world, an event that cracked open the solid realities of centuries. It had crept its way through the years until the slippage was too great to be ignored. Something had plucked the string that held the dragons, and now the vibrations were coming back as echoes.

She picked a long blade of grass and began to tie it into knots. One of the hawks overhead cried. Tam said, "Something changed. He could have killed you several dozen times over since you were born. Why is he doing it now? Did he just learn?"

"Ask Kelvan," he said. "He's seen him much more closely. At a guess it involves his sons. They're putting pressure on him, and he needs the dragons more than ever." It was a good question, though, and he had no real idea of the answer. The dragons would have found a way to keep their secrets, yet somehow Hadon had learned.

They were quiet. Corin looked up along the river, watching the way the sun fell on the meadow grasses and water and cliffs. There were streaks of black and red on the sheerer faces of the granite. He felt tiny and remote.

Tam said, "Have you ever seen anyone go mad?"

"I've seen them raving in a madhouse and on the streets."

"That's not how it always happens. Sometimes a person goes very quietly mad inside, and no one realizes it until it's too late. When they finally shatter there's nothing left."

He remembered a painting in a room in the Mycenean palace. It was of a battle. A man fell with a spear through his chest. In one hand he held a human-faced snake. It writhed in his grip. Above him a black bird with a red head stretched out vast wings. How often had Hadon stood in front of that painting when he planned his wars?

Corin said, "You're thinking of Hadon." He had had the thought more than once himself.

Her hands pulled at the grass and ripped it. She made it into a wad and tossed it aside. "He's bound to the dragons. I think that when he went mad he started to see what they can see. We don't want to believe in the dark place, Corin, so we don't see it. But when madness happens, there's no reason to keep closing one's eyes to it. If the rest of the world doesn't make sense, you give up that denial."

"By that logic, we could both be mad."

She shrugged one shoulder. "Once we go down that path, there's no point in doing anything, so let's not. And your premise is wrong. I did not say that madness was the only way to see it."

There it was, the cleverness he had missed. "I love you," he said. He pulled her into him and rolled her over so she lay on her back. He leaned over her. Her skin was very smooth. There were freckles on her nose and sun-browned cheeks. He kissed her.

It went on for a while. His hand found the hem of her shirt, and before he knew what he was doing he had pulled it up and placed his palm on her stomach. Her skin was very pale in the bright sun, and his hand was dark against it. He lifted the hem further and bent to kiss the roundness of her breast.

"Not here," she said, but her arm went back over her head, and her belly and hips twitched with desire. There was no sound but the faint rustle of reeds. As he slipped her trousers down, he realized he had never done that to a woman before. It was a little awkward, very different from removing a skirt.

Their lovemaking was fierce and hard. "Oh," she said, "oh," and then she bit his finger to suppress her cries.

Afterward they lay silently on the grass. Corin watched a creamy yellow butterfly flit about among the wildflowers. Then Tam sat up, pushed her hair back, and said thoughtfully, "It's an opportune time for the dragons, with Tyrekh on the one hand and the chaos in the Empire on the other. Could they have pushed it? Twisted his mind?"

It took Corin an instant to realize she was back in the conversation about Hadon. Fear pricked at his spine. He had the uneasy feeling that she was right. "I don't know what power they have," he said. "You told me so that night at the ball, but I haven't learned anything more. I think they could do it, though. You've ridden one now, what do you think of them?"

"I was too tired and frightened and sick to think of anything."

"You've been thinking plenty about politics."

"There wasn't much else to do when walking across fields or hiding behind trees. And it is my affair now."

"It certainly is." He sat up. "Perhaps the dragons gave you a push too. I need you, Tam."

She briefly gripped his hand and did not make light of it. After a pause, she said, "If I have Sight, it makes sense that they would push me. But why you?"

He found words for the thought that had only begun to surface in his mind in the past few days of solitude. "I think the dragons chose me because I would have access to Hadon's court, because I would have a reason to want to overthrow him. Because I could turn to the wizards for help. A farmer's son would not know the things I know."

"They chose you because it was politically expedient?"

"Yes. It's an ordinary struggle for power among princes, only the tools are different. The dragons are using me. I am using wizards. Hadon is using whatever he can."

"But it could have been your father or grandfather they chose, for the same reasons. It was you."

That had not occurred to him. He was too close to the problem. "I don't know," he said. "Tam, they don't live in time as we do. They may see already that I freed them. That I love you, that you are a Seer. They chose their time, and I was the one who fit into it. And it was because I fit into it that they chose it. It's all paradox." He was thinking aloud, words falling into place before he knew it. It felt right. He glanced down at his hands and noticed the clawlike curve of his fingers. They had given him their powers, but perhaps it was not a gift. Perhaps it was a transformation.

I will not, he thought fiercely.

"Have you ever asked them?" she said.

"No. Why don't you? You have no fear of prying into the secrets of those more powerful than you."

"I beg your pardon, my lord," she said, grinning. Then she turned serious. "They can't just want you to kill Hadon. That's too easy."

"Yes. And too human a solution. Whatever works, it will be something we can't think of."

"You can still decide to abandon them," she said. "Leave them to their own devices and do your duty as a prince."

"No," he said. He would not have sent for her if he still had that opportunity. "I've committed. If I try to withdraw now it will probably drive *me* mad. But I don't expect a happy ending. There will be a sacrifice of some sort, there always is."

To his relief she did not ask him which of them it would be. Her face was still. She raised his hand to her lips. They were a little rough, sunburned and wind-chapped. His body started to stir again.

Then Tam stood up. She said, "Must I bathe in the river?"

"Not at all." He picked up the basket. "There's a tub of water that's been sitting in the sun for hours. I'll stand guard."

"That's all you'll do," she said warningly.

But when she was clean, and her hair was combed and braided, and she was dressed in soft clothing he had cadged for her from the villagers, she took his hand and led him wordlessly into his room. Their room.

Kelvan and the dragon returned several hours later. Corin felt the approach and brought Tam outside to watch. She held his hand very tightly. The dragon landed without much grace and put its head down. Its folded wings shimmered in the sunlight. The front talons still had blood on them. Its tail extended into the shadow of the trees and twitched a little. He yearned for it, as he always did. For a moment he saw it new, as Tam must see it, all weapons and armor and cruel hardness.

Tam said, sounding startled, "It's basking." Her nose was wrinkled a little, and he realized how accustomed he had grown to the smell of sulfur.

Kelvan joined them. "Aye, my lady."

Corin half hoped Tam would not disclaim the title. Not because she should become practiced in being a princess—that was silly, here—but because he wanted to keep her name to himself. Kelvan was seeing her for the first time in daylight, and Corin watched the rider straighten, as men always did for her.

She did disclaim it, of course. "Tam," she said. "I'm sorry I called you a liar this morning."

"What? You mean about the wind? That's what people always say, I'm used to it."

She looked at Corin. "Did you?"

"Not the first time. Later, though."

"Could you take me up?"

He had only had a few flights by himself. He said, "Perhaps. Not very high. If Kelvan lets me."

"We'll see," said Kelvan neutrally.

The dragon's eyes were closed. Tam said, to Kelvan this time, "Does it have a name? And why is it an 'it'?"

"Its own name is something humans can't pronounce, my lady. There's no need for me to give it a name to speak with it. Dragons are neuter except when they are breeding, when they can be either sex."

"How often do they breed?"

"Once a year in the spring. Less often as they age. This one hasn't gone blue for several years now."

Tam's lips opened as though to speak, then went shut. She slipped her arm about Corin's waist and said nothing else. There was a tautness to her body that he attributed to fear of the dragon. "Let's get out of the sun," he said, placing his own arm across her shoulders. They never could have been this intimate with another person present in Caithenor.

Kelvan said, "Prince, there's news."

"What?" he asked, anticipation building sharply in him. He should have been angry that Kelvan had not said this immediately, but he was not. He was too foolishly pleased that Kelvan had given Tam preference.

"Your sister's been rescued."

He could hardly take it in. Tam's arm tightened. "How?"

"I don't know the details. But there was at least one rider involved, and several soldiers. Hadon's furious. He tried to send other riders after her, and the dragons wouldn't budge."

"Where are they taking her?"

"I don't know," Kelvan said. He took his gloves off and tossed them on the ground beside the dragon. "This only happened a few hours ago, my lord, and the rider isn't saying a word. What I know is from the riders still in Mycene."

"Do you trust him?" Corin asked. Hadon might have arranged the whole thing himself, to get Tai some place more secure. Or his sons, to gain an advantage against their father. Her husband was dead, she could be made to marry.

"Aye," Kelvan said.

Corin could not quite allow himself to hope yet. "My father can't have had another dragonrider spy."

"No. The man turned. I think others are ready. The dragons may be pushing them harder."

They had tried to free her once. Perhaps they had tried again, nudging the things Aram had laid in place.

Tam said, "Joce said the Mycenean soldiers won't like what Hadon's done."

"They don't," said Kelvan. "He broke allegiance, and that's a cowardly thing to do. They have their honor."

Corin kissed Tam's hair and stepped out of her touch. Tai's freedom was about the last thing he had expected, and he had not worked it into his considerations at all. Hadon losing command of the dragons was crucial too. With Tai free, Hadon had no hold on him. There was no reason to delay his own actions further. This was another fulcrum, a place where the decision he made could not be smoothed out or reversed. He realized with shame that a very small part of him wished Tai were still captive, because now he had to move.

He looked at Tam and saw the same quiet strength that had been on her face when he first told her about the dragons. *I'm still here*, she had said. He had sent the dragon for her and she had come back on it, trusting in him. If he weakened she was ready.

He caught hold of her hand and gripped it hard. "I need to think," he said. "Give me some time alone."

They nodded. Resolutely, he turned his back on them and walked to the river. Once he looked over his shoulder and saw that both of them had gone elsewhere. He was glad Tam was not watching, waiting. The dragon was obscured by the trees. The cottage looked bucolic in the afternoon light, a charming spot for a wedding tour.

He found a rock where he could sit and watch the waves break at the river mouth. The tide was coming in, and the river was rising. For a little while he stared mindlessly at the water. The sea was a different shade of blue where the sediment from the river was swept out to it.

Then he began to draw his thoughts together. If riders and soldiers both were ready to turn on the Emperor, the war would not last much longer. Hadon could not withdraw his soldiers and his dragons and leave Caithen in Tyrekh's hands, because that would only bring his men into open rebellion against him. He had to sit tight, or send reinforcements against the Sarians as he should have a month ago.

If he didn't, the soldiers might drive out the Sarians of their own accord. His sons would likely mass the Myceneans too. The princes would not want Hadon to be able to turn to Tyrekh for help, so they would do their best to smash the Sarian army, which would have the added benefit to them of reducing their father's troops in the process. If Joce succeeded in killing Tyrekh, the Sarians would turn tail and run. Caithen and Argondy would be the bloody battleground where two empires clashed, but in the end the Sarians would be gone.

But as long as Hadon held the dragons, he held the Empire. And Caithen.

Slowly Corin realized that was what mattered. Five hundred years ago Mycene had been a young Empire. Its history was full of tumult. There had been the revolts, the betrayals, the daughters, all the things that shifted the possession of the crown from one line to another.

But when the dragons came, it changed. The throne had been held father to son unbroken ever since. The Empire began its ascendancy. The dragons' power fed the emperors and was passed along with the crown. It gave them no power of magic or prophecy, no power like that of a wizard; it was the simple and unassailable power of might.

He had been approaching the question from the wrong direction. Instead of trying to find a way to free the dragons, he should try to find out how they had been taken in the first place. And he should not divorce the problem from the war. The dragons wanted to be freed, and they wanted the Empire to fall. He had said as much to Tam. If all it took to free them was magic, they could have picked a wizard centuries ago.

Perhaps they had, and that had failed. He might only be the latest in a series of would-be liberators as the dragons tried new routes. He did not think so, though. They had bided their time until a weakness in the Empire emerged. But he needed to go backward, to their taking.

He thought of the north, the Dragon Valleys. They made this valley look like a paradise. He had been there once, a dozen years ago now, a counterweight to luxury and ease. It had been late summer. He and his companions had walked on narrow twisting paths that vanished entirely at times among slabs of granite, loose scree, and chimney-like crags of jagged black rock. The only trees were conifers. Small grasses and mosses and tiny flowers snuggled into nooks on the stones. Here and there sulfurous steam came out of cracks on the mountainside, staining the grey rocks yellow. Dirty patches of old and crusty snow that had melted and refrozen several times lay in the shadiest parts.

He labored along with the others, breathing thin air and watching carefully where his feet landed. The paths dipped sometimes, or skirted small clear mountain ponds, but it was always an ascent after that. There was life—birds and rabbits and ground squirrels, even foxes. Meadows with bright purple and white flowers surprised them. As they went higher the plants and animals became sparser, the ground stonier and greyer. At night the stars were close and sharp. He slept fitfully, shivering.

Finally, after five or six days—he had lost count—they came to a large looming rough black crag. The mountain rose steeply to one side of it and dropped sharply on the other. The only way past the outcropping was over it. The last feet were more a climb than a walk. The stone was painfully sharp-edged and rough. By the time Corin reached the top his hands were chafed and sore. Lungs aching, he pulled himself up to a stand on the broad flat surface and sucked at a scrape on the heel of his hand, then looked out.

Below were the Dragon Valleys. The earth looked as though some vast dragon had raked its talons through it for miles, slashing across ridges and mountainsides with no regard for stone. In the distance were the white-capped peaks of higher mountains, impossibly close in the clear air. The wind was strong and smelled cold. The Valleys were black glass, shiny and sharp and straight. Even this high he could not see into the bottom of the nearest one. The topland looked barren and lifeless.

They pulled him. The descent from the crag seemed manageable. He traced a path out and, when it was fixed well in his mind, took a step down. Almost immediately he was grabbed and hauled most unroyally back up. He endured a tongue-lashing that made him turn red weeks later. He had done his very best to forget about it entirely.

At the time he had wondered what the soldiers thought would happen. The steepness of the descent was no greater than the one back down the way he had come. They could not really think he was going to run off into such desolation. It unfolded clearly to him now: Aram had feared if he went into those Valleys, the dragons would somehow seize him. He must have commanded an extraordinarily strict watch. But he had permitted the sight. Perhaps even intended it.

Corin knew he could not go there, at least not dragonback. Kelvan had said and the dragons had shown that the Valleys were outside the bounds of their prison. Tam, though, Tam had seen them in trance.

I can't use her so, he thought. *You must,* she would say.

He watched a line of pelicans glide low over the water, dipping occasionally to scoop up a fish. She would say it because she was brave, because she loved him. And because she was his subject. He had told her enough times that he used people, she would not want him to make an exception out of love. They had managed to avoid the conversation, to play at equality, but at the very deepest part she would obey him, just as he obeyed his father.

Tam, he thought, Tam. This was why he had never wanted to be in love. But he could not forsake it. And if he loved her, he had to set the choice before her.

He walked grimly back toward the hut. When he came to the sleeping dragon, he stopped. Then he leaned against it.

Its mind was asleep, and he traveled through strange dragon dreams before it roused enough to speak to him. It was cold, alien, inhuman. There was sound, thunder or breaking ice and bells and gongs. Wind. The crackle of fire. Everything was black. Then opal light. Vertigo. He was pulled, tossed. He plummeted downward into darkness while wind rushed over him and cold air stung his skin. Red light. The flickering shadow of a dragon writhed on Hadon's throne. Hadon stood before him, hands outstretched, and his eyes were the blackness of the void.

Go, the dragon was telling him. Go. You know what to do.

He broke the contact with his mind and simply felt the dragon. Its bulk, its heat, its scales. He ran the tips of his fingers along a scale over and over. So smooth. Water would bead on it and fall, a blade would crack, an arrow would bounce. He ventured the briefest of touches to the edge of the scale and pulled his finger back at once, bleeding.

There, he thought. Now you have my blood.

Then he hit it with his fist. Over and over, until his shoulder ached.

He leaned against it again, panting. It slept on. His rage died out of him. He hoped Tam had not witnessed the tantrum. When this is over, he thought as he sometimes did. He had no words to complete it.

CHAPTER SEVENTEEN

am could tell that Corin wanted to talk privately with her, but he waited until after the evening meal. It had been a simple supper of fish and beans and nuts. Corin made it, and did a far better job than she could have. She decided not to tease him about cooking again. Then, feeling that it was her turn to do a little work, she washed the dishes while Corin made the fire. Kelvan left the hut.

"He won't be back for hours," Corin said. "He has his own lover to see." He spread a blanket in front of the fire. "Sit here and pretend we're in the palace. The guards will keep everyone out."

She did not understand how he had been able to maintain his sense of irony through everything that had happened. Perhaps that was what kept him from brooding. Her back and legs still ached from riding the dragon, and the floor looked hard and far away. Carefully, wincing a little, she lowered herself down onto the blanket. She was glad to have clean hair again.

Corin sat, moved her foot into his lap, and began to massage it. His hands were warm. "It will ease," he said. "Walking is the best thing for it, you won't stiffen so much. Unfortunately good wine is hard to come by in the village. You have very nice feet."

"Really?"

"Yes. It was one of the first things I noticed."

"Why did you fall in love with me?" she asked. It was a dangerous question. She might well not like the answer, but she could not resist.

"Who couldn't?"

"You are ridiculously besotted," she said. "Mind you, I'm not complaining. But truly, why me? By all accounts you've been avoiding it for years."

"Because you are the first woman who paid me the honor of actually seeing me," he said. It was unexpectedly sober. "I'll concede I didn't give many women much of a chance to, but none of them were interested in it."

"I had no intent to lay you bare."

"That's why you could."

She turned Mari's ring a few times on her finger. If there had been no war, would Corin have continued to abide by the rules? Would Aram have agreed to the marriage? Or had it all come about because there was no real chance of winning the war and the rules no longer mattered?

"Without the war we never would have met," she said.

"I would have seen you at the ball. And without the war there would have been time aplenty to woo you."

"But not to marry me."

"Who knows," he said.

There was a hint of bitterness to his tone that made her sad. She looked at the fire. He had built it quite skillfully, and the flames were even and steady. His touch felt good on her foot, but it seemed absent of desire. Whatever was on his mind, he did not seem to know how to raise it. It was very unlike him. She had no idea how to break his silence.

It had turned cool with evening, and she was wearing his cloak again. She touched the pin and said, "I should give you this back."

He leaned forward a little, then relaxed. "Did I leave that in?"

"Yes. I wondered if your father saw it."

"I'm sure he did. It's no matter. Keep it, you have the right to wear it now. But it's a damn good thing no Mycenean saw you with it."

Tam nodded. She had thought of the possibilities many times, but it had seemed more dangerous to put it someplace where it could be lost. "I was careful. I don't know what I would have done with it if I'd made it back to Dalrinia."

"Joce could have kept it." He grinned suddenly. "What did you intend to tell your father?"

"Nothing, until I had to." It had seemed impossible. *Hello, Father,*

I married a man I had known only five days. Yes, we love each other. But you see, he's the prince, and the king was overthrown, and I don't know where he is and the Myceneans may come looking for me.

"Tam?" He sounded worried. She realized that only now, safe, was she allowing herself to admit what had happened.

"I'm all right," she said softly. She forced a smile.

He rubbed her foot some more, not speaking. The calluses on his palms from holding a sword were rough. He said quietly, "I can see how it would have been complicated. But if we win the war you will have to tell him."

"In that case I think you can tell him yourself." He would be much less awkward.

"If that's what you wish, love, of course."

"I wish my parents knew that I am safe," she said. "They'll be worried sick."

"There's no way to get a message to them. It would have to pass between too many hands. I'm sorry." He moved his fingers over the bones of her ankle. "Your skin is so smooth."

"What about your sister? Will we hear about her?" She had watched Corin's face go completely blank for an instant when Kelvan said that Tai was free. He had not been ready at all for that news.

"I hope we don't," he said vehemently. "I hope the rider delivers her safely someplace and she stays hidden."

There was anger in his voice, and pain, and she realized that was part of what he was struggling with. She reclaimed her foot and moved closer to him. "But that's not enough. What is it, Corin?" she asked carefully.

Instead of looking at her he stared into the fire. She watched the light shift on his face.

He said, "Tam, we won't escape Mycene even if the Sarians fall. Even if Hadon himself dies. Caithen will remain vassal as long as the dragons are held. That's why I must go on." He seemed to know something now that he had not earlier.

"Do the dragons mean to free Caithen or themselves?"

"Or," he said, and then went very quiet. She waited. At last he took her hand. "It's the same thing," he said. "There's no 'or' about it. I realized that this afternoon."

It was not fair. It made the stakes much higher, the burden heavier on him. If he failed the dragons he failed his kingdom, his father, his self. She put her other hand over his, so that his hand was clasped between her two. There was nothing she could think of to say. She hoped again that Aram wasn't dead.

He was very still, his hand motionless in hers. She closed her eyes and listened. His breathing was steady. She could hear the rush of hot air going up the chimney. She swallowed.

"Corin," she said, "tell me what you need."

He did not pretend to misunderstand her. "Tam," he said. He took a deep breath. He pulled his hand free of hers and faced her. "Tam, will you go into trance again?"

She had not anticipated that. He had been so opposed to it before. "What are you trying to do?" she asked.

"You saw the Dragon Valleys before. I want you to See into the past. See what happened when they were taken."

"That can't be done," she said, and heard the foolishness of it as the words came out. If she could See any thing, then why not any time? Especially when dragons were involved. "You can't do it?"

"God, Tam, if I could, do you think I would ask you?"

He was still avoiding whatever he needed to say. She gathered herself for a quarrel. "You're holding something back," she said.

"Yes," he said, full of fury. He got up and went to the door, jerked it open. The draft made the fire surge. All she could see beyond his body was darkness. It was like watching him that night on the steps. One wrong move and he would crack. She was afraid to either speak or touch him.

He swore a few times and slammed his fist into the palm of his other hand. Then something seemed to go out of him. He slumped a little, turned. He came back to her and lifted her hand. Gently, he brought it to his lips. She bit the inside of her own lip with sadness for him.

"I think it will be very dangerous," he said. He was sterner than she had ever seen him. "You could be lost, or you might set something free. I don't want you to do it at all. I think we were lucky last time."

"But you're asking me."

"You might say it's my duty to ask," he said, with a small, bitter laugh. He let go of her hand. "I can't let love protect you. But it is absolutely not a command. You can say no. I hope you do."

How hard that must have been for him to say, all of it. "You know I won't," she said gently.

"I do know that," he said. "I'm letting you choose your risk, because that is the only thing I have to give you. But please, Tam, don't do it just because you think it would be cowardly not to. Use your reason. Make a decision that would make your father proud."

The danger seemed unreal, a storybook danger, nothing to actually fear. She had to do him the justice of weighing everything carefully. "Come closer," she said.

He shook his head. "I don't get to be your husband in this."

There it was, that was the pain. She knew he did not want to be touched, but there had to be a way to ease him. She picked up the poker and used it to carefully reposition a log that did not need to be repositioned.

"What if I don't do it, or it doesn't help?"

"Then I'll have to think of something else," he said.

For a long while they were silent. Tam got hot and removed the cloak. Corin stirred at that, and when she had folded it into a neat square she put a tentative hand on his knee. He did not shake it off, and she moved it a few inches farther along his thigh. When he still did not react she brought her whole body closer.

He shifted. At first she thought he was retreating, but he took hold of her and pulled her in. She slipped her shirt over her head. The air on her back was cold. She watched the firelight on her body, then finally looked at him. "You are my husband," she said. "Always."

His lips moved. He put one hand on her side. She pushed him slowly down onto the blanket. It made a muscle in her back ache, and she winced.

"Thrice in one day?" he whispered.

"I could just be teasing."

"I dare you."

Tam lay awake long after Corin had fallen asleep. The bed was not really big enough for both of them. She was still wide awake when she heard Kelvan come back. She crept out of bed, dressed, and went into the other room.

He glanced at her from where he sat beside the fire. A single log still burned low. She raised her finger to her lips and dropped down beside him so that they could whisper. "My lady," he breathed.

"Do you know where the king is?" she asked. He hesitated, and she added quickly, "I'm not asking you where, I just want to know if you know."

"I do."

"How long would it take to bring him here?"

"Five hours each way in fair weather."

Ten hours. That was too long. She sighed.

"What do you want with him, my lady?"

"Nothing particular. It's just—if Corin dies—" She could not finish. The man she would really need was her own father, but there was no sending a dragonrider to get him. He would not be permitted in this valley. "Do you think there's a chance to win?"

"With the war, aye. The dragons will do their part, and the soldiers will go home."

"What will you do?" She was not sure why she asked.

He looked startled. "I can't go back to Mycene. I will do what the king asks of me, I expect."

"And if he asks nothing?"

"I don't know. I'm not fit for much other than what I am." There was a guardedness to his tone that told her not to pry further. He had spent years keeping himself hidden, as a wizard and as a spy, and he was not about to break that silence for her. She wondered if he approved, of her, of the match.

"Did you know about Corin and the dragons when Aram sent you?"

"Aye. He came in fall, not long after the prince was born. There was snow high up already, I remember that. He and Rois tested me, and then he said that what he wanted from me amounted to exile, and I asked him why. Then he told me."

"How old were you?"

"Fourteen."

It seemed absurdly young. It told her something about Aram, that he would entrust such a mission to a boy. He must have been a good judge of character even then. And able to think deeply and deliberately, even when taking risks. He would have been not much older than Corin was now; he had been crowned when he was only twenty-two. It made her feel inadequate.

As though he had heard her thoughts, Kelvan said, "I've known the king to be wrong about things, but never about a person."

Tam supposed it was both a rebuke and encouragement. *Trust yourself.* She remembered watching Corin in the drugged sleep, the king beside her. The room had been very still and cold but Aram's presence had managed to fill it. And from that Aram had decided she was worthy to marry his son. Had he known then that she had power? He had said that had nothing to do with it, but she was not naïve. He might have accepted her without it, but he certainly intended to make use of it.

They watched the fire a while longer without speaking. The log crumbled at the center and the two ends tilted down. The light faded. Kelvan stood up. "Good night, my lady," he said.

"Good night," she said.

He went to the door of his own room, then turned. "This valley holds stories," he said. "You have Sight. If you ask, it may give you one." He entered his room and shut the door behind him without waiting for her answer.

In the morning, over breakfast, Corin said, "Have you decided?" and Tam said, "I want to try," and that was all there was to it.

The dragon was still dozing midday when Tam walked with Corin up the hill to one of the huts. Her legs ached a bit, but the stiffness was improving.

It was a small, shabby-looking hut, with a pair of goats in a pen behind it and a thin grubby child playing in the dirt in front with a dog. The child, a girl Tam thought, gave them a glance as they entered and apparently decided they were not interesting enough to pay more attention to.

Inside was quite a different matter. She had been in the homes of very poor people many times with her father, and they were usually crowded and dark and in disrepair. The chimney smoked, if there even was a chimney, and the walls closed in. Sometimes two or three families would be living in the same two rooms. If there were windows, they looked onto filthy streets or a thin shaft of light that fell in the few inches between buildings. This place surprised her with its lightness and cleanliness.

Rois was very old, but she seemed spryer than Tam felt at the moment. When their eyes met Tam sensed the power, stronger than she had ever felt it from either Joce or Kelvan. She thought she should curtsy, but did not know how to do it without a skirt.

She gratefully accepted tea made of chamomile and a little valerian. It would help the stiffness. Corin stayed very close to her.

For a few minutes they engaged in polite idle chat. Then Corin said, with no lightness in his voice at all, "Rois, Tam needs to be tranced tomorrow."

"Tomorrow?" Tam asked, startled. She was ready to do it now.

"Yes. I think you need to go up on the dragon first, and it can't fly today." He turned back to Rois. "Can you do it?"

"Why?"

"To See the Dragon Valleys."

Rois looked at Tam. "Do you want to do this?"

"Yes," Tam said. "I've thought about it."

"Are you afraid?"

She shook her head. "No. I did it before."

"Tell me."

"It was dark," she said, remembering. "But I could see." It had been so easy to slip into trance. When Liko asked her questions, it had been impossible to provide full answers. It had been like trying to recount a dream. What she saw was so clear before her, but she could not describe it. To say the cliffs were high did not do justice to the two thousand feet or more that they towered above her, leaving her feeling the size of an ant. She had no words for the smell of the place, a coldness that might have been ice and a sharp scent of metal and ashes or old fire. It smelled angular and hard. There had been a faint and constant whistling that she thought was the wind shrieking across the top of the canyon.

Then she heard the piano and felt the needle pain of dragonspeech and told Corin to go to the roof. She heard the sound of wing strokes in the air before she jerked back into consciousness. Her eyes met Liko's, and he looked away. She terrified him.

"It took no effort to go into trance, and it took no effort to come back," she said. "I can do this."

Rois was silent. Tam could not read her face. The door was still open, and she looked out. A hen stood there, its golden feathers glistening in the sun, its feet scaled and reptilian. Dragon's feet.

"Were you alone?"

"Yes." Then, reluctantly, she said, "Until the end. The dragons spoke to me."

"What do you hope to gain?" Rois asked.

"To See the ghosts of centuries," she said.

"Why?"

Tam looked at Corin. His face was expressionless, but there was a tension in him that she recognized from the ball, when he had been so sure she was in danger. There was a way out for both of them, she realized. She only had to say that it was his thought, his idea, and Rois would refuse to do it.

Very deliberately, publicly, she put her hand over his on the table and said, "I want to See the taking of the dragons. That is what Corin needs to know, and he can't See it."

"And for this you will risk the dark place?"

"Yes."

"If you go deep enough, it might take you."

"I know." She did not want to explain it, to try to speak her loves and fears. They did not belong to anyone but her.

For a long time no one spoke. Tam heard the hen scratching at the dirt. Children's voices called to one another farther up the hill. The light coming in the eastern window shortened.

"Give me your hand," Rois said, as commanding as a king.

Tam did. She felt power at once, coursing hot through her, like wine, like passion. Steadily she lifted her head and met Rois's silver eyes.

Rois looked at Corin. "Outside, now," she said.

He went. Tam was a little amused.

Rois released Tam's hand and leaned forward. "You are willing and ready and brave enough to do it, but is it the right thing?"

"Yes."

"How far can you take yourself?"

Tam clasped her hands together in her lap and let her mind and body slip into the space Joce had shown her. She had to find the place of power within herself. She thought of Cade, the dryness of his skin as the life left him, the scent of stone that clung to him. When had she known she had power? Not when Cade died. But certainly she had known before Aram put it into words.

She remembered incense, candlelight, colored sand. The old woman must have had power of sorts. Perhaps she too had been a wizard. There was not a chance of remembering the words the woman had spoken, but she knew where to go. Back, not just into the stillness that she had felt before but into the stillness at the heart of time.

She began to sense presence, sparks of other moving creatures. Birds, dogs, quivering mice. The cold of a dragon's mind.

Pain, memories of pain. Heat rising from a blistering desert and the hollow wizened faces of those who had died in thirst and starvation, with the sun beating on them and the horrible consuming light everywhere. Then for a long time she felt only pain screaming at her from every cell in her body. She was blind but could not pass into unconsciousness. She could form no words or thoughts. Her head was heavy and hot and felt ready to burst into a thousand pieces.

The agony shifted into rage that she shrank from. It clawed at her. She crossed her arms before her. She had to hide. It pushed viciously against her. It forced its way through every protection that she had. She cowered against it.

It relented. Her mouth and throat were paper dry. There was a deep ache in her bones. They were there, the dead, their voices clamoring in her mind. They wanted her body, wanted to walk again on earth and under sky. It would be simple to yield to them. She was so very tired. Rest, a voice cajoled, rest. Her skin was numb. The spirits rocked her gently and sang a lullaby.

There was someone with her. It did not matter. There was no pain anymore, only weight and stillness. Light and silence. She could not lift her arm. All that remained of her was her mind. If she released it she would be done.

Sharp pain cut across her hand. She shouted. She was bleeding, damn it. What was Rois doing?

Then she realized she was herself again. Her whole body jerked violently. Her breath was ragged. Blood was running down her palm and fingers onto the floor.

Rois put down the knife and wiped Tam's hand with a warm damp cloth. It stung a little. The cut was very shallow.

"You'd better wrap it," Tam said tiredly. Her voice was hoarse and scratchy.

Without speaking, Rois spread a bitter-smelling paste across the wound. It numbed the skin. She wrapped it neatly with a strip of cloth.

"If you can go that deep on your own," Rois said, "trance is extremely dangerous. I may not be able to bring you back."

"You'll have to," Tam said. Her mind felt very clear. Whatever she had heard, whatever had spoken to her, that was what remained of the dragons' age. She drank some tea. "How many other worlds are there?"

"More than we can ever know," said Rois. "Or perhaps all worlds are one with ours but we can only see this if we step back."

There was a very long silence. Tam let it fill her, the valley silence, the voice of stone. It was far older than Caithenor. That was what Kelvan had meant about it giving her stories. The magma at the roots of the mountains, the wearing away by the rain, uncountable years of wind. It made the dragons look young, and yet they were like it too, snatched out of time to dwell in fire and rock.

She picked up the knife and wiped it clean with the damp cloth. One of the goats behind the hut bleated. She said, "How much do you remember, Rois? How old are you?"

Rois laughed. "I was not alive at the taking of the dragons, if that is what you want to know. Wizards live and die as other humans. But I am old enough to remember when Aram's grandfather found us and offered us this place. I was a girl then."

"Do you remember any stories about the taking of the dragons?"

"There is a legend, but I doubt its truth."

"Tell me anyway. Please."

After a hesitation, Rois said, "As the stories go, the Myceneans came and found a group of wizards to aid them. They were wizards who tried to increase their power with other magics, sorceries and spells from without, not wizards of ordinary sort. They took the Mycenean soldiers to the Dragon Valleys. They thought they would gain more power by becoming riders for the Empire. Somehow they made the dragons cold, froze them. Different versions say different things. They called the North Wind, shot arrows of ice, transformed the flames into rubies. Then the Myceneans killed all but one of them and took him and the eggs back to Mycene, and after the eggs hatched they killed him too. In one version of the story the wizards stole power from the rest of us and used it up, and that's why we weakened."

Made them cold, Tam thought. Something about it seemed familiar. She remembered the cold air when her hand plunged through the silver tray, the ice Corin had described when he tried to bring Tai back. It mattered. She could not quite see her way through to the answer.

"Why did your people come here?" she asked.

"It seemed a fair bargain," she said. "The service of a few to the king, whose subjects we were anyway, in exchange for safety and solitude instead of hiding and poverty. After the Fires things were very hard for us. There were some who objected to the bargain but they agreed in the end." She hesitated. The wrinkles around her eyes creased a little more. "But I remember, when we came here, it was the only time I ever saw my father weep. He felt free."

Tam imagined how he must have felt and shivered with the intensity of it. "What was that king like?" she asked. "Do you remember?"

"Big, black-bearded, impatient. Kind in an absentminded sort of way. He was said to be clever but not deceitful. I didn't know him, of course. I could not tell you if Corin is anything like him."

Tam had a hundred other questions, about Rois, about wizardry, about the people of the village. All of them seemed too much like prying. "Thank you," she said.

Rois rose. "He has waited long enough." She opened the door.

Corin came rapidly in and sat down beside Tam. "Well?" he asked. Then he saw her hand. "What the hell happened?"

"She wanted to be sure I could do it," she said. "It's all right. I'll tell you the whole story later."

He scowled. Tam did not try to appease him. She watched him exert control of himself. He said, quite calmly, "Will you do it, Rois?"

"Yes," she said. "Send for me tomorrow when you are ready."

"Thank you," he said. He started to rise, then dropped back down abruptly. He said, "How much power does she have?"

Rois included Tam in her answering look. "Sight, strongly. I think stronger in some places than others, places where there is power. But no wizard power."

Tam said, "Joce thought I might be able sometime to do more than See. Years from now. That was all he would say. The king seemed to think there was more."

"It depends upon how you use your Sight now," Rois said. "Upon what you will let in."

It sent coldness down her back and arms, and recall of wings fluttering against her skin. Was she ready to admit the dead? She swallowed and said, deflecting the question, "There's power in Caithenor."

"Yes. It did not become the seat of rulers by accident. That is what woke you."

"I didn't feel anything when I went back. There was no point in going." She remembered walking those ashy streets, sitting on the cobbles baking from the sun. It had been hot and frightening, and all that had happened was that her legs got more tired.

"You went back," Rois said, "because it is now the place you consider home."

Tam wanted to deny it, but the protest died on her lips. Even if Corin died, she would not be able to settle comfortably back into her parents' home. Rois was right.

"That," Corin said, "is why my father saw you as my queen."

She was afraid that if she looked at him she would weep. She stared fixedly at a knothole in a rafter. He put his hand on the side of her head and turned her slowly to face him. She swallowed over the swelling in her throat.

He stood up and drew her with him. She kept her hand in his. It felt more like a wedding than that moment in the palace had. He looked at Rois, started to say something, then shook his head. Tam looked back at Rois as Corin led her outside. The old woman held up a hand in farewell.

When they reached the dragon, Corin paused. It lay with its massive head resting on its forelegs, like a cat. The claws were a polished ivory that glistened where they caught the sun. Kelvan sat cross-legged on the ground beside it, inspecting a harness strap. He rose unhurriedly.

The dragon opened one eye and looked at Tam. She jumped. She knew she should not be afraid of the thing, not after having ridden on it for six hours with nothing worse than a queasy stomach, not with these two men here. But it was gazing at her with such intelligence, weighing her. The yellow of the eye was not really yellow, it was the color of straw and corn shucks, bright as new copper, striated with greens and browns that spoke of earth and evergreens and turning leaves. The pupil seemed to go forever, a liquid darkness, not like the darkness her hand had plunged into. It was deep and full of heat and profound knowledge waiting for her. It had a curving warm sensuality that brought her fingers to her mouth.

"Don't look it in the eye, Tam," Corin said, touching her shoulder. She jumped again and turned her head away. A pang of loss shuddered through her. Then she shook her head vigorously, as though she could shake the thoughts from it, and faced him with her back to the dragon. That seemed considerably less dangerous.

If I am going to free it I have to try to understand it, she thought. That was why he wanted her to ride it again first. "Help me look at it," she said.

He put his arm around her. It was warm, human. He walked her a few feet and turned her to look at the beast. Kelvan was now standing between her and the dragon's eye.

She looked. Do not be afraid, she thought. Do not. Do not. She tried to approach it as her father would: a body, a creature of skin and flesh and bone, with veins and lungs and spleen. It was her task to sketch and label it. The front legs were as long as the back, but less muscled, slimmer. Made for lashing out. The wing joint lay beside and behind the shoulder. The scales were darker there and did not gleam as much. The wing was batwing, not birdwing, with what looked like a vestigial claw at the end. There were no ridges or crests anywhere on the dragon except its head. It was a creature that could slip through air as a fish through water. The tail was long and the same thickness nearly to the end. It too looked ready to lash and strike.

Carefully she moved forward. Corin stayed close. She noted how the scales on the back toes were barely the size of a coin, while the ones on the flanks were as large as her palm. The body moved with very slow, shallow breath. She gripped Corin's hand with one of hers, and with the other pressed on a scale. The dragon did not respond. When she lifted her fingers from the dragon's side, iridescent fingerprints faded quickly out.

Without looking at Corin, because that would make her give in to fear, she said, "I should talk to it."

"Let me check," he said, and after an instant said, "Go ahead. But kneel, you will probably get faint. I'll be right beside you."

She went to both knees and leaned back on her heels. The grass was short and withered from dragonheat. A wave crashed on the beach, very far away it seemed. A small black beetle wandered along beside the dragon. A rosemary bush in bloom hummed loudly with bees.

Tam closed her eyes and put both hands on the dragon's side. Tell me your history, she thought.

The moon was high and full. It was cold. The trees were bare and straight and black, and the blue-silver light washed over everything. There was a scent of smoke lying under the cold scent of the snow and the frightened leaping scent of prey. Shadow fell over the open spaces, and the leafless trees trembled against one another. A dragon passed in a roar of wind. It was huge and dark and glistened like sun on melting ice. It screamed. Red fire flared across the sky. Sparks showered golden to the snow.

More wind then, swirling, a column of sound. It caught the flames and spun them like autumn leaves.

Around and around, rustling, each flame a thousand wings, each spark a hundred golden eyes.

The deer pressed against one another, and the hares huddled against the snow, and even the owls sat hunched and silent with feathers tightly drawn together. The wolves sang. The dragon called back to them. Fire. Wind. Darkness.

Dragon darkness, filling everything, cold and stretching endlessly. Scales fell from it and became crows, black and swift.

Wings beat and the dragon lifted. Moonlight sharp as a blade.

Tam fell back, gasping. Her vision was dark. She reached feebly for Corin and felt him take her hand. His fingers pressed painfully on the cut. "It's all right," he said, his words echoing a little. "It will pass. Lie still."

She got her breath back, and the darkness faded. The sun was warm on her face. She tried to look at Corin but had to squint at his shape against the sun. The sky was a burning intense blue behind him.

He helped her up. The earth whirled beneath her feet. She stumbled forward and almost fell. She grabbed at him. He put his arms around her and supported her, saying nothing. The sun beat on her hair. His shirt under her turned cheek was warm. He smelled good. She stayed limp for a while.

When she felt a little stronger, she looked carefully again at the ground. It stayed steady this time, even when she straightened.

"All right now?" he asked.

"Yes." She was far too unsure of it to say anything else.

He held her hand anyway and led her to the cottage. The interior was extremely dark after the brightness of the day, and she staggered again. By the time her eyes adjusted Tam realized she was famished. "I'm hungry," she said.

"I'm not surprised," he said. "That was a lot of effort. Sit down, and I'll get you something. Water first, I think."

She ate greedily, as though there had been no food for days. Cold spring water, fruit, meat. Her limbs had the weakness that followed an illness. Corin ate nothing. She reached for more.

When finally she was finished, he took away her empty plate and put another full cup of water in front of her. She drank, and wiped her mouth, and let herself settle back into ordinariness.

"You're very good at table service for someone of your upbringing," she said as he sat down.

"One can't talk privately of anything with servants hovering about ready to whisk away the dishes."

"Did you ever have to wait on your father?"

"No, thank God. If I was competent enough to hear it at all, I was competent to sit at the table. He never trusted me with the wine, though."

"Seeing how profligate you are, that was wise of him," she said. She extended a hand toward him.

He stroked her thumb a few times, then said, "Do you still want to do it?"

"Yes," she said. "I will See something. I wish I knew what the dragon said to me. Did it tell you?"

"No. Dragons keep confidences."

"I asked for its history."

"History is a human thing. Dragons don't have it."

"I thought you wanted me to See their past," she said.

"Well, yes," he said. "You've caught me in an inconsistency, which we could debate with Liden scholars for years. But don't try to figure it out. The meaning will come to you. If you need to wait a while, Tam, then we'll wait."

He seemed much calmer than he had since yesterday. Perhaps he was ready to talk. "What happens if we fail?" she asked.

"Assuming it is not so spectacular a failure as to kill us both, then we have to cede Hadon the dragons and fight an ordinary war."

If it turned into an ordinary war he would be always moving, hiding, planning. Tam wished she could spare him that. She said, "You won't stay here in the valley."

"No. But you might have to. We really will need to keep you hidden."

She stood and looked out the window at the dragon. It turned its head and seemed to look back at her. Avoiding its eyes, she watched its tail move.

She said, "What happens if you free the dragons before the Myceneans and Sarians are gone? Will the dragons still help us?"

"I don't know," he said. He was calm, not despairing. Something had changed in him.

"Aren't the Myceneans just as likely to leave us to Tyrekh, or even join with the Sarians as punishment for us?"

She heard him walk toward her. He put his hands on her shoulders and began to rub them. He kissed her hair. He said, "Tam, Caithen is the dragons' land too."

"But do they care about its people? What if all they want is to go back to the Dragon Valleys and be wild creatures again?" The dragon's images of snow and wolves were haunting her.

He was so silent that she would not have known he was there if she had not felt his hands working evenly on her shoulders. At last he said, "If they don't help us, we are still better off with them free of Mycene than with the Emperor using them against us. I don't have anything to hold hostage against them, even if I were so inclined."

"Can we try to bargain?"

He moved from her back to her side and faced her. His eyes were very green at the moment, nothing like dragon eyes. He traced her lips with a finger. Then he said softly, "What happens in the tales when someone tries to bargain with a dragon or a djinn or such?"

"If it's the hero he tricks them. Everybody else loses."

"Exactly. Never do both sides get what they want. The bargain always fails. I'm not playing that game."

He was right, but something about it stung her. She realized she had wanted to be the hero, to find the answer, to set things right. Perhaps that was the result of talking to dragons. It made one feel stronger, more important, cocky. She nodded reluctantly.

"I know you don't like taking things on faith," he said. "Nor should you. But sometimes it's necessary. A bargain is no bargain if you don't have faith the other party will keep it. That's why Hadon is losing his empire. He has no faith in his subjects, and they have no faith in him. A people can only be governed by its own consent."

"You said at the ball that power was making a person give something for nothing and thinking she had got the better deal."

"That's power, not governance. They aren't the same."

It was her turn to touch his face. She said what she would not have said to him last night when he was struggling. "You are going to be a splendid king."

She thought there was a faint blush to his ears and cheeks but could not be sure. He looked at the dragon. His face went quiet. Sad. However things turned out, he was going to lose something he loved.

"Corin?"

"Yes?" he answered, from someplace very remote and far away.

Everything she could think of to say sounded mawkish, so she said nothing. For a long time they just looked at each other.

At last he said, "Whatever you decide about tomorrow, Tam, you have my trust and my blessing."

"Thank you."

The dragon touched her mind then, a swirling darkness, and at its center was a spinning silver flame. No bargain, no contract, but it was giving her a promise.

CHAPTER EIGHTEEN

❦

Corin looked up at Tam on the dragon and said for at least the fourth time by his count, "Don't try to speak to it, just look at the land." Kelvan was in front of her, very adroitly managing to look at neither of them.

She gave him her most syrupy smile and said, "Yes, Your Highness." Then she prodded Kelvan in the back. The dragon rose before Corin had time to speak the farewell. Dust kicked up and whirled from the flap of wings.

He had vowed not to engage in any nervous behavior such as pacing. They would not take that long. Kelvan was going to circle the valley and bring her back and that would be it. He sat down with his back against the hut to make it impossible to pace and looked upward. They were very high already. He began stropping his sword.

He worked carefully, and they were back before he finished. Tam dropped to the ground beside him. Her face was pink with chill. "That was much better," she said.

"Good. How far could you see?"

"It's very clear. For miles. He took me high. I can see why dragons are useful in a war."

"Did he point out the Valleys?"

"The general direction. We're too far west to see much. There was no sign of any other dragons."

"Are you ready?"

"Yes," she said. "I didn't try to speak to it, but I think it spoke to me a little anyway. I had some strange images in my head. I can almost feel what it is to be a dragon. How much longer do you think you'll be about that?"

He gauged the work. "Ten minutes, perhaps. Drink some water if you haven't yet and I'll be right in."

She was not displaying any worry at all about the trance, which relieved him, since he was feeling enough for both of them. Last night she had asked Kelvan countless questions about dragons and riders, gathering information, and she knew nearly as much as Corin did now. He wasn't sure it was going to help her, since the taking of the dragons was just as remote to the riders. She had asked some other questions about the history of Caithen and the Empire and then declared herself done. Corin thought Kelvan was a bit relieved to have it over.

When he went back into the cottage, she was kneeling in front of the hearth, poking at embers. There was no wood laid for a fire. She accepted his hand and came to her feet as gracefully as if it were a court ceremony. He took her in his arms.

"What were you doing?" he asked.

"Seeing if the ashes were cool enough to sweep yet. I don't think they are." She pulled back a little and searched his face. "Kelvan went to get her."

"Do you want to do it inside or outside?"

"Outside, and near to the dragon." She swallowed. "You have to let me go as long as I can. Even if you think I'm in danger. It's not going to be the same as Liko's trance was; he did not really know what he was doing. I think she'll take me much deeper."

"Kelvan's going to follow if he can."

"I think the dragons will block him."

How calm and ordinary it was, as though they were discussing arrangements for a banquet. He knew he had to let her do it. When Rois had told Tam she considered Caithenor her home, his own heart had been briefly stabbed with certainty. She had made her choices, set herself on her course, and that was the very thing he most loved about her. She would not be swayed from what she thought in her core was right and necessary. Not even if he did command her. She was stronger than that. He had been underestimating her again, and Rois had placed her so that he could not fail to see it.

He said, "Tam, I'm letting you go into danger. You have to do the same when it's my turn."

"I know." She leaned against him. He was glad they would not quarrel about that. What was it his father had said? *She is far more sensible than you are.* She was not nearly so hindered by pride.

He held her a moment longer, then steeled himself and said, "It's time."

They found a spot under a tree eight yards or so from the dragon. The dragon had its head down, but Corin doubted it was sleeping. He touched its mind and found it calm. He had only the barest intimation of its vast consciousness.

He set a stool in the grass for Rois and worked at the ground a little to make it steady. Tam had nothing to sit on but a folded cloak.

When Kelvan and Rois came, Corin helped the old woman to sit. Tam sat in front of her. Rois said, "Sometimes, if one goes deep enough, it needs a memory to pull the person out. Give me something that is old and simple."

Tam tilted her face skyward to think. Corin loved that expression on her. The tiny purse of lips, the hint of a crease of the brow, the smoothness of her cheeks and eyelids. Sun coming through the tree branches dappled her hair. She said, "When I was ten, my brother brought a woman home to meet the family. I didn't like her. So I spilled water all over the front of her dress and pretended it was an accident."

Rois smiled. She said, "That will do well, unless—is it a bad memory? Were you punished?"

"Not really. My parents didn't like her either."

Corin felt himself grin. He had not heard that particular story before. He wondered if Rois had done it to set them all at ease. Tam looked at him, and he said, "If your brother spills water on me, I'll challenge him to a duel."

"He's never held a sword in his life," she said. "It wouldn't be gentlemanly." She turned back to Rois.

"Give me your hand," Rois said. "I will chant you into trance."

Tam did. Corin squatted where he could see her face. Silence was suddenly heavy and thick around them.

Rois chanted in a language he did not know. Tam's eyes closed.

Her face stilled and her breathing slowed. Still Rois chanted. Corin rubbed his own eyes as drowsiness began to overtake him.

Rois stopped chanting. "Who are you?"

"Tam Warin."

"Where were you tranced?"

"In the wizard's valley."

"Who is with you?"

"Corin, Kelvan, you."

"Very good. Now tell me where you are now."

She hesitated a little before speaking. Her voice got stronger as she went on. "The same place I was before. But I can see it clearly now. It's daylight. The cliffs are glossy and smooth, like glass. No one could scale them. Black, but not really, there are lines of grey and violet shot through it. It's silver where the sun catches it. Beautiful. The ground is grey and fine. Ashy. It's very dry. Nothing grows."

Corin bit the inside of his lip. He forced himself to relax. He heard Kelvan take up a place behind him.

"Turn around," Rois said.

There was a pause. Then Tam said, "I'm at the end of the canyon. There's only rock going up in front of me. There's a crack in it, not very wide."

"Can you go in?"

"Yes. It's dark. It's straight, mostly, I'm sideways but I don't have to bend. It's rough. It catches my clothing. Now it opens out, I can feel the space. I still can't see anything."

"You have a light."

Silence. An inhalation. "It's huge. I can barely see the other side. It's almost perfectly round, like a bubble. And black, so black. The light is reflecting off the walls. There's a chasm in the middle cutting it in half. The roof is high." There was no sound of fear in her voice, no tension in her body.

"Is there any light or heat coming out of the chasm?"

"I don't think so." A pause. "No, it's dead. It's very cold. The air coming out feels icy. It smells stony."

"Go back out."

The silence was longer this time. Corin heard something snap and realized he had broken a twig he was holding. A dog barked with excitement on the hill. Tam said, "I'm out, but it's night now. I see stars."

"Are you alone?"

"Yes. No. It's coming. It's like wind. I lie down. I can't hear anything but the wind's roar."

Corin tasted blood in his mouth from biting his lip. He swallowed. Her face was very calm. His legs were shaking a little from the strain of holding himself alert, so he gave in and sat down. He felt Kelvan's hands come to rest on his shoulders. Her mouth moved silently. He was a good lip reader, but he could not make sense of what she was saying.

She said aloud, "Now everything is spinning. The wind is holding me down. It stops. I'm still in the valley but it's changed, it's warmer. Oh! There are dragons. They are in formation. It's like a dance. I can't describe it. It means something." Her tone was joyous, delighted. For a breath he envied her for what she saw. The dragons tugged painfully at him.

"Go back to the chasm."

"I'm through the crack. The chasm is glowing now. It's hot. Something smells foul. It's not sulfur, not dragonscent. I can't go any closer, it's too hot. I hear steam. The smell is getting worse. There are wings. No, no." Urgency, fear. Corin jerked upward.

"Run," Rois said sharply, as Kelvan's hands pressed down hard, holding him in place. Corin took his eyes off Tam's face long enough to look at Rois and saw a disquieting expression of dread.

There was a lengthy silence. Then Tam said, sounding calmer, "I'm out. There are still dragons. It's all spinning again. There are men now, and it's cold again. Very cold. I see a dragon on the ground. It's alive but not moving. Its scales are black. It's the cold, that's what's keeping it slow. One of the men shoots it in the eye. Now they are gathering eggs. They have ropes and pulleys to lift them. There are no dragons flying.

"I go back through the crack. The chasm is dead again, they lost their heat, that's what happened. There is a dead man at the side of the chasm. His eyes are like the walls. Black stone. His fingers are cold.

"Wait. Wait."

Her lips did not move. Something made a sound behind him, and Corin looked over his shoulder. The dragon was standing. Its head was moving a little, back and forth, back and forth. Deep deep fear of it tightened his belly. He reached his mind out to it and sensed only a chaotic turbulence. It moved its front foot, scraping its talons against the earth. Kelvan's hands tightened.

Tam's face twisted in what seemed anguish. She said, "It's so loud. I see it. No. Bring me back, bring me back."

Rois chanted something rapidly. Tam's eyes opened. She flung herself at Corin, weeping.

He held her without saying anything. Kelvan had stepped back. He touched the dragon's mind and recognized it again. Her tears were warm on his skin. He smelled the salt.

She took a great, shuddering breath, and stopped crying. She straightened and looked at him. Her eyes were red and swollen. She wiped them.

"Corin," she said, and her voice trembled a little, "Corin. The thing that's trapped, it was once a dragon. I saw it, the Myceneans used the wizards to take its fire. They breathed it in and died. To free the dragons you have to set it loose, but it will kill you."

They sat by the river again in the sunset light. The sun was a huge red circle low over the sea. Tam's face showed signs of tears. She had been struggling against them all day. Corin felt only cold and empty. *It can't be,* he said, *it can't be,* even as his mind moved pieces into place and saw how well they fit.

Only after the sun had dropped beneath the ocean and the dark was gathering fast did Tam speak. "My love," she said, and stopped.

He still did not want to talk about it. But he knew that was a weakness he could not indulge any longer. "Yes?"

She surprised him. "Do you know what is happening in Caithenor?"

So strange a question, practical, ordinary. "It can be found out," he said.

"I think we need to."

She was right. He was afraid that whatever he learned, whether good or ill, would make him give up. But he could not go on blind. He got to his feet. It would have been very satisfying to have another fit of rage, but he knew better.

Tam said, "Are you going to ask the dragon yourself?"

"No. Too risky. I'll have Kelvan do it. Do you want to come?" *Would you like to have tea with me? Shall I take you to the theater tonight?*

"I'll wait here."

"Very well," he said, and heard the formality of it. He neither kissed her nor touched her before he went to find the rider.

He did not pause to speak to the dragon. That would make him too angry. He found Kelvan and issued curt instructions. There were a few bottles of wine the villagers had provided that he had not wanted to touch. He uncorked one, sniffed it. It had not gone to vinegar yet. He grabbed two earthenware mugs, almost dropping them, and stalked back to Tam.

She did not greet him. He filled the cups and handed one to her. The moon would not be over the mountains for a few hours yet, and the last of the sunlight was gone. They could not see each other's faces. If he tried he would be able to, dragons saw well at night. He did not want anything to do with their powers.

"Tell me," he said, a command. He was afraid she would call him "my lord." That would be the first breach.

She took his hand and kissed it. "Please don't interrupt me, Corin," she said. "I can only stand to do this once."

"I promise," he said, softening.

She released his hand. He heard her drink. She said, with that calmness he always marveled at, "The thing that came at me out of the chasm, it was a dragon. But it was wild and vicious and cruel.

It was not like these dragons. It saw me and it hated me. It wants to inflict pain, to steal back what was taken.

"And they need it, Corin. It's what they're missing. They were defanged. It's what's left after the Myceneans stole the fire. It's a shadow, a wraith. Without the fire, it can't get into the dark place where it belongs. Once they have the fire back, they'll be free. You have to call it to you and give it back the flame. And you'll be the first thing it has a chance to kill."

Every cell in his body told him she was right. Whenever he put on robes to sit in judgment he felt his mind sharpen, clarify, detach itself from the rest of him. He became a figure, the whole and real Corin covered by the anonymity of the formal costuming. His mind did the same thing now, abstracting what Tam said from the muscles and bones and nerves that screamed out for him to retreat.

"Yes," he said. "I see."

"I'm not going to able to explain it any better than that. My mind is too human. I can't See into their world. They showed me this, but I don't have words."

"It's enough," he said. He leaned toward her and found her lips with his. She was alive, warm, present.

They broke off the kiss. He said, "Hadon roused it?"

"I don't think so," she said. "I think the dragons drove him mad and followed him in. They couldn't free it, but they made it stir. He has nothing to do with it. He was just the opening."

"Bastards," he said, without force. He saw it clearly now. There was no way out.

She said, "You still have a choice."

"I don't," he said. "If I refuse either I'll go mad too, or they'll let Caithen be torn apart. It's not Hadon who holds the country hostage, it's the dragons." He could not even be bitter about it. He had accepted this when he turned to the dragons to try to bring his sister home, when he let them bear him from a burning palace, every time he went skyward and felt the rush of air over the dragonwing. They cared nothing for human love, for human loss; they were not human.

Tam said something he could not understand. It sounded as though she were crying again.

He put the mug down and pulled her into his lap, wrapped his arms around her. He would not lie to her and tell her he would live, she would not persuade him not to go. It was what he had to do. He was going into battle like a soldier, just not the battle he had expected.

"Tam," he said, "is there any chance you're pregnant?"

A sniff. "We've done our job trying," she said. "But I don't know. It's far too soon."

"If you are, and I die, Kelvan has to take you to my father."

"Don't say things like that, not now."

"All right."

They sat quietly again for a long time. Corin was aware of how alive they both were, their breath moving in not quite the same rhythm, her body warm and solid against his, the fingers of her right hand locked over his knee.

Desire roused. He resisted for a while, then gave in. His hand went to the inside of her thigh and clasped the muscle. The trouser-cloth was thin and soft with wear against his palm.

Footsteps. Tam scrambled off his lap. They both rose. She bent down again. When she straightened he could see that she was holding a mug in each hand.

"My lord," Kelvan said, with a bow.

For a moment it made him think his father was known dead. But no, if the rider were bringing that news he would have knelt. It was just a formality because Tam was present. Because Kelvan knew how tightly Corin was wound.

"Well?" he asked, hoping for a bit of news that would serve as a distraction. He adjusted his thinking.

"I've been speaking with a rider in Caithenor. You'll like this. Tyrekh's dead."

He felt a savage, pleasant sense of triumph. "How?"

"One of his own men threw a knife into his throat. They have not caught the soldier yet. He completely disappeared."

"I'll bet he did," said Tam, and Corin knew she had come to the same conclusion he had. He almost smiled. He realized that they were past the hardest part. They had decided to get on with it.

"I can try to find him if you'd like," said Kelvan.

"That won't be necessary. He'll have gone to Aram. What else?"

"The dragons are restless. Some are abandoning Hadon and coming north. And someone, I don't know who or how, has got the Myceneans to start to drive the Sarians out. It's easier now that Tyrekh's dead." He paused. "There have been a lot of deaths, on both sides, it's not pretty."

Corin took that to mean they were slaughtering one another. There were probably Caithenians dying too. He doubted his father was behind it directly, but the king was no doubt privy to it and consenting. With any luck it would be over soon.

"Any word of my sister?" he asked.

"The rider who took her has reappeared, but he won't say anything other than that she is safe."

"He probably doesn't know where she is," Corin said. "If he got her to the right man in Dele, she's someplace where even I couldn't find her by now. How is Hadon taking all this?"

"I only have rumor for that. But the rumor is that he's locked himself in his apartments with a fire weapon and won't let anyone in."

"So we're winning."

"It appears that way, aye."

He could not let this chance slip by. He had to take control of things before the battles became leaderless chaos, before the riders decided to do as they pleased. The dragons were using him, he would demand this as his price. He would make the devil's bargain after all.

"I need the dragons," he said. "And the riders. Can I gather them through your dragon?"

"You can summon them," Kelvan said. "I don't know that you can convince them. They're men, they'll want to see you, to measure you against Hadon. Especially considering all they have to lose if the dragons go. They'll have to see you're worth it."

Oh hell. He knew Kelvan was right, but the last thing he wanted to do now was make speeches or have debates. Politics was what it came down to, though. He looked at the mountains. All he could see was unmarked blackness rising into the starry sky.

"I can't do that here," he said. "And I'm certainly not going back to Caithenor or to Mycene."

"No," Kelvan said. "I think you should bring them as far north as you can, though."

It would have to be east and farther south. He did not want them too close to the valley and he was already at the northward limit. He turned the pages of mental map books and decided on a place. "Tower Peak," he said. It was remote, with a craggy ridge at the top that looked like battlements. He could not have a palace to speak from, but he could give a reminder of a fortress. Tomorrow was too soon, he would not have time to prepare, but the next morning, after sunrise.

"Good," said Kelvan.

"I'll be there shortly, then, thank you."

"You're going to do it now?" Tam asked as soon as Kelvan had retreated.

"Just the summons. Nothing else."

A quiet pause of relief. "Corin, this is terrible wine, why are we drinking it?"

"Give me my cup," he said. When she did, he gulped it down and put the mug on the ground. "Finish yours."

She made a noise of disgust but drank. She let her mug drop. It made a soft thud on the grass but did not break. Corin faced her, took her left hand with his right and raised it, slipped his arm around her waist.

"We're dancing," she said, not quite a question.

"Yes, my love," he said, moving his foot.

"I'm not very good without the music."

"Neither am I. We'll do it anyway. We never finished that one at the ball. Don't count."

She let him lead her, and they danced awkwardly along the

riverside. The ground was uneven, their course blocked by bushes or thickets of grass. At times when she stepped her foot into the inside of his, they stumbled, or banged ankles or knees together. He watched her the best he could with only starlight to see by. They were both quiet. A chorus of frogs started, one side of the river to the other and back, strophe and antistrophe. He tried to let nothing in but this time, this moment, her dark figure swirling.

They stopped, and held each other, and kissed hard.

Their arms dropped simultaneously. "Good luck," she said.

"This may take a while. Don't worry."

"I'll bring the cups in."

"Thank you." He kissed her quickly once and then strode to the dragon.

As Corin approached it he realized he had to ride. Kelvan was standing near. "Are the straps ready?" he asked.

"Aye, my lord."

He got on without help and tightened the straps. He put the helmet on. There seemed to be nothing to say. He nodded once at Kelvan, then prodded the dragon's mind. It leaped.

He had the dragon hover and let the wind take it. There was no sea scent, just wind. It stung his eyes. He feared that if he left the valley the wizard's barrier might keep him from returning. Then he decided that if that happened he could land the dragon somewhere nearby and send it to Kelvan to get him. So he turned it north and east, over the mountains, and urged it forward with a driving desperate passion.

It was difficult. Wind tossed the dragon with sudden drops and turns, and there was something almost terrifying about the darkness below. He remembered looking out over the garden with Tam that first night. This was different. It was hard and immense and threw no light back. Even closer to the high mountains with their white tips visible in the starlight there was no softening.

His cheeks and fingers went numb with cold. There were little sparkles of frost on the outside of his breeches.

Higher, he thought, higher, and urged the beast upward until he was gasping for breath and thought frostbite was beginning in his fingertips. The ache in his lungs pleased him. Then he turned it down, hard, plummeting toward earth. The air whistled around him. The stars were streaks of light above. I might die, he thought as he looked down into the darkness. He could not tell how fast it was approaching. He watched himself bend like a horserider to hold the straps tighter and keep the wind off his face. He watched the dragon extend its wings and catch the air. It spun and rocked before it got its balance.

He let it take its own path, sliding through the cold air while he lay on its back, empty and exhausted. Its heat seeped slowly into him. He listened to the beat of blood in his ears and closed his eyes. It rocked him from side to side. For a long time he thought of nothing.

Then he returned to himself and sat up. He directed the dragon back to the cottage. The air warmed, he could see the texture of the ocean, his eyes watered and his skin burned.

The dragon landed easily, almost lightly. He worked at the straps with numb fingers until the knots were free, then slid down. He took the helmet off and was surrounded by noise. He blew on his hands. When he tried to take a step forward he stumbled as the motion brought blood painfully back to his legs. He bent over, stretched, stomped his feet a little.

Now I'm ready, he thought. He felt as though he had been scoured inside and out. All that there was of him was his blood and his skin and his brain.

Kelvan was waiting in the same spot, as though he had not moved. Corin said with a dry mouth, "Have you any water?" He coughed with the effort. His chest still hurt.

"Here," Kelvan said, offering him a full cup. There was a bucket beside him.

Corin drank three full glasses. It tasted like stone. It was very good.

"Has Tam gone in?" he asked.

"Aye. You were up about an hour."

It had not felt that long, but he could never keep track of time when he was dragonback. He stretched again and went to the dragon's head. He knelt beside it.

There was no point in delaying. He looked over his shoulder at Kelvan and said, "If something goes wrong, pull me out. If something goes really wrong, get Tam and then Rois. I'm starting." He put both hands on the dragon's head and let his mind brush against the dragon's.

First there was just a jumble of images and colors. A mossy pool in a forest stream, a massive oak with a few tattered leaves still hanging on it, a spade leaning against a low sunlit wall. Then he saw only blackness. It was soft and velvety, without sheen or glitter. He heard the hums of dragonspeech. They ran through calls like a mockingbird, struck a slow deep minor chord, whistled like a carnival organ. He pulled for them everywhere, drew the hums to himself one by one. He sensed the dragons, a small silvery one and a bold young green one and a tired ancient red one. They were there, scaled and clawed, and they were the darkness without bound.

He pulled, and where he could not reach the dragons pulled for him, and the hums made blue lines in the dark that pulsed in rhythm. They cut across one another, longer and faster, making a net of light and sound. His bones hummed. His body vibrated.

Words came. You danced, he said to them. You used to dance.

He saw it, the loops and curves of dragons circling, sun or moon hitting their wings, their breath meeting to make a rushing pillar of fire, sparks falling earthward.

I know how to free you. I don't know if I can do it.

The hums deepened to a bell tone. Long and sonorous and echoing. It was the dark crimson of cooling lead, the rough darkness of charred wood.

Caithen was taken when the dragons were taken. I will go into the darkness for you and die, but Caithen must be freed too. If you will not help me, will you help my people?

Hums again, wordless, not quite song.

Give me your word.

A single clear chime, and then a birdlike trill, beautiful.

The net of light extended from him. He straightened.

I need also your riders. Call them. Even if they are not with you, call them. Tell them I must speak with them.

Presences began to gather, little flecks of color in the darkness. He sensed puzzlement, glee, anger, patience. He waited until the dragons hummed again.

He said, Riders, I summon you. You know what the dragons want. You know what you must do. Come, and hear me.

The bell, deep gongs, threatening. He felt his words affirmed. He reached to the sky for fire and let it flow from his fingertips. He found an image of Tower Peak in his mind, and pictured the angle of the sun he wanted, and fed it to the dragons.

There, he said. Two mornings hence. You are sworn to the Empire, and I am a prince of the Empire, and the dragons and I speak as one. You are summoned.

The dragon sounds rose in volume. The presences flicked out. He heard a cascade of hums. The bell once more. A flash of color. Images of the sea.

Silence, and a convulsive jolt.

He was lying on his back beside the dragon. His whole body ached. He felt as though he had been twisted and wrung and then thrown off a cliff onto sharp rocks.

There was torchlight. And moonlight. The moon wasn't supposed to be up yet. Someone was leaning over him. Tam. Kelvan stood a few feet behind her.

Groaning, he sat. His bones seemed to wobble and bend. She supported him, then offered him a cup. He took it carefully, with both hands. Water. He drank it empty.

He said, and was surprised to hear his own voice, "How long did that take?"

"Three hours. You hardly moved. We poked you occasionally to make sure you were still alive."

Between that and the ride, it was small wonder that he felt like hell. No one was going to draw him a hot bath, either. He stood, wincing and swearing, and shook himself lightly to try to get the stiffness out. Astoundingly, his legs did not collapse.

"Did it work?" she asked.

He had to remind himself of what had passed. "Yes. I think so. I have the dragons' promise. They won't leave until Caithen is free." I won't die for nothing, he thought. But he would not say that, it would hurt her for no reason.

"And the riders, will they come?"

"Not all of them. But most." He did not expect to have them all. Hadon had not lost their loyalty yet. But some would come because they sided with Corin, and some would come to challenge him, and some would come because they were curious. It would be enough. "It was an order, not a discussion. They'll obey the summons and oppose me at the gathering if they intend to." Then he could not endure any more. Exhaustion struck him, hard.

He took Tam's outstretched hand and let her guide him back into the cottage. The moonlight was eerie and beautiful on the granite peaks and shone bright on the ground. The shadows were very dark. He stumbled several times.

As they entered, he said, "I'm afraid I'm not going to be much of a husband tonight." His voice was thin and tired.

"It's all right." She pushed open the door to their room. He did not even have the mental strength to light the candle. Tam took it to the hearth while he sat down wearily on the pallet.

She came back in, the candle lit, the fire beautiful on her face. He wanted to desire her but could not. She put the candle back on the floor and sat beside him. Her hands moved up and down his back, soothing.

She said, "If the wine were any good I would give you some, but I don't think it will help."

"I'd rather suffer," he said. The pain was fading, or he was becoming accustomed to it, but the fatigue would not be shaken off.

Breeze fluttered the cloth over the window. Tam stiffened.

"What is it?" he asked.

"I don't know. Something just gave me the shivers."

"You had a very hard day," he said. The summoning of the dragons and the riders had been nothing compared with what she saw, what she held in her mind. He looked at the wall where he had seen the shadowthings and saw only a dark moth a few inches under the window.

Tam looked that way too. "Get it out of here," she said, "kill it, make it leave."

"It's just a moth," he said.

"It's not," she said, sounding on the verge of panic.

He could not help being irritated. He suppressed it, forced himself up without bothering to hide the discomfort, and carried the candle toward the window. He set it on the narrow sill and tried to cup the moth with his hands.

It flew away and circled the flame. The light twisted and contorted with the draft. The moth kept circling. It tipped its wings like a dragon. It was colored with dozens of bands of inky black and dark grey and deep deep blue, with small silvery-grey spots at the ends of the wings. The wings were delicate and feathery with edges scalloped like the trim on a lady's gown.

"Corin," Tam said anxiously.

Another moth came. They moved around the candle opposite each other, round and round, himself and Tam in the ballroom. The heart of the flame was nearly white.

He held the candle out the window to draw them back outside. One flew too close and went up in a crackle of smoke before the breeze blew out the flame.

He pulled the shutter closed and fastened the cloth across the gap. The moonlight was not coming in directly but it cast enough brightness for him to see by. He put the candle down and went back to the pallet.

She clutched at him. "What was that about?" he asked.

"Cade."

Of course. What a fool he was not to remember. His annoyance faded. "Tam," he said, "those were the moths no one else could See. These were ordinary."

"I know. But things are different here."

That was true enough. There was nothing he could say back. He pulled his shirt over his head. He did not think he could stay upright any longer. His boots took some doing to get off. He flopped onto the pallet. "I love you," he said.

She kissed him and wriggled out of her clothing. They settled down together in the darkness. He shifted to lie face to face with her and put his arm over her shoulders. There was very little room for her on the bed. Her warm body against his was soft and smooth but he could barely keep his eyes open.

Tam murmured his name. Her breath was warm.

"Mmm?"

"I'm coming with you," she said.

"We can't put three people on a dragon," he mumbled. It took a while for his sluggish mind to put the words together. It was not so much the weight as it was the havoc it could cause in wind, and the difficulty in arranging straps over that much of a dragon's body.

"It's time you had a dragon of your own."

Yes, he thought. They could give him that much too. Let him be a real rider, even if only for a day. He touched their minds and gave them the wish. A faint whistle sounded in his head. Then the dragons were silent.

CHAPTER NINETEEN

❦

Tam was shaking him. Corin opened his eyes slowly. His head hurt. The room was light, it must be well past dawn. He sat up groggily and ran his hands through his hair.

"That's not an improvement," Tam said. She was fully dressed and her own hair was pulled back and braided. "Wake up. The dragon came."

"I feel like I drank an entire cask of wine," he muttered. His mouth was dry and foul-tasting, and his back ached. He dressed as quickly as he could and splashed some water on his face. Tam waited patiently, then led him out of the hut.

Green and black. He woke immediately. Not jewel green, but deep green, the hue of very old bronze and several shades darker. It glistened and shone as old bronze never did. The wings were black. Gold scales banded its neck. It was smaller than Kelvan's dragon, feet more delicate, head more curved.

There was still a rider harness strapped to it. He realized Kelvan was nearby. "Do you know it?" he asked.

"Aye. Its rider died in the taking of Caithenor. No one will be claiming it back from you."

"Was it followed?" He knew the dragons would not have followed on their own, but it could hardly have left unnoticed.

"No," Kelvan said. "There's no rider anywhere near us, I'm certain of it."

Tam put her arm around his waist. "You should fly it," she said. "Come with me."

She shook her head. "Not this first time. It should be just you."

He put his hand on the scales and let his mind slip into its mind. At once he realized how much he had been restraining himself when he spoke to Kelvan's dragon. He had not wanted to intrude. But this, this was his. Anticipation churned under the surface images of its thoughts. It was expecting things to happen too.

The rider's helmet was attached to the straps by a loop. He put it on his head and climbed onto the dragon. Tam looked quite small. He waved at her. She blew him a kiss.

Kelvan said, "Fly fast, fly far, and fly well."

I'm a rider now, Corin thought, awed. Up! he said to the dragon.

And oh, this flying was different too. His mind fell into the dragon's and he saw with its eyes, felt the wind with its skin. His arms were wings. The air currents were pale ribbons that changed colors like opal or mother-of-pearl, and the colors told him where to go. Violet to descend and dawnlike pink to rise. The sea was a sheet of silver, etched and polished. Every edge and surface of mountain rock was marked, clear, distinct. The waterfall at the valley's end threw out droplets of clear glass that hung in the air before drifting slowly downward. Even the smallest ones had shape that he could see.

He swooped so low to the rock that claws nearly scraped, hurtled sideways through a gap between two crags, circled and looped with the slightest bend of wing, flick of tail. The air was a cushion, a bed, a buoyant thickness of light. Several goats stood on an outcropping, and his blood surged with hunger and the desire to kill. One quick swipe of claw across back, one taloned grip of neck and hindquarters, and the beast would be his, hot and rich.

No, Corin thought, exerting control. He brought the dragon out of its downward curve and back up. He looked down at the valley and as he tried to focus his human gaze on the huts his eyes blurred, and when he looked again there was nothing below but river and meadow. Illusion.

He had the dragon hover and sat still upon it, watching the movement of wings, feeling the air pass over him. The heat of the dragon's body worked its way through his trousers into his thighs and groin. His stomach tightened and curled, and his head pounded. He was holding on so hard that the straps wrapped around his hands dug painfully into his skin. He drew in all the air his lungs could hold and shouted so that his whole body shook. Again.

Then he retreated back into himself. Softly, he directed the dragon back downward. It landed with silence and grace. He slid off and put the helmet back on its strap. Sound rushed in. Birds, the ocean, a rooster crowing somewhere up the hill.

Tam was waiting where he had left her. The light on her shirt revealed the shape of her body perfectly.

With very great effort he took her hand and kissed it, courtly, polite. She looked at him and said, "You can ravish me later. There's work to do."

"Don't I know it," he said. "Damn you. We haven't any maps here, how good is your geography?"

The three of them came to Tower Peak the next morning an hour or so after sunrise. It was a two-hour flight, and Corin was tired and stiff when they arrived. He had kept an arm around Tam's waist nearly the entire time, even when he did not need to. Her hair was clean and combed, and she wore a vivid red and gold scarf wrapped loosely around her neck. It drew the eye from her plain clothing to her face, beautiful. She looked fit to be a queen.

The weather had held, and the sky was clear. By the time things started the sun would be high enough over the crenellations of the mountaintop to keep Corin out of the shadow, and the riders would not have to squint to see him against the mountain. The huge slabs of granite were almost white in the sun.

He had been there once before, on that long journey through the mountains to the Dragon Valleys. He had expected that it would be diminished, as so many things in memory were when seen again, but if anything it was larger than he recalled. The mountain sloped down to a narrow river valley that was gold with meadow and green with pines. On the other side of the valley the bare ridge above the trees was an uneven collection of fractures and lumps and cliffs. Smooth fans of grey ash spread above loose jumbles of rock. To the north and south the ridges continued as far as the eye could see, growing gradually higher northward. There was just enough wind to blow the ends of Tam's hair about.

They were on level granite below a fissured ridge of rough stone that had the appearance of a war-tower wall. The mountain curved behind him in a half-round with rocks protruding from either end, creating a natural amphitheater. There was easily space for five or six dozen riders without forcing them to crowd together. His dragon and Kelvan's would stay near, flanking him, but the riders' dragons would have to find perches on the crags and outcroppings. That was one reason Corin had chosen the place; he wanted the riders to feel somewhat naked.

Tam kept her hand in his. She was unusually silent. He thought it was more than fatigue from the early rising and the long ride, or worry over what might happen. She was looking everywhere, her gaze fixed and intent. Perhaps she felt lonely, there in the starkness of rock and sky. He was counting on it quelling the riders a little too.

Kelvan hollered, "One comes!"

"Go!" Corin shouted back. He watched carefully as Kelvan rode up to meet the rider. They would not be able to speak directly, of course, not at that distance even with only a light wind, but they had hand-signs. Kelvan would not speak to the other rider through the dragons unless there was some crucial need to; he was to act as Corin's lieutenant, not as the riders' peer.

Tam said, "Where should I wait?"

He had considered having her stand beside him, but they had decided it was better to keep the focus on him alone. It would be distracting enough to the riders that she was there at all. He had not wanted to bring her, but she and Kelvan both said her power might be needed.

"There will do," he said, pointing at a spot several yards behind him where the granite had cracked in a steplike formation. "On the top. Do you think you'll be able to hear?"

"As long as the wind stays light." She paused. "Corin, do you remember what Rois said about places of power?"

"Yes."

"This is one. The dragons may be able to use it."

"I will be careful," he said. It was a complication he could do without, but if the dragons used it, they used it. Kelvan and the rider were landing.

She took her hand out of his but waited until the other rider was approaching to bend her head and walk backward from him. He resisted watching her over his shoulder.

Several more riders were circling above. A few specks on the horizon betokened others. That was one thing one could say for them, they were punctual. As each came in and was separated from his dragon, Corin observed him closely. A handful were younger than himself, but most were Kelvan's age or older; some were grey-haired. They were all strong and graceful. If they rushed him with rider-quickness he would not have much chance, even with a dragon close by. Most looked at him with the same neutral expression. They would hear him out, but he had not won them yet.

When it became evident that no other riders were coming, there were fifty-three men standing before him. That was a good showing. If the dragons all left Caithenor and the other cities, the Myceneans might lose control of the Sarians too quickly.

The breeze died down, a stroke of fortune, and the sun on his back was suddenly hot. Corin straightened. He had better start. They were too well disciplined to shuffle, but he would lose their attention if he waited any longer.

"Riders," he said, and again, "Riders!" He saw his voice catch them. Confidence surged through him. He was prepared for this.

"Hadon betrayed me," he said. "Hadon betrayed you." Clear, simple sentences, but they would need reason behind them, not rhetoric. This was not a mass of impressionable peasants or fawning lords. He and Tam and Kelvan had debated at length about which language he should use and finally decided on Mycenean, to emphasize the depth of Hadon's betrayal.

"When the king swore his loyalty to Hadon, when I put my own hands between the Emperor's and swore the same, Hadon himself swore that in return for such loyalty he would provide the protection of the Empire. That is the compact of a liege with his vassals.

"And what has he done now? He has opened the way for the barbarian Tyrekh to conquer Caithen, and he has sent his own soldiers and servants to help. He has sent you. You! To burn a city that has never raised a hand in war against him, to destroy people who look on him as their own lord. You are the instruments he uses in his betrayal. It is not right, it is not just."

He paused to stare at them. They stared back. He lowered his voice a notch and said, "If you choose to take Hadon's way, I cannot stop you. If you continue to serve a coward in his cowardice, I cannot keep you from doing so. All I can do then is pity you. If you bring my head to Hadon and are rewarded, I can't even pity you. But your dragon will scorn you." He gestured sweepingly to the dragons scattered about on the rocks. As though prompted, several of them keened. A soaring raven made a sharp angle and winged rapidly south, away.

Corin lowered his voice a bit more and shifted his tone to something less emphatic and more conversational. "You know why he's done this, of course. Because the dragons have chosen me to serve them and to free them, to let them return north, where they belong. And that's the hard choice for you. Serve a traitor and keep a dragon, or lose your dragon and keep your honor."

He stopped again. He expected that one of them would speak. But they did not. They looked expressionlessly back at him, judging, thinking. On an impulse he changed tactics.

"But it's not really a choice, is it?" he said. He reached to the dragons with his mind and found the threads of light that joined them. He heard their hums. He sent them a thought. "Because I command the dragons. I speak with them."

He waved both hands like a conductor, and the dragons rose from their places and swooped across the sky. He was not sure what they would do; he left it to them to decide how they wanted to show their submission and their power. He waved again, and they gave a loud cry in harmony. It was piercing and beautiful. It vibrated in his chest. A rock cracked explosively on the opposite mountain. Something roared.

They all turned to the sound. A chunk of rock was falling, and bringing other stones with it in a rush. It sounded like the sea, like the wind, like the rattle of a hundred wagon wheels on the cobbles. The slide continued, pouring down the mountainside like a living thing. It reached the trees and crashed into them. They cracked and toppled. The rising dust obscured the slope. Ravens croaked and fluttered away in a line. Then silence returned.

Hastily Corin thought the dragons back. That was more than he had expected. His pulse was racing.

He and the riders looked at one another again. Some of the neutrality had worn off their faces. It was time to make them speak to him now.

He called a single name. "Ennoc." The word hung clear in the air. Kelvan had said this was the man the riders would follow. If he turned him, he turned them all.

From the back a rider came forward. He was tall for a Mycenean, with very dark hair cut helmet-short and golden-brown skin. He, or his parents, must be from some other vassal country. Corin saw antagonism in the lines of the man's body. Antagonism and strength. Dragon cold ran through him. He might be outmatched.

The rider stopped perhaps ten feet away from him. They looked at each other. The expression on the rider's face was not hatred or defiance but contempt. Corin's anger rose, but he checked it.

The rider spat, drew his sword, and charged.

Corin had been prepared for such a possibility, but it was the dragons that saved him. The man moved as though he were swimming through treacle. Corin drew his own sword and brought it up in one smooth curving stroke before Ennoc jerked into ordinary motion and brought his down. The sun glittered blindingly on the blades.

The swords clashed with a tone that reminded him of dragon-speech. After a few more testing strokes he and Ennoc stepped back and circled each other, assessing. Corin caught the rhythm of the man's movement and darted in.

Ennoc parried easily. Corin feinted, made a counterthrust, felt the quickness of his body. So fast. It felt like the swift descent of a dragon. The energy and ecstasy of it were almost unbearable. The swords struck in a blur of radiance. Again and again, the sound of the clash too high-pitched for him to hear more than a faint whine.

Abruptly Ennoc lunged at him with such speed that he seemed almost to disappear. Corin spun and ducked in one motion. Ennoc's blade struck his with such force that he almost dropped it. Not fair, he thought like a child. Not fair at all. He was not able to be so quick.

He reached to the dragons again. They stretched the moment out. Suddenly there were two Ennocs, then four, all of them bearing down on him. Their movements were not identical. This was no mirrored illusion: it was a sequence. His own sword was a beam of light. When the blades struck each other sparks went flying. He sped up himself enough to face only one Ennoc and hold him off, again and again, but could not attack. Sweat poured from him. His arms shook with effort. His lungs were aching from the altitude. The rider had the advantage of him in that. When the blades struck, he could tell that he was stronger, but he was getting short of breath too quickly.

He began to feel desperate. That meant he would soon be getting careless. His mouth was drying up. There was so much sweat on his sword hilt and hands that it was hard to keep his grip. The granite did not yield, and his feet were hurting. There was no room for slipping or drawing back.

Why couldn't the dragons help him more?

They had given him their magics, maybe he had to find it in himself. Something more than rider quickness.

He parried another thrust and felt himself weaker. Fire, he thought. They gave me fire.

Flames licked along the blade of Corin's sword and sprang up at Ennoc's feet. They writhed around the rider's arms and wound their way, hissing, up his legs. The man cried out. Corin thought it was more in fear than in pain. He looked at his arms and saw the sweat gleaming on them like scales. He took his left hand off his sword hilt and watched the fingers elongate and curve into claws. With one swipe of his hand he could tear Ennoc to pieces.

He was consumed with dragonthoughts. The sweetness of blood, the rippling colors of flight. He was bound. Time only went one way now. Space was a confining net. It was wrapped around his wings and claws. He was trapped in ice. There was no way out. It would only break when fire roared again from the earth and filled him with light and heat and motion. Made him light and heat and motion.

He stopped moving and looked around. There was light wrapped around Tam's neck and shadow falling down her back. The sky was the pearl of dragon eggs and the mountain was the darkness of coal. The riders were outlines of colored lights. The wind drifted silver among them. Somewhere, deep below, heat waited to hatch.

He had not that strength. Not yet.

Fire burned around his head in a band. It reminded him that he had been born a prince, not a dragon. He let go.

Ennoc was on his knees before him, swordless. Corin put the point of his blade at the man's neck.

"Are you going to make me kill you?" he asked harshly in Mycenean. His throat was raw from the thin air.

The rider looked up at him. His eyes were a surprising green. After what seemed a tremendously long time, he shook his head.

"Say it."

"I yield."

Corin pressed the sword tip slightly harder.

"I yield, my lord."

Corin sheathed his sword. "Stand up." He had to play this delicately now. He raised his voice and said, "I command the dragons, and they command me. I will die to free them if that is what it takes. I will die to free your dragon, even if it is your sword that kills me. Would you do the same?"

"Why should I?" There was a measured quality to the tone, not defiance.

"I will not bargain with you," he said, hoping he had imbued his tone with just the right amount of arrogance. He looked over the crowd of riders. "With any of you. But I can make a promise. When it is over, I will allow you to return to Mycene if you wish, or stay in Caithen. I will not force you to my service, nor will I turn you away. When the dragons are free, you have your freedom. What happens between you and the dragon is up to the dragon."

"You are not the king."

"In this matter I speak for him. And equally he will honor my promises if I die."

To his great relief, Ennoc did not challenge him again. The man stood quietly, considering. He said, "If the dragon stays with me I can fly where I wish?"

"Yes."

The mountain silence was immense. Not even a bird called. Corin had no idea what he would do next if the man refused him. He was tempted to have Ennoc's own dragon engage in some theatrics, but better not. He did not need to show off might as a dragonlord now, he needed to show himself a better man than Hadon.

"And if the dragon does not stay I am not bound?"

"You are a free man," Corin said. "Freer than you are now. While the dragons are slaves, you are slaves." It was the one thing he could offer that he thought would tempt them away from the luxuries and privileges of Hadon's court. He expected few if any to remain to serve him; they would want to be their own masters. That did not matter.

"If you fail I cannot return to Mycene. I am an exile."

"There are always risks. But I won't fail."

"Do you know how to free them?"

"Yes," Corin said. He could not help glancing at Tam.

The crevice glowed with heat. Flames shot up as though from a furnace. On the roof of the cavern was the shadow of a dragon. It writhed in pain. It screamed, and fire jetted to the cavern roof in a white-blue glow. A man with eyes that flashed silver stood on the edge of the crevice and drew the fire to him. He breathed it in. His skin shimmered. He became a puff of ashes that fell softly down.

That was what she had seen. He made fire curl above his hand and said, "I will go into the earth and stir the embers. The dragon is roused, it needs only to catch fire again."

Ennoc stared at him. For the first time he looked frightened. There was a very long quiet. Corin kept himself focused on Ennoc. Just the two of them, and whatever the other riders did while watching was less important.

"What do you need?" Ennoc asked, and Corin knew he had him.

"To do what Hadon should have done," he answered. "He betrayed you. You must turn against him, be the knife that slips in his hand, the axe that falls to his foot. Drive out the Sarians, and then send the Myceneans home. Caithen is not theirs for the taking any longer. This is what the dragons want. And when it is done, you will be free."

He pressed his left fist into the palm of his right hand and folded his fingers over it. "I am your lord. And this I promise," he said.

Another stillness. Then one rider raised his right hand, palm outward, in answering salute. Then another, and another. Then they all were doing it.

He was proud, and sure, and exultant. This is what it feels like to be the king, he thought. Very very briefly he let himself enjoy it. Then he gestured Kelvan toward the riders and went to Tam.

She was still and quiet. He could not read her face. He wondered if he had somehow disappointed her. Then she caught his hands with both of hers and looked at him as she had that night on the roof, that fierce demanding loving gaze. She nodded slightly and released her grip.

"Well?" he asked.

"You did very well, my love." She brushed his hair off his forehead with soft fingers. He briefly put his arms around her, not caring if the riders saw. "My lord."

He did not deny it, but he bent his head and kissed her.

"What next?" she asked.

"I'll go among the riders, but it's not a social event." He glanced up and saw that by the sun nearly an hour had elapsed since they arrived. The fight had gone on much longer than it felt. "They have to get back to Caithenor and the other cities and pass orders to the soldiers. There's probably at least one here who will be going back to Dalrinia, do you want to send a message to your parents?"

It was too bright for her face to show any paling, but he saw it in the sudden tension of her body. He caught her hand and held it while she thought. He knew that for her hard moments still lay ahead.

At last she said, "No. If I could send a letter I would, but there's too much explaining."

"I'm sorry," Corin said. He wished he could make it easier for her. But she had to come through this one on her own; he was not going to send a royal proclamation of marriage with a herald, nor was he going to appear alone and announce that he had married Hyrne's daughter. He kissed her forehead. "Go sit down, you don't have to be noticed anymore. I expect we'll be done here within an hour."

He expected her to protest, but she did not, which told him how tired and worried she was. He watched her find a sheltered place against the rock and sit before he went to speak to the riders.

Perhaps half an hour had gone by, and several of the riders had already called their dragons to them and departed, when sudden coldness froze his spine and set his teeth and head to aching. His skin pimpled. Then a dragon screamed, and he clapped his hands over his ears and fell to his knees with the dread of it.

Kelvan was at his side, helping him up, rushing him to his own dragon. Tam was there too, clutching at him.

"There," Kelvan said. Corin followed his arm and saw them in the distance. A line of dragons, not many, only a dozen perhaps, but there was force and hatred coming from them that made him want to do nothing but run away.

"Get her out of here," he said. "Go with him, Tam, go, go, back to the village."

She straightened and took her hands off his body. She drew her knife. With pride and love he watched her decide it was the beginning, not the end.

"I see them," she said. "It's Hadon. He'll want to talk to you, Corin, the dragons won't attack yet."

He clenched his fists and looked at Kelvan. The rider nodded and turned. They had not planned for the possibility of Hadon himself coming, but they had considered that there might be a battle of dragon turned on dragon. Kelvan knew what to do.

He looked back and saw the phalanx much closer. He could make out the colors of the dragons. Kelvan and two other men were directing his riders while dragons tore from their perches and hurtled toward them. They would all be in flight in seconds, ready to hold off the approaching enemy.

Corin said, "Stay here with the dragon, love. Don't let him notice you. This is between Hadon and me."

She kissed him. This may be the last, he thought, and hugged her to him as tightly as he could.

CHAPTER TWENTY

T am crouched beside Corin's dragon where she hoped she could not be easily seen. As soon as she looked at the approaching dragons an image of Hadon had come to her mind. She did not know if it was Sight, or if the dragons themselves had given it. She could play no part in a battle of swords or dragons, there was nothing to do now but stay out of the way and wait. She tightened the grip on her knife nevertheless. The sky was very blue and very bright. The wind had died down entirely. Corin's riders were up, circling, waiting.

The dragon carrying Hadon landed. It was the biggest dragon she had seen yet, red-bodied, black-winged. It had none of the serenity to it that she had come to associate with Kelvan's dragon. Its tail swished, its wings were pulled back, steam came from its nostrils. It was full of rage.

Hadon's other dragons circled above, guarding, keeping a wall between the Emperor and the riders who had come to Corin's summons. Hadon dismounted slowly, but with nothing of an old man in his movement. He took his helmet off, revealing white hair. Tam knew he was ten years or so older than Aram, but he did not look it. She had imagined that he would be frail, a husk of himself, but his back was straight. Sunlight glittered at his neck. He was wearing armor of some kind.

Oh, why did we not expect this? she thought. Corin approached him with drawn sword. Tam did not think she could bear to watch.

"Highness," the Emperor said, making it an insult.

"Betrayer," Corin said. "Get to the point, if you have one."

"Impatience is your weakness. You lack cunning. But I have no desire to extend this either." He raised his hand. There was a sharp click.

Corin's head jerked. Tam followed his eyes. The rider whose

dragon had brought Hadon held a Sarian fire weapon, pointed at Corin.

No. No. She remembered the patches of greenfire as they fled Caithenor, the things Joce and Corin and her father had told her. The rider had several chances; even if he missed Corin once the prince would not be able to move before the next one, and the next one. She looked upward and saw, unsurprised, that the other riders who had accompanied Hadon had the weapons too. This was not how it was supposed to end, not now, not when he had won the riders.

She trembled with the tension of keeping herself from running. Go to him, she thought at the dragon beside her.

The rider fired. White flame burst from the end of the weapon.

Dragonspeech came to her mind, images of deep deep cold. Time slowed. The flames unfurled like a flower in the morning. She saw the silver ball hurtling toward Corin. His breath plumed in the air. The blade of his sword had feathers of frost on it.

A loud explosive crack made her drop the knife and cover her ears. The earth shook. Tam swayed back and forth and watched unbelieving as her knife slid jerkily away from her. A crevice was opening in the rock, splitting the mountain, ripping it apart like a seam. Corin threw out a hand, palm outward, warding. Instead of striking him, the silver ball dropped vertically into the crevice, bursting into greenfire as it did. Steam roiled. Hot air roared around her as Corin's dragon flew to him.

She steadied in time to see Corin sheathe his sword. Fast, so fast, he grabbed Hadon and pulled him onto the dragon. It rose. The Emperor writhed and struggled in Corin's grip. Neither of them was strapped on. Tam bit her cheek.

Corin's voice was clear and sharp, carrying well from the height. "I'll let you fall, so help me."

To Tam's surprise, Hadon stopped moving. It's a trick, she thought. The oldest trick of them all, to feign weakness and then turn. Corin had to know better than to fall for it.

His dragon rose higher. Hadon shifted. He's going to jump, Tam thought, looking at the angle of his legs against the dragon's side.

He would jump, and another dragon would catch him, and the battle would take to the air. She did not think Corin had seized the Emperor as a shield; it had been a fury-driven attack directed at Hadon. But when Hadon was no longer in his grip, the riders would have no reason to hold back.

A fire weapon went off again, from farther away, high up. Tam's attention turned toward the sound. One of Corin's riders was hovering on his dragon with his own fire weapon pointed down toward Hadon's man. Others had their weapons out and were firing. A rider near Hadon fell forward in a burst of greenfire as his dragon screamed in pain. It was the most horrible sound she had ever heard. Another weapon fired.

I'd better get away from here, she thought. The dragons were too close; a poorly aimed shot could continue downward and land in front of her. She picked up her knife and ran to where one of the spurs of rock began to extend from the mountain and climbed over it. When she was on the other side she climbed down until she was protected by the rock, then raised her head cautiously to keep watching. The stone was almost steplike, and she had solid footing. A wide flat area spread behind her.

Hadon was back on one of his own dragons. He must have dropped and been caught, Tam concluded. Corin was higher. She saw in panic that he was hanging over the side of the dragon, arms extended to grip the straps, legs dangling. He looked small and toylike. His body swung from side to side. She covered her eyes.

Coward, she thought, and looked again. She was certain she would see him striking the ground. The dragon had tilted to the side and Corin was pulling himself back up. She bit her cheek again. He was sitting straight. His hands moved. It was too far away to see what he was doing, but she was sure he was securing himself with the straps. She exhaled deeply. Her hands shook.

The riders were exchanging fire aloft. Bursts of white, then green flame consuming the bodies of falling men and licking along the stone. The air reeked of smoke and burning meat and some bitter chemical. There was nothing to burn on the stone, but the flames would not go out until they had exhausted their own fuel. A line of flames between the rock spur and the rest of the area had sprung up, cutting her off from a direct run now. She would have to go up the mountain if she needed to get away. She realized the dragons were not flaming at each other; it was a battle of men, not dragon set on dragon.

Another patch of fire broke out near her. It suddenly seemed like a very good idea to go higher. The slope was steep. There were cracks in the granite that she could put her fingers and toes in, and though the stone was uncomfortably rough on her hands it was not particularly difficult. She was panting anyway from the thin air by the time she thought she was safely out of the way of any rogue fire.

She looked back at the battle in time to see green flame burst from the base of a dragon's throat. It fell downward like a stone. When it landed flames of mingled red and green shot up in a pillar of light. The rider was engulfed. He screamed and screamed. Tam thought she would be sick.

When she could stand to look again, she saw Corin still high up, watching, and Hadon's dragon the same. They'll have to confront each other again, she thought. They can't resolve anything through proxy. One of them has to kill the other.

The spurts of fire began to lessen, and then were done. Three dragons had died and more than a dozen men. Greenfire still burned in places, but there were long streaks of char now on the granite where other fires had gone out. The crevice widened as it went outward. Tam was at no good angle to tell its depth, but she was certain it would be more than light could show. It reminded her uneasily of the crack she had seen in trance.

The memory of the cold air touched her skin, raising the hair on her arms. She felt horribly exposed. It would be no effort at all for a rider to land, grab her, and use her as hostage against Corin. She had lost track of whose men were whose.

Corin's dragon began to spiral down in wide, graceful loops. Hadon's followed. They landed, not far from the crack. The men faced each other, swords drawn, as their dragons retreated.

Corin did not want to do it at all. Tam could tell from the way he stood, the angle of his shoulders. It must go against everything he had been taught, everything he believed, to fight an old man. But Hadon held his sword with steady hand. There was no sign of weakness in his stance. Tam did not know if he was drawing power from the dragons or if it was his madness that gave him strength, but she was certain he was Corin's match right now. Whatever edge Corin had in youth and practice, Hadon had its opposite in experience and wiliness.

The Emperor thrust. Tam jerked with anticipation. Corin countered it, apparently with ease. She recognized some of the moves from things Joce had taught her. Hadon was on the offensive. She thought Corin was letting him do it, taking his measure. The fight with the rider had been a chaos of movement and sound; they had been far too fast for her to see what was happening. This was slower. She wondered why Corin did not move so quickly now and realized that he was being fair and honorable. And perhaps tired.

The riders were watching, some from their dragons, others standing well to the side. Patches of fire hissed. The only other sound was the loud clash of blades. She had just realized that Kelvan was not among the riders when his dragon landed on the slant of rock above her and he hurried to her side. She glanced at him, acknowledging, but said nothing.

Now Corin thrust. Hadon parried as easily as he had. A flurry of blows, followed with silence and circling, then more blows. She understood, ridiculously, why Corin's shoulders were so strong.

The sun was hot even to Tam, unmoving. She could not imagine how hot the men must be. Both were sweating. Corin still wore his leather riding clothing. His face and hands glistened, and his hair was soaked. She hoped he would not lose his grip.

She looked at Kelvan. "Can he win?"

"Aye," said Kelvan. "But it may take a while. Hadon's fighting well."

"How—how—why do the dragons help the Emperor? How could he bring them here?"

"They aren't free. And those riders are still loyal to Hadon."

And if Corin killed Hadon, then what? She could not even imagine the possibilities. She caught a glimpse of the Emperor's face and shuddered. His madness was not frenzy, it was the death of all feeling.

Corin quickened his blows. She saw him slide through Hadon's defenses, then heard a ring as the blade struck the mail Hadon was wearing. That was extra weight, it should have caused the Emperor more difficulty than it seemed to.

Corin stepped back a few paces, huffing. Hadon did not press him, he must need the rest too. This could go on until they were each too weary to raise a sword, what would happen after that? Would they go for each other's throats? Tam forced her arms to hang looser, her fingers to spread wide.

Stroke, parry, thrust, counterthrust, feint, stroke. Corin appeared to be pushing Hadon harder. He had a longer reach. In rapid succession he made a pass to Hadon's thigh, one to each shoulder, two more to the legs. Hadon whirled and spun and held him off, but for the first time Tam saw him begin to falter.

It appeared that Corin saw it too. He was darting, stabbing in and out, moving quickly. The effect was to push Hadon backward. Tam realized that Corin was driving the Emperor to where the granite began to slope downward more steeply.

One of Corin's slashes struck Hadon on the forearm. Bright red splotches appeared on the granite as the Emperor moved.

"First blood," said Kelvan in satisfaction.

"He didn't hit an artery," Tam said. It looked like a serious wound but not anywhere close to a fatal one.

"It will weaken him, though."

Hadon struck Corin in the leg. Tam gasped. Kelvan's hand came down impossibly hard on her shoulder, restraining her.

There was no fountain of blood, and Tam could not even tell over the darkness of the leather if it had gone through. Corin's posture changed a little, though, she thought it had. The granite was full of cracks and humps and uneven patches, and she was afraid he would stumble if he had to bear weight on an injured leg. He parried a thrust aimed at his shoulder, countered a downward stroke at his thigh, swung at Hadon's bleeding arm.

They were getting too close to a patch of greenfire. Their long shadows flickered on the granite, crossways to the stubby shadows cast by the sun. They coughed simultaneously. Tam did not know how Corin could see at all through the sweat running down his face, but now he raised a hand to wipe his eyes. The fire must be making them water. He retreated, which drew Hadon back onto level ground. Their breath was loud and ragged.

The blood flowed steadily from Hadon's arm. His posture had changed too, perhaps he had pulled a muscle somewhere. Tam knew that he would not yield. Corin would have to slay him even if they were in exhausted crawls. She realized she had made her hands into fists again and once more forced them to loosen. Why could it not be over?

Sparks seemed to fly from the swords. Corin slashed, but Hadon countered perfectly every time. The Emperor raised and lowered his sword with a precision that might have belonged to a machine. Yet his face was paling.

There were only a few spots of greenfire left, but the smell of smoke was getting stronger. Corin started driving Hadon toward the slope again. They were drawing near to the crevice. Thin black tendrils of smoke were coming from it. Tam saw Corin realize it. He was limping now, and he made an off-balance swing. Kelvan's hand came over Tam's mouth, holding in her scream before she could even draw breath for it.

Hadon's sword struck Corin's. Tam watched in horror as the blade waved and he nearly lost his grip. He turned the blow back somehow and let his blade slide down the edge of Hadon's to the hilt. They jarred loudly and Corin forced Hadon's sword down. Blood ran down Hadon's blade. She thought it was his own.

The light changed. It darkened as though the sun had gone behind a cloud. But there were no clouds. Instinctively Tam looked upward. The blue of the sky was tinged with purple. She wanted to cower in a huddle behind Kelvan but could not move.

She made herself look again at the fight in time to see Corin pull his sword back and Hadon's momentum carry him forward. Corin swung in a graceful backstroke. The sword went flying from Hadon's hand.

Corin pushed the point of his own sword against Hadon's neck and said in a hoarse voice that Tam could barely hear, "On your knees."

Hadon grinned at him and said, "Kill me."

It threw Tam into vision. A room, magnificent with carved and colored stone. Pillars, statues, tile. It was a long hall that blazed with light. There were patterns on the floor wrought with gold and silver. At the end was a dais, and on the dais a throne, gilt and elaborate and glittery with gems. Dragons were carved on its arms. A dark-haired man, thin and cruel-looking, sat on it.

A man approached, struggling under the weight of the silver box he carried. He knelt, spread a cloth on the floor, opened the box. He removed a large shimmering egg and laid it on the cloth.

The Seeing jerked, reshaped. The room was dim. The king stood on the lowest step of the dais. Facing him stood a man whose eyes flashed silver. A nimbus of light flickered around them both. The man held a glass vial with a dark red liquid in it. Slowly the liquid lightened and changed color, until it was the color of pale yellow wine. The king drank. He convulsed, twisted, almost fell. Then he recovered. The shadow of a dragon loomed behind him and danced like fire.

The man's eyes had changed from silver to black stone. The king said something, and he knelt. The king dropped the vial, which shattered on the stone floor. He placed his hands on the man's shoulders. It seemed a blessing.

Then he raised one hand and gestured, and the light flickered, and the man fell over with an arrow in his back.

Tam surged into awareness, breathing hard. Evil, she thought, evil. But now she knew what had happened. That was the hold, that was the spell. Father to son, in the blood.

Hadon's words were a taunt. That was why he had come, to bait

Corin into killing him. His madness was the dragons' way to freedom. If he died now the bonds would snap closed again. Corin had to know that, had to hold back.

"Don't!" she shouted. Wind gusted, and he did not hear.

A knife of dragonpain stabbed her mind. It reached to her belly before it stopped. She gasped. The air on her arms went abruptly icy. She started shivering as the cold settled into her. She smelled dust and ash. Her body realized what was happening and broke away from Kelvan before her mind did. She drew her knife and slid and climbed frantically down back to the level surface. She ran toward Corin, strands of her hair blowing into her open mouth.

A dragon shrieked. Hadon's face changed and he fell. Blood poured out of his ear.

"Corin!" He had to get away, get down, fly off the mountain, anything.

This time he looked toward her. Several riders screamed. A dragon let out a cry of pure terror that made Tam think her heart might burst on hearing it. Corin's sword fell from limp hands.

Black smoke was rising out of the fissure in the stone, black smoke and heat and sulfur, and as it rose it gathered in the shape of a vast dragon. Lightning played along its flanks. Fire poured from its mouth. Its claws were iron. Blood and fire had called it forth. Tam had watched it come out of the chasm in the cave once, and whether that was memory or prophecy she did not know, but this was the same. The smoke dragon was a shadow, yet it was real, with claws and teeth that could kill, breathing fire that could burn.

Corin was staring at it, motionless. Tam knew that Corin would be the sacrifice, not Hadon. He would stand there and submit.

She looked at the blood pooling under Hadon's head. His link to the dragons was not gone yet, and when he died the door would shut. Corin's death must come first to feed the dragon shaping itself into being. Otherwise it would dissipate back into the place where the Myceneans had kept it trapped for centuries and Kynos would become the dragonlord. She could save Corin's life with a knife slash to Hadon's throat.

The dragon was entirely airbound now, unspeakably huge. It made the other dragons look like its young. Perhaps they were.

Tam reached Corin's side. He looked exhausted. Smoke still curled up from the crack, and there was a faint reddish glow very far down.

"It's not done," he said.

She remembered trance, remembered snow and rock. She knew what she had to do. They had chosen her too, after all. She was their messenger. "It's not. But your part is. Go join the riders."

"Tam—"

"Don't, Corin," she said. "I love you. It's my turn. Go." She planted her feet. Yards away from her one of the patches of greenfire flared and went out. She glanced over her shoulder. "Go!" she said, feeling that she might breathe fire herself, and he finally moved.

She lifted her knife and pointed it at the sky as Joce had shown her. Power surged through her, locking her feet and arms in place. It crackled on her back and flowed from her knife blade. She was drenched in radiance.

The dragon saw her and ripped through the air until it was almost directly above her. It avoided the path her body made between sky and earth. It stank of death and sulfur and smoke and stone. Its eyes were cruel and knowing. It wanted life again, and she stood between it and its prey.

Not so different from Hadon, are you, she thought. But it was. It was not human. It did not know compassion, nor did it know evil or selfishness. It had neither loyalty nor blame. She stood in its shadow and watched the sparks flicker along its body. It was terrifying and beautiful, and she could speak to it.

You don't need blood. You need life. They aren't the same.

It fixed its flickering golden gaze on her. Slowly, carefully, she began to give it back its past. All the images the dragons had shown her, moon and snow and tree. Whirlwinds of sand on a tray. A twisting fire-cast dragon shadow on stone and a man falling in a puff of ash. The rock and cinders of the Dragon Valleys. The swirling infinite cold her hands had felt. And the touch of it, the air currents catching the membrane of dragon's wing, the silkiness of scale. Pain.

Moths fluttering out of Cade's mouth. Shadows of wolves in the moonlight. Sun on a slow river.

I am the repository, she thought. She looked up and met its eye. The gold was steady now, mortal. The liquid darkness of the pupil spread around her like silk, warm, inviting. She let it take her.

Light, everywhere was light. Steam passed across her face like a veil. The sweat on her arm refracted back hundreds of tiny rainbows. Her memories drained from her. She watched them go with a small, mournful wave, and as they went the light got brighter and deeper, until she was standing at the white center of the flame. She spread her arms out wide and watched the sparks flicker away from her. The roar of fire was like the sea or the wind. Here, she thought.

Agony brought her back into her body. The dragon had scratched her on the chest. It burned and stung. Blood was blossoming on the ruins of her shirt. She felt her face contort with pain.

That's all you need, she thought fiercely, fighting back tears. Just a little blood. You have my memories, you have the dragons' past. You have smoke, and a mountain, and wings.

It stared back at her. Muscles moved under its hide as it hovered.

Go, she said. It's over. You're free. The Dragon Valleys wait. There is fire moving again beneath the rock. You live.

It flapped its wings. She coughed and choked with the odor. It held out its claws. Her blood darkened the tip of one.

Take it. It's enough. Go.

It ascended in a shower of cinder and ash. Its scales were red and gold and hinted at the blue of flame. The colors rippled along it as it moved. Its huge shadow covered the granite.

It swooped suddenly, and Tam dropped the knife and recoiled, throwing her arms over her head. It glided over the last of the burning greenfire and inhaled it, drawing it upward in ribbons of incandescent green. It turned and began flying north and east.

Then Corin was holding her, seated on the granite. She had no recall of him coming to her or of sitting down. She had lost time. Fainted, probably. The light had changed back to ordinary daylight. Her clothing was smoke stained and burned in places, and the back of her left hand was red and shiny and already blistering. Blood continued to soak her shirt. It had been cut open to her stomach, as neatly as if with shears. The shadow dragon, the living dragon, was nowhere to be seen.

She looked past Corin to Hadon. There was still life in his face, and pain, and sanity.

You can die now, she thought. You're free too.

She would never know if he heard her thought, or came to it himself, or if it was simply chance, but she watched his eyes go slowly dim. She could tell when his heart stopped.

"Tam," Corin said.

"Water," she tried to say. Her swollen lips cracked with the effort, and she tasted blood. He made some sort of gesture with his hand. Kelvan stood in front of her with a waterskin. It was far too fast, even for a dragonrider, and she realized she must have briefly fainted again.

Corin dripped the water into her mouth, splashed it over her face. She swallowed greedily. Her throat was raw and sharp. It hurt. But she drank as much as he would let her have. Then she gave in and let herself weep with the pain in her chest.

He unwrapped the scarf from around her neck and lowered her down. He cut the rest of her shirt and looked at the wound. He poured water on it, and she jerked with hurt. "Steady, love," he said. He pressed the scarf hard against it. Her eyes wanted to close, and she let them.

When she opened them again, Corin was still sitting beside her. Blood was sticky on her breasts and stomach, but the pain had subsided. She looked at herself. He raised the scarf. It was a long slash down her breastbone, neck to stomach. The dragon could have ripped her open. The blood was clotting.

He said, "There's some burn around the edges, you'll have a scar. I think we can wait to clean it until we get medicine, though, instead of opening it again here. I'll find you something to wear."

She clutched his hand. "Your leg," she whispered.

"I'll get it tended to. It's shallow, nothing to worry about." He bent to kiss her, then raised his head. He said, sounding awed, "Look."

Holding her shirt closed with one hand, Tam struggled up and looked. The dragons were dancing.

They circled and dove and matched formation more gracefully than dancers at any ball. Fire came from their mouths in perfect spheres of red that slowly faded. Their tails twined, their wings flicked to catch refulgent sun, they looped around one another. They swirled like leaves caught in wind, ashes carried upward by heat. Their colors glittered against the blue sky and the white stone.

Tam leaned into Corin and watched. His arms came around her, carefully, avoiding the slash. She smelled smoke on his skin and clothing too. She let her eyes follow the dragons, round and round. She wondered if they would ever speak to her again.

After some measureless time, dragontime, no time, had passed, a dragon left the circle and returned to a crag where it sat, alert, watching. Slowly, one by one, the other dragons left the dance until there were only two left. They faced each other as though doing battle. They breathed fire at each other.

The flame rushed upward, a moving column of light and color, and fountained off in sprays of red and gold that faded into sparks. It cast its color on the dragons, on the rock. The dragons fanned it with their wings and swirled around it, then let the fire go out. They soared and crossed and returned and breathed fire again.

Two more times the dragons danced around a pillar of flame. After the third one, they circled, then parted and flew back to the mountainside.

Tam let her breath out. It made her cough. Corin handed her the waterskin.

She drank deeply. She said, "I'll live. Now go attend to the riders, there's still the war to win."

He kissed her forehead. Then he lifted Hadon's body and limped away.

Evening. Kelvan had left the cottage to them for the night. Corin's wound was more serious than he had thought, and the village healer had commanded him to keep weight off it for a few days. He lay on the pallet in front of the fire. Tam sat beside him with her legs crossed. She had been treated too, and aside from some tenderness in the burned hand she felt perfectly fine. The healer thought the scar on her chest would be nearly invisible to anyone who didn't have Sight.

She was very tired. She said, "You would think we had had enough of fire."

"Humans can never have enough of fire," Corin said. His hand touched her cheek.

She knew there would not be many more such quiet moments. As soon as his leg started to heal he would be agitating to leave, to go back to Caithenor, to get about his business. It had to be safe, of course, but the accounts they were already getting from the riders were that the Mycenean soldiers were following the riders' orders. Hadon's body had been taken back to Mycene. Tam wondered what the tale of his death would be, and what would be told of her. Probably very little of the latter; the riders would not want to describe anything that had happened.

Corin said, surprising her, "Do you want to go to Dalrinia, Tam? Kelvan could take you tomorrow."

"How long have you been waiting to ask that?"

"A while. I thought I would take you myself, of course. But there's no reason for you to suffer out my convalescence here."

"No reason except that I married you."

"You know what I'm saying." There was a bit of sharpness to his tone that made her think the wound was starting to hurt more. He said, "I don't want you coming back to Caithenor until it's stable, and that might be a while. We have no idea what Hadon's sons might do with him gone. I don't know if they'll blame me or thank me for his death, but they will certainly be furious about the dragons."

"I'll go to Dalrinia, but not with Kelvan, with you. I'll wait." Worry she thought she was past surged suddenly. "What am I to tell them? Especially about you?"

"Love, they will be so relieved to see you they won't care whom you married. And I am hardly going to hang about expecting to be entertained like a gentleman of leisure. Once you're settled I may not even stay there. I'll have a great deal to do."

"I'm not going to laze about either."

"Of course not. It will resolve itself, Tam, don't fret over it now." He touched her again. "You were so brave today. How did you know what to do?"

She had turned that over in her head more times than she could count. "I couldn't let it kill you," she said. "The dragons wanted something from me too, I knew that much. All I could think of to do was give it back what they had given me. There was nothing else I had. So I did."

"And it worked."

"It worked. What are the dragons going to do now, Corin, once the Sarians and Myceneans are gone?"

That made him sit up. "I don't know," he said. "They won't be coming back to me, it's getting distant already. They'll go to the Dragon Valleys, but I don't know that they'll stay there. I think many may choose to stay with their riders. It's upset the balance of the Empire rather nicely. We'll have to keep other countries from trying to steal them again."

He was in that world already. "I love you," she said.

He stroked her hair. They sat in silence for a while. Then Tam said, "What happens to me when we go back?" She certainly was not going to stay at her parents' home longer than she needed to, but in Caithenor there might not be much to do besides let Corin storm and pace his angers out in her presence. There would be plenty of that.

"You're going to hate it," he said cheerfully. "We have to cram years' worth of royal schooling into you as fast as possible. You'll read. And read and read. History and law, mostly. It gets dull much faster than you think it will. And you'll sit in councils and hearings and court sessions. You'll have to have dinner with the Lord Justice, who is very loud, and host dinners of your own, and help my mother plan the Midwinter festivities." He sobered suddenly. "Such as they are. I expect there will be scarcities. That will be hard for you, love. You'll have to listen to courtiers complain about a shortage of Liddean oranges and smile sympathetically when you know there are people in the city who haven't had enough to eat for days."

She closed her eyes. He was right about the difficulty that would pose. "I can help the doctors," she said.

"Yes," he said. "At least at first. But when the urgent times are over, your education will be more important."

"And when I have it, what am I to do with it? Besides giving you redundant advice? Your mother does not hold court or sit in council."

"That's by her choice," Corin said. "She sat beside my father whenever she could until I was fourteen or fifteen. If he had died she would have had to rule for me. Now she prefers to speak with him in private. As, I confess, do I. But when we have a child you will need to be able to sit in my place."

It was not quite overwhelming. She had never imagined she would be a queen. When he asked her to marry him, all she could think of was how much she loved him. She said, trying to keep her voice light so he would not take her too seriously, "No wonder you weren't supposed to marry a commoner."

He put his arm around her. "Tam, name me three unmarried women of rank who are more prepared than you."

She thought about it. Jenet, Elyn, they were certainly not prepared. "I can't," she conceded. "But I don't know very many such women at all."

"It doesn't matter," he said. "I know them. And I can't think of three. And you've seen more of the world than they have."

"Not really." She had been to Argondy and Illyria to see the famous sights, the Illyrian mosaics and the Grand Avenue in the Argondian capital, but wealthy women all did such visiting. Or had, before the war. "I've never even been to Mycene."

"You've been to warehouses and hovels and apothecary's shops. You know what a bill of lading is and how to tell a bookkeeper is cheating. That's much more useful to me than sitting in the Mycenean capital drinking juices and playing with a pet monkey."

"All right," she said. It did not make her feel any more ready, but there was no point in arguing it further. "I'll take your word for it."

"Good." He slid the edge of his hand under the hem of her shirt but left it low and warm on her back.

"What about the other women? Are they going to hate me for leaping over them into the matrimonial bed?"

"No doubt some of them will," he said. "But they would hate anyone I married. It won't be about you. I suspect most of the women will be pragmatic about the whole thing. And you'll have my mother and sisters as your allies. If I had married a woman they despised, it would be much harder for her to win the court than it will be for you."

"There are still going to be people who think you married beneath you." There would be flattery to her face and sneers and insults behind her back.

"They can take that up with my father," he said forcefully. "Tam, don't forget that quite a number of lords and their heirs have died. It's going to be a different court. People who were fourth or fifth in line for a title will suddenly find themselves in possession of it. They will be so busy scrambling to establish themselves that they won't care much about you."

"A different court."

"A different court and a different kingdom. Caithen will change, my love. Our marriage is only a small part. You can tell that to your parents."

His voice dropped a little near the end of the sentence. Tam shifted so she could see his face. It was full of exhaustion. He needed to rest. It was not just the wound, it was everything else that had happened as well. She would never forget how he had looked standing in front of the riders while they raised their hands. He didn't need a crown to make himself a leader.

She said, "I wish your father could have seen you today, Corin. He would have been proud."

"I'm glad I'm not the king."

"So am I. But when it's time, you'll be ready." She kissed his cheek. "Would you have killed Hadon?"

"I don't know. I don't think so, not unless something pushed me into fighting him again. It felt wrong the entire time. Even though I hated him. He hadn't chosen to go mad." He was definitely sounding weaker.

She counted hours. "How is your leg?" she asked.

"It hurts," he admitted.

"I think you need some more medicine," she said. "Let me get it for you."

"It will put me to sleep."

"It's supposed to. You'll heal faster that way. Wine or water?"

"That's an evil choice. Water."

The healer had provided a powder with ingredients that Tam knew worked quite well. After some consideration, she mixed it a little stronger and brought it back to Corin.

He made a face and drank it quickly. She gave him more water to wash it down with. She settled him on the pallet despite his protests. He would be asleep in minutes. Softly, she kissed his lips.

He mumbled something. She leaned closer to hear. He pulled her down onto him. "Caught you," he said. Then he fell asleep.

Tam rolled off and adjusted the blankets over him once more. Already some of the lines of pain were softening. He was very beautiful, the dark eyebrows and the flop of mussed hair, the shape of his lips. The light on his face was the comfortable glow of a tame fire. "Sleep well, my love," she said. "Heal fast."

She went into her room with the lit candle and carried it to the window. She pulled the shutter closed. A black moth fluttered in. She looked at it and was not frightened. You too have come in from the dark, she thought. She blew out the flame.

EPILOGUE

C orin shifted again but kept himself from making any nervous
adjustments to his clothing. If he had been allowed any
choice in the matter he would have worn a soldier's uniform,
which had the virtue of being both plain and comfortable. But when
he said something about the weight and heat of ceremonial clothing
in late summer, Tam said, *No one is going to lace you so tight you can
hardly breathe*, which put him in his proper place. As it happened,
the day was perfect, borrowed from fall, crisp blue and gold.

There was scant pageantry, though. A wartime wedding was necessarily subdued. And it was still wartime, even though the Sarians
had been driven out of Caithen and the Mycenean troops had
returned to Mycene. In Argondy the battles continued, and in Mycene
violence raged as the princes battled for their father's throne. Caithen
was an island of quietness. Its safety for the present was assured—the
Sarians had been routed not only by arms but also by a deep fear
of the city that had taken their god Tyrekh's life. The Mycenean
princes had no interest right now in reclaiming a small northern
country across the sea. But the wars that went on around it cast
their shadows. Joce, who had made it safely out after killing Tyrekh,
guarded Tam no less closely than he ever had.

Corin looked at the guests. There were many gone who should
have been there: the marshal, three dukes, a score or so of minor
lords and ladies, his father's clerk. The occupation of Caithenor had
been brief but deadly. There were places in the palace and city where
Tam could not go because she stumbled into visions of atrocity. The
list of the known dead was long; the list of the missing much longer.
Among the guests, many still bore scars or signs of captivity or flight.
Faces were thin, clothing hung loose, women wore scarves to conceal
hair they had been forced to crop short to rid it of mats and lice.

Bron had a persistent cough from breathing smoke. Seana was there, a widow now and looking ten years older. They had made their peace.

His mother and sisters were in the front row on one side, Tam's family on the other. He liked her brother. The dreaded introduction had gone smoothly. He stayed back while she embraced and was embraced by her startled, grateful parents. Then she drew him forward and said, blushing, *This is Corin. My husband.* Her mother said, *Tam!* Her father, who was taller than he was, looked him up and down very carefully several times, then said, *Would I be correct in supposing that upon a different occasion rather more titles and formality would be called for?* He said, *Yes, but not now.* Tam told him later that each had remarked separately to her on how polite he was.

A sparrow fluttered down and began rustling about in the grass between the flagstones. "You're early," he said to it. "Come back after the meal." He pretended not to notice the look his father gave him. Aram was amused by his anxiousness and not trying too hard to hide it. He supposed that in six months or a year he would be amused too.

He heard a dragon. No one else seemed to have noticed. He looked up and saw only a high silver spark. They did not speak to him anymore, not directly, but he still had that acuity of hearing and vision. They were gone, free, most with their riders, some without. No one knew yet how it would shift the balance of power.

The musicians started playing. He straightened. The crowd went silent. In the front row Cina most improperly took her husband's hand. It had been hard for her too. Soldiers had managed to bring her out of the palace, but then there had been weeks of hiding. Tam's parents twisted to look down the aisle.

Then she came. He had not seen her since yesterday. She had refused to spend the night with him, and his mother and sisters had weighed in on her side. The fact that they were already married and had spent the last two months sharing a bed was apparently irrelevant. But as she walked closer, he understood why she had done it. He saw her new, and she was more beautiful than ever.

He noticed vaguely that the dress was a shimmering sapphire and that her hair was wound around her head in a braid. His attention was all for her face, though. She looked up and caught his eye and smiled. When they joined hands before his father he repeated the words he was to say without hearing them. He managed not to drop the ring as he slid it on her finger.

Aram said in a low voice, "Kiss her, Corin," and he realized he had missed hearing it the first time. He drew her to him and kissed her for a very long time.

They did not have to go through the ritual of formally ennobling her; that had been done weeks ago. As soon as the kiss ended he drew her arm through his and walked back toward the palace. There was cheering, and they were showered with flower petals and even a few coins. He saw white petals, for purity, and red, for fertility. She was laughing.

When they passed through the arch of greenery at the end of the aisle, he broke a rule and kissed her one more time before they stepped apart and waited to greet the guests.

The remainder of the day seemed to take decades. After the receiving, there was a meal, for which he was not hungry, and then the dancing. He danced with her, then gratefully retreated to the side while she danced with her father, his father, and her brother. Aram said something to her that made her embrace him. Then it was Corin's turn again. And again. When she was not dancing she was moving about the room, talking to people he did not even know she knew, although he recognized some of the women. He had not realized how much work it was to be a bride, especially a royal one. Her friend Jenet, who had been captured by Myceneans but survived and was herself now newly wed, seemed to be giving her hints.

He said to Bron, who was standing next to him, "What are you going to do while I'm gone?"

Bron looked at him as though deciding whether the question was even worth answering. He said, "Without you to keep me in line, I suppose I'll just drink and wench, sir."

Corin snorted in a manner most unbecoming to a prince and bridegroom. Then Tai came to his side. She was very pretty in green and silver, and looked happier than he had seen her since Ader died. "I'm going to give you your present now," she said, and went to the musicians. When the dance stopped she sat at the piano.

She played the drinking song—the cheerful version—through once, and got enthusiastic applause. Corin wondered how long it would be before someone else figured out what it was. When she came back, he kissed her and said, "Thank you," grinning. It made him think of the dragons. That was a small sadness.

Tam touched his arm and drew him away from his sister and Bron, who were now blocking them from view. "Should we go?"

"My God, yes," he said, relieved. "I wish we could do it unobserved." He was taking her away from Caithenor for a week, but it would probably take another hour to get out of the palace with all the farewells they would have to make. He envied Joce and the guards who had gone ahead.

"Be patient, my love," she said.

The wine steward was opening another cask, the Illyrian red. He poured a glass for the king, who had appeared from somewhere. Corin thought he had left long ago. Aram sampled the wine. Someone rang a bell. The room quieted and the king began to speak.

"Now," Tam whispered.

"We can't—" Corin began, but Tam was already pulling him toward the door. His mother would skin him alive for walking out on his father like that, but he gave in and followed her.

The corridors between the ballroom and the bedroom were strangely empty. The guards they passed all seemed to be standing down side corridors with their backs turned. In the bedroom Tam began to rapidly undress. She pointed toward his wardrobe. "Change," she said.

When he opened the wardrobe and saw the unprincely clothing he had worn to the fair hanging in front, he began to understand. He changed quickly. He was not very surprised when she led him to the private entrance. A plain coach was standing ready. He looked up the drive and saw the royal carriage and its team of six at the main entrance.

She almost pushed him in. The coachman helped her up nearly as inelegantly and shut the door hard and fast. He heard the whip snap in the air, then the coach began to roll.

"There," she said, sitting back and reaching for his hand.

"How on earth did you arrange that?" he asked her.

"It was your father. It was his wedding present to us."

"Long live the king," he said.

✿

They kept the curtains of the coach closed while riding through the city, but when the road beneath them turned to dirt, Corin slid them open. He almost wished he hadn't. He looked over a field with fire-blackened earth and nothing growing but weeds. In the distance, a farmhouse chimney stood by itself among a pile of rubble. The only leaves remaining on the trees were withered from heat.

When he had come to Caithenor dragonback two weeks after the war ended, it was the first time he had seen the city and surrounding land. The ruin had made his stomach hurt. Outside the city mass graves were raised in mounds of bare earth, while villages were reduced to charred timber and streams were clogged with decaying bodies. Fields that should have been green and lush with young grain were bare. Slaughtered animals lay bloated and stinking in the pastures. In the city itself swaths of burn and destruction cut across every neighborhood and shopping district. The river wound blithely through with far too few boats upon it. When he went horseback through Caithenor, he saw everywhere the same things: thin, hopeless faces, ragged blankets in haphazard lean-tos constructed among the ruins, small cairns to mark a place of death, newly made shrines crowded with god-offerings.

There was money; there would be no tribute paid to Mycene this year. But timber and medicine and food were scarce. Some things could not be purchased at all. The blacksmiths forged, the carpenters nailed, and the masons troweled, but it was not enough.

When winter came, too many people would still be homeless and hungry.

Corin left the curtain open. It would not do to block things out, not even on a wedding journey.

Tam said his name. He looked at her and said, "We have a lot of work to do." At night he dreamed sometimes of white-faced Sarians gleefully putting houses to the torch. Those dreams would not be banished until much more of the country was restored.

"We do. But you of all people deserve some rest. The task that only you could do is done. Give things over to everyone else for a few days." Her voice was soft. She knew how he felt.

They had had this conversation before. He said, *I can't possibly do enough*, and she said, *You freed the dragons, no one could do more*. It felt a hollow victory.

But he owed her what joy there was. "I'll try. You too."

"I'm hoping to try quite a few things," she said devilishly.

That was an interesting thought. He put his hand on her leg. "Should I close the curtain again?" he asked just as the coach tilted precariously to one side and she slid away from him.

"Not on this road," she said.

"Then find some other way to distract me."

She pretended to consider it. "I could tell you about your sister, but that won't take very long. Let me think of something else. Perhaps you could answer some questions about the laws of taxation."

"Never. What about my sister? Which one?"

"Tai." She came back closer to him and gave him a kiss. "She's pregnant."

"That's why she looked happy," he said, happy for her.

"She looked happy because she can keep her food down again," said Tam tartly, nipping any comments about the blessed state of pregnancy in the bud. "And she's not going to try to find someone to marry right away, so don't even think about looking."

"I wouldn't," he said honestly. Tai was a princess and did not need a father to provide for the child. She should at least be given her time of grief. "Am I allowed to know?"

"Yes, now. I've known for a month."

That meant Tai must be further along than she looked. Or had there been a slight swell to her belly that he had not noticed? He said, "When is the babe to be born?"

"A few weeks after Midwinter."

He counted. That made her four months along. "Good. There will be no doubt it's her husband's child."

Tam looked appalled. "Would anyone suggest anything else?"

He hated to remind her now, but he was certainly not going to lie. Everything was political. "If it becomes known that she was held for a week in Mycene, yes. That's the sort of vile rumor people most love to spread. But if she conceived two months before Ader died, it is clearly his."

Tam shook her head and pressed against him. He put his arm around her, and she reached up to pull his hand over her shoulder. He could tell that it was a desire for comfort, so he did not move it anywhere else.

She said, "People can be so vicious."

"They can," he said. War had showed that yet again, not just in the bodies of the dead but in the subtler cruelties of young girls lifting their skirts for a loaf of bread and taunts directed at a burned and disfigured man. It was nothing like dragons. "I'm afraid you're going to have more than your share of such people to confront, Tam."

"Ah, but I'll also have you."

"No regrets?"

"Not a one." She gave him another kiss. It lasted until a bump and a swerve almost unseated them.

He said, "If we had taken the other coach we would have been more comfortable."

"If we had taken the other one we wouldn't have left yet."

❧

When they arrived at the manor, the night was as perfect as the day had been, cloudless with bright stars and clear noises of crickets, frogs, cows lowing far away. There was just enough of a chill to make it pleasant to stand close beside her with a cloak tossed over them both. A light came on in the house, and the door opened.

"Whose is it?" she asked.

Of course she would want to know every detail. He wondered if she was teasing him. He took her hand to lead her up the steps. "Mine," he said. "I was thinking of giving it to you."

She said drily, "You mean all your property didn't pass to me automatically upon the marriage?"

"Now there's a silly law," he said. "When we get back you can use all your influence to try to convince the dukes to let it be changed. Father would sign. I didn't get anything from you, did I? I didn't even think about it. I should have married someone else."

They were in the hall now. It was lit, the floor a lovely red-gold wood that glowed invitingly in the lamplight. The servants had taken heed of their orders and were nowhere to be seen.

"I think you got quite a lot," she said, and slipped her arm around his waist under the cloak. One of her fingers went between his waistband and his shirt.

He pushed her against the wall and kissed her hard. He began to unbutton her shirt. Her hand went to his belt.

They stumbled their way past expensive paintings and fine sculptures to the stairs. By the time they reached the landing he could barely restrain himself. Her hair was in disarray. His shirt was open to the waist and hers was halfway there. They continued upward and somehow found the bedroom.

He kicked the door shut. She reached over him to bolt it. Her breasts brushed his bare skin.

They made it to the bed, leaving a trail of abandoned clothing behind them.

They exhausted each other, but she fell asleep first. He propped himself against the headboard and watched her in flickering candlelight. She looked younger when she slept, her face relaxed from its usual intensity. He loved the curve of her shoulder, the fall of her hair. He kissed her forehead. Her breath stayed soft and even.

He blew out the candle and went to the window. He opened it enough that the curtains moved gently. Light from the kitchen shone on the garden. He could hear the servants talking. If he tried he would be able to hear more: the creaks as the boards settled themselves in with night, the small animals of darkness, the wind on the grass. There was no reason to.

He got back into bed and put his arm over her. Clever, beautiful, fearless Tam. He adjusted himself and closed his eyes. Once she had said to him that what they had was grace. Even now, married properly, rank bestowed, it still was. And always would be.

ACKNOWLEDGMENTS

This book would not be what it is without the work and goodwill of many people. First and foremost I thank my husband, Adam Louis Hill, and our son, Benjamin, for their love, support, suggestions, and patience. Also: Andy Kifer and David Gernert at The Gernert Company and Emily Murdock Baker at Viking, none of whom let me get away with cheating; Tom Williams, whose geology field trip to the Eastern Sierra helped me see the ending; Rachel Smith, for the awesome map; and Panna and Carl, for sharing Osa the black dog with me. Finally, I am indebted to Jane Austen, whose language I liberally borrowed.